Double Agent

Double Agent

Tom Bradby

Atlantic Monthly Press
New York

First published in Great Britain in 2020 by Bantam Press
an imprint of Transworld Publishers

Printed in Canada

First Grove Atlantic hardcover edition: November 2020

Library of Congress Cataloging-in-Publication data available for this title.

Typeset in 11.5/16pt Palatino LT Std
by Integra Software Services Pvt. Ltd, Pondicherry.

ISBN 978-0-8021-5764-5
eISBN 978-0-8021-5766-9

Atlantic Monthly Press
an imprint of Grove Atlantic
154 West 14th Street
New York, NY 10011

Distributed by Publishers Group West

groveatlantic.com

20 21 22 23   10 9 8 7 6 5 4 3 2 1

To Claudia, Jack, Louisa and Sam.

Prologue

KATE COULD NOT decide whether the woman before her had a keen sense of humour, a deep-seated social autism or both. 'Why do you think *you*'d be a good fit?' she'd asked, after a long explanation of the critical role her former deputy and friend, Rav, had played in the day-to-day work of MI6's Russia desk.

'Like for like diversity replacement,' Suzy had replied, without the slightest hint of a smile.

Suzy Spencer was slim, pretty, northern, state-educated and half Vietnamese. 'The smart half,' as she'd put it. She didn't take prisoners, but that was perhaps no bad thing. 'I'm keen to spread my wings,' she said, 'I really am. The Security Service has been good to me and I love working there, but I've always had half an eye on a life across the river here – the chance to expand my horizons, play on a wider field. I'm sure you understand.'

Kate supposed she did, though it was harder to recall, these days, as that wider playing field seemed ever more threatening.

'I'd be grateful, though,' Suzy went on, tucking a half-curl of neat black hair tidily behind her ear, 'if you could tell me a little more of what really happened to your deputy, Rav.'

'That case is closed, I'm afraid.'

'But I would need to know the background, would I not?'

'I don't believe so, no.'

'But if my life is also to be at risk—'

'It won't be.'

'Given what happened, I don't see—'

'The file is sealed. That's all I can say.'

'But these allegations that the prime minister is a Russian spy—'

'Unproven, which is why the file is sealed.'

Suzy didn't flinch, or back down. 'If I'm to take this role, Mrs Henderson, I'd appreciate knowing the background. That's all.'

Kate was tempted to wonder aloud why she was under so much pressure from her superior, Ian, to take this woman as her new deputy. Good for interdepartmental relations, he'd said airily, though he'd been fiercely territorial at even the hint of an incursion from MI5 across the river until his ambition to be the next chief had got the better of him. He'd been turning himself into the ultimate Whitehall warrior.

She leant back in her chair and stared out of the window at the morning commuters hurrying through the rain outside Vauxhall station – the unchanging backdrop to her working life. She'd ideally love to send this woman back across the river where she belonged, but she recognized that, given the questions over her own recent past, she'd probably lost the ability to determine this aspect of her future – and many others. 'It was called Operation Sigma,' she said. 'We received intelligence that a group of senior Russian intelligence officers used to meet regularly on a super-yacht owned by Igor Borodin, a former head of the Russian Foreign Intelligence Service, the SVR.'

'Of course I know who he is.'

'We – I – recruited a young au pair to take a job as nanny to Igor's grandson onboard. We persuaded her to plant a bug in his study. Shortly afterwards, we recorded him and his colleagues discussing the fact that the former prime minister had cancer and was about to resign. It was clear that one of the candidates to replace him was working for Moscow.'

'Which one?'

'Well, you'll have seen the leaks in the press—'

'The current prime minister, yes, but was it correct?'

'In the end, there was no way of proving it either way, which is why the case was sealed.'

'Did you agree with that decision?'

Kate hesitated. 'We cannot afford to see a democratically elected leader's mandate undermined without hard evidence.'

'Do you think he was guilty?'

'My view is immaterial. We need to be an evidence-based organization, particularly in this world of disinformation and lies.'

'What happened to Rav?'

'He was murdered.'

'But the coroner's verdict was suicide?'

'Look—'

'And as I understand it, he – indeed all of the work of Operation Sigma – was betrayed by an agent in your midst, planted here to assist the current prime minister's rise to office.'

Kate gazed at her icily. Bloody Ian, she thought. This woman was far too well-informed. So much for the file being sealed. 'That matter is also closed.'

'The agent – Viper – was your husband?'

'If you already know the answer, there is no need to pose the question.'

'I'm sorry, that must have been extremely hard.'

'I'm looking for a deputy, not a therapist.'

'And you won't regret hiring me. I'm very thorough.'

Kate watched the rain hammer the glass. She stood, determined to draw this audience to a close. She offered her hand. 'Thank you for coming in, Miss Spencer.'

'Was that all right?' Suzy asked, a sudden and rather startling hint of humility in her gaze. 'Did I get the job?'

'I'll let you know.'

Kate sat again and watched as Suzy retrieved her coat, then headed down the corridor. She couldn't really have had graver reservations about the woman, but that was beside the point. On this, she accepted, Ian would have his way.

But the much bigger question was simple enough: why was he so determined to inflict this outsider on them? It wasn't his idea, of that much she was certain.

1

Three weeks later

SAVE FOR A thin skein of mist that curled its way around the dome of the Basilica di Santa Maria della Salute on the far side of the Grand Canal, it was a bright, crisp, clear morning in Venice. The kind of day, in fact, that Kate Henderson might have been enjoying in any other circumstances. Sometimes being away with your family was murder.

'Why do you keep drumming your fingers on the table?' Gus asked. 'You hate it when people do that.'

Kate forced herself to stop. She smiled at Julie, who was sitting opposite. 'Your mum's a bit nervous,' Julie said. 'Under the circumstances, I think that's understandable, don't you?'

They lapsed back into silence and watched a gondolier paddle slowly past. The tables on the breakfast terrace were full of Chinese tourists, mostly glued to their phones. They didn't seem to be eating much either.

Kate couldn't resist returning to a study of her daughter's plate. 'Please eat up, love,' she said. Fiona had ordered a poached egg, Kate had insisted on toast, but neither was going anywhere near her daughter's stomach as yet.

'Just eat it, for fuck's sake,' Gus said. Remnants of his hearty breakfast were visible across a wide arc of the once pristine tablecloth.

'Gus, please!' Kate admonished. 'Don't talk to your sister like that. And don't swear.'

'Like *you* don't.'

'Not long to go now,' Julie said. 'And then we'll all be a lot happier.'

No one returned her cheerful smile. Normally, Julie's tumbling auburn hair, startling green eyes and full-figured beauty were enough to keep Kate's son mesmerized, but not that morning. 'Does Dad have a new girlfriend?' Gus asked his mother.

'For God's sake, Gus!' Fiona glared at him, her piercing blue eyes radiating fury. She'd applied make-up for the first time in months and pulled her hair back into a neat bun, which served to highlight her increasingly gaunt cheeks. There was no question that her conflict with food was on the cusp of robbing her of her looks. She got up from the table and stormed off.

'You haven't eaten,' Kate called after her. But Fiona was already halfway across the terrace. 'We're leaving in five minutes!'

'Well, *does* he?' Gus asked, once his sister had gone. In contrast to Fiona, his cheeks were becoming chubbier by the day and the pudding-bowl haircut he'd instructed her to carry out wasn't helping matters.

'Not so far as we know,' Julie said.

Gus glanced at her, then returned his gaze to his mother. 'But you said you can't ever get back together with him, so why would it be a big deal?'

Neither Kate nor Julie answered that. What could you say? Gus pushed himself to his feet. 'I'm going for a dump,' he announced.

'It's just the way you tell 'em,' Kate said, as he departed. 'I hope time spent with my children is proving a useful contraceptive,' she told Julie.

'Don't be so hard on yourselves. You've all got every reason to be tense.' Julie absent-mindedly tucked into a second croissant. She ate as she drank, as she lived, really: with an easy nonchalance.

'Have you got a cigarette?' Kate asked.

'I thought you said not in front of the children?'

'Well, they're not here, are they?'

Julie retrieved a packet of Winston's from her bag and threw them across the table. Kate took one, lit it and waved at the waiter, who reluctantly changed course and swung towards her. 'Yes,' he said abruptly. The Venice Charm School had worked a treat. She ordered another coffee.

'Because that will definitely help,' Julie said.

Kate inhaled deeply and leant back to face the Grand Canal. A half-empty vaporetto glided past in the direction of the Rialto bridge. The mist had reached the dome of Santa Maria della Salute and was now curling up into a clear blue sky. 'How are you feeling?' Julie asked.

'I'm not entirely sure. Nervous. Angry. Raw. Upset. Take your pick.'

'Do you have any idea what he *has* been up to in Moscow?'

Kate shrugged. Since she had discovered that her husband had betrayed not just their marriage but his country, she'd had no direct contact with him. After his defection, all communication had been routed through a consular official at the British Embassy in Moscow.

'*Does* he have a girlfriend?'

'I should think so, knowing him.'

'What will you say to him?'

'Nothing. What is there to say?'

'"You fucking bastard."' Julie smiled. 'That would be a start.'

'I said that already.' Kate took another quick puff and stubbed out the rest of the cigarette. 'Come on. We can't put this off any longer.'

Kate went to brush her hair and touch up her face. She studied herself in the mirror, concluding she'd aged at least a decade in considerably less than a year. She sat on the bed, stared at the ornate ceiling and closed her eyes. This hotel had seen better days and she knew that feeling. The knot of tension in her stomach had been steadily tightening ever since she'd boarded the plane at Gatwick.

Fiona and Gus were on time for the brief stroll through to St Mark's Square. And once they were there, Julie distracted them from the slowly marching hands of time on the clock tower by reading aloud from the guidebook. 'Okay. This area by the water's edge is known as the Molo and these columns were carried home from Tyre by the Doge Michieli in 1125.' She turned the page. 'In fact, he brought back three, but one fell into the sea as it was being unloaded here. Huh. How about that?'

No one was listening to her. Kate glanced at her watch, as if it were a more reliable mark of time than the clock above them. She returned to surveying the groups of tourists across the square.

'Relax, Kate,' Julie whispered.

Kate didn't answer. She felt foolish for agreeing to meet here now. Venice was a hostile intelligence service's dream location. 'Why would they try anything?' Julie said, reading her mind. 'Stuart would never let them.'

Kate tore her eyes away from the survey of the square and glanced at her watch one more time. 'All right.' She looked at Julie. 'Just give me ten minutes, okay?'

'Yes, as we agreed.'

'What are you going to say to him?' Fiona asked. Her voice was softer now.

'I don't know, love.'

'It would help if you told us.' She glanced at her brother, who looked uncomfortable in a way he usually reserved for encounters with members of the opposite sex.

'I'm just going to talk about the arrangements for this visit and how we might work things in the future. If there's some-where you'd be able to stay with him and so on.'

'Are you going to talk to him about what happened?'

'I don't think so. I'm not sure how that would serve any of us.' She rubbed her daughter's shoulder affectionately, but got no response.

Kate set off across St Mark's Square, weaving her way through the shoals of slow-moving tourists, then turning into Ala Napoleonica. Once she was out of view of Julie and the children, she paused by a shop and pretended to browse the jewellery display in the window as she glanced back the way she had come.

Nothing was amiss. Perhaps Julie was right. Why would anyone be watching her?

Kate walked on and paid her entry fee for the Correr Museum further down the street. She went into the cool, quiet interior and browsed through the costume section, with its fine collection of ancient fashions and silk banners.

'Hello, love.'

She swung around. Stuart was dressed in black jeans and a blue T-shirt, with a stylish leather jacket and trainers. He had shorter hair and designer stubble. He'd lost some weight, half a stone, perhaps more. He looked much more like the funny, irreverent young man she'd fallen so heavily in love with all those years before.

The one she'd known instantly she wanted to build a life with.

'You look well,' he said.

'I don't.' The sense of contentment she'd convinced herself she'd embraced appeared to have deserted her. She felt like a teenager again, giddy, uncertain, embarrassed.

'Where are the kids?'

'They're with Julie. They'll be here in a minute. I thought it was best to have a few minutes together first, just to . . . discuss practical things.' But even as she said it, she knew that wasn't true. Did it show?

'Of course. How are they?'

'They were all right for the first few months, but things have got a lot more complicated since then. You'll . . . see. Gus is taciturn, even by his standards, and Fi has got very weird around her food.' She felt on surer ground discussing their children.

'Is she seeing a therapist?'

'They both are. She's perilously close to anorexia, but we're monitoring it closely.'

Stuart nodded. It had always been so easy to talk to him. And it was, strangely, still. 'I'm sorry,' he said. 'How are you?'

'I'm fine.' She looked up at him and suddenly, through her disorientation, anger burst through. What did he expect her to say? That after seventeen years of marriage, more than twenty together, she had felt cleaved in two by his departure? 'I'm fucking fantastic, Stuart. What do you think?'

'I'm sorry.'

'And stop saying that.'

'What else would you like me to say?'

Kate bit her lip. She breathed out slowly, her head spinning, her stomach churning. It was like their first evening together, but without the giddy sense of possibility. 'How's life in Moscow?'

'Not much fun. I get a paltry pension for my betrayal, which is hard to live on. I'm trying to find work, but they have little interest in helping. They treat me as if I'm a vaguely infectious disease.' He smiled bitterly. 'Which perhaps I am. The British Embassy does a good job of killing off my chances with any company that checks in with them, so I'm a bit screwed, to be honest. But no more than I deserve.'

'Do you get a flat?'

'Yes. And a car. But both are pretty decrepit.'

They were silent for a moment. Kate stared at the floor, which seemed the safest place to look. 'I just wanted to discuss how things are going to work with the children in the future,' she said. 'I'm sure we'd both agree that their interests are paramount.'

'Of course.'

'I don't know what you were thinking, but—'

'I'll fall in with whatever you want to do. I'm sitting in Moscow, doing nothing. So . . .' he shrugged '. . . this will be all I'm living for. And they don't seem to care what I do or where I go.'

'Of course they care. They'll be watching.'

'I doubt it. I think my days of usefulness, or at least relevance, are at an end. The only issue is cash. I don't have much spare money, so I don't know how frequently I'll be able to travel around Europe.'

'You're surely not expecting me to—'

'I'm not expecting anything, Kate. I deserve everything that's coming to me.'

Tears crept from the corners of Kate's eyes and rolled down her cheeks. She wiped them abruptly away. 'My love . . .' Stuart stepped forward. Kate raised her hand and took a pace back. 'You know I'd do anything for a shot at redemption, right?'

'That's never going to happen, Stuart, and I'll stop bringing the children to see you if you go down that road.' She was surprised at how definitive that sounded.

'I'm sorry,' he said again.

The pain in him cut her like a knife. 'I need to go,' she said. 'I'll be in touch about how you see the children.' She turned away.

'Why did you come, love?' he asked.

She faced him. 'What do you mean?'

'You could have sent the children up here on their own or with Julie. So why did you come?'

'I . . . I don't know.'

'Did you want to see my pain, to see if it looked anything like yours?'

'Perhaps.'

'Well, if you hoped to see a ruined man, I trust you weren't disappointed.'

'This is perhaps going to come across more harshly than I really mean it to – since I'm still too confused to know what I think about anything – but I would say that it's that kind of self-absorption and, indeed, self-pity that got you into this mess in the first place.'

She turned away and walked out. Julie and the children were waiting just outside the entrance. 'He looks well,' Kate said to Fiona and Gus. 'You go on up.'

Kate watched them disappear inside. Despite herself, the tears began to roll down her cheeks again. Without a word, Julie linked arms and led her friend slowly back towards St Mark's Square. They walked past the Doge's Palace and sat by the water's edge. Julie waited while Kate composed herself. 'So,' she said eventually. 'How was he?'

'Let's not talk about it.'

It was a glorious spring day now, the lagoon busy with the morning traffic. They watched a glistening white cruise liner heave into view. It seemed vast, a giant from another world entering a Toytown harbour. 'You want me to fetch you an ice cream?' Julie asked.

'Getting even fatter is the last thing I need.'

13

'Somehow that seems to be the least of your worries.'

'Perhaps you could explain one day how you eat so much and stay so trim.'

'I don't think about it.'

'That can't be true.'

'It is.' Julie was watching a shifty-looking man standing by the waterfront. He was theoretically selling leather bracelets. 'Perhaps we should just lie in the sun and smoke something medicinal.'

Given their employer's strictures in relation to illegal drugs – and the questions on the subject in routine positive vetting – there were many things Kate could have said to this, but she'd decided long ago that Julie's weekend penchant for dope and possibly more had better remain off-limits. She was the most loyal friend and colleague you could wish for. 'Could you at least pretend that you understand the rules of our employment?'

'You think anyone cares?'

'Yes.'

'It would do you good.' Julie waited. 'All right, so what do you want to do?'

'Drown myself.'

Julie stood. 'Come on. That isn't your style. It's a beautiful day. Let's go for a walk.'

Kate had agreed that Stuart would have Fiona and Gus for three hours, so she and Julie had plenty of time to fill. They headed for the Rialto bridge, then the Ponte degli Scalzi by the station and then to the Campo Santa Margherita, finally coming back across the Ponte dell'Accademia. 'You sure as hell do like to walk,' Julie observed, once they had returned to the tourist hordes in St Mark's Square. They had intended to catch a boat across to San Giorgio Maggiore, but they were out of time and patience and opted to go for a drink in Harry's Bar instead, which was a mistake. 'It would have been cheaper to be mugged,' she concluded.

Stuart had agreed he would WhatsApp Kate with a place to meet in the vicinity of St Mark's, but at two o'clock she still hadn't heard from him. She sent him a message, but there was no reply. 'What's he playing at?'

'Did you definitely say two?'

'Definitely.'

They left the bar and went to wait in the square. Two fifteen came and went and then the clock tower crept past the half-hour. Kate messaged again: *We can't do this if you won't keep to your word.*

At two forty-five Kate started to worry in earnest. 'Do you think we should call the office?' she asked Julie. Kate's bosses at MI6 in Vauxhall had concluded a meeting between a traitor and his children was not a matter for them to worry themselves with but had agreed to allow Julie to accompany her superior 'just in case'.

'Not yet. Give him another fifteen minutes before we start to panic.'

They watched the clock in silence, but a few minutes later, Kate's phone buzzed. *So sorry, didn't see the time. Just finishing pizza. Could we meet in the Chiesa San Giuliano – a couple of minutes from St Mark's?*

All right, she shot back.

It was a short walk to the church and Kate asked Julie to wait outside. The interior was chilly and her breath hung in the air as she glanced around at the church's baroque splendour. She could see no sign of Stuart or the children, so she walked up to the front of the nave and looked up at the giant oil painting of the Crucifixion on the wall beside her, a brooding, even foreboding window to a different, more spiritual age. She turned back to face the entrance. 'Stuart?'

As she started to retrace her steps, she swung around to confront a shadow shifting in the corner of her eye. A man in a dark raincoat was pointing a Browning at her stomach.

2

HE HAD A lean, angular face, with severely acne-scarred skin. Two colleagues emerged from the darkness to join him, pistols hanging loosely at their sides. 'What do you want?' Kate asked.

'Your children are safe. Come with us and they will not be harmed.' The men spoke Russian, of course. She cursed her complacency.

'Come where?'

'Do as you are told.'

'I need to tell—'

'No! Don't be foolish,' the man told her. 'It is not worth the risk.'

They ushered her out of the side door of the church and hurried her along the smooth cobblestones of Campo de la Guerra. It was a relatively wide street that led down to the canal, lined with pastel-coloured houses, shops and cafés. It was quiet by the standards of central Venice, but there were enough people for her to make a scene if she wished to. Kate glanced over her shoulder. The men had slipped their Brownings into their pockets.

At the end, she was forced into a launch. She turned to face them. 'Where are you taking me?'

'Save your voice,' the acne-scarred man told her.

'My children will wonder what's happened to me.'

'They're safe with your husband.'

'Is this his doing?'

The man motioned for her to sit. She refused. The launch set off gently, motoring deeper into the heart of the city in all its rambling, faded glory, the buildings around her a patchwork of peeling paint, plasterwork and exposed brick. As they crossed under the first wrought-iron footbridge, a group of Chinese children watched her pass.

The canal swung to the right, opening out to the baroque splendour of the church of Santa Maria della Fava, with its ochre bridge and peaceful square, full now of tourists sheltering from the city's busier thoroughfares.

Just beyond the church, the launch swung right again and immediately glided to a halt by a villa, with stone steps that stretched down to the water's edge. A young man in a smart white uniform was waiting for her. He offered his hand. She did not take it. 'Please follow me, Mrs Henderson.'

He led her through a cool, damp, spartan lobby, which looked as if it flooded when the tide was high, and up another set of stone steps to a richly furnished hall. A chaise longue upholstered in burgundy velvet lined one wall beneath what looked like a Picasso. A coffee-table stood alongside what looked like a solid gold Buddha the size of a small horse.

She followed the man up to a sitting room on the floor above, where the furnishings were lighter, to fit with the sun streaming in from full-length windows opened to the balcony. 'Please wait here,' the man said.

Kate stepped outside. It was very bright now, the sun warm on her face, the palms and bougainvillaea in pots curling over the lip of the iron railings. She returned to the room and walked around it, assessing the art that graced its expensive walls: a Monet certainly, another Picasso probably – no, for sure, now she looked closer – a Cézanne, Van Gogh's self-portrait with a bandaged ear.

'You have an eye for a master?'

Kate swung around. Mikhail Borodin stood in the doorway, six feet two of tanned, lean muscle. 'I have an eye for value. The paintings in this room must be worth two hundred million or more.'

'More, I think. But this is my home, my true home. And it is my indulgence. As my father says, you cannot take it with you.'

'The art, or the money?'

'Both. Can I get you something to drink?'

'What have you done with my children?'

'Nothing. They are with Stuart, as Alexei should have told you. They are quite safe and I will return you to them within the hour, however this conversation progresses. I give you my word.'

'Your word's not worth a great deal.' Mikhail Borodin was the son of Russia's former intelligence chief, Igor. They had history from Operation Sigma, and not of the good kind.

'Well, let's see. I am sorry for the guns and the strong-arm tactics, but I didn't think you would come otherwise. Now, can I get you a drink?'

'Just get on with it.'

He gestured at the sofa. 'Please, sit . . .'

'I'd rather stand.'

'Come on, Kate, please . . . I am not going to hurt you.'

Kate did as she was instructed. Mikhail poured a glass of water from a jug filled with ice and fruit on the table. 'Cigarette?' He offered her a silver case.

'I'm trying to give up.'

'Wise. How have you been?' Perhaps it was Kate's imagination, but he seemed nervous suddenly.

'You've just kidnapped me in the heart of a European city. You're on very thin ice. So get on with it – and whatever you have to say had better be good.'

'Oh, so it is like the time you filmed me having sex with a man I had met in a bar and then tried to blackmail me?'

Kate didn't answer.

Mikhail swirled the water in his glass. 'As you can probably tell, I am here on my own. My wife, my son and my father are all in Moscow.'

'So what?'

'Well, there is a reason for that. They are being prevented from leaving.' He leant forward. 'I'll cut straight to it. There has been a coup in Moscow. The GRU has finally seduced the president and got what it has always wanted. Control.'

Kate kept her eyes locked on him. The rivalry between Russia's Foreign Intelligence Service, the SVR – successor to the notorious KGB – and the GRU, the country's military intelligence organization, was legendary.

'Durov has been suspended,' Mikhail said.

'When?' Vasily Durov had been hand-picked by Mikhail's father, Igor, to succeed him as head of the SVR.

'Last week. He is being interrogated at an old KGB summer camp outside Moscow. Yesterday my father was supposed to join me here with my wife and son. They were all prevented from boarding the aircraft in Moscow.'

'Why?'

'No reason has been given. They were allowed to go home, but they are under house arrest and are being watched around the clock.'

Kate kept her eyes on Mikhail, who was sweating now. His father was a long-standing friend of the Russian president, so she didn't think it likely he had been suddenly cast out from his inner circle. So unlikely, in fact, was it that it might just be true, however. 'How did Vasily and your father fall out with the president?'

'I don't know and neither do they. But . . . he's an unpredictable man. Normally it has to do with money, or loyalty, the only things he cares about. You understand that. No one can ever consider themselves truly a friend, and the closer you get, the more in danger you may be.'

'What does this have to do with me?'

'My father has been around long enough to know that the wind has changed. They will interrogate Durov until they have squeezed everything possible out of him. They will then put him on trial for corruption. In a week, or two at the most, they will arrest my father and take him to the same place. They are not going to bother with a trial for him.'

'My heart bleeds for you both.'

Mikhail ignored the remark. Having finished the first cigarette, he took another and pushed the case across to her. She accepted this time and leant closer so he could light one for her.

'My father has an offer. But we would need to move very quickly. In return for residency, the guarantee of a passport, freedom of movement in America and Europe, assurance that he will be able to keep his wealth, and security protection for life, he is prepared to bring you evidence that your prime minister is a spy working for Moscow.'

'Oh, yes?' Kate could feel the knot tightening in her stomach. The threat, even the likelihood, that this had long been true was unsettling enough, but hard evidence would be like a nuclear device exploding at the heart of British democracy. She shuddered at the thought she might be the one to detonate it.

'You should not make light of this.'

'What kind of evidence?'

Mikhail leant back, dragging deeply on his cigarette, as if to allow time for his offer to sink in. 'Payments, very large ones,' he said. 'Made to your prime minister, James Ryan, over many years.'

'The evidence my friend Rav managed to find before you killed him?'

'That had nothing to do with me – or my father.'

'We're not interested.'

'Oh? And what if I said we have even more than that on offer?'

'Such as?'

'Kompromat.'

'Our prime minister's lax personal morals are legendary. There can hardly be anyone in the country who doesn't know of his many affairs.'

'He would not survive this.'

'Oh, Christ, don't tell me – animals?'

'Your flippancy does you no credit. Underage girls.'

Kate felt the ground being cut from under her. Mikhail's gaze was locked on her. 'How young?'

'Fifteen – fourteen in one instance. He can be heard asking their ages *before* he has sex with them.'

Kate tried to compose herself. 'Where? He can't have been stupid enough to do it in Moscow?'

'Kosovo, during the war there.'

It made sense. The prime minister had once been an army officer and he had certainly served in Kosovo. Before he died, Rav had identified Ryan's female interpreter at the time as a probable Russian agent.

'If you always had this kind of kompromat on our new prime minister, why did you need to pay him?'

'As well as being profoundly immoral, your prime minister is extremely greedy. At the time, we were not certain even the kompromat was enough.'

'How do we know the video isn't fake?'

'Because when you see it you will know it is not.'

'Let me watch it now.'

'No. Only when they have accepted our offer.'

Kate finished her cigarette, stood up and went to the window. She watched the shifting eddies in the water below. 'You have a nerve, I'll give you that. Why should I trust you at all? I recruited Lena Sabic. She was a blameless young girl who'd had life stacked against her. I bullied and blackmailed her to come and work for you. And you murdered her. You cut her throat and left her for me to find in Greece.'

'I didn't do anything.'

Kate wasn't listening. 'And then, when my beloved friend Rav had managed to unearth some evidence of those payments you made to our prime minister, you murdered him, too, and tried to make it look like suicide by hanging the poor bastard from the light flex in his flat.'

'Not my decision, either.'

Kate turned to him. 'So, just to be really clear about this, hell will freeze over before I do anything to facilitate your very kind offer.'

'Is that so? We ask for nothing but a passport and protection in return for the greatest gift any intelligence agency has ever been offered and you turn me down flat? What would your superiors make of that?'

'Right now, I don't care.'

'I don't believe you. You want to know how your file in Moscow Centre concludes? The most conscientious – and *ambitious* – officer currently working for MI6 in London, tipped to be the first female head of the Secret Intelligence Service. A woman who regularly drives herself well above and beyond the call of duty, an officer who always appears to be trying to prove herself to someone or something, whose life has been dominated by the single-minded pursuit of exceptionality.' He looked at her steadily, daring her to deny it. 'And yet you want me to believe that this same officer is going to turn down an offer of such gravity without even passing it on to her superiors?' Mikhail shook his head. He held himself with the poised self-confidence common to all old Etonians. And, unlike his father and many others in Moscow, he had a sophisticated understanding of Western institutions and social mores, gained while he was educated in Britain, which had been Igor's intention.

'If I'm as ambitious as you say, I'd keep it to myself. You think my bosses want to know that you have cast-iron evidence their new prime minister is a Russian spy? They had a heart attack at the idea he *might* be. Certainty would kill them.'

'Come on, Kate.'

'You can call me Mrs Henderson.'

'Well, whatever you want me to call you, we both know one thing is true beyond doubt. Right now, our agent in Downing Street is passing the details of every file that crosses his desk – which, since he is the prime minister, means *every* file of any note, secret or otherwise – straight through to Moscow Centre and the office of our president. And I am offering you the chance to stop this calamitous threat to everything you hold dear.' Despite his polished air, a note of panic had crept into Mikhail's voice. But, then, fifty years with hard labour in a modern Russian gulag was probably an even less enticing prospect than the KGB hellholes of old. Even Eton wasn't preparation for that.

'You're a murderer.'

'We both know I am nothing of the kind.'

'Lena and Rav would say different if they were here.'

'I understand how upset you have been. We will offer something in good faith: the next step in the war on the West.'

'Which is?'

'A revolution in Estonia. The Night Wolves have bought a farm, just over the border, close to Narva.'

'Where?'

'We don't know precisely. It is a GRU operation. There will be unrest, the Wolves will burst from their lair and come to the aid of the Russian minority . . . so you will have something like war, as in Georgia and Crimea, but this time in a NATO ally. What will your prime minister do then? Will he consider himself to be bound by the famous Article Five? Is an assault on one really an attack on all?'

'When is this going to happen?'

'Soon. That is all I can tell you. But we will want to know you accept our offer by tomorrow night at the latest.'

'That's impossible, as you well know.'

'Then make it possible, Mrs Henderson. That is your job and everyone agrees you are good at it.'

'Show me the video.'

'Not here, not now. First, we need to know you accept our offer in principle. Then we can agree to meet again. But we have very little time. I have been summoned back to Russia and I can hold them off only for so long.' He shook his head. 'We have our backs to the wall, Kate. If you won't accept what I propose, we will go to the Americans or the Germans. And once the deal is done, your superiors in London will inevitably learn that you rejected our offer.' Mikhail came towards her with a small scrap of paper. On it was written a number. 'That's how to contact me. But I ask you to be quick. I don't think we have more than a few days at best and, whatever you might think of me or indeed my father, you may have many years to regret this opportunity being lost.'

Kate slipped the paper into her pocket. 'Don't ever use my children like this again,' she warned, as she moved to the door.

'It was not your husband's doing. You should know that.' Kate stopped, turned back to face Mikhail. 'He cuts a somewhat pathetic figure in Moscow. For what it is worth, I think you are the love of his life.'

'Goodbye, Mikhail.'

'I think you mean *"au revoir"*. We'll meet again.'

Kate walked down to the ground-floor lobby and out on to the launch. 'Take me back to my children, please,' she instructed the man with the pockmarked face. Her chest had constricted so violently that she felt as if she was about to have a heart attack, the anxiety that had been her constant companion for months now threatening to consume her.

3

KATE WAS MET back at the church by the implacable set of her fifteen-year-old daughter's jaw. 'Where the hell were you?'

'I—'

'You promised you weren't going to work while you were here.'

'How did you—'

'Dad said you had to take a work call.'

'Yes . . . yes. I'm really sorry.' Kate knew better than to choose this moment to get into an argument with her daughter. She could see the hurt in her eyes. There were also scratch marks on her arm, a recent worrying indication of her tendency to self-harm. Gus, meanwhile, stared resolutely at the floor. Whatever had happened in the meeting with their father had evidently shaken them both. 'Let's go,' she said. 'Maybe we can find an ice cream.'

As the children turned away, Julie whispered, 'What the hell happened?'

'*Pas devant les enfants.*'

'I do speak French, you know,' Fiona threw over her shoulder, 'and in six days' time, I'll basically be an adult anyway.'

That sounded like a threat rather than an abstract statement of fact, but Kate let it ride. They did get ice creams on the way back, and sat on a wall by the canal in front of their hotel, eating them in silence.

Once inside, Kate left her children in their room to simmer down, and tackled Julie first. 'Mikhail and Igor's thugs,' she explained. 'They took me at gunpoint to Mikhail's fancy palazzo.'

'What did they want?'

'To defect.'

Julie looked at her as if she had just gone mad, her vivid green eyes clouded by confusion.

'They are offering us the video they claim to have been using as kompromat against the prime minister. It shows him having sex with underage girls.'

'Did you see it?'

'No. Only if we accept their offer in principle.'

'What if it's a fake?'

'He claims we'll know it isn't.'

'I thought they could fake anything, these days . . . But why would they want to defect?' Julie couldn't keep the incredulity from her voice. She sat down on her bed.

'Mikhail says his father and Vasily Durov have fallen out with the Kremlin and been ousted in a coup orchestrated by the GRU. He says Durov is under arrest, which likely means bound for Siberia at best, execution at worst. He and his father are desperate to flee to the West before the net closes on them.'

'Did you believe him?'

'It doesn't matter whether I believe him or not. If the video exists, if it's real – and he promised evidence of the payments they've made to the prime minister, too – then we have no choice. There was more. As a gesture of goodwill, he said we should know the Kremlin is planning some kind of coup in Estonia.'

'What?'

'There will be a "threat" to the local Russian population in Narva – protests or riots or civil disorder. The Night Wolves have bought a farm just outside, stacked it with enough weaponry to start a war. They will come to the aid of their "countrymen".'

'Why the Night Wolves?'

'Plausible deniability. A bunch of old army vet bikers. How would we prove they took their orders from the Kremlin?'

Julie contemplated that in silence. Neither of them needed to articulate the fact that this was the kind of confrontation that could spark a third world war. 'Are you going to call London?' she asked.

'No. I was thinking about driving to Rome to file from the embassy, but we don't have time. Let's go straight to the flight. I'll have to drop the kids off at home, but I'll text Danny now and see what he can find out. The CIA is bound to have good coverage on the border.'

'I've never actually seen the Night Wolves in action, so what—'

'Just volume at this stage. Any farm with a lot of out-buildings or barns, any sign of lorries moving or parked on a significant scale. Motorbikes, obviously. Any recent transactions recorded in the Estonian Land Registry, otherwise a list of all properties owned by ethnic Russians.'

'Should I talk to Karen in Tallinn?' Karen White was their station chief in the Estonian capital.

'No. And don't do anything to alert the Estonians either. As soon as I've dropped the kids I'll tackle Ian and the chief and we'll go from there.'

Kate went next door to speak to her children. Fiona was in the loo. Gus was on his bed, playing Angry Birds on his iPad. Kate came to sit next to him. 'Was it all right?' she asked, caressing the back of his head. He pulled away. 'What happened?' she asked.

'Nothing happened.'

'You both seem . . . upset.'

'I'm fine.'

'Was it nice to see Dad?'

The bathroom door opened and Fiona stepped out. 'Dad burst into tears. He said he was miserable in Moscow. He has no friends, no money and no life. He told us he had made one terrible mistake and he would pay for it for the rest of his life.'

Kate shook her head slowly. 'He shouldn't have said that.'

'Why not? It's true.'

'Because it loads the burden of his mistakes on to you.'

'He only made one.'

'Well, that's not quite true, is it?'

'It's absolutely true.'

Kate could see her daughter was spoiling for a fight. Fiona took off her hairband and shook her hair free. It was never a good sign. Kate knew she should walk away. 'He betrayed us and chose to betray his country,' she said quietly.

'He didn't betray Gus and me.'

Kate stood up. 'I'll meet you in Reception in twenty minutes. We're a long way past the check-out time I agreed, so don't be late.'

'Why won't you accept his apology?' Fiona asked. She looked as if she was about to smash something or burst into tears, or both.

'Let's talk about this calmly when we get home.'

'That's just an excuse not to talk about it at all.'

'I'll see you in Reception in twenty minutes.'

Kate went to her own room and sat on her bed. She noticed that her hands were shaking, got to her feet and went into the bathroom. She stared at herself in the mirror. Her face was white, her eyes bloodshot. She looked exhausted, which was no surprise. The acute stomach and back pain that had been plaguing her had returned with a vengeance. It was as if someone had wrapped a belt around her chest and was slowly tightening it.

She felt physically terrible. She walked to her bed, lay down and tried to concentrate on the breathing exercises the psychologist she had been seeing had recommended. They seemed to make no bloody difference at all.

She forced herself upright, packed the last of her belongings and walked down the grand staircase to Reception.

They caught the four o'clock flight home, the entire journey conducted in more or less total silence. Julie had made a concerted effort to jolly the children along before they boarded the plane until she received a text at Passport Control. After that she'd retreated rapidly into herself. Kate made no headway in winkling out of her what the trouble was.

She left Fiona in theoretical charge of her brother at home in Battersea and reached MI6's Vauxhall Cross headquarters just after eight. She stopped off at the ops room on the second floor, where she found Julie sitting next to Danny in front of a bank of computer screens. 'I think we've found it,' Julie said.

'Grab a seat,' Danny instructed. He had long dark hair, piercing blue eyes and pretty much always wore a black T-shirt, blue jeans and threadbare sneakers. He had a Chinese dragon tattooed around the side and back of his neck and the kind of easy smile that could stop grown women in their tracks. Or perhaps it was just Kate. She suspected he and Julie had once been an item but, if so, it was a rare outbreak of common sense on her friend's behalf: her taste in men was usually abysmal.

Kate did as she had been told. The floor was covered with styrofoam coffee cups and takeaway food cartons that had yet to make it to the bin in the corner. In his eating habits, and the curious absence of any visible impact on his waistline, Danny provided another painful reminder of her former deputy, Rav, who'd had a similar penchant for chaining himself to his desk in a tunnel of intense concentration. It was what made Danny – and had made Rav – so good at his job.

The images streamed from the CIA satellite covering this section of Estonia were so clear you could have seen a pebble in the grass. They were looking at a collection of outbuildings, but the screen next to them had a wider view of a village. 'Puhlova,' Kate said.

'You know it?' Julie asked.

Kate had met a Russian Army colonel there about a decade previously. He'd promised information on the state of

Russia's nuclear arsenal in return for very large cash payments, but she'd not believed a word he'd said and had turned down his offer flat.

'It changed hands two months ago,' Julie said. 'The new owner is a business registered in Helsinki.'

Danny closed in on the tyre tracks in the mud. Kate could see exactly what he was thinking: a lot of tracks, too narrow for a tractor, much too wide for a car. 'Hard to be sure until we see some movement,' he said. He zoomed in on a patch of grass just outside one of the buildings. Cigarette butts lay everywhere. 'A lot of workers for a small farm.'

'You find anything on the firm?'

Julie shook her head. 'A holding company in Geneva, another in Bern, then to Belize and finally Panama. If it's not the Russians, it's someone else with a lot of cash to spend covering their tracks.'

'How far back can you go?'

Kate's question was to Danny and he pulled up another screen and started to rewind the footage on it rapidly. 'Only a week, but that's what's weird. I checked the Met Office records. It rained really heavily nine days ago, so these tracks would have been obliterated if they'd been there before then. They must have been made after the deluge. But there's been no movement in or out of these barns in the past week.' He stopped rewinding and minimized the screen, pulling up another. 'We started casting around. We looked closer to the border . . . but neither of us could find anything. So then we went further away.' He froze the footage and closed in on a building by the Baltic. 'This is a hotel in Silamae on the beach. A congenial place to plan a coup.'

Beneath a lean-to beside the hotel, the rear wheels of several motorbikes were clearly visible. 'Not an army, exactly,'
Danny concluded, 'but maybe the vanguard.'

'That's great,' Kate said. 'What's that on?'

'PCR2.'

'See what else you can find on both sides of the border.'

Kate left them to their work, then thought better of it and
doubled back. She sat again, so that she was close to Danny:
the people at the other end of the ops room would be out of
earshot. 'Talk me through faking a video.'

'What kind?'

'If someone wanted to create a fake kompromat video, is
it possible to do it convincingly enough to fool us?'

'I guess that really depends. What kind of video are we
talking about exactly?'

'A sex tape.'

'It's hard to know without seeing it. I guess it would
depend on the quality of the lighting, the camera angles . . .'

'But, in theory, is it possible that we could be completely
convinced by a fake?'

Danny glanced over his shoulder to check no one was listening. 'In theory, yes. Who you are talking about?'

'The prime minister, say, or the US president.'

Danny nodded. 'You could fake footage of either of them
giving a speech they never gave saying things they never
said – and people have.'

'How?'

'Well, they've given thousands of speeches, so you feed
all those into a powerful piece of software called a neural
network. You direct the software to learn the visual associations between particular words and their mouths as they

say them. And if you want the final version to be particularly convincing, you'd get the software to compete with a copy of itself, one generating the imagery, the other trying to spot the fakes. They call them generative adversarial networks and it's very effective. The computer goes on improving its work until it finds a way to beat the competing network that is trying to weed out the fakes, so you get pure computational hallucinations.'

'What about a sex video?'

'Same principle, though probably easier in reality. You just need to make the statistical connections between the individual you want to focus on and the aspect of his behaviour you wish to fake – in this case movement.'

'Could you spot a fake?'

'Probably. The GAN images have a creepy edge, though the software is improving all the time. The Russians might be ahead of us on this.'

'Could I spot a fake?'

'It all depends on the clarity of the image. If there is plenty of light and the visual and audio quality are good, you'd probably have a good sense of whether it's real or not. But the lower the quality, the easier it might be to pass off as a fake.'

Kate touched Danny's arm. 'Thanks.' She made a brief phone call to their liaison officer at GCHQ in Cheltenham to check whether they had any information on the claims Mikhail had made of a coup inside Moscow Centre against his father and Vasily Durov. She said they had heard nothing of the kind.

Kate walked up to the chief's office on the fifth floor. C, otherwise known as Sir Alan Brabazon, was waiting for her,

looking out at the lights of the House of Commons twinkling on the far side of the river. As he turned to face her, she
thought how much he had aged these past six months, his
thick curly hair now flecked with grey and his hooded eye-
lids locked under a permanent frown. His wife, Alice, had
seen her cancer return – this time to the liver – and her life
was now almost certainly measured in weeks rather than
months. He walked to his desk and picked up the phone.
'I'll get Ian up here.' He dialled and waited. 'She's here,' he
said, and replaced the receiver.

He went to the sofa and chairs in the corner and motioned
Kate to sit. He tapped his tortoiseshell reading glasses
against his knee, his hands weathered from the hours he
spent in the garden at his country home just north of
Winchester. 'How was Stuart?' he asked.

'He burst into tears when he was alone with the kids.'

'I'm not surprised. A lifetime in Moscow probably wasn't
what he had in mind.'

'He says they're treating him like a pariah.'

'Perhaps, but I doubt it.'

Kate had only a moment to consider this before Ian
Granger burst in, as was his habit these days. He'd always
liked to stage an entrance. *'Aghamo mshvidobisa,'* he said.
Even by the standards of the service, he had a gift for lan-
guages and liked to remind everyone of this by peppering
routine conversations with different greetings – in this case,
Georgian.

'I fear this is not going to be good news.' He crossed his
legs to reveal a brand new pair of suede Chelsea boots that
matched the designer black jeans he had recently taken to
wearing to the office. He now eschewed Savile Row

tailoring, the qualities of which had once been one of his standard dinner-party riffs, and rarely seemed to bother with a haircut either, his long blond curls tumbling over the collars of his Ted Baker shirts. Sir Alan was much too aloof to notice Ian's cry for mid-life attention.

'Coffee, tea?' Sir Alan asked.

'Not at this hour,' Ian said. He'd discovered 'wellness' lately and told anyone who would listen it was 'dangerous' to drink caffeine past noon.

'Something stronger?'

Ian was about to decline, but then had second thoughts. 'Well, if you're offering.'

Sir Alan went to a cupboard in the corner, took out a bottle of Glenfiddich and poured three glasses. He didn't ask Kate whether she wanted ice or water.

Ian didn't wait for Sir Alan to take his seat before turning to Kate. 'Give us your worst,' he said, with what he considered his megawatt smile.

Kate tried not to let her irritation show. 'Mikhail Borodin and his father, Igor, want to defect. Mikhail says that Igor and Vasily Durov have been the victims of a coup in Moscow Centre, orchestrated by the GRU. He says that both men are under house arrest already. He's offering the video he says was used as kompromat to force the prime minister to work for them, along with evidence of the cash payments made to him over the years.'

'Do I dare ask what the video shows?' Ian said.

'He claims it's of James Ryan having sex with underage girls while he was an army officer in Kosovo. I asked to see it, but he said he would only show it to us once we accept his offer in principle.'

'What do they want?' Sir Alan asked.

'Residence here, passports – and a guarantee they'll be able to use the assets they have stored in the West. They also want to ensure freedom of movement throughout Europe and America. I said that wasn't in our gift.'

'And, no doubt, they're in a hurry.'

'Yes. There was one other thing. He offered what he called a parting gift. He says the GRU has been planning a coup in Estonia, which is now imminent. The Night Wolves have bought a farm just outside Narva and stored enough weapons there to start a small war. The Kremlin will create some kind of crisis involving the Russian minority and the Night Wolves will come to their aid.'

'And the Center Party will call for Moscow to intervene,' Sir Alan said, tapping his glasses against his leg again. Kate noticed some dark stubble beneath both sides of his chin, missed with careless shaving. It was most unlike him.

'We think we've probably found the farm. It's on PCR2.'

Sir Alan got up and went to his desk. Ian and Kate stood behind him as he put on his glasses and looked at the satellite feeds. 'The place by the beach on the right is where we think some of them are staying. If you close in, you can see the rear wheels of a line of motorbikes.'

'How long have the CIA got?' Sir Alan asked.

'Only a week. No movement in or out in that time. But it rained heavily nine days ago, so those tyre tracks outside the barn have been made since then.'

Sir Alan closed the feed and led them back to sit in the corner. He took a sip of his whisky and swirled the ice around in his glass.

Ian jumped into the silence, as was also his style. 'I'm suspicious,' he said. 'That's my first reaction, I'm afraid.'

Kate resisted the temptation to point out that he was always suspicious of anything he hadn't originated. Sir Alan continued to stare into his glass.

'I don't think this needs to take all night,' Ian went on, which invariably meant he had a dinner to attend, or an assignation, or both. 'We can monitor the situation in Estonia to see how it develops, but we shouldn't – *couldn't* – accept their offer to defect.' He looked at his superior. 'I'm sure you agree, Alan.' It wasn't a question.

'And why would you think that?'

Ian made a show of appearing incredulous. 'Because it smacks of a well-organized disinformation plot designed to take us for fools. They know Kate is in a vulnerable state—'

'Come on, Ian,' Kate said. She had not expected his assault on her to be quite so obvious.

'Withdraw that,' Sir Alan instructed him. 'And apologize, please.'

'All right, I'm sorry,' Ian said easily, without bothering to look at her or sound as if he meant it. He ran his hand languorously through his hair. 'But the stakes are damned high here. Just imagine if the PM gets wind of the fact that we're taking this seriously. He *is* the prime minister, after all, and likely to remain so, unless I'm missing something. The damage that could be done – the havoc he could wreak – on our organization might be terminal.'

'So you'd rather have a Russian spy running our country?' Kate asked.

Ian faced her. 'Well, first, we should be careful in our language. If we accept your theory, he isn't a Russian spy but an agent of influence. Compromised, yes, if it were true, but unlikely to be doing much more than simply giving their arguments a fair hearing. And, much more importantly, there is absolutely not a shred of hard evidence that he *is* working for the Russians.'

'That's what they're offering us,' Kate said.

Sir Alan was sitting back in his chair, watching the pair of them fight this out.

'It's a trap, Kate. Surely you can see that. They've offered us some tasty bait again. We'll be drawn in again. And then they'll seek to embarrass and confuse us. Again. They hardly need to bother with any serious operations, these days, because we do all their work for them.' Ian looked at them, waiting for a response, and, when he didn't get one, simply ploughed on. 'It's too damned *neat*. Last time, they drop in the intelligence that our prime minister has prostate cancer. We don't know this, so we discount it. Then, hey presto, he suddenly walks out into Downing Street to announce both his illness and resignation within twenty-four hours. We take this as clear evidence that the original operation was a stroke of genius and the intelligence it gleaned thus one hundred per cent genuine and correct. And the rest is history. Weeks of total chaos and confusion not just inside these four walls but in our country at large.' Ian paused to draw breath. If his frustration was confected, it was very convincing. 'And now here we go again. They offer us another juicy morsel. *Proof*, this time, in the form of some disgusting video of our new prime minister – and who can argue with that? It couldn't *possibly* be faked – that the original intelligence was correct. They know Kate will be inclined to believe—'

'Do not personalize this, Ian,' Sir Alan said. 'And that's an order, not a request.'

'But we're going around the same mountain.'

'Perhaps we are,' Sir Alan said, 'but if there is a video and a chance it proves that our prime minister is a liar, a traitor and a cheat, then we would be neglecting our duty if we failed to mount even a cursory investigation into its credibility. I have enough faith in our organization to believe us capable of determining whether a piece of video is faked or not.'

'But that's exactly the point. No one can ever determine that with one hundred per cent accuracy. So they've just put this fly out on the water, waiting for us to come up and swallow it whole, like a lazy trout.' Fly-fishing was another of the new hobbies Ian liked to show off about, along with skiing, shooting and an apparently endless succession of Ironman competitions. He glanced at his watch. 'Time is money' was another of his favourite phrases. 'I have to go or I'll be late.'

'For what?' Sir Alan turned his gaze towards him.

Ian was briefly flustered. 'I just promised not to be late for dinner.'

'I understand that your reputation for good timekeeping can't be held hostage by important matters of state, but all the same . . .'

Ian bridled. Only a short time ago, his brazen insubordination, even rudeness, would have been unthinkable, but his insolence was a testament to Sir Alan's fading power. He had been in the job for seven years now, his standard five-year term extended twice, but it was unlikely to be amended for a third time, and Ian's attempt to woo the prime minister to appoint him Sir Alan's successor was Whitehall's worst-kept secret.

'We really can't take this any further now, Alan.' Ian was addressing him as if Kate wasn't present. 'I'm happy to stay all night, if need be, *as always*.' He shook his head. 'But nothing is going to be said, I fear, that will persuade me to change my mind. I propose a keen watching brief on Estonia, but as for the rest . . .' he shrugged '. . . we should let it go.'

As Kate watched the two men squaring up to each other, like stags long past their prime, she was reminded of Stuart's succinct summary of Ian Granger. 'He's just a bit of a cunt,' he would say. 'Everyone has a boss like that once in a while.'

If thinking of Stuart wasn't in itself so painful, it might have made her smile.

Ian departed. Sir Alan peered at the whisky in his glass, then drank it straight. 'If he ends up as your replacement, I'm going to kill myself,' Kate said.

Sir Alan went to refill his glass. 'You'll have to excuse his manners. Ella has just filed for a divorce.'

'Christ. Why?' Ella was Ian's long-suffering wife. The pair had met at Oxford and he liked to boast of her incredible success in building an online retail empire selling sleep-wear. 'I mean, I always assumed she must know about his affairs.'

'Suspecting is one thing, but it turns out knowing is another. She found the phone he'd been using to arrange his assignations.'

'With Julie?'

'He wasn't in a mood to be specific. It only happened this afternoon.'

'Oh, shit. That would explain it. She got a text while we were travelling back from Venice.'

'He tells me he's in love and fully intends to marry her.'

'Julie? He thinks he's going to marry Julie?' Kate was aghast. If the two of them having an affair was puzzling enough, marriage would be incomprehensible. 'She thinks it's just sex. Expedient, because she can't be bothered to date properly. I feel sorry for him.'

'I doubt that. I don't. Somewhere in there, beneath the vaulting ambition and the deep-seated insecurities, is a man whose heart is basically in the right place, but I'm afraid I lost sight of that individual a long time ago.'

'Subtlety has never been his strong point.'

'Or loyalty.' Sir Alan turned to her. 'How are you?'

'I don't know.' She thought about it. 'I just don't know.'

'Try not to take this the wrong way, but you don't look on top of the world.'

'Thanks. How are you?'

'As you would imagine. Alice decided in the end that she would go through another round of chemo, but the oncologist was fairly clear that he thought it unlikely to have much effect. If it doesn't, we're to be transferred to palliative care.'

'I'm sorry, Alan.' She watched him in silence.

He was as still as a statue. Then he shook his head, as if to dismiss a morbid train of thought. 'Tell Karen to go down to Narva tonight. I'll send out someone to help her and speak to the Estonians. We'll need a Cobra in the morning. I'd like them to know we were ahead of the curve if Mikhail is right and it does kick off.'

'What do you want to do about their offer?'

'Ian's objections are understandable enough. In the end, the only thing all that grief brought us six months ago was the knowledge that your husband was Agent Viper. So . . . I need to buy some cover. I'd like us both to brief the foreign secretary after Cobra. I think, for once, I'll conspire to leave Ian behind.'

'Is that wise? Briefing the foreign secretary, I mean.' The prime minister had sent one of his early leadership rivals, Meg Simpson, to the grandiose office overlooking Whitehall that had once ruled an empire. The press generally considered it a dull, uninspiring choice, designed to make sure he had no rival anywhere near him. Imogen Conrad, the dynamic younger woman who had given him a run for his money in the final round of the leadership contest, had remained where she was at Education.

'I think so,' Sir Alan said. 'Meg may not be as dazzling as either the prime minister or Imogen Conrad, but she's a hell of a lot more reliable than either. Did you check with Cheltenham for any traffic to support the idea of a coup in Moscow Centre?'

'Yes, and they've heard nothing of the kind either.' Kate stood. 'I'd better go. The children are looking after themselves, which is not ideal.'

She went downstairs and put her head around the door of her department. Only Suzy was there, which was far from untypical as Kate had quickly learnt. Suzy shared her predecessor Rav's work ethic but, sadly, not his charm. 'Julie briefed me,' Suzy said, with clipped Mancunian vowels, in such a way as to indicate Kate should really have done so.

'I'm sorry. Do you mind if I fill you in properly tomorrow? I have to run for the kids.'

'I understood the situation in Estonia was potentially critical.'

'We're watching it closely. Karen is going to Narva tonight. She'll report back in the morning.'

'Do you want me to do some work on anything?'

'No, don't worry. And don't stay late . . .' Kate got a few paces down the corridor before she had second thoughts and went back. If Suzy was determined to staple herself to her desk, they might as well make it count. 'Actually, it would be useful if you could do a briefing note on the Night Wolves for the foreign secretary and the PM, their links with the Kremlin and the GRU, their role in Ukraine, that sort of thing.'

Suzy looked pleased. 'Thanks,' she said. 'I really appreciate that.'

'There's a Cobra meeting first thing. I'll give it to the PM and the foreign secretary there.'

Suzy's smile broadened. Kate had already worked out that nothing pleased her new deputy quite as much as the prospect of catching the eye of their superiors.

4

KATE CHANGED INTO her trainers by the lift and walked out
into the chill night. The wind was biting, so she took a
cashmere beanie from her coat and pulled it down tight
over her ears. Normally, this daily walk helped bring some
order to her thoughts, but tonight, the rhythmic pace of the
journey seemed to accelerate the rising tide of her anxiety.
Now that Stuart had gone, the only person she shared her
true state of mind with was her aunt Rose, who combined
the role of mentor at work – as the long-time head of the
Finance Department, it had been she who'd first encouraged Kate to apply for the Service from Cambridge – and
surrogate mother at home. Kate's real mother was in a home
nearby with Alzheimer's, which was a relief to everyone
who knew her.

But even Rose was not aware of the long sleepless nights
and the sense of a world closing in so fast that it was almost
suffocating her niece.

As had been so often the case, it was a sense of duty that came to Kate's aid as she walked into the light and warmth at 17 Khyber Road. The single driving force of her life now was to try to limit the damage of her husband's departure on Gus and Fiona.

Not that she had any sense they appreciated it. Her thirteen-year-old son was hunched over his iPad on the sofa in the corner of the kitchen. Kate gently removed the headphones from his ears (which, she could not help noticing, were full of wax). 'What are you watching?'

'*Mission Impossible*.'

'Sounds like my life.'

He didn't smile. 'Is that a joke?'

She tutted in despair. 'Where's your sister?'

'She went out.'

'Where? I told her—'

'That *is* a joke. She's upstairs. With Jed.'

'Oh. What time did he come around?'

'About ten minutes ago.'

Kate went to put on the kettle. 'What did you have for supper?'

'Salmon, like you suggested.'

'Did she eat her—'

'I'm not going to be your snitch, Mum.'

Kate came to sit next to her son. 'You know this is serious, right? They say anorexia is the hardest mental illness to treat.'

'She isn't anorexic.'

'With respect, you're not a doctor.'

'And neither are you. If it's so serious, why haven't you taken her to see one?'

For all his detachment, Gus sometimes had a knack for putting his finger on the key question and she winced inwardly. She'd been asking herself the same question for some weeks. 'Right now,' she said, 'what with everything else, I worry that it might actually make it worse, not better. I'm hoping if we can just keep her on the straight and narrow for a little longer, the pressure will ease off.'

'You know that's not how it works, right?' Gus said.

'What?'

'Psychiatrists don't make you worse. That's not the point of them.'

Kate had no comeback to that. She kissed him thoughtfully, made a cup of tea and opened the bin to throw in the teabag. As she did so, she noticed the remains of what looked like an untouched piece of salmon fillet.

With a heavy heart, she went upstairs to knock on Fiona's bedroom door. 'We're fully clothed,' her daughter replied. Kate pushed back the door to see Fiona and her tall, rangy boyfriend lying in front of what appeared to be homework on Fiona's bed. Jed leapt to his feet and came to kiss Kate on both cheeks. Despite his tattoos and piercings, Kate had come to be very fond of him over the past few months. She wondered sometimes what they would have done without him. It was almost as if he was the glue holding their family – or sanity – together.

'Hi, love,' Kate said.

'Hi.' Fiona didn't move.

'Did you manage to cook supper okay?'

'Uh-huh.'

'Have you eaten, Jed?'

'Yes, thank you, Mrs Henderson. I had supper at home. How was the rest of your day at work?'

'Er, complicated, if I'm honest.'

Fiona's demeanour suggested there was every chance she would continue to ignore her mother, so Kate retreated to her bedroom. She ran a bath and soaked in it, then contemplated once more how lonely she felt in the middle of the night – or at any time, for that matter.

She had one more task, so she reached for the house phone and dialled the number for Rose's London home. It was a gorgeous four-bedroom townhouse just off the King's Road, in a row characterized by many shades of pastel.

'Is that you, Kate?'

'How did you know?'

'No one else calls this late.'

'I'm sorry.'

'How was your trip?'

'Oh . . .' Kate realized she hadn't had time to reflect upon the impact of seeing Stuart. 'I don't really know.'

'How was he?'

'Sad. A bit pathetic. He burst into tears on the children and told them both how much he hated his life in Moscow.'

'Oh, God, how selfish. And bloody unhelpful.'

'Yes . . . yes. I guess so.'

'Was that all?'

'Yes. Other than that, it went smoothly.' Kate had learnt to her cost over the last six months that, in the house of secrets, it was better to keep knowledge to herself, even if Rose was the reason she had joined the Service in the first place. 'Look, I'm so sorry to do this to you, but something's come up that's going to keep me in London this weekend, I think, so we'll have to cry off the trip to Cornwall.'

'That's a shame. We were so looking forward to seeing the children.'

'I know. I'm really sorry.' Rose and her husband Simon had a newly built holiday home – a temple to oak and glass – between the beaches of Polzeath and Daymer Bay, one of Kate's favourite places. As she thought of it, she realized she was disappointed too.

'Why don't you let us take them?' Rose asked. 'If you're going to have to work, it doesn't sound as if they'll have much of a weekend. And, of course, there's your mother. She'll never let us forget it and I'm not sure I feel saintly enough to take her on our own.'

Kate thought about this.

'It's settled, then,' Rose said. 'I'll drop by your office in the morning to work out the arrangements.'

'I don't know what I'd do without you.'

'You'd be fine. But . . . have you seen Dr Wiseman yet?'

'No.'

'Kate—'

'I actually have an appointment tomorrow lunchtime.' Kate had clean forgotten about it until then. And she had fully intended to cancel.

'Well, go. Whatever else is happening, make sure you go. Please. Or I really won't forgive you.'

'All right, all right . . . Oh, one more thing.' Kate bit her lip. 'Any news on Lena's sister?'

'I'm still waiting for the report from Belgrade.'

'What's taking them so long?' Kate had recruited Lena Sabic to work for the Service with the clear promise that

they would free her young sister Maja from terrible circumstances in Serbia and bring her to England. Kate naturally
felt Lena's death reinforced this promise rather than freed
them from its implications, but it was not a universal view,
with the cost and complications of an extraction in danger of
triggering a major row at the top of the Service. As head of
Finance, Rose was overseeing the operation, at Kate's behest.
At least she would have one ally when it came to the crunch.

'It's complicated, Kate, you know that. I'll chase it up in
the morning. In the meantime, get some sleep – and make
sure you see Dr Wiseman.'

Kate replaced the receiver. Although she had been seeing
a counsellor for months, sometimes singly, sometimes with
the children, Rose had insisted the change to a psychiatrist
was what she needed now.

Kate's phone buzzed and she picked it up to see a message from Suzy, sent via the secure in-house service they
used amongst colleagues: *Julie just told me about the potential
video. Jesus, what a fucking sleaze bucket. Am sorry, but you are
absolutely right. You have to follow it up.*

Kate put her phone face down and switched off her bedside light. She stared at the ceiling, thinking of the phone
call with Rose. There was no way she'd see Dr Wiseman
tomorrow. It felt too much like opening Pandora's Box.

5

KATE WAS AWOKEN the next morning by another message, this time from Julie. *Switch on the TV.*

She glanced at her watch. It was 6.24 a.m. She pushed herself upright, reached for the remote and turned on the television.

The banner running along the bottom of Sky News read: 'Estonia: Kremlin calls attacks a "provocation".' It was emblazoned over footage from late last night of a mob wielding sticks and attacking a group of protesters in the centre of the Estonian border town of Narva.

The presenter, a slim woman with riotous blonde hair and the cadaverous air of someone who hasn't eaten properly for a decade, was talking to her political editor, a slim young man who looked like he was filling in between school and Cambridge. 'Well, the temperature seems to be rising rapidly,' the young man said. 'As you know, this all started when a group of men tried to pull down a statue of Lenin in the Estonian border town of Narva. Some of the local ethnic Russian population protested and were then attacked. Now, in the last few minutes, we've seen the Center Party in Tallinn, which principally represents Estonia's quite substantial Russian minority, issue a highly provocative invitation to the Kremlin to formally intervene – militarily, if necessary. Russian people are simply not safe in Estonia, it says. No word from the Kremlin in response, yet, but Estonia is of course a NATO ally and, under its Article Five, an attack – or a threat – on one is an assault on all.'

'So what has been Downing Street's response?'

'It's early in the day, of course, and I understand there is to be a Cobra meeting within the next few hours, but the briefing I received a short time ago suggests that the prime minister's overwhelming mood is likely to be one of caution. In the words of one source in Downing Street, it's not worth risking World War Three over a few punches being thrown in Estonia. But the Germans and the French are taking a much more robust line and I guess we'll wait to see exactly what emanates from the White House in the course of the day.'

'Would it be overly cynical,' the presenter asked, sitting back in her chair with a sly smile, 'to cast our minds back to those allegations in the leadership election six months ago that the prime minister might in some way have been . . . how shall I put it? . . . compromised by the Russians – and to worry that this could be a factor?'

The political editor permitted himself an equally sly smile back. 'I think it's a thought you would whisper very quietly, unless you wanted to earn the PM's undying enmity. "Trash of the social-media age" is what they call all that in

Downing Street. But opposition MPs will, no doubt, level the charge at him once again that he is in some way Moscow's stooge.'

Kate switched off the television and went to shower. By the time she was out, she had a message from Sir Alan warning that the Cobra meeting had been brought forward to 8 a.m., so she left an apologetic note for Fiona, asking her to make sure she got her brother on to the bus with her for school, and caught a cab direct to Whitehall.

She walked through the entrance just next to Downing Street and swung right to go down the stairs past the carefully preserved Tudor remnants of the palace that had stood there in Henry VIII's time. She handed her phone in to the guard sitting by the security portals at the bottom. Her pass didn't give her automatic clearance, so she waited for him to check her details against the names on the list, then open the door for her. She glanced through to the anteroom, where the more junior aides sat, sifting any last-minute intelligence coming in.

The prime minister, James Ryan, was already seated in the Cabinet Office Briefing Room, the setting for all Cobra meetings, waiting for everyone else to arrive, a very different approach from his predecessor, who had always liked to arrive last, preferably having kept his audience waiting. The PM was fifty-five, the same age as C, of whom he had been an exact contemporary at public school. He had the carefully cultivated crumpled air of the truly vain. His shirt did not appear to have been ironed and his thick, wavy dark hair seemed not to have seen a brush for days, giving him the appearance of a student who'd just crawled out of bed. He'd put on weight since crossing the threshold to Downing

Street, his once handsome features now puffed and jowly. But he still liked to share his legendary charisma with anyone in his orbit.

'Kate Henderson, as I live and breathe. What a pleasure to see you.' He gave her a beaming smile.

'Good morning, Prime Minister.'

'Is it? I've been up for hours. It feels like lunchtime.' He glanced at the cabinet secretary, who sat beside him. She was a tall, grey-haired, mostly serious woman called Shirley Grove, who, it was said, occasionally exhibited a flash of supremely dry and rather cutting humour. She didn't find her boss funny in the least. 'Must be why I'm getting so fat,' the prime minister went on. 'I keep inventing extra meals.' He leant forward on the table and fixed Kate with a steely, half-amused gaze that was another of his stocks in trade, as if life was one long P. G. Wodehouse story. 'How *are* you, Kate?'

'I'm well, Prime Minister.'

'Sorry to hear about your husband. Sounds like a wretched fellow. Better luck next time. That's my motto.' He smiled again. His latest girlfriend had just departed Downing Street after what was said to have been another tempestuous row. 'I'm on the market,' he had quipped at a recent dinner.

Kate coloured. She couldn't think of anyone else tactless enough to make a joke of the breakdown of her marriage. But she was saved further embarrassment by Sir Alan's arrival, which chilled the air by several degrees. He nodded at the prime minister and sat at the far end of the table from him, as if deliberately trying to keep his distance. The two men were said by contemporaries to have been close friends at school, but, if so, Kate had yet to identify the cause of the current hostility between them. He was followed by the defence secretary as the room quickly filled. The foreign secretary, Meg Simpson, and her senior team were the last to arrive.

Simpson was smaller and broader in the flesh than she appeared on television and looked quite a few years older, too, with thick-rimmed reading glasses on a chain around her neck and a tight bob of grey hair. She wore barely any make-up and betrayed few signs of vanity. She looked flustered to have arrived last.

'Let's begin,' the prime minister said, as if they were about to have a party.

Sir Alan stood up. He sure as hell wasn't the entertainment. 'As you know, we scheduled this meeting yesterday evening, before the events in Narva. We had received a tip-off from a reliable source that the Russians were about to roll the dice again. Our working assumption is that the GRU is the agency responsible and they appear to be following the playbook that worked so well for them in Crimea: create unrest, claim the local Russian minority is under threat, and intervene.'

Sir Alan had the remote control for one of the screens at the end of the table and he flicked it on. It was showing the feed from PCR2 on SIS's internal server, which Danny must have switched out to line. 'This is a farm in a small village called Puhlova, which was bought from a local man by a firm registered in Helsinki some months ago. The true owner is hidden behind so many holding companies that it will take us some time to get to the bottom of it, but I think we can safely assume we will find it's one or other agency of the Russian state.'

Sir Alan zoomed in on the muddy ground and moved to point at the screen. 'It's hard to make out unless you look very closely, but you can see here the tyre tracks of lorries or heavy trucks. Our understanding is that the Night Wolves – which is a Russian paramilitary group mainly made up of veterans from the war in Chechnya and closely allied with the Kremlin – have stored enough weapons here to mount a serious challenge to the Estonian state.'

'Looks like any other farm,' the prime minister said. 'What have they got hidden in there? Pitchforks?' He was smiling, as if this was still some kind of joke.

'We don't know yet.' Sir Alan closed down the feed and clicked on another. 'Kate here and her team found this hotel nearby on the Baltic, which we think at least some of the Night Wolves are staying in.'

'Looks tempting,' the prime minister said. Kate glanced from one man to the other. It was hard to imagine that these two had once been school friends. If they were faking their disdain for each other, they were great actors.

Sir Alan flicked on Sky News, which was still showing pictures of last night's violence. 'We have no doubt that the original attempt to pull down the statue of Lenin, which of course triggered the protests and then the counter-violence, will have been orchestrated from Moscow. Indeed, the entire event, from beginning to end, appears to have been their work.'

'Why?' The prime minister leant forward on to the table again, his demeanour more serious now.

'To expand their sphere of influence, as they have in so many other places that used to be part of the Soviet Empire. That has to be our working assumption. The Night Wolves will come to the protesters' aid, possibly tonight. They will clash with Estonian security forces. The tension will ratchet up. The local Russian population will increase their demands for Moscow to intervene, possibly for the entire region to secede, as we saw in Crimea.'

'It's possible the whole thing is just a feint,' Ian said, desperate to be in on the act. Sir Alan didn't deign to look at him.

'A *what*?' the prime minister asked.

'A feint, Prime Minister, a manoeuvre, just designed to test us out.'

'I should say it's obviously designed to test us,' the prime minister said, turning to Kate. 'What do you think?'

She was acutely conscious of all eyes in the room being upon her and of the fury in Ian's flushed cheeks. He'd forgotten that a stilted formality was the hallmark of all Cobra meetings – at least, all those she'd attended – and his easy insouciance jarred, even if the sentiments were designed to appeal to the man at the head of the table. He looked underdressed for the occasion, too. He was the only man in the room without a jacket.

'Ian may be right,' she said, throwing him a lifeline, on instinct. 'Perhaps they just want to see how we react. But then we have only to look at what happened in Crimea and even in Montenegro, with that attempted coup. So it might be wiser to assume they mean business again.'

'We've got about a thousand troops there?' the prime minister asked the defence secretary.

'That's right, Prime Minister,' he said. 'Nine hundred men and women, principally from the Queen's Royal Hussars and the Rifles, armed with Warriors and Challenger II tanks.' He was a relatively young man for such a post, with a dramatically receding hairline and flawless skin. Like so many politicians, these days, he had been a special adviser before becoming an MP and always carried with him the air of a teenager pretending to be a grown-up. 'Of course, NATO can quickly move reinforcements in from neighbouring countries.' He pushed a sheet down the table. 'That is the list of deployments in the region. We can also look to reinforce swiftly from here—'

'It's too soon for that.' The prime minister glanced around the room, deliberately making eye contact with his audience. 'Ian here may be right. Perhaps it is a feint. We need to be careful not to overreact. And, in any case, I'm not sure the public is ready for us to go to war over a country few have heard of.'

There was a stunned silence in the room, its occupants carefully avoiding catching anyone's eye. Meg Simpson broke the spell. 'Prime Minister, I've spoken to the French and the Germans already this morning. We're talking about a fundamental tenet here of the most important and longest-lasting security alliance our nation has ever known. They want NATO to send reinforcements to Estonia today. We must—'

'I'm aware of all that, thank you, but not yet.' The PM was looking at the list of deployments in Lithuania, Latvia and Poland on the table in front of him. He had a reputation across Whitehall for chronic indecision, but there was no sign of it this morning. 'I have a call scheduled with the White House as soon as the president is awake. I imagine he will share my caution. For the moment, we remain as we were. I will circulate a draft press statement.' He stood abruptly and walked out, taking the list of deployments with him.

For a moment, nobody moved or spoke. There were a few coughs. Then the politicians and their staff stood and filed out in silence. Only Shirley Grove, the cabinet secretary, held back. 'Good work, Mrs Henderson,' she said, then headed for the door.

It was a strange aside, since Kate had never before met the woman, but perhaps she was just making up for her superior's bad manners.

6

KATE, SIR ALAN and Ian were the last to leave and they stood together for a moment in the morning sunshine on White-hall. 'One can't blame his caution.'

Ian must have been aware that Sir Alan was intending to brief the foreign secretary on Mikhail's offer to defect, but the chief skilfully deflected him with a request that he return to monitor the unfolding situation in Narva and inform Downing Street directly if there were developments. It was a role Sir Alan knew he would be unable to resist.

Ian jumped into a taxi. Sir Alan and Kate walked the long way around to the front entrance of the Foreign Office in King Charles Street, perhaps to give them time to talk. 'If we needed anything to focus our minds,' Sir Alan muttered, 'it couldn't have been planned any better.'

'Exactly.'

'You're not convinced?'

'It feels a bit too neat, I suppose.'

'Which part?'

'This crisis blows up just as we need convincing that Mikhail's offer to defect is serious.'

'You think we should share that thought with the foreign secretary?'

'No. You?'

'Agreed. We need to see if this video exists and appears genuine. We can then take a sober view. But if they potentially have evidence, we have to see it.'

Sir Alan appeared lost in thought as they walked across the courtyard, up the grandiose staircase, and were ushered into the foreign secretary's enormous office, with its magnificent array of leather-bound books and treasures from the days when the UK had bestrode the globe. Meg Simpson sat behind her mahogany desk, looking out over Horse Guards Parade and St James's Park.

Normally, the foreign secretary received guests in the spacious red leather seating at the other end of the office, but perhaps she wanted to keep the great bulwark of the desk between her and the secrets they were about to impart. There was a single-page briefing note Sir Alan had evidently prepared on the desk before her and she plunged straight into its contents, without any reference to the strange Cobra meeting they'd all just sat through.

'I'd like to walk back a few paces,' the foreign secretary said. 'I obviously understand that the allegations about the prime minister's Russian connections first surfaced in the leadership election and have been a thorn in his side ever since, but I seem to recall that when I asked you about them in our first meeting here, you said that there was nothing to the charges and the case was closed.'

Sir Alan leant forward in his chair. In Kate's experience, he liked to dominate politicians and clearly felt uncomfortable at the expanse of wood between them. On reflection, perhaps that had been Meg Simpson's thinking. Kate's respect for her crept up a notch. 'In the end, the evidence we had was not conclusive.'

'Walk me through it from the beginning.'

'Kate recruited a young nanny called Lena Sabic to help us plant a bug on a super-yacht owned by Igor Borodin, who used to be the head of Russia's Foreign Intelligence Service and is – or was – a close friend of the Russian president. We planned the operation because we knew that Igor likes to keep in touch with what his successors are up to and has been in the habit of inviting them to join him on his yacht. The operation was Kate's idea and it was one of the most successful of the past decade. We managed to record a meeting of Russia's most senior intelligence officials, who were discussing our former prime minister's prostate cancer before it was known to anyone back here, including us. The way in which they were discussing the leadership election that would ensue from his resignation suggested to us that one of the candidates to replace him was working for the Kremlin.'

'I have not received a transcript of that conversation?'

'We closed the file.'

'Not to me.'

'I'll send it across later.'

Meg rewarded him with a thin smile. 'In any event, I assume that once the prime minister had declared his prostate cancer and resigned, that reinforced your notion that the conversation you recorded was genuine.'

'Yes.'

'So how did you proceed?'

'We began an investigation into the candidates.'

'All of us?' There was a twinkle in her eye. 'Even me?'

'Once the contest narrowed to Imogen Conrad and the prime minister, we focused our attentions there.'

'Perhaps it was me the Russians were referring to all along and I just didn't make the final cut.'

Sir Alan didn't smile back at her. 'Perhaps.'

'And what did you find?'

'Nothing conclusive, but a great deal of circumstantial evidence that James Ryan was recruited by the Russians as an agent many years ago, probably while he was an army officer in Kosovo. Kate's deputy, Ravindra, followed a lead to Geneva and may have uncovered details of the payments the PM has received over the years, but he was found hanging from the ceiling of his flat after his return. We later discovered that the woman he had gone to see in Switzerland – a former secretary to one of the Russian president's lawyers – had been killed and dumped in a wood.'

The foreign secretary turned to gaze out over St James's Park again. They watched the prime minister's convoy turn out of the back of Downing Street and speed away down Horse Guards Parade.

'As you will see from the file when I send it across,' Sir Alan continued, 'the original operation also pointed to a spy named Viper working somewhere in Whitehall, who had been helping their agent of influence.'

Meg Simpson turned back to face them. 'I don't recall you mentioning an agent in Whitehall.'

'It was my husband,' Kate said. 'The Service has kept the matter top secret at my request.'

Simpson's dark green eyes flicked from Sir Alan to Kate and back again. 'It sounds to me as if the decision to close this file was rather too hasty.'

'I don't think we had any choice but to pursue the original intelligence to see where it led,' Sir Alan said. 'But, equally, given that we could find no proof of anything, I felt it was our duty to let the matter rest once the prime minister had taken office.'

'I don't understand. You just told me the operation to bug the yacht was a great success.'

Sir Alan could see immediately where this was going. He edged forward still further in his seat. 'It yielded exactly the kind of intelligence we hoped it might.'

'That the prime minister was working for the Russians?'

'That our country's security might have been compromised at the highest level.'

'Might have been?'

'That's correct, yes.'

'So you think the intelligence was accurate and that the man or woman they were originally referring to in the bugged conversation was our current prime minister?'

'Yes.'

'But you closed the file?'

Sir Alan wasn't enjoying this. 'Froze the file would be a better way of putting it. We pursued every available lead, but came to a series of dead ends. We had to take a view. He is our democratically elected leader. To put it simply, I felt we had to put up and shut up.'

'So it doesn't matter to you if our leader is working with – or for – the Russians? Given what is happening today and, if I'm going to be frank with you, his tendency to inaction on the subject, I should have thought it was all pretty relevant.'

'Perhaps we should have done more to keep the investigation alive.'

'It would seem so.'

'But there was no proof and we had to bear in mind that the Russians might have been attempting to deliberately mislead us.'

'Which would make the original operation less a success and more a catastrophic failure, I should have thought.'

Kate glanced at her superior, who seemed suddenly to be tying himself in intellectual knots in a very uncharacteristic manner. But, then, he looked dead tired.

'And what do you think, Mrs Henderson?'

'About which aspect in particular?'

'Is the prime minister a Russian spy?'

'Yes.' Meg Simpson gazed at her steadily. 'I mean, I can add caveats about what exactly we mean by that term. But if you're asking me whether he has been compromised in some way by the Russians, then, yes, I think he has.'

'What did you make of his behaviour in the Cobra meeting?'

'It confirmed my suspicions.'

'Not everyone in your organization agrees with you, I believe.'

Kate glanced at Sir Alan, whose flinty gaze gave not a hint of anger. Fucking Ian, she thought. 'Not everyone agrees with me, no.'

'Then what makes you so sure?'

'I believe the original operation was well set up, so there is very little chance the intelligence was planted. I don't know

how they could possibly have known the PM had prostate
cancer—'

'Unless Viper told them,' the foreign secretary shot back.

'My husband was not aware of the PM's illness.'

'Are you sure?'

'Yes.'

'What about some other source? Perhaps you have another
traitor in your organization who picked up the information
from somewhere?'

'Perhaps, but the knowledge of the PM's illness was kept
to such a tight circle around him.' Kate shrugged, tired of
the interrogation suddenly. 'If you're asking me, I think the
original intelligence was correct and the prime minister is
very lucky we were unable to produce any direct evidence
of his treachery.'

'And yet here it now is, popped into our laps by the hands
of a potential defector.' Simpson was looking directly at her
now.

'Potentially.'

'Do you believe it to be credible?'

'We'll have no idea until we see the video,' Sir Alan said.

'So what is it you need from me?'

Sir Alan glanced at Kate, as if he was unsure quite how to
answer this.

'Cover,' Simpson replied for him.

'If this video were to prove genuine and the allegations
surrounding the prime minister true, the controversy and
potential damage to our democracy would be incalculable,'
Sir Alan said.

'And if it were to prove a fake, you might end up with egg
all over your face, which you would much rather was *our* face.'

'I don't think you'd thank us if this blew up without warning,' Sir Alan said.

'I doubt I'm going to thank you either way.' She flipped the file containing his single-page briefing note shut. 'You should know that I'm a patriot more than a politician and I came into politics motivated more by love of country than party. And if that sounds unbearably pompous, you may yet live to be glad of it.' She stood. 'I recognize from your note that time is pressing, not least because the events in Estonia make it so, but I would nevertheless like the weekend to think about it. There is a lot at stake here, as I hardly need tell the pair of you.' She nodded at them. 'Thank you for coming over.'

They walked unescorted to the door and let themselves out. 'She's a lot more impressive than she looks,' Kate said, as they descended the stairs.

'She's a ball-breaker.'

'That's a bit sexist.'

'Why?'

'You wouldn't call a man a ball-breaker, would you?'

'I might.'

'No, you wouldn't.'

'I'd call Ian a parasite. Does that count?'

Kate smiled. 'No, I don't think it does.'

They discussed Ian's evident deceit in the car on the way back to Vauxhall, exactly how and when he had communicated his reservations about the Russians' intentions to the foreign secretary.

They parted company at the lifts and Kate went first to the operations room, where Danny and Julie were seated in front of the screens in the corner, surrounded by empty coffee cups. It had clearly been a long night. Julie glanced up at her. 'You're going to want to see this.'

Kate bent closer to the screen. The video feed was of the farmhouse in Puhlova. It showed an enormous lorry, which had backed up into one of the barns. 'I don't know what they're doing, but . . .' Danny clicked a button in the corner and brought up another stream of video, which showed a group of bikers – perhaps a hundred or more – driving along a highway. 'They left their hotel about ten minutes after your Cobra meeting ended. They drove straight to the border, which they crossed about ten minutes ago. It looks like they're headed home to St Petersburg.'

Kate stared at the screen. This made absolutely no sense at all.

'There's more,' Danny said. 'I traced the lorry back. It took me a while.' He was now rewinding some footage. He hit play. 'It left this army base just outside St Petersburg at nine last night. I guess we can't say for sure it's a pull-out unless we can get sight of what the hell they're loading into that lorry, but it sure looks like one.'

'They knew we were on to them,' Julie said, her big green eyes fixed on Kate. She didn't need to add that, at nine last night, the circle of knowledge within MI6 had been very small indeed. Kate picked up the phone and dialled C's extension. He answered immediately. 'It's Kate,' she said.

'I know.'

'There's good and bad news. So far as we can tell, the Night Wolves are pulling out, with all their kit. I'll get Danny to put the feed back on PCR2 if you want to take a look.'

She waited while he got the correct screen up. 'Split the screen on PCR2,' she told Danny, and he did as instructed so

Sir Alan could see the lorry being loaded up and the bikers on the St Petersburg highway. 'What's the bad news?' Sir Alan asked.

'Danny tracked the lorry back to its point of origin. It left a military base just outside St Petersburg at nine last night.' There was a long silence, as he absorbed the implications of this. 'What time did you inform Downing Street you wanted a Cobra meeting?' she asked.

'I called the cabinet secretary at midnight. I wanted to reduce the risk they would leak it to the morning papers. So . . . to state the obvious, to save you the trouble, the circle of knowledge was still very small at nine p.m., and restricted entirely to people inside this building.'

'You think Ian could have tipped off the PM, or someone close to him?'

'I'm starting to think Ian is capable of almost anything.'

Kate bit her lip as she turned this over in her mind. Blaming Ian was reasonable – his appetite for promotion was voracious – but also, perhaps, too easy. 'It doesn't make any sense, though. If they were really trying to stage a coup, why back off now?'

'Because they know we're on to them,' Sir Alan said. 'Because they've lost the element of surprise. Because, after the car crash that was the attempted coup in Montenegro, they don't want to look clumsy and amateur again.'

Kate glanced at Julie and Danny. Both were transfixed by the screens in front of them. 'Or because the whole episode was designed to convince us of Mikhail's good intentions,' she said. 'They stage an effective but brief theatrical show, which they know very well will be marked down as a quick win for us.'

'A train of thought that leads us to a still darker and more confusing place, because, if they're in a position to do that, it hardly suggests that Igor and his son have one foot in a Siberian gulag already.'

Kate didn't know what to say to that. It felt as if, every day, her work became a more complex and confusing mental jigsaw. If the question in Operation Sigma had been simple enough – was the original bugged conversation on Igor's super-yacht genuine or faked for their benefit? – the same could be said of this latest twist: was Igor and Mikhail's story true and their offer real?

But how to be sure of the answer? If what everyone sought was incontrovertible proof, all they ever had to fall back on was instinct – and primarily *her* instinct at that.

But it didn't waver. Not truly. She knew politicians were always going to want the comfort of proof, but intelligence rarely worked like that. Sometimes rock-solid instinct was all you were going to get. Thank God for Sir Alan. He, at least, understood this implicitly.

'I'd better call Downing Street,' he said. 'I'll place a small bet they'll spin this as evidence of the wisdom of caution – which is, of course, another aspect we should think about carefully.' He ended the call.

'You look like you've seen a ghost,' Julie said.

Kate mumbled a vague reply. She turned away and walked up to her office. Suzy was waiting for her. She had a way of addressing people – both hands on hips, her angular body tilted slightly forward – that they certainly didn't teach in Charm School. 'The original Operation Sigma case file is still locked,' she said.

Kate was tempted to reply, *Of course it bloody is*, but her brain was clouded by the conversation she'd just had with the chief, and its implications. 'Yes,' she said.

'Why?'

'Because we couldn't prove the prime minister was working for the Russians, we had exhausted all potential leads, and, under the circumstances, it felt like locking away the allegations was the responsible thing to do.' Kate almost added that it had not been her choice, but decided against it. She sensed that, with Suzy, every word was likely to be taken down and used in evidence against her.

'But I need to read it.'

'I thought we went through this before you joined.'

'The allegations are still part of the political conversation. I don't think we can just bury our heads in the sand and prevent—'

'I can tell you what you need to know.' Kate dropped her bag beside her desk and sat down. Suddenly she felt shattered.

'I need the file, Kate.' Suzy was in the doorway. She seemed to fill it, despite her narrow frame, but perhaps that was just her demeanour. She tucked a strand of jet-black hair neatly behind her right ear. 'I don't want you to think I'm a stooge for the Security Service during my time here, but I'm really surprised they – we – were not called in to have a look at this. The director general would have a coronary if he knew the scale of the intelligence you'd kept from him. I mean, the prime minister potentially working for the Russians . . .'

'Well, to be clear, that is exactly what I will think if you take that kind of tone.'

Suzy stood her ground. 'I'm part of this team now, Kate. I've been around long enough now to know what that involves.'

Kate got up, went to the filing cabinet in the corner, unlocked it with the key she kept in her pocket, took out the file marked *Operation Sigma* and handed it to her colleague. Suzy looked pleased, as if she had expected the conversation to reach a different conclusion.

Kate logged on to her computer. She'd barely had a chance to glance through her emails when their team assistant, Maddy, put her head around the door. She had an unerring ability to gauge instantly Kate's state of mind. 'You all right?'

'Why wouldn't I be?'

'O-kay.' She pulled a face. 'Glad I asked. Your aunt Rose called.'

'What did she want?'

'There's a problem with your expenses.'

'What?'

'All right, bad joke. She said she'd spoken to Fiona and would pick her and Gus up at four. She's sorted your mother with the nursing home. She'll pick her up just afterwards and they'll all head down to Cornwall together. You're welcome to join them at any point if you can get away.'

'Did she hear back from Belgrade?'

'Not so far as I know.'

'Will you check?'

'Of course.'

Maddy didn't retreat. There was clearly more. 'And?' Kate asked.

'She said I was to make sure you kept your appointment with Dr Wiseman – and walk you there myself if necessary.'

'All right, thank you.'

'What time is your appointment?'

'Two.'

'Are you going?'

'No.'

'Why not?'

'Maddy . . .' Kate faced her assistant, whose concern for her welfare sometimes felt intrusive.

'You have to go, Kate.'

'Last time I looked I was a grown woman. So I don't *have* to do anything.'

'You're not well.'

Kate frowned. 'What do you mean?'

'We all know what you've been through and you're not yourself. Surely you can see that.'

Having dropped her bombshell, Maddy withdrew. Kate was caught between irritation and despair. Was it that obvious? She'd barely had time to fashion an answer when Julie came in with questions of her own. 'What was their answer on Mikhail's offer?' she asked, as she sat on the desk beside Kate.

'The foreign secretary wants the weekend to think about it.'

'Lucky there are no time pressures, then. Do you think she'll go for it?'

'Sir Alan didn't leave her much choice. He was there buying top cover and she was smart enough to grasp that. She seems pretty thorough. I didn't realize he'd basically kept the original file from her, so I think she just wanted the time to go through it carefully. Ian had been there before us.'

'What do you make of the Night Wolves pulling out?'

'It's confusing.'

'Convenient, though. I mean, a quick win for us. It makes Mikhail look good.'

Kate was staring out of the window as she sifted the various different explanations for what had just happened in Estonia. None entirely made sense.

Julie stood and went to the glass wall overlooking the rest of the office. 'I guess you know that Ian's wife has booted him out,' she said.

'I do. I was a bit surprised, to be honest.'

'Not half as bloody surprised as I was.'

'What's your reaction?'

'I'm horrified. It was just casual sex, and now he's suddenly saying he wants to marry me.'

'What will you do?'

'I'll have to break it off.' Julie's voice betrayed no hint of emotion. She could sometimes, Kate thought, be a cold fish. Her hair was greasy, her T-shirt stained with a coffee spillage, but it did nothing to diminish a radiant, vibrant beauty. 'I see you gave Suzy the Sigma file,' Julie said. She was staring at their colleague, who was hunched over it on her desk.

'I didn't feel I had a choice. She'd have gone running back to her friends the other side of the river and they'd have made trouble.'

'Who do you think she's really working for?'

'The correct answer is that we're all on the same team. Isn't it?'

Julie rolled her eyes and walked out. Kate watched Suzy for a moment. So what if MI5 ended up knowing everything? Perhaps it didn't matter.

Kate picked up her bag. The foreign secretary's desire to have the weekend to think about it left open the possibility she could join her children and aunt in Cornwall and she couldn't think of a good reason to stay behind. But Rose would kill her if she missed her appointment with Dr Wiseman.

Before she went, Kate took the number Mikhail had given her from her pocket and sent him a WhatsApp message. *The foreign secretary has asked for the weekend, but I anticipate a positive response. Will keep you posted. K.*

Kate thought the mention of the foreign secretary would probably be enough to convince Mikhail they were taking his offer seriously and prevent him from approaching anyone else with his secrets, at least for a couple of days. The idea of the CIA, or indeed any other foreign intelligence service, having cast-iron proof of the prime minister's treachery – with all the leverage, complication and even humiliation that that would involve – didn't really bear thinking about, especially as it would come with the knowledge the British had deliberately chosen not to take up the offer.

He replied in a couple of seconds. *I am in Berlin. See you at 10 a.m. on Monday. Head for Alexanderplatz. Do not be late.*

Kate sent back: *Monday too soon. I can't make the wheels turn faster. Let's say Tuesday at 10 a.m.*

It was a long wait before she finally received a reply: *All right. No later, or the deal is off. And you're welcome, re Estonia.*

Maddy was at the door of her office again. 'The PM's just about to make a statement.' Kate joined the rest of her team in front of the big TV screen in the centre of the office, which was switched to Sky News. The prime minister swept up to a makeshift podium in Downing Street. 'I will make a full statement on the events in Estonia to the House this afternoon . . . but it is our understanding that if the Russians did intend to provoke unrest on the border, as some have alleged, then that threat is now receding. The protests have petered out and we do not believe there is a meaningful threat to Estonia's integrity and security. I have spoken to the Russian president directly this morning and he assured me that this is indeed the case, though he did ask that the Russian minority in Narva and in eastern Estonia be adequately protected, which is a perfectly reasonable request.' There was a pause as he looked up from his script and directly into the camera. 'I take this as further evidence of the advantage of a cautious, nuanced and balanced attitude to international relations. Nobody wants to rush into a war over a country few have heard of. That's the rub of it, like it or not. Thank you. Good day to you!'

He turned and walked back in through the door of Number Ten. 'That's going to make the Estonians feel good,' Julie said. 'He's a lot more bloody Neville Chamberlain than Winston Churchill.'

Kate didn't reply. She picked up her bag and went to the lifts, trying to shake the sense that she had just been manipulated in a way she couldn't yet quite articulate.

7

DR WISEMAN WAS a man of angular leanness, with a pair of square reading glasses that he took on and off as he alternated between asking questions and writing down her answers long-hand in a huge exercise book in the centre of his wood and chrome desk. He had a wide forehead, curly dark hair and a steady, level gaze. He reminded Kate of her first tutor at Cambridge, and her faltering attempts to explain herself were an uncomfortable echo of those encounters.

'It's really hard to describe,' she said. 'I usually feel all right when I first get up in the morning. I think. When I've slept. But then, as I said, I'm not sleeping well, and sometimes barely at all. In any event, once I get into the flow of the day, it's as if someone has crept up and injected some kind of diabolical chemical into my bloodstream, adrenalin or cortisol – or whatever. And then I just feel . . . *awful.*'

'In what way?'

'Just this nameless sense of dread, of being permanently on guard and anxious, as if someone is about to come around the corner and shoot me at any moment or, worse, the children.'

'And you say you felt like this before the events of six months ago, your husband's betrayal and the deaths of the young woman you recruited as an agent, then your deputy, Ravindra?'

Kate hesitated. Unburdening herself was painful. She felt as if she was standing on the edge of a precipice and all she could see was how far there was to fall. 'Yes, I suppose so.'

'When would you say it started?' He was looking at her over his glasses.

'I don't know.'

'Did you feel anxious as a child?'

'No. I was pretty confident.'

'One can be confident and anxious.'

There was a long silence. Kate stared at the floor as she racked her brains. And suddenly it was as if a window opened to allow a chink of light into the darkness. 'I guess I was, yes. Anxious, I mean.'

'About what?'

'Not the usual things, like exams. I was pretty cool about all that. I didn't mind very much what other people thought of me, either. I wasn't anxious about friendships, or whether anyone did or didn't like me or approve of what I was doing. But . . . I suppose loss . . . death.'

'Loss of what? Or whom?'

Kate thought hard about that, too. It was bloody difficult casting her mind back across the years and trying to unravel the complex weave of thought and emotion. 'Death, generally. The loss of someone or some people I loved, or of letting them down in some way. My own death, too, I suppose. Just the vagaries and impermanence of human existence. There were times when that uncertainty, the unpredictability of life, was paralysing.'

'Did you fear you would lose your mother?'

'No. I never had a relationship with her. I wasn't close to her as a young child, and after I learnt of her infidelity – she had a long-running affair with my best friend's father, a guy called David – I would say I came actively to hate her. I was brought up by my father. I understood from an early age that my mother was unreliable and often quite undermining, even poisonous.'

'Did your father challenge that?'

'No. That was the only issue I ever really had with him. I could never understand how he could love my mother. And, particularly, how he could go on loving her after she had treated him so badly. But he just quietly took me out of her orbit, which wasn't difficult because she is the most self-absorbed and, indeed, selfish woman I have ever met.'

'You were worried about losing your father, then?'

Kate had never thought about it like that. 'Yes, I suppose I was.' She stared at her hands. 'I definitely was. I had no siblings, so I guess my father was all I had. I was petrified something would happen to him.'

'Or that he would leave, that your mother would drive him away? Is that what lay beneath your resentment of her?'

'I knew he would never leave me.'

'Do you think you were the reason he stayed?'

Kate had never thought about it like that, either. It was an uncomfortable idea. 'I suppose so.'

81

Dr Wiseman continued writing. Kate glanced at the clock on the wall beside her. They had only ten minutes left and she was starting to panic it would not be long enough. Reluctant as she had been to start this process, now that it had begun she didn't want it to end. When was she going to get an answer? 'Was your father anxious?' he asked.

'About what?'

'Anything. You, your mother, life in general.'

'No.' She looked through the blind at the blurred figures hurrying by in the rain outside. 'Actually . . . yes, perhaps he was. I . . .' She sat up straight. Memories were crowding in on her. 'When I was about eight, or maybe nine, a friend of mine at school died very suddenly of meningitis. She sat at the desk next to me and she said she had a headache. I told her to go and see the nurse. The following day, the teacher came into the class to say that Jane had died in the night. I didn't know what to think or how to react. It was incredibly sad, but I didn't know what death meant. And in an awful way, life went on as normal.'

'But not for your father.'

'Exactly. Not for him. You see, Jane was also an only child. I think I understood then that my father was terrified of losing me. I remember him being quite strange around me for a while. I'd always been a bit of a tomboy, into climbing trees and fighting with the boys, and he had been very relaxed about that. But after Jane died, he was much more tense around me for a long time.'

'In what way?'

'Every way, I suppose. If I was going out into the garden, he wouldn't forbid me to climb the trees, but he'd come out and watch me, just to check I came to no harm.'

'How long did that last?'

'I don't know. A year, maybe.' Kate thought about it. 'But I suppose, in another way, a lifetime. I mean, he really worried about me a lot. I knew that. If I came home for the weekend, he would always say, "Drive carefully," at the gate when I was leaving.'

'Doesn't every parent say that?'

'I suppose so. But there was an intensity to it that I haven't really thought about until now.'

Dr Wiseman nodded. 'Given everything you've said, what do you make of the profession you've chosen?'

Kate took a long time to answer. It was a good question. 'I suppose there is a disconnect, as with many people, I should imagine, between what drives my intellectual curiosity and what ideally suits my psychological temperament.'

'Except that cannot be true. I imagine your job requires high degrees of natural empathy. How else would you have persuaded the girl you lost to work for you?'

Blackmail, Kate thought. Bullying. But she decided not to share that. 'I think I feel more in control the closer I am to the things I fear. I always worried about someone hurting someone I love, but this way I can seek out threats and defend myself and those I care for against them.'

'In order to keep your home life pure?'

'In what way?'

'To avoid the hurt your mother's betrayal caused?'

'I . . . don't know. Perhaps. But there is no perfect spy. We're as flawed as everyone else.'

Dr Wiseman glanced at the clock. He shuffled his notes. 'All right, I suggest we continue in a week or two. Please call Sarah to make another appointment.'

'How do we proceed? I mean, what's happening to me?'

He stapled his notes together. 'I'm going to refer you to Cognitive Analysis. That should take around twenty sessions—'

'Twenty?'

He didn't blink. 'We'll explore issues relating to your work, your past and your family of origin. I'll continue to see you at the same time. We'll need to consider pharmacology—'

'I really don't want to take drugs.'

He looked up at her sharply. 'Medicines,' he said. 'We call them medicines.' He smiled. 'And how interesting. You would take penicillin without a moment's hesitation, I have no doubt, so why would you not take a medicine that might help you recover from the highly anxious state you find yourself in?'

Kate felt pretty stupid. She didn't argue. 'What is wrong with me?' she asked.

Dr Wiseman closed the file. He took off his glasses, placed them carefully in the centre of the folder and looked up at her. 'I suspect that some genetics is involved and some imprinting. You may have a natural predisposition to anxiety, as it seems your father had, and in turn his behaviour, his fears over your safety, may have helped further imprint that natural tendency into you.' He wiped his forehead and began to clean his glasses. 'You spoke earlier of the impact of your father's death. Up until that point, you had looked to him to soothe your fears. After his departure, there was no one left to do that for you, save your husband, whom, as you also said, you clung to with too great a force.'

'But what can I do about it?'

'You will need to learn to self-soothe. To care for yourself, rather than rely on others to provide comfort. In short you must leave the anxious child behind you and learn to be comfortable in the adult and capable Kate, who is a mother to two children and a senior executive officer in one of our nation's most demanding professions.' He put his glasses back on the folder. 'It would help, I think, to begin that conversation quite consciously.'

'Between?'

'Your adult self and the frightened child within. The adult Kate Henderson is an incredibly accomplished and confident woman, making decisions of enormous importance for the nation at large. She is surely the person you need to soothe the scared child. If you can open up that conversation within you, it would help.'

That made a lot of sense. She stood. 'Thank you . . . thank you, Dr Wiseman.'

She left his consulting room and hurried out into the light drizzle. She turned her face to the sky and let the cool drops fall upon her cheeks, then roll over her chin and down her neck. The relief was immense. Someone understood.

Dr Wiseman's room was in Ealing Broadway, so she caught a cab all the way back to Vauxhall Cross and returned to her office with a spring in her step. She had barely got back to her desk before her new deputy was slipping through the door behind her. 'Kate . . .'

'Hi.'

Suzy closed the door. 'I read the file. Operation Sigma.'

'Good.' Kate waited, but nothing further was forthcoming. 'So now you're up to date.' She turned to her computer.

'Are you sure your analysis on Viper was correct?' Suzy asked. Kate turned back to her. 'I'm not trying to be difficult,' Suzy went on. 'It's just that, over at Five, I did quite a lot of mole hunts. You might even call it my speciality. And I'm not sure it makes sense that your husband was Viper.'

Kate tried to contain her irritation. This was about the last thing on the planet she wanted reopened. 'My husband admitted his betrayal.'

'I'm not disputing that, only the conclusion that he was actually Viper. We know how much effort the Russians have put into seducing and corrupting people across Whitehall. It makes sense that they have more than one – perhaps multiple – corrupted agent of influence. Stuart was expendable.'

'Not to me.'

'I'm sorry, bad choice of language.'

'Indeed.'

'I just mean . . . if you go back to the beginning of the operation on Igor's yacht, he's overheard saying, "Viper can help." If you consider the stakes, does it really make sense that Igor would be referring to a relatively tangential player in those terms?'

'Stuart worked for the prime minister's principal rival. He was married to me. I am not sure he was tangential.'

'I get that. Stuart was betraying you. In the heat of an operation, I totally understand that, as you began to appreciate his treachery, you would naturally conclude he was Viper.'

'But I was wrong?'

'I'm not saying that. It's just, to me, as an outsider, looking at this afresh, it doesn't make sense of Igor's comment. "Viper can help" implies someone more important in the food chain than your husband.'

'Perhaps, perhaps not.'

'And yet how could they possibly have known what Rav was up to in Geneva? According to the file, your husband had no idea of that.'

'They must have been monitoring his phone.'

'Rav was surely much too experienced and capable to have communicated with anyone in a manner that was less than secure.'

'He called the *Guardian* journalist.'

'True. I saw that. But he was unlikely to have told him what he was really up to.'

Kate thought about this. On Rav – perhaps – Suzy might have a point. And now that she had brought it up, Kate wasn't sure this doubt hadn't been nagging at her ever since Rav's murder. 'Okay,' she said. 'Thanks.' She debated telling her of the way in which someone in the Russian hierarchy had started the Night Wolves retreat from Estonia at nine the previous evening, but thought better of it.

The circle of knowledge had been the same small group: C, Ian, Julie, Danny and Kate. The betrayal of one or another was unthinkable.

'I'm not trying to be difficult, Kate.'

'I understand that.' She nodded. 'I do. You make valid points. I don't know how profitable it's likely to be to reopen this right now, but I will give it some thought.'

Suzy slipped out and Kate closed her eyes. 'Fucking hell,' she whispered to herself.

8

KATE TOOK THE opportunity to leave Vauxhall early that afternoon. She chose one of the six aliases common to officers at her level and asked Travel to book her on to the first flight to Berlin on Monday morning. She warned Operations to put Danny, her favoured team leader, on standby to manage the surveillance on the ground in the city, pending the foreign secretary's approval. And then she walked up to Victoria to catch the Circle line to Paddington.

The train journey to Bodmin Parkway should theoretically have been a time of relative peace and relaxation, but the temporary relief she had felt after her appointment with Dr Wiseman was overtaken by a tidal wave of further anxiety. If she had heard 'We have a solution' as she left his office, all she could hear now was 'You have a problem.' The questions crowded in: was she going to have to take drugs? Would she become addicted? Would they affect her ability to do her job? Why did she think like this anyway? When was she going to feel better? *How* would she feel better? What would happen if she got worse, if she lost control, if things began to spiral? Would she lose her job, her children? Who would look after them then?

The questions clattered in her mind. And that was before she had even got around to turning over whether she might really have been wrong about Stuart being Viper. Suzy had a point. But if not Stuart, then who?

She hoped to see Rose at the station, but instead she got only the cheery face of her husband, Simon. Perhaps it was a relief. She just about managed to make small-talk on the short journey up to the coast. Simon looked as if he had been in Cornwall for a month already, dressed in a T-shirt and shorts despite the season, his curly white hair as wild as the wind, which was blowing in hard from the west.

Rose knew something was wrong as soon as Kate walked through the door. 'Are you all right, my love?'

'I just need a few moments.'

'Well, you know where you are.'

Kate went straight upstairs to the main spare bedroom on the first floor, without saying hello to her children or her mother. She closed the door, drew back the curtains and looked out at the moonlight shimmering on the flat, calm water. She started to cry and, before she could contain herself, she was sobbing uncontrollably.

Her chest constricted again, as if she were having some kind of heart attack. She lay down on the sofa by the window and put her legs into the air. She tried to slow her breathing and bring some control to her quickening pulse.

There was a soft knock on the door and Rose crept in. She came closer. She'd bought a new pair of oval glasses, which somehow served to exaggerate the kindly expression that was her default demeanour. Her long dark hair was shot through with more grey now, though she seemed disinclined to do anything to hold back the march of time. 'Anxiety attack?'

'I don't know. I—'

'They are horrible things.'

'What the hell is happening to me?'

'You mean physiologically? You've been driving yourself too hard for too long. Too much stress. Too much trauma. The release of adrenalin and cortisol has become your body's learnt reaction and now your mind and your body are winding each other up, collectively panicking that things appear to be spinning out of control.'

'Have you ever had it?'

'Yes.'

'When?'

'It's a long story. It was in the period we were trying to have children. I was very busy at work and I invested too much hope in . . . and . . .' Rose shook her head, clearly reluctant to go back there. 'The main thing you need to know is that it will pass. You will get better. As long as you take action now.'

'Did Dad suffer from anxiety?' Kate's father had been Rose's much-loved younger brother.

'Not that I was aware of, but . . . perhaps. He certainly wasn't himself after he found out about your mother's affair with David Johnson.'

'David Underpants.' Rose permitted herself the ghost of a smile. 'You know,' Kate went on, 'he used to wear these really tight swimming trunks that stretched high above his waist. Even as a child, even when he was supposed to be still our friend, I could see he was a ridiculous figure.'

'I'm not sure that helped your father.'

'I can still remember the call to Helen like it was yesterday. I was sitting on the stairs. I could tell from the moment she answered the phone something terrible had happened. She said she couldn't see me any more and when I asked why, she said my dad could explain.'

'Did he?'

'Not really. He said there had been some difficulty with Helen's father. I thought maybe he'd gone bankrupt, or they'd lost their house or . . .' Kate's voice trailed off. 'But then I couldn't understand why that was causing so much tension in our home.'

'Did he ever talk to you about it?'

Kate shook her head. 'You know how he liked to avoid confrontation. But I don't entirely blame him. What would he have said? "Your mother is poisonous, deeply selfish, dishonest and unreliable"? I already knew that.'

'I assume you have seen Dr Wiseman.'

'Yes.'

'How did it go?'

'When I walked out of his office, I felt as if a huge weight had been lifted from my shoulders. But as I came down on the train, I lost sight of the potential for a solution and all I could focus on was the certainty that I have a problem.'

'Well, you're in a very volatile state of mind. And you will be for a while. But the first step to recovery is to admit you're not well. Did you talk about work?'

'What do you mean?'

'Taking some time off.'

'I can't do that.'

'Kate—'

'I can't, Rose.' Kate sat up. The pain in her chest was still searing. 'Please don't push it. I just absolutely cannot take any time off now and that is all there is to say on the subject.'

Rose nodded in a way that made it crystal clear she was far from convinced and the matter was certainly not closed. 'All right. Just stay here for a while. I'll bring you up a cup of tea and tell the children you had to rest.'

'Did you hear from Belgrade?'

Kate's aunt hesitated a moment too long. 'Let's talk about it at work on Monday.'

'What happened?'

Rose was now staring at the floor. 'It's complicated.'

'How?'

'You know it is. We have to find a couple willing to adopt Maja there. Then we have to go to court to force the state to remove her from her mother, see through the legal adoption, then bring the entire new family over here. It's long-winded, extremely expensive, and success is far from certain.'

The anxiety in Kate's chest was exploding again now. 'We don't have a choice.'

'Ian thinks we do.'

'No . . . No. We made a promise!'

'Calm down, Kate. That's why I suggested we deal with it on Monday or whenever you're in a fit state to have a rational discussion about it.'

'We'll do it outside the law!'

'We can't, and you know we can't.' Rose's gaze was steely. 'Look, I'm on your side. I think Sir Alan will be, too, so I suggest in the strongest possible terms that you let it go for now.'

Once Rose had gone, Kate closed her eyes and started to cry again. She had never felt so hopeless and ashamed.

Rose came back with a cup of tea. 'Take your time,' she said. 'And if you can't make it down to supper, that's fine.'

'Can I help?'

'No. Absolutely not.' Rose pointed to the huge rolltop bath in the bay window. 'Run yourself a hot bath, look up at the moonlight, drink your tea and relax for a few minutes. I'll bring you something stronger in a while.'

'Thank you,' Kate said, as Rose reached the door. 'I don't know what I'd do without you.'

'With any luck, you won't find out for a while, because I intend to hang around for as long as I possibly can.'

'You'd better.'

Rose slipped out again. Kate ran a deep bath and tried to relax into it. But neither the hot water, nor the tea, nor the moonlight did much to alter the basic physiology of her body, which felt as if it was vibrating constantly.

Rose returned with a gin and tonic. 'You probably shouldn't,' she said. 'But I'm not sure it'll do any harm.'

Kate took a sip. 'Christ! What did you put in it?'

'Five parts gin.'

Rose went back to her cooking and Kate came down twenty minutes later as supper was being served. She felt quite drunk and consequently played little part in the conversation, which, in any event, didn't cover much of substance. They mostly talked about what they would do tomorrow.

It was at this point that Kate's mother chose, incomprehensibly, to pipe up. 'Where is Stuart?' she asked.

There was a stunned silence. The children stared at their food. 'Stuart went away,' Rose said quietly. 'You know that.'

'Where to?'

'Russia.'

'*Russia?* Why on earth did he want to go there?' She turned slowly to her daughter. 'Was he running away from you?'

'That's enough, Lucy,' Rose said. 'Would you like some more chicken?'

'I don't understand. Why did he leave?'

Kate nodded at Rose to indicate that she could and would handle it. Her mother always had the ability to rile her, if nothing else. 'Stuart is still my husband and the children's father, Mum, so I'd be grateful if you'd drop the subject.'

'Well, I did warn you.'

'About what?' Fiona asked.

'Leave it, love,' Kate said.

'I just want to know what Granny warned you about.'

'Oh, you know what. Your mother is awfully difficult.' Lucy looked from Fiona to Gus and back again. 'You both know that. She drove him away. I knew she would. I told her she'd never be able to hold on to a man.'

Even by her mother's standards, this attack was so vicious and brazen as to take Kate's breath away. But that didn't stop the rage exploding inside her head.

'I think you should go to bed, Lucy,' Simon said. 'No good is going to come of you sitting here with us at supper in this mood.'

They all turned to him. Simon was normally emollient, generous, munificent, steady. None of them had ever heard him talk like that before. Even Lucy was a bit taken aback. 'That wasn't a request,' he added, smiling.

Lucy put down her knife and fork, thrust her plate away and left the room. Rose waited a few moments, then pushed back her chair. 'I'd better go and see if she's all right.'

'Thank you,' Kate said to Simon.

'It's my pleasure.'

'Sometimes, I think the Alzheimer's is actually just a front to allow her an old age full of the pleasure of dispensing poison as and when the mood takes her.'

'Don't say that,' Fiona said. 'She's ill.'

Kate didn't fancy an argument with her daughter, so the rest of the meal passed off in small-talk.

Rose insisted Kate leave the washing-up and go straight to bed, but her fevered state of mind seemed to accelerate with the night. She climbed beneath the huge duvet ready to pass out, but something in her brain prevented her from drifting off. And the more she thought and worried about it, the more awake she felt. Worry became fear, then panic.

She didn't know whether it was better to lie there and hope that sleep crept over her or get up and distract herself, so she ended up doing both in turn. She switched on the bedside light and tried to read the new William Boyd novel she'd brought with her.

Then she switched off the light and lay still.

She got up, drew back the curtains and gazed at the moonlight, which shimmered on the still waters of the bay.

But as the hours of the night crawled slowly by, she had to acknowledge to herself that sleep would not come. As a consequence, the dawn was a kind of relief. The sun came up over the estuary with a crisp amber hue. Kate watched the light creep across the landscape, freeing her inch by inch from the terrors of the night.

She let herself out and walked around the headland towards the small town of Rock, crossed the golden sands of Daymer Bay and climbed to the top of Brae Hill, where the view took in a contrasting patchwork of green and blue all the way down to Padstow on the far side of the inlet.

Rose and Simon were already at the breakfast table by the time she returned, but there was no sign of her mother or either of the children. Rose poured her a cup of coffee. 'Did you sleep?'

'No.'

'Not much or not at all?'

'Not at all.' Kate shook her head. 'It's weird. It's a long time since I managed to go all night without any sleep.'

'It's not weird at all,' Rose said. 'You've been under the most incredible pressure. Something has to give.'

'I guess so.'

Kate pulled the newspaper across. 'NATO in Crisis' was the headline on *The Times*. 'The Germans say they still want to send more troops to Estonia, even if NATO refuses to do so officially,' Rose said. 'The French will follow suit.'

'Any word from Downing Street?'

'Still the same line, that the crisis is receding. It's a time to cool tempers, especially as the British public wouldn't wear being drawn into a conflict over a country like Estonia. Or words to that effect.' Simon put down his copy of the *Financial Times* and poured himself more coffee. 'Makes you proud to be British, doesn't it?'

Kate's phone buzzed. There was a message from C. *The foreign secretary has asked to see us at Chevening tonight.*

I hear you're with Rose in Cornwall, so will send a car to Padding-ton to bring you down there.

'They want you back,' Rose said. Kate nodded, wondering how Sir Alan had known where she was spending the weekend. 'One of the advantages of not actually being your mother,' Rose went on, 'is that I don't feel obliged to nag. So just take this as a statement of obvious fact. I don't think you're in any fit state to be at work and I'm sure Sir Alan will understand if you explain it to him. And if you don't want to, I'm quite happy to do so.'

'I'll be fine. I'll catch the afternoon train back. I'll sleep tonight.'

Rose didn't make any attempt to hide her disquiet. 'All right, but let me know when you're ready to acknowledge that things are stacking up against you. There's no shame in admitting you've reached your limits.'

Kate buried herself in the paper. She had absolutely no intention of admitting she had reached her limits. She wasn't even entirely sure what that meant.

She woke the children at nine, so that they would have time to eat before their scheduled surf lesson. It took three attempts to get Gus out of bed, but once he was awake, he ate his breakfast with the speed of a gulag prisoner finally offered a square meal. Fiona had coffee, black, no sugar. Her once dappled cheeks looked gaunt, her greasy blonde hair tied back in a tight knot. Her vivid blue eyes were in danger of being the only trace of the beauty she'd once been.

Normally, she would pretend to eat something – usually cereal, which she would then push around her bowl until it looked as if she'd had some. But this morning, she didn't even do that.

Kate tried to get her daughter on her own on the way down to the beach, but Fiona wedged herself alongside Jed the entire way, as if she knew what her mother was trying to do.

Simon and Rose went back to the house, so Kate watched the surf instruction alone on the beach. Despite the sunshine, it was cold, and she kept her hands thrust deep into her pockets. Polzeath was a small community that swelled in the summer months. Drab in the rain, it could pass itself off as quaint when the sun was shining, as it was that morning.

All three of the children got up easily on their surfboards at the second or third attempt. Jed was by far the best and Fiona consequently lost his company to her brother on the walk back to the house. Kate thought her son's admiration for Jed bordered on adulation these days, but perhaps there was no harm in that.

Kate saw her chance and accelerated to fall into step naturally with her daughter. 'I knew you were waiting to pounce,' Fiona said.

'That's not kind.'

'I had breakfast.'

'Did you? I only saw coffee.'

'I wasn't hungry. I *am* eating.'

At least she hadn't said, *It's none of your business.* 'How are you feeling?' she asked, changing tack.

'About what?'

'I don't know. Life. School. Jed. We don't seem to discuss things as much as we used to.'

'Jed's lovely. I don't deserve him.'

'That's a bit harsh. He really loves you. And he's right to.'

'I don't need a pep talk, Mum.'

'I'm not—'

'What is it you want? Why don't you just spit it out?'

Kate felt unconscionably like bursting into tears. Was her daughter turning into her mother? 'We haven't really talked about how things were with your dad.'

'We have.'

'Not in any meaningful detail.'

'All right. What do you want to know? It was a bit shit. It was *obviously* a bit shit.'

'Was it nice to see him?'

'Of course. We still love him, even if you don't.'

'What did you chat about?'

'School. Friends. Jed. How he was doing in Moscow. When we might see him again. Whether it would be possible to live with him . . .'

Fiona had speeded up now, so that Kate had to jog a few steps to come back alongside her daughter. She could feel her throat constricting. 'I'm sorry, *what* did you just say?'

Fiona didn't slacken her pace. Kate was forced to take hold of her arm and spin her around. She was confronted by five feet seven of pure teenage fury: a young woman who seemed unsure as to whether to spit at her mother or burst into tears. Or both. Kate knew exactly how she felt. 'What do you mean, whether you could live with him?'

'Exactly what I said.'

Kate stared at her. She knew when Fiona was trying to provoke her and that she should not take the bait. 'I'm going to forget you said that.'

'Why? I meant it.'

'I don't think you did.' Kate couldn't keep the anger from her voice. 'Not just because it's grievously insulting, but because we both know it would be impossible.'

'Why? I'm sixteen in two weeks' time. Old enough to have sex. Officially. An adult. If I want to go and live with Dad in Russia, I don't believe there's anything you can legally do to stop me.'

'That's not true, as you should know. Anyway, what about your brother?'

'He wants to come too. And he can, as soon as he's old enough.'

'And what about Jed?'

Fiona's face clouded. She didn't have an answer to that one. Kate was tempted to press her advantage, but she held her tongue. You really didn't need to be a psychiatrist to discern what was going on here. It was her job, as a mother, simply to suck it all up.

Fiona hurried to join her boyfriend. When they returned to Simon and Rose's house, Kate went upstairs to her bedroom and burst into tears. Again. Never in all her life had she felt so alone.

9

IF, FOR A contented mind, time is peace, then for a fevered one it's precisely the opposite. The nearly five or so hours it took for Kate to return to London were close to torture. The worse she felt, the more she wondered what was wrong with her.

C had promised a car would be waiting for her at Paddington. Kate got into it and closed her eyes for much of the journey down to Chevening, the foreign secretary's country residence. She was only interrupted by a text from the education secretary, Imogen Conrad. *Crazy times again, hon. You about?*

Kate had once enjoyed an artificial friendship with Imogen of the only kind one can with a husband's boss. But the education secretary did not appear to think that being filmed having sex with Stuart and breaking up their marriage should be any kind of barrier to her future relationship with Kate. Using the pretext of having been appointed a governor at the children's school, she had bombarded Kate with texts ever since the scandal broke.

Kate mostly ignored her in what she hoped was a dignified way, but Imogen was insanely persistent and had a skin as thick as that of a rhinoceros. *Can we chat?* Imogen messaged, when she did not immediately reply. About bloody what? Kate was tempted to ask, but so far she'd held her tongue and was determined to continue to do so. Her dignity demanded she treat Imogen with the amoral vacuity she deserved.

Hun? Imogen texted again. She had once been so annoyed with one of Stuart's deputies in the Department of Education that she had suggested it would be easier to send around a message in a bottle. When he had been slow to respond to a subsequent text, Imogen had actually sent a message in a bottle. Stuart had thought that clever, sassy and really quite funny. Perhaps it was.

Kate stared at her phone. *Am in Cornwall with Rose and the kids*, she lied.

Assume you'll be home tonight for school tomorrow. So can I pop around at 10 p.m., say?

Kate didn't answer. What was the point?

She stared out of the window for the rest of the journey, trying to think about how she would manage the next two or three days. Rose could step in and look after the kids. She herself would take a sleeping pill tonight to make sure she finally got some rest. It was manageable. Of course it was.

Before long, the car crunched across the smooth gravel and swept past a tinkling fountain to the front of the red-brick Palladian Inigo Jones mansion that was the week-end home of serving foreign secretaries.

A uniformed member of staff ushered her into the grand hallway and showed her through to a small anteroom. She was surprised to find her new deputy waiting for her. 'Suzy?' she said.

'The foreign secretary asked me to come along.'

Kate was tempted to enquire as to how Meg Simpson had even known of Suzy's existence, but she made a mental note instead to keep an even closer eye on her deputy. 'Where is Sir Alan?'

'I believe he's in a meeting here already.'

Kate sat down on a stiff-backed cream chair by the door. The Sunday newspapers were carefully laid out on a coffee-table in front of an empty fireplace. She picked up *The Sunday Times* and glanced over the front-page story. She'd intended to catch up on the train, but the tiny shop on Bodmin Park-way station had not yet stretched to newspapers. 'Any read-out on the NATO summit beyond the headlines?' she asked Suzy.

'I only had a chance to speak to Sir Alan briefly on the way down here.' Kate noted they had not offered to share a car with her and that Suzy appeared keen to underline the fact. 'The read-out from the room is worse than the headlines. We're looking at a total split in NATO. Germany, France, the Benelux countries, everyone on Europe's eastern flank – in fact, pretty much everyone else – is keen to send reinforcements to Estonia, even if the crisis is receding. Washington and London insist that would be provocative.'

Kate wondered if this fissure in NATO had been the true purpose of the entire episode. If the Russian president's primary foreign-policy aim was to fatally divide his enemies, he was doing an exceptional job. He'd regained control in Syria, was busy attempting to hold the whip hand in Libya. Who knew where his ambitions really ended? 'What does the foreign secretary have to say about it?' she asked.

'I don't know, but I guess we're about to find out.'

The butler – if that was what he was – put his head around the door. 'Mrs Henderson?'

Suzy got up with Kate. The butler raised a hand and an eyebrow at her. 'Just Mrs Henderson, please.' He led Kate along the hallway to one of the drawing rooms, where the windows were open to the expansive gardens and a lake in the distance, illuminated now by a bright moon. Despite the chill breeze, there was a hint of spring in the smell of newly mown grass.

Meg Simpson and Sir Alan sat opposite each other in stiff-backed chairs. There were gloomy old masters on the walls, an ornate white fireplace in front of them and a rich Afghani rug on the floor. As an image, Kate thought, it was every conspiracy theorist's fantasy of how a British foreign secretary and the head of SIS might conduct their business.

The foreign secretary, in particular, looked tired, as if the last few days had aged her considerably. 'I've reviewed the files,' she said, without introduction or small-talk. 'And it's my view that we should proceed to the next stage of this operation. You have the offer to meet Mr Borodin's son in Berlin?'

'That's right, ma'am. I've suggested Tuesday at ten a.m.'

'What would it involve?'

'In terms of resources?'

'If you could just give me an outline . . . I'm not familiar with how such operations work.'

Kate glanced at Sir Alan as she tried to assess what was really being requested here. No minister she'd dealt with before had wanted to know the nuts and bolts of such a relatively simple operation. 'I would go with one or both of my deputies as back-up. Then we'd have a team on the ground to conduct the requisite covert surveillance, just to ensure that neither side was being watched or followed and that the meeting would be able to take place in relative security and secrecy.'

'Will you be in a position to assess . . . to see the material?'

'You mean the kompromat video, ma'am?'

'The alleged kompromat, yes.'

'That is essentially the purpose of the meeting. As I'm sure Sir Alan has outlined, the potential defection of the former head of one of Russia's main intelligence agencies is highly unusual, not to say unheard-of, and down the line will require enormous effort, expenditure and a great many resources on our part. They will come to the meeting with the material. I'm sure of it.'

'It's the unusual-bordering-on-unheard-of bit that bothers me.'

'But that is why it's important I see the material first-hand. Once we've assessed it, we'll be in a position to say whether the defection is a risk worth running. But if they're prepared to bring us evidence that the Russians have been blackmailing our prime minister, I think it's a chance we must take.'

Simpson stared at the empty fireplace. The decisive air she'd cultivated at the start of the meeting seemed to have dissipated in Kate's discussion of the detail. 'You have my permission to go to the next stage,' she said finally. 'But no further. Assess the material, then let us speak again immediately.'

Kate realized she was expected to answer. 'Of course, ma'am. I'll come in to brief you as soon as I'm off the plane, although . . .'

'Yes?'

'Mikhail will want to know for sure whether we're prepared to offer his father and family sanctuary.'

'That's what we'll decide once you've assessed it.'

'He will almost certainly want an answer on the spot. And we may lose them if I can't give him that assurance.'

'Lose them to whom?'

'Another foreign intelligence service. The French, the Germans. Perhaps even the Americans. And they will know we turned Mikhail and his father down.'

The foreign secretary evidently didn't like the sound of that. 'Very well. Say what you need to say. We can always change our minds at a later date.'

'That isn't how we do business.'

Simpson looked up sharply. 'These people are sharks. I won't be lectured on morality by them, thank you very much.' That wasn't what Kate meant and both women knew it, but she let it go. 'If the material is legitimate, we will almost certainly go ahead with the exchange, repugnant as it may be. But we will take one step at a time.' She rang the bell and waited for the butler. Rather like the Queen, Kate thought, but didn't say. 'Could you bring Suzy in?' Simpson asked.

Suzy, Kate noted. Not Miss Spencer, or even Suzy Spencer. Just Suzy. They were clearly better acquainted than she'd imagined, but the question was how and why? Kate tried to catch Sir Alan's eye, but he was staring out of the window at the moonlight.

Suzy walked crisply in. 'Foreign Secretary, Sir Alan,' she said, nodding at each in turn. She sat. She was dressed in a tailored dark suit and a white shirt: a model of cool professionalism. Kate glanced down at her weathered trousers and scuffed brown suede flats. Perhaps she should have made more of an effort.

Suzy took a folder from her shoulder bag and placed it on the walnut coffee-table. It sat there like an unspoken accusation.

'Tea, coffee, a drink?' Simpson asked.

'No, thank you, Foreign Secretary.'

They waited. Suzy was enjoying her moment in the ministerial limelight. 'Get on with it, Miss Spencer,' Sir Alan said.

Suzy glanced at Kate nervously. Whatever she was doing, perhaps she was having second thoughts. 'I've been looking at the Operation Sigma file. It was extraordinarily well conceived and carried through, so none of this is meant to be a criticism in any way, but rather a reflection of the fact that we all know some things are bound to be overlooked in the heat of the moment.' Kate kept her eyes on her new deputy. 'I agree with Kate's analysis that many of the facts do fit the idea that her husband, Stuart, was Viper. While he did not know the details of the original operation in Istanbul, he was aware that it was a significant success and he clearly had some general idea of what it was about.'

Kate could feel her face reddening. In reality, Suzy was protecting her here, since she had clearly worked out her boss had been somewhat economical in the file as to how much she had shared with Stuart.

'So, assuming Stuart passed on to his controllers the fact that Kate was returning to Greece to continue with the operation, that might well have been enough for Moscow to swing into action and put a team on her tail. Until this point, Stuart as Viper adds up.'

She flipped open the file and handed around some sheets stapled together. 'I've run a precise spot check on Rav's phone for the last twenty-four hours of his life, including the time he was in Geneva investigating the lawyer with close links to the Kremlin. As you can see from this timeline, there was virtually no activity. He was entirely off the grid. There is the call to the *Guardian* journalist, which Kate reported. I have spoken to the journalist in question directly. He seems a pretty straight guy and insists Rav just wanted the lawyer's name and told him nothing of what he was up to. He insists he spoke to no one about it and I'm inclined to believe him. Then there is the incoming call from Kate while Rav was in Geneva. After that, there are no calls and no spikes in any kind of electronic activity, save for here, at around six p.m. I think that's the message that Kate also logged in the file.'

Kate handed her sheets back to Suzy. The others followed suit, as they contemplated their contents in silence.

'I'd also say Rav strikes me as much too experienced and talented an officer to have breached operational security in any significant way,' Suzy added.

'Perhaps he was followed,' Simpson said.

Kate glanced at Suzy, who waited for her to answer. 'That kind of surveillance requires a great deal of manpower, ma'am. And, as Suzy says, Rav was experienced enough to have taken anti-surveillance measures and to have reported any activity back to us in London.'

'So someone knew what he was up to in Geneva and tipped off the Russians?' Simpson said. She was looking directly at Kate.

'It looks that way, yes.'

'And it could not have been your husband?'

'That's correct, ma'am.'

'To be honest, I'm surprised these questions were not asked before,' Suzy said. They all turned towards her. Even Simpson was frowning at what felt like a gratuitous twist of the knife. 'I didn't mean . . .' Now it was her turn to redden.

'Who knew enough of what Rav was doing to tip off the Russians?' Simpson asked.

'Chiefly me,' Kate said.

'I knew,' Sir Alan added. 'So did Ian and Julie.'

'Just the four of you?'

'I would say so.'

Kate stared at the floor. My God, she wished Operation Sigma had never darkened her door. Nothing good had come of it, nothing at all. Kate wondered if Sir Alan would mention that the Russians seemed to have been tipped off about Estonia as well, but he must have decided that discretion was the better part of valour and she was not about to argue with him.

'Well, we can't pretend this is anything but uncomfortable,' Simpson said.

'My colleagues in Five will certainly want to know why these questions weren't asked before,' Suzy said.

Sir Alan looked at her. 'You are a very clever and ambitious woman, Miss Spencer, but you are in danger of overplaying your hand here, if I may say so.' Sir Alan's voice was at its most acid. 'We did not involve our colleagues at Five because we wanted to protect our operational integrity and the security of its ultimate source, Lena Sabic, the au pair we recruited to bug Igor's super-yacht. Once the operation was complete, we had no reason to believe anyone other than Stuart was Viper.' He glanced at Meg Simpson, before turning to Suzy and leaning forward to emphasize his point. 'Your logic makes several fairly enormous leaps. We have never determined who killed Rav or why. Perhaps it was the Russians, but it may have been someone else entirely, for motives we have not yet uncovered.'

'The file makes it clear you thought it was the Russians,' Suzy said tartly. She did not look as if she was enjoying her ticking off.

'Supposition and fact are two entirely different things. We don't know what Rav was up to. He was off the grid and not following orders from anyone here. Perhaps he met someone we are not aware of, or made a call using a land-line. Or it may just be that the Russians had the lawyer or his assistant under surveillance.'

'I acknowledge all those possibilities, but I still think we should—'

'Close this down now.' Sir Alan smiled at her again. 'We have bigger fish to fry. We are potentially being offered evidence that our prime minister is a traitor, who seeks to undermine our response to Russian aggression. Nothing is more serious than that, and we cannot allow anyone to stand in the way of pursuing this matter to its logical conclusion in Berlin over the next few days.'

'But if I'm right, we'll be putting Kate and her team in danger if we allow them to proceed. Their entire operation could be compromised before it has even begun.' Suzy sounded almost plaintive.

All three looked at Kate. She shrugged. 'You raise an interesting question over Rav's murder, Suzy. We shouldn't and won't sweep it aside lightly. But I'm ultimately confident my husband was Viper. And I agree with Sir Alan: nothing can be allowed to stand in the way of this operation.' Kate was aware of the formality of her language. It almost sounded like she and the chief were in a police interview, but perhaps that was what having a member of Five around did to you.

The foreign secretary nodded. 'All right, we'll leave it there for now. Kate, you and your team will go to Berlin and we'll assess where we stand on your return. But, I repeat, I want to take this step by step.'

It was clear their audience was over. Kate and Suzy both stood, though Sir Alan did not move. Kate turned back at the door. 'Would you like us to wait for you, sir?'

'No, thank you. We have other matters to deal with.' He smiled again at Kate.

She wished them both goodnight and walked out to the car waiting by the fountain in the driveway. Suzy got in with her. Neither spoke for some time, though even the driver must have sensed the tension in the back. Eventually, Kate could contain her curiosity no longer. 'How come you know the foreign secretary so well?'

'I don't.'

'Then why did she call you "Suzy"?'

'I don't know. I only met her earlier this afternoon.'

Suzy was staring out of the window to avoid Kate's gaze, but she was plainly lying. 'I think you tried to go a bit far in there, if I may say so,' Kate suggested.

'I wasn't trying to do anything except my job.'

'You could have fooled me.'

'I was asking a question you should perhaps have asked. And I think you know that.'

Her sanctimony stung Kate into a response. 'Don't they throw a spell at Charm School into the training programme for the Security Service?'

Suzy was visibly upset. 'I'm really sorry, Kate. I know my manner can be tactless. My last boss at the Security Service said as much and couldn't wait to approve my transfer.'

If the vulnerability in Suzy's eyes was not genuine, then she was a damned good actress. 'Look, forget it. You're right on both counts. I should have asked the question and I do know it.' Suzy smiled at her. 'Let's talk about it when I get back from Berlin.'

'I really think I should accompany you to—'

'I need you here.'

'I have to be there. I mean, I want to be. This is exactly why I asked for the transfer from across the river. Please.'

Suzy's transition from snake in the grass to vulnerable young woman and back again was bewildering, but Kate no longer had the energy to fight it. 'All right,' she said, but it didn't stop her train of thought. If Suzy knew the foreign secretary much better than she was letting on, then the question was how? And was she Simpson's eyes and ears inside the Service? Was that why she had been foisted upon them? Kate resolved to treat her with still more caution.

'Thank you,' Suzy said. 'Thank you very much.'

10

KATE WAS RELIEVED that the house was still empty when she got home, the children having not yet returned from Cornwall with Rose and Simon. The respite she'd felt during the meeting at Chevening receded with the onset of fatigue, and the energy drained from her once more. She put on the kettle to make a cup of tea, then thought better of it and poured herself an enormous glass of white wine instead.

She sat at the table to drink it, wondering if this was what being an alcoholic felt like. She looked at Nelson, quite possibly the laziest beagle she had ever come across, gazing up at her without much enthusiasm from his basket in the corner. She got down on her hands and knees to rub his head and scratch his tummy, then lay flat so that she could put her head alongside his in the basket. He didn't much like to travel, these days, so she relied on a neighbour to look after him when she and the children were away.

Good God, his breath smelt. Perhaps that was what old age did to you. She shifted position so that her head was resting on his back instead and closed her eyes. It wasn't exactly comfortable on the tiled floor, but she was as likely to get to sleep there as anywhere else.

She lay there until the smell of him got too much, then stood and walked through to the living room. She switched on the TV and channel-surfed for a few minutes.

She'd managed an entire vacuous half-hour watching *Game of Thrones* before the doorbell rang. She glanced through the keyhole to check that it was Fiona and Gus, no doubt having forgotten their keys, only to see Imogen Conrad standing there.

Damn, Kate thought. The very last thing she needed. Was the woman stark, staring mad? She waited, pretending no one was in and hoping her unwanted guest would get the message and turn away.

Fat chance. The bell rang again. Kate gritted her teeth, opened the door and smiled. She was determined not to give her former friend the satisfaction of seeing just how much hurt she'd caused.

When she was talking politics, Imogen rarely drew breath, and Kate could tell tonight was going to be no exception. 'What do you think?' she asked, as she marched through the kitchen to the living room beyond. 'Oh, God, wine on a Sunday night. I shouldn't . . .'

Kate hadn't been intending to offer, but she filled a glass more or less to the top, since she'd long ago learnt that Imogen really *did* like to drink, and returned to the living room. '*Game of Thrones?*' Imogen said, looking at the screen, paused on a dragon in flight.

'Better late than never.'

'I couldn't watch. Too much violence and all the energetic sex just reminded me of what I miss with Harry.' Imogen took a large sip of her wine. 'Too much information?'

'I should say so.'

'I'm sorry. I suppose you're single again.'

'I suppose I am.'

The silence that followed this reference to the fallout of Stuart's betrayal was awkward enough to have both of them avoiding each other's eye. In the immediate aftermath of Stuart's admission of his affair with Imogen – or, rather, their episodic trysts, since both denied it had ever been more than that – she had bombarded Kate with phone messages containing ever more profuse and abject apologies. They had been followed by letters, then unannounced visits.

Kate knew then as she did now that she should have been angrier with her erstwhile friend, but she couldn't quite summon the bitterness the circumstances seemed to demand. Imogen was every clichéd politician writ large: engaging and entertaining, but unfaithful and untrustworthy. Kate had never laboured under any illusions regarding her, but Stuart was the rock she herself had built her life on. She reserved her rage, therefore, for him and allowed herself to be bludgeoned into submission by his former boss, knowing that Imogen's desperate attempts to preserve some vestige of their friendship were nothing more than an attempt to salve her own conscience. 'So, what do you think?' Imogen asked, still staring at the TV screen. Kate quickly turned it off.

'About dragons?'

'No! What's going on in Estonia.'

'Oh, that.'

'What do you mean, "Oh, that"? What else would I be talking about? I'm surprised you're not stuck at your desk.'

'I've just come back from seeing Meg Simpson.'

'What did she have to say?'

'About what?'

'The prime minister's response, of course! I mean everything we said – *you* said – during the leadership election looks like it must have been true. He's a Russian spy, isn't he? How else do you explain his utterly bizarre reaction unless he really is working for the Russians?'

'Innate caution?'

'But he isn't a cautious man, is he? In fact, we'd probably agree he's reckless by nature – and pretty bellicose when it suits him.'

'I suppose so.' Kate wanted to get out of this conversation. She was relieved to see the wine disappearing at a rate of knots.

'What are you going to do?'

Not refill the glass, she thought. 'About Estonia?'

'The suggestion that he's a Russian spy!'

Kate sat down on the arm of the sofa. She suddenly needed to. 'There's nothing we can do. We have no evidence. The case is closed. He's the prime minister, after all.'

'Have you spoken to Meg about it?'

'No.' Kate avoided Imogen's penetrating gaze.

'Are you all right?' Imogen asked. 'You don't look well.'

'Just tired.'

'I'm sorry. I know the past six months have been . . . very difficult.'

Kate smiled weakly. She had forgotten: Imogen also had a gift for understatement. 'I should probably get some rest. I understand what you're saying, but I honestly don't think there's very much we can do about it.'

Imogen drained her wine and stared at the floor, deep in thought. She started waving the glass in a circle, and Kate worried that she would ask for a refill. But she placed it decidedly on a side table. 'I'm going to have a word with Meg myself. I won't mention you – don't worry – but I think I should at least raise it with her. And perhaps the home secretary as well.'

'Why?'

'Because we can't let him get away with it.'

'As you wish.' Kate didn't doubt her former friend's political skills. She was one of the great survivors, after all. But she wasn't about to launch a leadership challenge so soon after losing her battle against James Ryan for the premiership.

Imogen hovered. 'I'm sorry, Kate. I really don't like to see you this way and I know I . . .' She smiled again and made her exit. What else, Kate supposed, was there to say?

Kate drained her own glass and went up to lie on her bed while she waited for the children to come in. It was strange to feel dog-tired, but not at all like sleeping, as if she were being hollowed out from within.

It was a shade after eleven when she heard the door go. Neither Fiona nor Gus bothered to come and say goodnight, so she had to haul herself off her bed to do so. She went to Gus first. He'd flopped face down on to his mattress. 'How was today?'

'Fine.'

'Long journey back?'

'It was fine.'

'How was Fiona?'

'Fine.'

'You all okay for tomorrow?'

'Yeah.'

'I have to go away for a couple of days, so Rose said she'd be here.'

'I know.'

'Will you be fine?'

'Yeah.'

Kate allowed herself a smile as she kissed his head. She moved on to her daughter's room. Fiona was lying in bed, staring at her phone. 'You'd sleep better if you didn't look at that all night, you know.'

'Because you're the expert.'

Kate smiled again. Perhaps it was despair. 'I have to go away for a few days—'

'I know. Rose said. I'm staying with Jed this week.'

Kate recognized the incendiary device for what it was, but trod on it anyway. 'You can't do that, love.'

'Er, actually, I can.'

'This is your home. You can't just leave.'

'I'm going to Jed's house. Not Moscow or Beijing, or the moon. His parents are both doctors. I'm fairly sure I'll come to no harm. I'll be back by the time you finally get home anyway, so you'll hardly notice the difference.'

'But it isn't really fair to leave Gus here on his—'

'He won't notice either. Whenever he crawls out of whatever gaming hole he chooses to occupy this week, Rose will be there to spoil him. He'll be like a pig in shit.'

Kate was tempted to go on, but, for once, discretion got the better of her. Fiona was right: Jed's parents were responsible people and she was unlikely to come to any harm.

She retreated, without kissing her daughter goodnight, took Nelson down the road for a night-time pee – he didn't bother – then came back to bed. She took 15mg of her sleeping drug of choice, zopiclone – double her normal dose – and lay down to stare at the ceiling until chemistry finally overwhelmed her worried mind and gave her at least a few hours of fretful sleep.

11

WHEN THEY ARRIVED, it was a flat, grey, cold March day in Berlin, a city that had been comfortably in the mid-teens for most of the weekend. Suzy revealed an unlikely eye for luxury in the choice of a hotel overlooking the Tiergarten, with a giant wooden sculpture of a crocodile's jaws in Reception, a nod to the proximity of Berlin's zoo and perhaps the situation in which they were about to place themselves.

It was called Das Stue, meaning 'living room' in Danish, and beneath the grand split staircase in the entrance lobby, the reception area had been designed to capture the warmth and intimacy implicit in the hotel's name. It was very Berlinerisch, from the doorman dressed in bowler hat and Dr. Martens to the inverted art-deco lights arranged in the shape of a grand piano hanging from the ceiling.

Kate was shown to her room on the fifth floor, which had a long balcony overlooking the treetops of the Tiergarten. She ordered tea and sat outside in her winter coat drinking it, then took herself across the road for a walk in the park as the light was beginning to fade. Berliners were hurrying home with hands thrust deep in pockets and hats pulled low to ward off the chill. And yet, the signs of spring were all around: the daffodils were coming into bloom, the lime blossom drifting on the evening wind.

There were joggers and cyclists, dog-walkers and lovers out for an evening stroll. And it was so *quiet*. Berlin was the only capital in Europe that could pass for a town or even a village, and Kate had always had a particular affection for it.

She walked as far as the Brandenburg Gate, where shoals of tourists were still being talked through the days when this monument to a nation's bellicose past had stood just beyond the wall that had divided a city, a country and a continent. It occurred to Kate to wonder if it hadn't all been a touch easier for her predecessors when the threat from the East could at least be contained in part *behind* that wall: the days before they could come and go at will in all places at all times, whether it be to murder former spies in Salisbury or attempt to rig elections across the democratic world.

It took longer than she'd anticipated to complete the circle back to the hotel, so she skipped a shower in favour of touching up her make-up, then headed down to join her colleagues in the bar.

Julie was curled up with her feet tucked beneath her on a long aubergine-coloured sofa, opposite doors open to an internal courtyard. It was cosy in there too, with a low ceiling and black-and-white photos on all the walls.

A girl was singing slow jazz to the accompaniment of a keyboard player. A couple at the next table seemed grateful for the excuse to avoid conversation, the woman deep in her phone. Beyond them, two young parents also watched the singer in silence, apparently oblivious to their young son playing a game on his iPad between them. In the courtyard, two girls chatted, feet beneath thick rugs and an empty champagne bottle upside down in the ice bucket beside them. Kate joined Suzy at the bar and asked her for a gin and light tonic, then returned to sit next to Julie. 'Where is Danny?' she asked.

'Don't know.' It was standard practice for the covert surveillance teams to stay somewhere different for an operation such as this and to avoid communicating, except via the agreed method.

Suzy returned with their drinks. They listened to the singer for a while and Kate glanced about her once more. With its pastel rugs, parquet floor, the glass and chrome bar, this salon felt like a temple to modern Berlin: slick, stylish and low key, as if the city's violent, tumultuous past had belonged to a different world entirely.

Half an hour later, they caught a cab to a restaurant called Borchardt, which Suzy insisted was a 'Berlin institution'. It was a German twist on a French brasserie, with high ceilings, grand pillars, waiters dressed in black waistcoats and white shirts, and French café chairs and tables packed in close together, save for the upholstered maroon velvet booths along the far wall.

The waiter brought the menus and Kate glanced around her. It was the kind of place where people spend the evening watching everyone else – and eating *Wiener Schnitzel*, which seemed the main course of choice for every second table.

They ordered. Kate decided on *Schnitzel* – when in Rome – and gazed around the room again, as Suzy and Julie appeared to be getting along like a house on fire, until Suzy turned the conversation to the internal politics of their own organization and brought up Ian's ill-disguised ambition to succeed Sir Alan as C. 'Do you think he'll get it?' The question was directed at Julie.

'I have no idea.'

'But he wants it badly, right?'

'I should think so. Wouldn't you if you were in his shoes?'

'What's he like?'

'He's okay. A bit chippy sometimes.'

'I heard he's a bit of a player. On the romantic front, I mean.' Kate watched Suzy's expression. Either she was spectacularly ill-informed – since Julie's affair with Ian was now pretty much common knowledge inside the building and probably beyond – or she was being provocative, malicious, or both.

Julie shrugged to indicate she had no idea, or did not want to be drawn. 'I just need to go the Ladies,' Suzy said.

Julie waited until she was out of earshot before she exploded. 'What is she – fucking autistic?'

'I don't think she can possibly know. Even she isn't that stupid.'

'Everyone knows.' It was said with a disconsolate shrug.

'I'm not going to say I told you so.'

'Good!' Julie said. 'What a mess. I should have listened to you. He proposed to me last night.'

'What did you say?'

'No! Of course! I told him I was not the marrying kind and never would be. He burst into tears and said he was heartbroken and he would now be on his own for the rest of his life and . . . Oh, my God, I thought he was never going to leave. He just cried and cried like a baby.'

'That doesn't really strike me as a normal kind of reaction.'

'Well, I'm not normal, am I? Maybe I pushed him to it.'

'Is that what he said?'

'No. He was pathetic, rather than angry. But that always makes it worse.' Julie nodded towards the Ladies in the corner. 'What's the deal with her? One minute she's really engaging and good fun and the next she's a monster.'

'That might be a bit of an exaggeration.'

'She told me she was investigating you.' Kate frowned. 'Yeah, exactly,' Julie went on. 'There's nothing like actually announcing you're the snake in the grass. She said she didn't think Stuart was Viper and that she'd been given permission to open the investigation. She said she'd narrowed it down to a choice between you, me, Ian and Sir Alan. I replied that as career strategies went, I thought she was on to a guaranteed winner – all three of her bosses and one of her juniors. That should see her floating in the River Thames fairly soon.'

'I think she might be getting carried away.'

'She can really get in the way, that's for sure.'

Suzy came back. They sat in awkward silence for a moment. 'Have you been talking about me?'

'Of course not,' Julie said.

'Is it true you're having an affair with Ian Granger?' Suzy asked.

Julie looked as if she'd been punched in the face.

Kate gasped. 'I really don't think—'

'Given the work I need to do,' Suzy said, 'it would be better for me to know.'

'This would be the investigation you've just been told to park by the leader of our organization?' Kate asked.

'It's just that I heard he'd left his wife and was having a relationship with someone else in the organization. One of my colleagues thought it was Julie. I really feel that's something I should be made aware of.'

'Well, if you're really desperate to know,' Julie said, recovering some of her poise, if not shedding her anger, 'then, yes, we had a brief affair. It was just sex. His marriage was breaking down anyway. He has now left his wife. We are not going to be together. Our relationship is over. Would you like to know what sexual positions we preferred?' Suzy's face was reddening. 'Isn't that the kind of information you find important at the Security Service?'

'There's no need to talk like that. It was a legitimate question.'

The food arrived, just in the nick of time, and conversation really flew along after that.

Kate was grateful to get back to her room. She brushed her teeth, took another double dose of zopiclone and crawled beneath the sheets. The last thing she recalled of that night was a message from Julie that said simply, *What a bitch.*

12

THE FOLLOWING MORNING, Kate was awake early after a short, disturbed and not very restful sleep. She made herself a cup of tea from the kettle in the corner of the room and sat on the balcony outside with a thick oversized coat on her lap.

She glanced at her phone. She opened and closed Whats-App, flicked through Instagram, then depressed herself with a few minutes on Twitter. She mostly followed politicians and political journalists, and the rage these days was disheartening. It felt like the place everyone went to shout at each other.

She forced herself to put her phone in her pocket and leave it there, which was always surprisingly hard when she was on her own. The sky over the Tiergarten was a brooding, portentous grey, with only the faintest lick of dawn light. The silence felt oppressive. Once upon a time, trips abroad had been accompanied with the regular buzz of the phone in her pocket relaying messages from Stuart, just the everyday frustrations – and sometimes pleasures – of a man left alone to look after his children. And of love. For the first time since his departure, she was aware of truly missing him: his laugh, his smile, his episodic thoughtfulness and concern for her, not to mention the physical affection and warmth.

She wondered when she would next have sex. Before she died? When she was eighty?

Kate finished her tea and was about to get up when her phone buzzed. It was a WhatsApp message from Sergei. *How are you?*

She stared at it. Was he telepathic? She messaged back, *Am good. Are you in London?* Her heart raced with the same kind of force as it had in the days when they had almost become lovers as students in St Petersburg, a world and half a lifetime away.

No, at home in St Petersburg. Be great to see you sometime.

Kate looked at that for a long while. What was he up to? What was it about? She couldn't think straight. She hadn't seen him since a meeting at the US ambassador's party in London at the height of Operation Sigma. And she hadn't heard from him since she'd travelled to his family's dacha in the Gulf of Finland, north of St Petersburg, expecting to have everything explained – his role in the GRU, the reason for tipping her off about the meeting of the Russian intelligence elite on Igor's super-yacht, the identity of the secret mole, Viper, in MI6 – along with confirmation that the prime minister really was working for the Russians.

Instead, she'd found Stuart waiting on the beach, with confirmation that he was Viper, and it was all over.

Except nothing was over. In her more troubled moments, she thought the game the Russians were playing might only just have begun.

She put the phone into her pocket and immediately took it out again. *How?* she typed. *Where?*

But there was no reply. She opened the photograph attached to his feed. It was of him smiling against the backdrop of a long beach and the Gulf of Finland, his family's dacha just visible in the distance. She waited and waited – and then could contain herself no longer. *Are you there?* she asked.

He didn't answer.

Eventually Kate forced herself from the chair and went to shower. She had to resist the temptation to look at her phone while she dressed, but when she could stave it off no longer, there was still no reply from Sergei.

The sense of anxiety, of dread, even, wrapped itself around her, but she forced herself through it, as if in a fog, and found herself the first at the breakfast buffet. She filled her plate and went to a remote corner table. She ordered coffee and drank it too fast. She didn't feel like eating. She wondered how Fiona and Gus were getting on at home. She called Rose's mobile, but got no reply there either.

Neither Julie nor Suzy made it to breakfast, so they met at eight forty-five in the lobby as agreed. Kate had her earpiece in and she set off on the route they had all arranged in advance with Danny.

She walked through the centre of the Tiergarten, skirting the Rose Garden, and then under the Brandenburg Gate to allow Danny and his team time to assess whether she was being watched and followed by members of any foreign intelligence service, most notably, of course, the Russians.

The idea was to move from crowded areas to open ones and back again, while officers on the streets worked behind her to get a sense of what they might or might not be up against. Danny, meanwhile, monitored the electronic activity in the immediate vicinity of her progress to check for any spikes that might suggest hostile officers communicating with each other while in pursuit.

Kate was halfway down Unter den Linden when the tiny microphone in her ear came to life with Danny's calm, steady voice. 'Take a turn into Bebelplatz.'

She did so, ambling slowly to the centre of the famous square, in which the Nazis had burnt books, to look through the glass window in the cobbles at its centre, which afforded a view of the library built in memorial beneath.

She returned to Unter den Linden and continued on past Museum Island to Alexanderplatz, which still had the bleak air of the square in east Berlin it had once been.

Despite her leisurely pace, Kate reached the corner of the square early and Danny instructed her to carry on beyond it. 'Need a bit more to be sure,' he said.

She walked on under the S-Bahn and swung left into Münzstrasse. Halfway down it, she turned into a vintage shop, where 'The Eton Rifles' by The Jam was playing on an old turntable. It was a pick-and-weigh store, where your choices were measured by the kilo, full of ripped jeans, denim shorts, leather belts, bags and jackets, sunglasses and every kind of hat that might have been fashionable in the sixties, seventies or eighties.

As she stepped back on to Münzstrasse, Danny's voice rang in her ear: 'Clear. Go back to the meet point.'

Kate retraced her steps, past the homeless people sleeping beneath the underpass, until she was standing by the bus stop in the corner of Alexanderplatz.

She waited. Julie had slipped a packet of cigarettes into the pocket of her jacket before she'd left the hotel and she lit one now to pass the time.

It started to spit with rain, so she joined the bus queue beneath the shelter. An old woman in front of her waved away the smoke.

A phone rang in her pocket. It was not her own. She took out an old-fashioned Nokia and answered it. She had not felt anyone place it there. 'I said come alone,' Mikhail said.

'We're not at the stage yet where I'm prepared to take that risk.'

'Go to the S-Bahn station. Head for Westkreuz. Keep the phone with you.'

Kate put the Nokia back into her pocket and crossed the road. 'He's asked me to get on an S-Bahn train to Westkreuz,' she whispered quietly into the microphone hidden inside the lapel of her jacket. 'How the hell did someone get a phone into my pocket?'

'Sorry, Kate,' Danny replied. 'We didn't see anything.'

Kate bought a ticket and walked up the stairs to the plat-form on the floor above, which was shielded from the elements by a grand semicircular metal and glass roof. The station was crowded for this time of day, a large group of French school-children moving slowly along it. Kate walked on beyond them to where a young man was circling on a battered scooter.

A train pulled in and she got on to it. The students boarded with her and she listened idly to the meaningless chatter of someone else's children. The train pulled out. Grey buildings slid by beyond a rain-splattered window. The burner phone buzzed in her pocket. She answered it. 'Get off at the next stop. Don't end the call.'

The train rattled slowly into the station at Hackescher Markt. As the doors slid open, Kate did as she had been instructed. The voice at the other end of the line was silent. She waited. 'Get back on. End the call.'

She did, just as the doors closed. The train pulled out. 'I don't know if I like this,' she whispered into her lapel.

'Let's stay with it.' It was Suzy, who must have been assigned to the makeshift control room. 'We're sticking with you, not far behind.'

'Easy for you to say,' Kate muttered. The train rolled on, past Museum Island and across the canal. The phone rang. 'Get off at Friedrichstrasse. There is a coffee shop on the platform called Cuccis. Buy a coffee and wait.'

Kate was on the cusp of telling the voice at the other end of the line where he could stick his meeting, but he ended the call before she had the chance.

In the coffee shop, she ordered a black coffee and stood drinking it as the platform emptied, then slowly filled again.

The minute hand on the station clock crawled around the dial. Five minutes became ten, then turned into fifteen and finally twenty. 'I'm crying off,' Kate said.

'It's your call, boss,' Suzy said, to which Kate very nearly replied, *Of course it's my bloody call.* But with the same uncanny sense of timing, the phone rang again. 'Go down the stairs, cross Friedrichstrasse and head east.'

'Is this leading anywhere? I'm close to calling it off.'

'You were followed.'

The call was ended. Kate gritted her teeth. She did as she'd been told, emerging again into the spitting rain on the cobbled street the far side of Friedrichstrasse. She followed its passage east, past a series of down-at-heel cafés and restaurants.

She stopped to drop money into a busker's hat. 'Talk to me, Danny,' she said. 'He says I've been followed.'

'We don't know what he's on about, Kate. We think you're still clean.'

Kate walked on. She reached the end of the road, where the S-Bahn bridge crossed the canal. She lit another cigarette and turned around. There was nowhere she could sensibly proceed to without further instructions, so she paced and smoked with choking unease. 'Fucking hell,' she muttered. 'This isn't right.'

The phone rang. 'Get out of there,' Mikhail said. 'We've been compromised. Get out of there now.'

Kate threw away her cigarette. Two men emerged from the shadow of the S-Bahn bridge. One blocked the road she had come down, the second a potential escape route to her left. She instinctively turned right, only to be confronted by a car that screeched into view and swung around in the middle of the street. Kate was cornered, with her back to the canal, both men armed with thick steel bars. 'I've got trouble,' she whispered. 'Big bloody trouble.'

Kate glanced behind her. To swim or try to run?

She faced the men again. One was short, stocky and bald, with tattoos that climbed from his neck up either side of his shaved skull. The other was surprisingly slight, with a thin moustache and the kind of wispy half-beard you'd normally see on a teenager. He was the more dangerous.

The short guy got out of line, came on too quickly and swung with too much force. Kate stepped aside, tripped him and smashed his skull on to the top railing of the fence by the canal. He collapsed with a low grunt.

Two more men had got out of the car and were advancing towards her. One had a knife, but her immediate concern was the guy who looked like an overgrown adolescent. He advanced with stealth. They circled each other for a moment.

He feinted one way, then brought the bar down in a vicious arc towards her skull. She swerved, but only just in time – she felt the tremor in the air as it passed her cheek.

He tried again too swiftly and this time she caught his arm, blocked his leg and used his momentum to send him tipping over the rail and straight into the canal.

But the other two men had split up, blocking any realistic chance of escape. Besides, one was now armed with a pistol. Kate edged along the fence as they closed in. The man she'd sent into the canal was yelling at his colleagues in Russian.

There was no way out of here. Kate wondered how Rose would cope with the children and whether Fiona's fragile state of mind would deal with the death of her mother as well as the loss of her father.

There was nowhere to run and no place to hide. And even if by some miracle she could disarm the man with a knife – a hundred times more difficult in real life than they ever made it look in films – a single bullet from the other advancing thug would end this encounter in a heartbeat.

She had all but given up and resigned herself to her fate when she heard a single cry: 'Kate!'

The man with the pistol turned, but he was not quick enough. Suzy pushed his arm up so that a shot pinged harmlessly off the metal strut of the bridge above, then slammed the heel of her palm into the brachial nerve on the side of his neck.

Danny and his colleagues were only half a pace behind her, so that the thug with a knife, who had seemed so menacing only seconds before, now found himself surrounded by four men and a female officer with a pistol trained at his chest. He didn't need any further warning: he ran for his life.

They all watched him go. Kate leant back against the rail. Suddenly she felt very faint. 'Thank you,' she muttered. No one seemed to have heard her. 'Thank you, Suzy,' she said. 'All of you.'

13

KATE TOOK THE decision to make a swift exit from the scene to avoid any operational fallout with the German police and their intelligence colleagues, whom they had deliberately chosen not to inform of their plans.

She went straight to her room once they had got back to the hotel, washed her face and sat on her bed. She noticed her hands were shaking violently. Her phone rang: C. She didn't answer it, but as soon as it rang off, he called again. 'Yes, boss?'

'What happened?'

'I don't really know. We stuck to the plan. Danny and his team allowed plenty of time for the covert surveillance and he was confident I was clear. Somehow Mikhail got a burner phone into my pocket. I don't know where or how – I didn't spot that and neither did the ops team. He called and said I'd been followed. He instructed me to get on to the S-Bahn and off again at Friedrichstrasse. He directed me to a spot under the S-Bahn bridge that did feel as if it had been deliberately designed for an ambush and then . . .' Kate gathered herself. 'I thought I was done for, to be honest. Suzy came out of the darkness at them like a wild cat. I wouldn't be here without her.'

'Who betrayed you?'

'I don't know.'

'Get back here and we'll work it out.' Sir Alan ended the call. Within a few seconds, her phone lit up again. This time it was Ian. But hearing his reproachful analysis was the last thing she needed, so she ignored him entirely.

She lay on her bed, but that didn't help. She made herself a cup of tea, but that had no positive impact either. Eventually, she used the in-house service to send a message to Julie and Suzy, instructing them to book everyone on to an evening flight, the operational teams included.

She went back out into the Tiergarten and walked fast, the events of the morning and all their possible implications churning in her mind. As she passed the Rose Garden for the second time, she pulled out her phone and sent Sergei another message. *You there?*

She still did not get an answer.

Kate continued on autopilot until she emerged from the Tiergarten just opposite the Holocaust Memorial. She made a point of visiting it on every trip to Berlin, and perhaps its unconscious allure today was a connection with something bigger, of greater importance.

At first sight, it seemed an inconspicuous, underwhelming memorial to the many millions of Jews killed by the Nazis, but as you moved from the low tomb-like slabs of smooth grey concrete on the periphery and into those of monstrous scale in the interior, a sense of the awesome nature of this, the greatest crime ever perpetrated against humanity, became at first unnerving and finally overwhelming.

It was two o'clock in the afternoon by the time she returned to her hotel room. Ian had called three more times, but she decided on a visit to the spa and sauna over responding to any of his messages. She sat next to a very fat, determinedly manspreading German in the sauna and kept her towel tightly wrapped around her. She swam afterwards and felt, in the round, a tiny bit calmer.

She returned to her room, only to find it much colder than she had expected. She came around the corner and saw the window was open, a man sitting in a deckchair outside with his back to her. It was Mikhail. He had a bottle of beer in his hand. 'I hope you don't mind. I helped myself from the mini-bar.'

'What the hell are you doing here?'

'You were followed.'

'Our ops team was confident—'

'Then they need a kick up the arse. We have been watching you ever since you landed at Tegel. And so have my former colleagues in the SVR. I am sorry you ran into trouble, but it was not of my doing.'

Kate felt acutely vulnerable standing opposite him in her dressing-gown. 'This is incredibly unprofessional.'

'Relax. You're safe with me, as I think you know.'

'What do you want?'

'Asylum. As we discussed.' He picked up a bag on the floor beside him and came into the room. He closed the doors to the balcony, took out a laptop and placed it on the desk.

'Take a seat.'

She did so. Mikhail opened the computer and logged on with touch ID. 'You'll recall that your prime minister was once an army officer in Kosovo back in the late nineties, attached to army intelligence. As you have guessed, his interpreter was working for us. He had an affair with her, which provided plenty of useful information, but the most important revelation was the sheer scale of his greed and sexual appetite. The latter included a penchant for young girls.'

Mikhail pulled up some video and hit play. It was evident straight away that the room had been rigged with more than one camera of the highest possible quality – and lit to ensure maximum visibility. There seemed absolutely no doubt that the man entering the room was James Ryan, now Prime Minister of the United Kingdom and First Lord of the Treasury. There was an old woman with him, who pointed at three girls rapidly getting to their feet by the coffee-table in the corner. 'Two virgin, but third also very young.'

The girls looked thirteen or fourteen – fifteen at most – and were dressed in high leather boots and short miniskirts. Their faces were caked with make-up, which failed to conceal their ages or their anxiety. The old woman departed. Ryan took a packet of white powder from his pocket, poured a thin line of it on to the table, rolled up a US twenty-dollar bill and encouraged the girls to partake. He was the last to bend over and snort cocaine, before the orgy – if you could call it that – began in earnest.

One thing was quickly evident: this was not his first time in such company. He knew exactly what he wanted for his money and directed the girls with all the confidence of a man who had done this countless times before. Initially, he only watched, but eventually he rose from a seat in the corner, unbuckled his belt and dropped his trousers and boxer shorts. He didn't bother to take off his shirt or socks. 'You don't have to watch the whole thing,' Mikhail said.

'Given what is at stake, I'm afraid I do.'

'It doesn't get any better.'

To begin with, Ryan was content to let the girls pleasure him, but he then insisted on having intercourse with each in turn – in the missionary position, while the others waited. All three of the girls cried as he entered them. 'Just fast forward to the end.'

'The end is the worst bit,' Mikhail said, but he did as he was instructed. When he reached the part where James Ryan was putting his trousers on, he hit play again. One of the girls was still crying. 'Tell her to shut up,' Ryan instructed the others. 'At least you will eat well tonight.'

He put on his jacket and left the room. Mikhail stopped the video. 'That's it,' he said. 'Not pleasant, but you can see there is no doubt it is him.'

'How can we be sure you haven't faked it?'

'Don't be absurd.'

'We both know it's possible.'

'Not with that kind of quality. Ask your experts.'

Kate nodded. 'You look like you've seen a ghost,' Mikhail said.

She glanced up at him. 'It's a lot worse than that, isn't it?'

'No, it is not. It is really very simple. I am offering you a quick and easy solution. No one can doubt that he is the man in this footage, or that its contents don't amount to a resigning matter, so all you have to do is get myself, my family and my father into Britain with this computer intact and then you can release the pictures and it will all be over.'

'You honestly think it's going to be that straightforward?'

'Why not? They say the foreign secretary is an honest woman. As long as you don't make the mistake of consulting anyone else, I don't see why it should be complicated.'

'How do you want to proceed?'

'Do we have your promise of asylum?'

Kate hesitated a moment too long. 'Yes.'

'Signed off by the foreign secretary, and with the stipulations we made, we are afforded your meaningful protection and are allowed to keep all our assets in the West?'

'Yes.'

'Where is the letter?'

'I'll have to get it. We—'

'We can take this shit anywhere!' The tension Mikhail had been doing his best to hide was starting to show. 'And embarrass the hell out of you in the process.'

'I said yes.'

'I need a letter from the foreign secretary.'

'I'll get it.'

'You should have brought it with you!'

'Come on, Mikhail. She was never going to authorize that until she knew the material was genuine.'

He slammed the computer shut and put it back into his bag. 'Well, now you have seen it.'

Kate stood. She walked to the window. She went to her jacket for a cigarette and offered the packet to Mikhail, who waved her away airily. She lit up, if only to give herself a few moments to think. 'We have a deal,' she said. 'I want to know how to proceed.'

He watched her, hands thrust deep into his pockets. 'I don't know if we should trust you.'

'Yes, you do. That's why you came to me in the first place.'

'Don't be so sure of yourself.'

'We have to lay our hands on this material. You know we do. So let's get on with it.'

He watched her smoking, his gaze unblinking. She wished she wasn't standing before him in a dressing-gown, hair unkempt, but perhaps that had been part of his calculation.

'My father's family was originally from Georgia, as I am sure you know. We still have a home in Tbilisi and another in Kazbegi, just over the border. He thinks he can get himself, my wife and son there. So that is where we will meet. The Russians have the commercial airport covered, so you will need a private plane on standby to come in and pick us up – or, better still, to remain on the ground until we are ready.'

'When?'

'This week. You can send me the letter from your foreign secretary tonight – tomorrow at the latest. I will find a way to show it to my father. You will need to unfreeze the assets you have seized in the UK, including the house in Knightsbridge, where we will have to live. The letter will need to confirm we are free to move around as we please in both Europe and America.'

'As you know, that's not in our gift.'

'You can deliver it. We will come with this video and incontrovertible evidence of the money we have paid to your prime minister over the course of the time he has worked for us – more than thirty million pounds in all – along with a global paper trail, which will allow you to seize the cash and arrest those who have helped launder it.'

They looked at each other. 'All right,' Kate said. 'You very much have a deal.'

Mikhail forced a smile. 'And hang the consequences.'

He picked up his bag and slung it over his shoulder. 'You'll be the most famous British MI6 officer since Kim Philby.'

'Just what I always wanted.'

He walked to the door. 'Sorry to have caught you off guard.'

'There is one other thing.'

He turned back to face her. 'You're getting more than enough for your money.'

'This concerns both of us. Is it true that my husband Stuart was the agent codenamed Viper?'

A flicker of alarm crossed Mikhail's handsome face, all the more noticeable for the speed with which he tried to hide it. 'What do you mean?'

'Are you sure Stuart was Viper?'

'Yes. Why?' He was looking her in the eye now. Perhaps with a little too much intensity, as if he was determined to hide the momentary flash of alarm she'd witnessed a few seconds earlier.

Kate leant back against the desk. 'Well, since you murdered my old deputy I was forced to acquire a new one, and she has some questions about our original operation that I'm having to admit I struggle to answer.'

'Such as?'

'Stuart didn't know anything about Rav's trip to Geneva.'

'So . . .'

'And Rav was much too smart to have drawn attention to himself while he was there.'

Mikhail shrugged. 'If I recall correctly, he went to see the lawyer François Binot. Maybe one of my colleagues had him under surveillance.'

'Why? Binot worked for you.'

'Exactly. Perhaps it was Binot who alerted us.'

'Rav wouldn't go anywhere near a man like Binot. And, besides, he would have called us straight away if he had sensed he was being watched.'

'I don't know . . .' Mikhail looked exasperated. 'Why does it matter?'

'Was Stuart Viper?'

'Yes.'

'Are you sure?'

'Yes. It was my father who recruited him.'

There was something about Mikhail's expression that unsettled Kate, not so much that he might be telling a lie – which he would likely pull off with consummate ease – so much as the sense that she, in turn, had unnerved him. But why?

'How did Moscow Centre know what Rav was up to? Because Stuart could not have told them.'

'Who says we killed Rav?'

'You did.'

'*If* we did, it was done without my father's knowledge.'

Kate thought about that. She had kept her gaze fixed on Mikhail's face. 'What do you mean *if*? You must know.'

'You are starting at shadows, Kate. It was not our work. That is what I am saying.'

'What if there is someone else?' she asked.

'Where?'

'In SIS, working for Moscow Centre.'

'You mean someone whom my father, the head of our foreign intelligence service until two years ago, was unaware of?'

'Perhaps he or she does not work for the SVR.' Kate moved to the window and looked out at the grey clouds illuminated by the dying rays of the sun. 'What about someone recruited and run by the GRU?' She turned back to him. 'A man or woman in a position to tell his or her masters in Moscow that Rav was circling close to Binot, a lawyer with intimate connections to the Russian president.'

She waited. 'A man – or a woman – in a position to warn his masters that we had come to Berlin with the aim of persuading you to defect.'

'You think anyone in the GRU gives a fuck what happens to us?'

'I imagine, if they succeed in removing you, your father and his successor from power in the SVR, they would be rather interested in inheriting the British prime minister as an agent of influence.'

'Stuart was Viper,' Mikhail said, with finality. 'The rest is just conjecture. I shouldn't let it keep you awake at night.'

But as he left, she knew with utmost certainty that this particular piece of conjecture would be keeping them both awake for many nights to come.

14

C WANTED TO see them once they had landed back at Heathrow, but there was a complication: his wife Alice was dying. Kate called him directly to reassure him it could wait and they would deal with the foreign secretary directly if need be. He would not hear of it, so the car delivered them in driving rain to the Lister Hospital, just down from Sloane Square. They had to cross no more than twenty yards of open ground, but they were dripping when they arrived in the Lister's hallway.

Kate had been instructed to go directly to room 307, but she asked Julie and Suzy to wait in the third-floor reception area.

The door to 307 was wedged ajar and she could see her superior in a chair with his back to her, reading quietly to his wife. Alice's eyes were closed, her pearly white face turned towards the window, classical music playing softly on a portable CD player in the corner. Kate watched for a moment, feeling like a voyeur. Middle age had written a few lines on Alice's elegant features, but illness had not robbed her of her beauty.

Sir Alan sensed Kate's presence and turned slowly, without breaking the rhythm of his reading. He nodded at her to indicate he would be with her shortly and returned to his wife.

Kate re-joined her colleagues. 'How is she?' Julie asked. Kate shrugged. She felt incredibly uncomfortable just being there.

'What does she have?' Suzy asked.

'Cancer,' Kate replied.

'What kind?'

'Originally breast, but now secondary in the liver.'

'That's bad.'

'Yes. But, for God's sake, don't say anything about it.' Kate didn't have a great deal of confidence in Suzy's ability to adhere to social norms.

'My mother had liver cancer,' Suzy added, cutting the feet from under her. 'The doctor said she would die in three weeks and he was right – to the day.'

Kate went to get herself a cup of coffee from a machine opposite. 'You want anything?' she asked the others. They shook their heads.

'That should definitely help you sleep,' Julie said, as Kate returned with a plastic cup of dirty brown liquid.

A few minutes later Sir Alan emerged. He'd arranged for them to talk in an empty room at the other end of the corridor. Kate sat in a chair in one corner, Sir Alan stood by the window, while Julie and Suzy perched on the empty bed, like children visiting their parents.

'How is she?' Kate asked.

'She has a throat infection and a fever. She can't swallow and is in a lot of pain. The doctors think she has a few weeks left, so I'm keen to get her home again, but for the moment we're stranded here.'

'Sir, I'm sure we can deal with the foreign secretary directly.'

'Let's just get on with it. Talk me through the video.'

Kate couldn't think of a worse time or place to be discussing this. 'I'm not an expert, but, to me, there's no doubt that it's him. The entire thing is shot with very high-quality hidden cameras. He enters the room. Three very young-looking girls dressed in high leather boots and short skirts get up from a sofa in the corner. An old woman, who is clearly the madam, promises him that two of the girls are virgins and the other still very young. He takes a packet of what looks like cocaine from his pocket and encourages them to snort it first, before doing so himself with a rolled-up twenty-dollar bill. He asks them to undress and to . . . well, to pleasure each other, which they do not very convincingly. He is clearly no newcomer to this kind of scenario and he directs them to do a series of specific things to each other.

'Then he stands, unbuckles his belt and comes to the bed. He has removed his underwear, but keeps his shirt and socks on. The girls then pleasure him, before he has intercourse with each of them in turn – in the missionary position. All three girls appear to be crying as he enters them. Afterwards, one is still shedding tears and he instructs the others to "tell her to shut up". He adds that all three will "eat well tonight", then dresses and departs.'

There was a long silence. Sir Alan had his back to them. He was staring out across the rooftops, which were just shapes in the darkness. 'You watched the whole thing?'

'Yes, sir. It was unbearably sordid.'

'And you are absolutely one hundred per cent certain it was him?'

'Yes. It was the way he talked, the way he moved . . .'

'It could not have been faked?'

Kate hesitated. Had she been too quick to believe what had appeared to be the evidence of her own eyes? 'It's real – it has to be,' she said. 'And it is definitely him.'

Sir Alan looked like a man trying to hide frustration, anger or both. 'What arrangements did you make?'

'He and his father want a letter from the foreign secretary guaranteeing protection, free travel in Europe and America, and the ability to enjoy their assets in the West unhindered, which I promised they would have tomorrow. They will assemble in Tbilisi, where Igor's family were originally from, or a home they have in Kazbegi, close to the border, by the end of the week. They want a private plane to fly them direct to London, so that they do not have to pass through the main airport terminal, which he said was watched by the Russians. They also promised to bring with them evidence of the cash they have paid to Ryan – more than thirty million pounds in all.'

'The foreign secretary wants to see us tomorrow morning at her London house,' Julie said. 'Just Kate and me.'

Suzy looked as if she might object, but thought better of it after catching sight of the expression on Sir Alan's face. Ice radiated more warmth. 'Talk me through the operation,' he said. He was still addressing Kate, as if the others were not there.

Kate shook her head. 'I'm still confused by it. Danny and his team were convinced I was clean by the time I arrived in Alexanderplatz. I don't know how Mikhail got a burner phone into my pocket. And I have no idea how they managed to ambush me at that point in Friedrichstrasse.'

'Did you raise it with Mikhail?'

'I asked him whether Stuart was Viper.'

'What was his answer?'

'He said Stuart was definitely Viper, but he seemed less sure about the possibility of another mole. I suggested that a second source was working for the GRU.'

Sir Alan fixed each of them with a steady gaze in turn, his pale blue eyes tinged with a melancholy Kate had never witnessed before. 'Who knew about the meeting in Alexanderplatz?'

Suzy stood up, as if this had been her cue. 'The same group. You, Kate, Julie, Danny.'

'And you,' Kate told Suzy.

'And me, yes, though I can be ruled out since this mole, if he or she does exist, was part of the original Operation Sigma.'

'That's merely your conjecture,' Kate said. Suzy flushed. For a woman so tactless, she appeared to have a strange aversion to confrontation.

'What about Ian?' Julie asked.

'I informed him,' Sir Alan said. Kate tried to conceal her surprise. Ian had not bothered to ask her the details of the operation in Berlin – which, now she came to reflect on it, was odd in itself – and it would have been all too easy for Sir Alan to keep them from him. If there was a potential leak, then the need-to-know principle ought to have been paramount.

The thought came to her unbidden that Sir Alan's actions could be interpreted as a deliberate attempt to widen the circle of knowledge.

'What about the foreign secretary?' Julie asked.

Sir Alan shook his head. 'She didn't know the time or the place of the meeting.'

'She was aware of the time,' Kate said quietly. 'And she knew it was in Berlin.'

'All right,' Sir Alan said, moving towards the door. 'We're going around in circles. It's quite possible they've been monitoring Mikhail. Kate and I will pick this up with the foreign secretary in the morning. Suzy, I want you and Julie to start preparing the ground in Tbilisi. Work on the assumption that we'll get approval for the extraction and permission to hire some kind of private jet. And whatever security detail you think we might need, double it.'

'Should we inform the Georgians?' Suzy asked.

Sir Alan looked incredulous. 'Of course not,' he said, and Kate could see Suzy privately cursing her inexperience.

As they moved towards the door, Sir Alan put his hand on Kate's shoulder to stop her. 'One moment,' he said. The others hesitated, but he gestured at them to continue. 'I'll see you in the office in the morning,' he told them, 'and very well done. For all the issues, we got what we went to Berlin for and that is a feather in all of your caps.' That seemed intended more for Suzy than the rest of them and she smiled for the first time since they had left Berlin.

He waited until the door was closed, then sat on the bed.

'Are you all right, sir? As I said, I'm very happy to—'

'I'm as all right as you are,' he said, 'which is not very bloody okay at all. But neither of us has any choice but to plough on, do we? Anyway, that's not why I asked you to stay behind. We may have a problem with the foreign secretary.'

'In what way?'

'She's getting cold feet.'

'Why?' Kate couldn't quite believe this.

'Because it's a very big call and she simply isn't used to making them. She's about to authorize an operation to oversee a major defection – which, for all that we're recommending it, is still a significant step for someone new to this kind of decision-making. The controversy it will bring with it would likely test the bravest of politicians and Meg Simpson is not one of them.'

'You think she'll refuse to send the letter?'

'I don't know. But all I am saying is that it's not a given she'll agree to this tomorrow and we may have to work hard to persuade her.' He stood again. 'I'd better go back to Alice. Get some sleep, Kate. You look like you need it.'

By the time Kate passed the room further down the corridor, Sir Alan was seated at his wife's bedside again, head bent as he read to her. Kate watched him for a moment, envious of his devotion and loyalty. It made her feel lonelier still.

She walked home, despite the rain, which had slowed to a drizzle. She found herself wishing Sir Alan had not left her with that departing instruction about sleep, which loomed larger with every step she took homewards. She recalled the days when the house in Battersea had represented only comfort, love and rest. Now it served as the instrument of her torture, and that alone made her feel guilty. What kind of mother doesn't want to return home to her children?

She passed her own mother's nursing home and felt the familiar pull of filial duty. She overrode it and had almost reached her front door before guilt got the better of her and she doubled back. Why did she feel any loyalty to the woman who had spent a lifetime traducing and belittling her? It made no sense at all.

But Lucy was a shadow of her normal self today. She sat in an armchair, facing the window, gazing out into the darkness. 'Hi, Mum,' Kate said, as she installed herself in a corner of the window seat beside her.

'Hello, my love.' Her smile was full of quiet warmth. 'I was just thinking about you.'

'Glad I stopped by, then. Can I get you a cup of tea?'

'No, thank you. And I'm pleased you came. I'm so sorry for the things I said in Cornwall. I don't know what got into me.'

Kate stared at the floor. Her mother had resolutely refused to seek any psychiatric or psychological help over the years, determined to view even the suggestion she might as a sign – or, rather, an accusation – of weakness. It was impossible to be certain whether she was a depressive, or bipolar, or was dragging around some other psychological disorder, but the speed with which she oscillated between two entirely opposing personalities still took Kate's breath away. And even now, after all these years, she couldn't help the rush of warmth she felt at even the slightest expression of love or affection.

'I know I've made it hard for you and I'm sorry.'

'That's all right, Mum.' It wasn't, of course, not by the longest shot. But what else could she say?

'I think your aunt Rose brings out the worst in me.'

That wasn't true: her mother was capable of being equally poisonous at all other times, but she let that ride as well. 'I don't know why,' Kate said.

'She's always wanted to think of you as her own child.'

'She does her best to look after me.' If there was an accusation in that, it was designed to stop her mother in her tracks.

Lucy nodded, as if to acknowledge this. 'All right. I don't want to pick a fight. I know she's the mother you never had. But she's more competitive than she lets on and I'm never certain she's as generous – or perhaps I mean as straightforward – as she appears.'

It was said without rancour, or bitterness, or the twinkle in the eye with which Lucy usually delivered her malicious barbs, so if it was an impression she took issue with, Kate didn't doubt it represented, for once, her mother's genuinely held view. Lucy was looking at the picture of her former lover on the side table. 'I think you'd better put that away now. Perhaps you could retrieve the photograph of your father from the drawer.' Kate did so and they both sat in silence for a while, as if determined to enjoy this momentary contentment. Kate could hardly take her eyes off her father's kind, smiling face.

They retreated into safer subjects after that: the weather, Fiona's dress sense and Gus's gaming habits. Kate waited for the wheel to turn, for the malice to creep back in, but her mother retained her equanimity throughout and they parted, much later than Kate had intended, with a hug. 'You do look tired, love,' Lucy said, as she released her.

'I am.'

'It must be hard without Stuart.'

'Yes.' Kate couldn't help bridling. 'Nothing I didn't bring upon myself, I'm sure.'

'I didn't mean it like that and you know it. I understand that trying to have it all – and do it all – on your own must be impossibly difficult. But you must sleep. And if you need help, please ask for it – from whomever. Rose. Even me.'

Kate didn't pick that up immediately, but neither did she walk away.

'I know we've had our differences over the years, but I've never shown the children anything but love, and I'm not so gaga that I can't look after them now and again.'

'I understand, Mum. Thank you.'

'You can't look after them if you're not well yourself.'

'I'm fine.'

'I don't think you are, but I'll leave it there.'

Kate walked home slowly, as if to make the feeling of relative warmth last. She wished she had stayed longer. Why hadn't she lingered awhile?

It wasn't until she turned the key in the door that her rational mind reasserted itself. It said everything, surely, about her upbringing that twenty-five minutes of relative normality could have elicited such a response.

Rose had cleaned the kitchen so that it was immaculate. She sat at the table, reading an old copy of *Vogue* and drinking herbal tea. She stood to hug Kate. 'What can I get you?'

'Valium.'

'As bad as that?'

'Basically. It's been a long day. Is Gus still awake?'

'He might be.'

Kate threw her coat on to the sofa. 'I could murder a glass of white wine, if I'm completely honest.' She went up to find

Gus face down on the bed with Nelson beside him. For once, she didn't feel inclined to move their ancient dog.

'Don't take him,' he said, as she sat gently on the bed.

'I don't know how you can bear the smell.'

'You don't notice it after a bit, though Rose gave him fish skin for dinner.'

'Yuck.'

Gus turned on to his back and looked at her. 'How was your trip?'

Kate couldn't remember the last time he'd asked a question like that. It was the night all her ships were coming in. 'Complicated.'

'Why?'

She smiled. 'State secret.'

'Did you see Dad?'

'No. I'll arrange another meeting with him very soon.' Kate couldn't miss the longing in her son's eyes. 'You miss him?'

'Sometimes.'

'Me too.'

'Will you ever get back together?'

'I don't see how. Quite apart from all the emotional damage, it's a practical impossibility.'

'Will you get another boyfriend?'

'I sincerely doubt it.' She squeezed his leg under the duvet. 'You are my priority and always will be. Have you spoken to Fi?'

'No.' There was a long pause as Gus stroked Nelson's ear. Kate sensed he had more to say. 'It feels a bit strange here without her.'

'It's only for a few days.'

'Maybe. She's behaving very weirdly.'

'How was Rose?'

'She's great. She's so kind. I guess she's how Granny should be.'

'Granny has her own issues.' Kate bent down to kiss her newly articulate son and ruffled his hair. For the first time in a very long while, he held her tight. She stood and moved to the door. 'I'll see you in the morning,' she said.

'Will you leave Nelson?'

'Of course.' She paused. 'Things might be a bit busy for the next week or two at work, but it will calm down after that.'

'Like it did last time?'

'Fair point. I'm going to consider asking for a period of absence so I can spend more time with you.'

'Okay.'

'Would that be a good idea?'

'It's up to you.' She took that as a massive endorsement. 'Why is work busy?' he asked. 'Matters of life and death?'

'Political life and death, perhaps.'

'Fiona told Jed you're basically James Bond.'

Kate had to stop herself laughing. This was turning into a very surprising conversation. 'My work is *supposed* to be secret,' she said.

'Not to family. And I guess Jed is family now.'

'I guess he is.'

'Is it true?' Gus persisted.

'No one is James Bond. He's a bit ludicrous, really.'

'Jane Bond, then. That's kind of cool.'

'Sleep well,' Kate said. She was still smiling as she walked into the kitchen. 'I don't know what you've done to him,' she told her aunt. 'I just had an articulate, affectionate conversation with my teenage son.' She glanced at the wine. 'You'd better make that a double.'

'He's a lovely boy. So funny.'

Kate sat opposite her aunt. 'He seems to be missing his sister, which is an even greater wonder. Is she all right? I texted her earlier and got no reply.' Kate took a large slug of wine.

'She's fine. I imagine she'll be home in a day or two. I sense the Jed exile might be wearing a bit thin for both of them . . . I'm not going to preach,' Rose continued, 'which would be incredibly tedious, but, my God, you look tired.' Kate glanced at her aunt, whose gaze radiated concern. 'Are you still on the sleeping pills?'

'Yes.'

'Zopiclone?' Kate nodded. 'Be careful,' Rose went on, 'they're highly addictive.'

'I know, I know. I'll be fine. I won't need one tonight. I'm dead beat.' She took another slug of Pinot Grigio. 'Did you have anxiety or depression?'

'The one tends to lead to the other.'

'Yes, I guess so.'

'But mainly the former.'

'About what exactly?'

'I came to define my self-worth by my ability to become a mother. The more times I failed, the more anxious I got about never succeeding. But, as Dr Wiseman will already have told you, I'm sure, it's rarely just one thing.'

Kate nodded. 'You said you were very busy at work?' The question was genuine: the Finance Department had always seemed to be a pretty sedate place.

'It was in the period I was attached to Operations.' Kate looked at her aunt, gobsmacked. Rose permitted herself a wry smile. 'I know, I probably should have told you about it long ago.'

'When – I mean, how long ago? Where? Doing what?'

'I joined as a Finance trainee straight from university. But in those days you could opt to transfer to Operations for an attachment. The idea was to give those of us who were going to spend our lives bean-counting a sense of life at the sharp end. I guess it would have been 'ninety-two to 'ninety-six. Something like that. I was mostly working in Bosnia.'

'With Sir Alan?'

'Yes. And Ian at the tail end.'

Rose was staring into her wine as she swirled it in her glass, as if to conjure old memories.

'How come you never told me about it? I feel embarrassed not to have known—'

'I had my breakdown straight after that and had to take four months off work.'

'Do you know what tipped you over the edge?'

'Everything. Alan was mostly focused on Mladic and his Bosnian Serb friends. Ian took over from him. I came in and out, trying desperately to get pregnant in between and repeatedly miscarrying. I pushed myself far too far and was very stupid about it. I'm anxious you don't do the same.'

'So what did you do when you returned to work?'

'Transferred back to Finance, prioritized my marriage and my mental health and tried to wipe the period from my memory.' Kate could see that her aunt was now determined to change the subject. 'How was Berlin?'

'It went to plan, mostly. The foreign secretary has a very big decision to make, which Sir Alan predicts she is not going to enjoy.'

Rose knew better than to ask any more. She got up and went to wash up her mug. While she did so, her phone buzzed. Kate glanced at the screen. It was a message from Sir Alan. *Call you later*, it said.

Rose turned, noticed the message, picked up her phone and slipped it into her pocket, without meeting Kate's eye. She kissed her niece tenderly on the head and headed for the stairs. 'Sleep well,' she said.

Kate finished her wine in melancholy silence. *Call you later* . . . What was that about?

Almost certainly none of her business.

In fact, definitively none of her business.

But still . . .

She washed up and followed Rose up the stairs. She removed her make-up, brushed her teeth and collapsed into bed, convinced she would go straight to sleep.

But the more she circled closer to it, the more her mind began to torture her again. For a long time, her patience held. Just rest, she told herself. Sleep is close. It will happen. But it didn't. Not quite.

Her pulse quickened. She recognized the signs and got out of bed. The digital alarm clock told her it was just after two in the morning: four hours until she needed to be up.

She went down to the kitchen, switched on a side lamp and sat in the chair in the corner reading *Vogue*. After twenty minutes, she didn't know if she was tired or not. Was sleep creeping up on her? It didn't feel like it, but the clock on the wall was closing in on half past two, which meant her window to sleep was closing fast.

She returned to bed. Her self-discipline held for what seemed like an age, but as the minutes marched past the panic crept back in. She tried some yoga, slowed her breathing right down. She felt better and attempted again to drift off. But it was ultimately always the same threshold she couldn't cross. She realized she was sweating it too much and tried to roam far and wide with her thoughts. They returned, like a dog with a bone, to her inability to sleep.

The dawn was once again a relief, the sun inching along the painted terraced houses opposite. She had a shower, dressed and put on her make-up. She faced the day, momentarily uplifted by the fact that, for now at least, she was roughly able to function.

15

IF IAN GENUINELY saw himself as the next C, Kate thought he was going a strange way about getting there. Even by his own standards, his outfit for the breakfast meeting at the foreign secretary's grand stucco residence on Carlton House Terrace was eccentric. He'd grown his hair long so that his blond curls tumbled over the collar of a shirt that might have been appropriate for an evening in the Caribbean. His black jeans were ripped above the knee, his ubiquitous suede Chelsea boots scuffed and dirty, as if he had walked there across a field. He wore a black cardigan, half done up to lend his cry for attention – or possibly help – an air of vague respectability.

Perhaps *he* thought he was James Bond. This certainly appeared to be the message he was conveying to the foreign secretary, of a man too busy, important and, frankly, dangerous to bother with the conventional Whitehall dress code.

What was more surprising was the way Suzy was watching him. Even while he warmed them up, as they waited for the foreign secretary, with the story of his last Ironman event – he had done many and could talk about them at vast length – she barely took her eyes off him. My God, Kate thought, there really is no accounting for taste.

Sir Alan stood with his back to them, looking out over the Mall. Kate thought he held his emotional pain in his upper body as if it were a physical affliction, which she supposed in the end it was. She tried to think of something that might comfort or distract him, but he seemed far removed from everything around him, as if he was preparing to make the journey to the other side with his wife.

As a superior, she reflected, he had always been broadly supportive: encouraging when she got it right, steely when she screwed up. She was far from beyond wanting to please him. For a moment, she thought of how it would be if Ian managed to claw his way into Sir Alan's chair. Intolerable, really. Unimaginable. She'd have to quit. But now that her family was supported by her salary alone, what, exactly, would she do?

Their 'breakfast', which consisted of croissants and other pastries, fruit salad, orange juice and two large pots of coffee, lay untouched in the centre of the table and as Ian droned on and wretchedly on about his training regime – 'You have to cycle for two hours before dawn or you never get enough in' – Kate had to restrain herself from getting stuck in. It was hardly a scientific revelation that chronic sleep deprivation left one absolutely *ravenous*.

Meg Simpson stormed in like a thundercloud. She didn't bother to wish any of them good morning. And more pressingly, from Kate's point of view, she did not show any inclination to reach for the pastries or even the coffee. Kate weighed the social acceptability of opening the score.

C hadn't bothered to join them at the table. 'Would you care to join us, Sir Alan?' Simpson asked, with more edge than the situation appeared to demand. Kate wondered if she knew of his wife's illness. He did as he was asked, looked at Kate and, as if reading her mind, reached for the coffee and a pastry. She mouthed her thanks and he allowed himself a smile.

'Sir Alan has briefed me,' Simpson said.

'It was an excellent operation, conducted with the utmost professionalism,' Ian offered, 'but I hold to my initial view that—'

'I am well aware of your views,' Simpson shot back. Ian's face reddened. It occurred to Kate that if Ian was Viper, or some other agent working for the SVR or the GRU or any other arm of the Russian state, he was not subtle in covering his tracks. Simpson shuffled uncomfortably in her seat. She stared at the coffee pot in front of her. 'I do not find myself willing as yet to write the letter you say you need, or to set in train the actions it would instigate, or deal with the consequences that might arise.'

They waited for her to elaborate.

'You may be inclined to view that as political cowardice. I would prefer to see it as caution.'

'The difference is academic,' Sir Alan said. 'We are not interested in motive, only conclusion.'

Now it was her turn to look stung. 'I am aware that this is not what you wanted to hear.'

'We have a bounden duty here that is not, I think, in question.'

'I disagree. Our greatest duty is to preserve the integrity of our democracy, which, I am afraid, includes an essential belief in it.'

'It's hard to think of anything that would erode it more swiftly than the idea that we all sat here knowing the prime minister was working for our mortal enemy, not to mention his past actions, and resolved to do nothing about it.'

'But that is where all this falls down for me. Upon reflection, and taking into account what you've told me, I don't think I do yet believe that.'

'Kate has watched the video, in full, revolting detail, an act of conscientious duty in itself. She is not in any doubt that it is genuine.'

'I understand that. I have always found our prime minister's personal morals repellent, though even I did not believe he would sink this low. But the fact that he is a profligate adulterer – even in this repellent way – does not *de facto* prove he is a Russian spy. And if we were to go ahead and accept this defection, we would be destroying him.'

'We have a former head of the SVR – or at least his son – categorically stating that they recruited James Ryan to work for the Russian government while he was serving in Kosovo and that they used this video and enormous cash payments, the details of which they will bring with them, to blackmail and induce him.'

It occurred to Kate that she had never asked Mikhail if the video had been sufficient of itself to turn James Ryan, but the conversation was moving too fast now. 'This is my point,' Ian said. 'What if the Russians are just using this to destroy the prime minister and cause maximum possible chaos and disruption to our political system?'

Normally a master of self-control, Sir Alan visibly struggled to maintain it. He stared at Ian with barely concealed disdain. Kate glanced at Suzy, who had the good sense to remain silent. She wasn't looking at Ian with quite the same admiration now.

'I'll be honest,' Simpson said. 'What really troubles me here is the context. In the very first briefing note to me on this matter, you made very clear that you were not aware of any putsch within the SVR, the GRU, or at the apex of any other part of the Russian political system. This news has come out of nowhere.'

'That is because we very rarely get a break at this level. We're being offered an unprecedented opportunity that we cannot in all conscience turn down.'

'But isn't it just a bit *too* convenient?' Ian asked, all innocence once again.

'We lose nothing by proceeding. We have to give two people, who mean nothing to the public at large, asylum. Once they are here, we can all assess the video and the evidence of bank payments for ourselves. If we do not believe them to be genuine, we argue they came here under false pretences and act as we see fit.'

'Except they will have a letter with my name on it. What would be our explanation for why I wrote it if we decided this offer was not genuine? I'd look naïve at best, downright stupid at worst. The prime minister would be livid that I had even entertained the idea and I wouldn't blame him.'

Sir Alan shook his head curtly. 'You have no choice, ma'am, I am afraid.'

It was Meg Simpson's turn to redden. She didn't like to be lectured by anyone, but she was on shaky ground and she knew it. 'I'm not saying I won't write the letter and authorize this operation, just that I need more. If you can find further detail on the context, on what is really going on in Moscow, then I would feel a great deal more confident. Has there really been a putsch? If you can confirm there has, without equivocation, then I guarantee I will sign that letter.'

To Kate, this information seemed theoretical at best, irrelevant at worst, and she could see Sir Alan felt the same, though he chose to internalize his anger, in front of the group at least. He stayed behind as she, Suzy and Ian filed out.

They didn't speak until they were on the Mall. Suzy ordered a taxi and Ian let her climb in before he turned to Kate. 'Do you fancy walking back?'

Her head was so paralysed now with sleep deprivation, coffee and the strange tension of that meeting that she had already decided as much. Not that she would normally have welcomed Ian's company.

It was a lot warmer that morning, the daffodils blooming in St James's Park, which was more or less deserted. They were level with the great expanse of Horse Guards Parade before Ian finally blurted out what was on his mind. 'Have you spoken to her?' he asked.

'Who?'

'Julie, of course!'

'About what?'

'Don't be obtuse, Kate.'

She tried to think of any subject she less wanted to discuss with him. 'What was that all about?' she asked, gesturing back to the foreign secretary's residence behind them.

'You know what it was about,' he said. 'The Russians love playing games and sooner or later we need to stop responding. I just don't agree with you and Alan on that, but it's an honest difference of opinion and I'm perfectly entitled to express my views, convenient or not. Isn't that his mantra? "We are not here to agree"?'

'This is different and you know it.'

'You both think it is. But I'm less certain. I don't blame her for her caution. You'll probably get your letter, whether it's a good idea or not, but she's just covering her arse. I don't see any harm in making us go through the hoops.'

'We have a week at most until the offer disappears – perhaps to a rival, who may be in a position to embarrass us.'

'Everyone else will have exactly the same reservations, Kate. All Alan has to do is write a moderately convincing brief and you'll have your letter. And she's right to question it – even you can't deny this has all come out of the blue. Have we heard a single other source talk about a coup in Moscow Centre? Don't you think we would have seen *some* other reporting of it?'

'Not necessarily. You know how long it takes for news of any change at the top in Moscow to leak. Besides, I have seen the video.'

'If it's real.'

Kate could see further argument was pointless. She turned her attention to a group of Japanese tourists feeding the ducks. The enthusiasm of their children, their joy, was briefly distracting.

'Besides,' Ian continued, 'don't change the subject. Have you talked to her?'

'About what exactly?'

'Us, of course! Jesus, Kate, you can be wilfully dense sometimes.'

'What aspect of "us" would you like to discuss?'

'She won't return my calls.' Ian stopped and faced her. Kate noticed that the chest hair that poked out from his open-necked shirt in tufts was grey now. He suddenly looked older, too. Not that she could talk. 'This is serious, Kate.'

'What is?'

'I'm in love with her, goddamn it.'

Kate did not know whether to laugh or cry. She felt as if she was being hollowed out from the inside with exhaustion and nervous tension, and here was this absurd man-child pouring out his heart – and to her, of all people. 'You'll have to talk to her, Ian. I really can't help you.'

'But you're her friend. She trusts you.'

'I'm also her boss and you're mine, so this conversation feels inappropriate on any number of levels.'

'Oh, for God's sake! Don't be a prig. I just told you I loved her. This isn't some wretched office fling. I care—'

'But that is exactly how she sees it. I'm fairly sure it was just sex for her. She's told me that often enough.' Ian looked as if she had slapped him across the face. 'Don't look so surprised. Isn't that what most extra-marital affairs are supposed to be about?'

'No! Jesus . . .' Ian was clearly bewildered. 'What do you mean, just sex?'

'Oh, come on, Ian. This is like talking to one of my teen-agers.' Much too like, Kate wanted to add. 'Julie is a very tough and, if we're being honest, somewhat damaged young woman. She has many demons to slay, which I'm sure she'll manage to do in her own good time. She was having an affair with you because it came without baggage. Your declaration of undying love is the last thing she wants to hear.'

'Damaged?'

'Her mother! You must know that her mother abandoned them when she was still a child?' He seemed mystified. 'And her brother?' Kate added.

'He was killed, yes . . .'

'On that bus on 7/7. They'd had an argument. She was more or less a mother to him and she blames herself because he skipped school that day.'

'But that's why I love her. She's complicated . . . interesting.'

'You have a wife, Ian.'

'Had! I must be the only man in the country whose calls are rejected by both wife and mistress. It's absurd!'

Kate thought that probably took them to the nub of the matter. Only Ian could mistake a bruised ego for a broken heart. 'I have to get back,' she said.

'I'll see you there. I'm just going to drown myself in the pond.'

'You'll have a job,' Kate said. She walked on through St James's Park, enjoying the feel of the sun on her face. It was still early. Civil servants were arriving for work in a steady stream at the front entrance of the Treasury building. She skirted Parliament Square and walked on down towards

Millbank, past a group of Kurdish protesters demonstrating against the depredations of the Turkish state outside the House of Commons.

She joined the morning rush through the space-age security pods at the front entrance to the SIS building and exchanged small-talk in the lifts until she reached her floor. Julie was waiting for her, and no sooner had Kate run through the essentials of the meeting with Meg Simpson than Julie was bringing her back to her least favourite subject of the moment. 'What is wrong with him?' Julie asked.

'I assume you mean our boss?'

'He keeps pestering me, day and night. I'm going to have to report him to HR if this goes on. And I really don't want to do that – for either of our sakes.'

'He just declared to me his undying love for you in St James's Park.'

'To *you*?'

'Try not to make that sound like an insult.'

'Don't be ridiculous, Kate. You can't stand the man.'

'True. I can think of people he would more logically choose to confide in.'

Julie left with a departing shot at her former lover: 'He's a total idiot.' Kate almost replied that she could have told her friend that, and had, but she managed to swallow her words. She closed the door and watched Julie walk across to her station on the other side of the office. Kate closed the blind, sat at her desk and logged on to her computer. She shut her eyes, fatigue overwhelming her.

Her phone buzzed and, for a surprising moment, her heart skipped at the thought it might be Stuart. Ian's declaration of love for Julie had reminded her of the early days of Stuart's courtship at Cambridge, when he had refused to take no for an answer. But it was C: *One p.m. at Grumbles restaurant, Pimlico.*

It wasn't a request, much less an invitation. He could be Olympian in his detachment, though as he nursed his wife in her death throes he had more than excuse enough.

Kate slipped the phone into her pocket. Why had she thought it might be Stuart? And why had her heart skipped a beat at the prospect?

Comfortable, comforting Stuart: she was conscious again of missing him and the steady to and fro of everyday domestic interaction. But it left a bitter taste in her mouth. Why had he thrown all that away for a few nights in bed with Imogen Conrad? For the rest of her days that would make her feel about two feet tall.

16

IT WAS THE kind of instinct born of long experience, but it took Kate some time to be sure.

She walked on up Belgrave Road as planned and turned into Churton Street. She passed the blue awning of Grumbles and carried on towards C's house in Churton Place. It was bright now, the sky a clear and vivid blue. The customers of a café called the Roasting were sitting at small metal tables outside, their faces turned towards the sun.

Kate stopped at a flower shop just beyond it and lost herself in there for a moment or two, as if killing time.

She emerged again and, without looking back, walked on beyond Churton Place and turned left into the street market in the pedestrian section. The vendors mostly sold food and she drifted past their stalls, picking up some vegetables and fruit to test their quality and bending closer to smell some of the cheese on the trestle at the end.

She quickened her pace, heading towards Victoria, but it took her until she was on the other side of the station to be absolutely sure she was right. She had come up the escalator to the small shopping mall on the first floor and now doubled back. Almost immediately – coming up on the opposite escalator – she saw the young Indian man in a grey T-shirt and leather jacket she had first spotted as she had turned from Lupus Street into Belgrave Road.

Kate went into WHSmith and bought a copy of *The Times*.

She walked across the station concourse, then swung quickly right on to Wilton Road. As she passed Rosa's Thai Café – inexplicably another of C's favourite local restaurants – she saw the girl with the green chinos and brown pumps.

Kate didn't break her stride. She went to a café called Pimlico Fresh at the end of Wilton Road and ordered a latte. She took it to a vacant seat outside and looked up and down the street to see if she could make out any more of her watchers.

She wasn't in much doubt as to who they were or what they were doing, but she wanted a few moments to think about it. She had toyed with the idea that the men and women following her might be Russians, but she had dismissed it. Unless Moscow's operational teams had made epic strides in their ability to assimilate convincingly into a London scene, it was not conceivable. Besides, why on earth would the Russians want to follow her to lunch?

Kate took out her phone and called Suzy. Her deputy answered straight away. 'When were you thinking of telling me you've put a tail on me?'

'I haven't done anything, Kate.'

'All right, let me rephrase the question. When were you thinking of telling me that your friends at the Security Service have put a tail on me?'

'I think I made clear they are not really my friends.'

'Could you at least deny it?'

'I told you they'd opened an investigation. The plain fact is you almost certainly have a mole. It's their job to find him or her.'

'I thought C had expressly forbidden this?'

'The DG made a courtesy call. C tried to claim that, if there was a problem, it was an internal matter and any investigation would breach operational security, but the integrity of all government agencies is MI5's business, as you well know. I did inform them of my questions about Viper, but it's out of my hands now. It's out of all of our hands, to be honest.'

'Did they put their most incompetent team on me, just so I would know they were watching?'

'I doubt it. They don't really think like that.'

'What do they hope to achieve by trailing me to lunch?'

Suzy sighed. 'This isn't really going anywhere. I'll see you when you get back.' She ended the call and Kate nursed the rest of her coffee in cold fury. Her mood hadn't lifted by the time she arrived at lunch with Sir Alan.

He was in the corner booth, which she knew to be his regular, opposite a sign for 'Rue Mozart'. It was a cosy place, with wood-panelling on the walls and an eclectic mix of street signs and photographs from around Europe.

Kate was so used to the air of authority that her boss always carried with him, consciously but also effortlessly, that the sight of him shorn of it seemed more shocking than it should have been. He looked tired, his shoulders hunched uncomfortably and eyes hooded. 'I'm sorry,' he said, gesturing at their surroundings. 'I've just managed to get Alice home, so this is about as far as I want to stray from her at the moment.'

'We can go and have a coffee at your house, if that would be easier.'

'No, it's actually a relief to be out of it for half an hour.' He glanced at his watch, as if to double-check that that was all it was likely to be. 'There is only so much of the impending tragedy any man can cope with.' He shook his head. 'It's funny, I suppose others might say we're more acquainted than most with the tenuous and temporary nature of human existence, but even that doesn't stop you being holed below the waterline.'

'I'm sorry.'

'Everyone is. And it doesn't make a damned bit of difference.' Sir Alan gestured at the waiter, who had just arrived at a table opposite. 'Part of the trouble is that she doesn't want to go. Neither of us has ever felt much need to consider the possibility of a life hereafter, but now she's so close to the threshold that seems a bit of an oversight.'

The waiter came. Sir Alan ordered salmon, Kate cod. He asked for a glass of red wine. 'I can't remember the last time I drank at lunch,' he said.

'I'd order a bottle if I were you.' Kate looked at him seriously. It had never occurred to her before in how much affection she held him. If he were to step down, she would certainly miss his phlegmatic wisdom and easy temperament, but also the kindness he had displayed after Stuart's departure for Moscow. She wished there was more she could say or do. 'If it's not an impertinent question, how much longer?'

'Less than two weeks. Our youngest son, John, is coming back from South Africa, so she's determined to hold on until he makes it.'

'How heartbreaking.'

'In all those years together, you never really contemplate what it will be like to say your final farewell. And I can't quite decide whether this slow, steady route – in which, at least, everyone gets to say goodbye in the way they see fit – is better than an abrupt exit.'

Kate found herself wishing that Stuart was dead rather than divorcing her. But she kept that thought to herself.

'Were you followed here?' he asked.

'Yes. I called Suzy and she didn't deny it.'

'She's got some ambition, that girl, not to say a fair degree of brass bloody neck.' The waiter brought his red wine and he took a healthy swig. 'Well, you may be encouraged to hear that they've been following me also.'

'You?'

'Don't look so surprised. If you are a suspect, then I must be, too. They appear to have assigned me their least experienced team. I spotted them as soon as we left the hospital and I assured them that my wife was dying and I would be unlikely to stray far from home until she had departed to the other side.' He took another sip of his wine.

'I could murder a smoke,' Kate said. 'I'm not sure what's happening to me.'

'You look how I feel, so I'm not surprised.' He glanced at his watch once more. 'I spoke to Andrew Blaine in Moscow this morning and I had a long conversation with Ian. None of our sources have picked up the rumours of Vasily Durov's demise inside Moscow Centre, though those we have managed to contact acknowledge they've not personally seen him for some time.'

'That's hardly news, given how reclusive he is.'

'Exactly. I've spoken to the foreign secretary again. She's digging her heels in, adamant she's not going to write that letter unless we can give her greater reassurance that what Mikhail says about the changing of the guard in Moscow is true.'

'That'll take time we don't have.'

'Have you heard from your friend Sergei?'

Sir Alan's blue eyes were on her now. She thought about lying to him, but rapidly changed her mind: this was neither the time nor the place. 'Yes and no,' she said.

'Meaning?'

'He did contact me. Just something very innocent.' She got out her phone and found the texts. '"How are you?" I replied I was good and was he in London? He answered, "No, at home in St Petersburg. Be good to see you sometime." I sent a message back and never got an answer.'

Sir Alan was looking out of the window. 'I'm guessing you received the message in Berlin?'

'Yes.'

'Have you had any contact with him since then?'

'I tried a couple more times and gave up when I didn't get an answer. I have enough on my plate without wondering about someone I used to like.' Kate realized that was more information than she'd needed to share.

'Would you still say his motives for that first tip-off about the meeting on the *Empress* in Istanbul were personal?'

Kate stared at her hands. How often had she asked herself this question? So much seemed to hang on it – and more with each passing day. 'I think so, but it's impossible to be sure without spending a little time with him. I'm going on a friendship of half a lifetime ago and the man I knew then. But people change. So . . . I don't know.'

'Has he been in touch with you since Stuart's defection?'

'Not until that exchange in Berlin.' The waiter came with their food. Sir Alan tucked into his as if he hadn't eaten for a week. 'I could try to make contact again,' Kate said.

'I thought you said he wasn't replying?'

'I know where his parents live in St Petersburg.'

'We could ask Andrew to send someone up. But it seems a long shot.'

'I meant I'd go myself.'

He looked up at her sharply, his lunch forgotten. 'I'll pretend you didn't suggest that, Kate.'

'Just hear me out.'

'No. It would be a ridiculous risk, which I couldn't countenance and nor should you.'

'It has to be me,' she said. 'They grew up in the old Soviet Union. They wouldn't dream of talking to someone about their son unless they knew him or her.'

'I'll have a word with Andrew, see what he thinks.'

It was said with finality, but Kate couldn't let go of the idea. It was against every conceivable current procedure and protocol for a senior serving officer to travel undercover into Russia alone. But C was right: everything that had happened had begun with Sergei and they would make no real headway until she could see him and get a sense of what his motive truly was. Meg Simpson had said she needed certainty, and Kate could see only one way to get it.

She pushed the food around her plate. Sir Alan stared out of the window. 'There was one other thing,' she said.

He faced her again. 'Go on.' Kate finished the last of her cod, though she wasn't in the least hungry. 'The suspense is killing me,' he said.

'I know what you're going to say, but I do feel really strongly about it.'

'The wrong sort of preamble for a successful negotiation, but never mind.'

'When I recruited Lena Sabic to go and plant that bug on Igor's yacht, I looked her in the eye and swore that, if she kept her side of the bargain, I would make sure we rescued her sister, Maja, from Belgrade, and brought her to this country.'

Sir Alan didn't blink. 'And we assuredly would have done so if Lena had survived.'

'But that's just it. Lena paid for this deal with her life, which, from my – from *our* – point of view, writes it in blood.'

'Interesting use of terminology, which I don't know that I accept.'

'I made a promise. I can't break it.'

'Meaning?'

'Well, for a start, I'd have to resign with immediate effect if we refuse to implement it.'

'The implication being that you would be unable to oversee this current defection, which would make it unlikely to happen?'

'I didn't say that.'

'I should hope not,' he said, 'because that would be black-mail, which I do not respond to well, as I hope you know.'

'I'm not blackmailing you or anyone else. I'm just trying to tell you I feel very strongly about it, to the extent that I'm prepared to sacrifice my career, if need be.'

Kate had expected this to be difficult, but the depth of his annoyance took her aback. 'I admire the true nature of your moral compass, Kate, but we have to separate dream from reality here. Of course we would all like to make good on that promise to Lena, myself more than most. But "saving" Maja, as you might see it, cannot be more than a fantasy. Leave aside the epic expense of a protracted legal process and her resettlement here, who is she going to end up with now Lena is dead?'

'Me.' The shock on Sir Alan's face was genuine. 'I'll adopt her.'

'Have you lost your mind?'

Kate had not given this outcome any thought before it emerged from her mouth, but she moved from instinct to certainty in a heartbeat. 'I feel more in possession of it than I have for quite some time.'

'What would Gus and Fiona think?'

'I have a hunch they'd wholeheartedly support it.'

'They lose a father and gain a deeply damaged refugee sister? Are you sure?'

'If that is the only way it can happen, then so be it.'

He leant back and, finally, smiled. 'I'd braced myself for a fight on this subject, but even I didn't expect you to go this far.'

'You talked about it with Rose last night?'

There was a hint of something in his eyes for the most fleeting of moments – surprise, perhaps, or was it guilt? – before he recovered his composure. 'I asked her to prepare the report so, yes, we have been conferring, if that is what you mean.' He shook his head. 'Look, I'll promise to give it some thought. That's all I can do.'

'You can promise you'll do everything in your power to make it happen. And that is the price of me remaining in the Service.'

His gaze was steady, remorseless even. 'You're a tough woman, Kate. That's why I admire you. But this is a test of leadership. I understand the promise you made to Lena, but circumstances move on. This is a financial and legal mine-field and it would be foolhardy for all of us to embark on it.'

'Nevertheless, it is the price I've set.'

'I've always seen you as a potential successor, one day. I think we should view this as a test of whether you have the necessary emotional and analytical clarity for such responsibilities.'

'If it is, I fail it. Willingly.'

He smiled, as if impressed, despite himself. 'Fair enough.' He picked up his coat. 'I'd better get back. I have a tab here, so no need to wait for the bill. Thank you for taking the time to see me.'

Kate stepped out with him and watched him all the way to the turn into Churton Place. He didn't look back.

She walked on towards Vauxhall Bridge, trailed by her MI5 watchers, her resolve stiffening both in relation to adopting Maja – what else could she honestly do? – and the idea of going to find Sergei in St Petersburg. Although it occurred to her the latter might be an attempt to escape the consequences of the former. She told herself going to St Petersburg had nothing to do with the loneliness that was becoming an aching chasm within her.

Back in the office, she closed her door. Sir Alan would fire her. Of course he would. Julie would advise against it. Ian would dance cheerfully on her grave. Suzy would probably take it as clear evidence she really had been working for Moscow all along.

She'd crossed the border from Finland before. What was the chance that the guards there would be on the lookout for a lone intelligence officer from London travelling under an alias she had never before used? She looked at the picture of Rav on the edge of her desk. He would have told her she was mad. And that, more than anything, decided it.

She had to go. Were it not for the prime minister's rank treachery, her former deputy and friend would be sitting here, she was sure. If she had to walk through hell to prove it, so be it. There was a knock and Kate swung around. It was Julie. 'I can tell you have a plan,' she said. 'It's the way you hold your shoulders.'

'Close the door.'

Julie did as instructed. 'Go on then. Hit me with it.'

'I'm going to St Petersburg.'

'What? Do you have a death wish?'

'Meg Simpson is not going to write that letter. Not unless we can find some corroboration of what Mikhail told us. We have to know that Vasily is definitely out. I have someone who will know and might tell me.'

'The same guy who tipped you off about the original meeting on the super-yacht, you mean? The one you have never quite admitted to?'

'Yes.'

'The one Ian claims was once your lover?'

'He was never my lover.'

'That's not the story doing the rounds.'

'I'm not interested in what story is doing the rounds.'

'Is C aware of this? Or Ian?'

'Neither of them. I floated the idea to Sir Alan and he expressly forbade it.'

'You'll get fired, whether you succeed or not.'

'Probably. But I'm doing this for Rav and I can live with the consequences. If I don't, there's the very real chance that our prime minister will get away with murder.'

'I'll come with you.'

'No. I go alone. It's the only chance I have of getting what I need.'

'Well, I'll travel with you at least as far as Finland, like last time.'

'They'll fire you, too.'

'No, they won't. I'll threaten to sue Ian for sexual harassment. And, anyway, I couldn't care less.'

'I'm going to book myself on the morning BA flight to Helsinki. Do not tell another soul, Julie.'

'You are stark, staring mad, but perhaps that's why I like you.'

Suzy had arrived back in the office during the tail end of that conversation and was looking at them quizzically. Kate debated what they should tell her and decided that nothing was the only sensible answer.

Eventually, Suzy could restrain herself no longer. She knocked and came in. 'Anything I can help with?' she asked.

'I had lunch with C,' Kate said. 'We were just talking about it. He says Meg Simpson is not inclined to write that letter. So this will have to go back into the long grass.'

Suzy looked personally affronted. 'Surely she has to write it.'

'Politicians don't have to do anything.'

'What are her reasons?'

'The risk that we're being played. She wants more evidence that what Mikhail says about the changing of the guard in Moscow Centre is true. Without it, she won't take the risk.'

'So how do we get that?'

'C is talking directly to Andrew in Moscow. We'll have to see what he can find out, but time is not on our side.'

Perhaps it was the effects of lunch, but Kate felt overwhelmed by fatigue. She sat down at her desk and faced her computer, which was intended as a clear signal to Julie and Suzy that this audience was over. They took the hint.

Kate struggled to think clearly about what she needed to do. Her mind seemed shrouded in fog. She closed her eyes, but that didn't improve matters. All she could think of was her overwhelming desire to lie down in the corner of her office.

She stood again and went along to the Ladies at the end of her floor. She glanced at herself in the mirror. She looked about sixty.

The only private space in the entire building was the shower in the corner. She went in, locked the door and sat on the bench where she used to change on the days when she ran into the office. Her heart was thumping again, getting faster as fear and anxiety threatened to overwhelm her. She lay down in the basin of the shower cubicle, with her feet up against the bench, trying to slow her breathing. She felt as if she were having a heart attack.

Eventually, the panic subsided, but the feeling of total depletion did not. She curled up in the bottom of the shower tray, like a dog in a basket, and closed her eyes. She could feel the damp beneath her, but didn't care. All she wanted was some kind of release. It didn't come, but as she began to plan how she would make it to Russia she could at least begin to focus on something else.

Eventually, Kate stood up. She left the cubicle and ran a basin of cold water. She splashed some on her face and looked at herself in the mirror again. She texted Dr Wiseman's secretary and asked if there was any possibility of speaking to him – urgently.

She returned to her desk. She took two of the passports with fresh identities, neither of which she had used before, from the drawer and waited until Suzy left the office, then collected a thick wad of dollars, euros and roubles from the safe in the corner. She emailed Julie to say she would meet her at Heathrow in the morning, put on her trainers and started to walk home.

It was a relief to be in the house alone, but that didn't last long. She had only been home for ten minutes – just enough time for her to be seated at the table with a cup of herbal tea – before her mother called. Kate had an instinct, based on years of experience, that today she shouldn't answer, that everything would be different. She let the first few calls ring out, but picked up on the fifth. 'Yes, Mum,' she said.

'They're trying to poison me.'

Kate took a deep breath. A tear crept on to her cheek at the prospect of the familiar downward spiral. 'Who is?' she asked quietly.

'The fat black one.'

'You mean Lisa?'

'I don't know her name!'

'Because why would you?' Kate whispered.

'What was that?'

'Nothing. I don't know how many times we've been through this, Mum. Or how many more times we're going to have to. I've met every single one of the nurses in the home and they are, without exception, nice and caring individuals. No one is trying to poison you.'

'Perhaps you put them up to it!'

'I'm going to end this call now.'

'Telephone the police! I want to report the black bitch.'

'Mum! Do not speak about Lisa like that. It is grotesquely racist and frankly unforgivable.'

'If only David was here. He was the only one who ever cared for me.' Kate bit her tongue. She didn't doubt that the photograph of David Bloody Underpants on the beach in his absurdly tight swimming trunks pulled high above the waist had by now been swapped back to pride of place on her mother's side table.

Kate ended the call. The phone immediately started buzzing again. She pressed call reject repeatedly, and they engaged in this terrible game until, somehow, a call from the home itself managed to slip between her mother's frantic redialling.

It was from the long-suffering care manager, Jessica. She said she felt she needed to inform Kate that her mother had punched Lisa that afternoon. Lisa had been so upset she had gone home sick. The home could not, Jessica said, tolerate this behaviour much longer and they would soon be asking her mother to move elsewhere unless matters improved rapidly.

There was nothing Kate could say in her mother's defence. She promised to come round and speak to her. She wondered if she would one day be forced to care for her here at home, on the grounds that nowhere else would take her.

Kate rang off and immediately broke her promise. There was no way she could face her mother or her issues. She went to the sitting room and lay down on the sofa. Rose kept an immaculate house and the place was spotless.

She closed her eyes and put a cushion over her face. She had given up trying to sleep. The phone rang again and she saw that it was Dr Wiseman's surgery. She picked up. 'Dr Wiseman.'

'I'm sorry it's taken me some time to return your call.'

'No problem at all. Thank you for taking the trouble to ring.' Kate waited for him to open the dialogue, but she had recognized already that he used silence to draw his patients out. 'I don't know what to do,' she said eventually. 'When I left your clinic, I felt a degree of relief, elation even, as if someone finally understood me, as if I might even understand myself. I took it that, yes, I had issues, but I could see the possibility of resolution and that brought great hope.

'But whereas I saw a potential solution in the light of day, in the dead of night all I could think of was that I had a problem. And my mind just wouldn't – couldn't – switch off. I took sleeping pills one night, then worried I'd get addicted to them, so last night I was determined to doze off without them—'

'Why were you determined to do that?'

'Because I know they're addictive.'

'Who told you that?'

'A friend. Well, my aunt, actually. So I didn't sleep a wink on Friday – or maybe Saturday night. Then I took a zopiclone and did sleep, before I didn't take one and didn't, if you see what I mean . . . So I was wondering what I should do.'

'Take the medication. Do you have a decent supply?'

'Yes, yes. So I should just take them every night?'

'Yes.'

'Every night?'

'Yes.'

'But I don't sleep well with them. I only get three or four hours and I still feel terrible. I think they stop me sleeping properly.'

'You're not sleeping well because your mind and body are in a highly agitated state.'

'I see. So. Every night?'

'Until you next come to see me, yes. Then we can talk about moving you to a different medication.'

'What kind?'

'There are various options. Mostly likely, one of a group that are known as SSRIs – serotonin reuptake inhibitors.'

'Antidepressants?'

'Are you going to google this?' It was said with just a trace of bite.

'I might.'

'They are medicines that will help with your anxiety, but also have a strong sedative quality to help you sleep at night.

They are not physically addictive in the longer term and there is no reason to think they will be required for a lengthy period in any event.'

'But if there is a strong sedative quality, I won't be able to work properly, surely.'

'You take them at night to help you sleep. In the morning, you'll be fine. Perhaps a little groggy, but otherwise you'll carry on as normal. However, regarding that "normal", I would strongly suggest you consider taking an extended leave of absence from your work.'

'I can't do that.' There was a long silence. 'I'm sorry, Dr Wiseman, but I just can't. I have some very important operations running.'

'To which you are indispensable?'

Kate thought long and hard before answering. She could sense already there was no beating this man. Not in the logic stakes. 'I know this will seem egotistical and, most of the time, you'd be right to question me, but in this particular instance, it's undeniable that I must remain involved.'

'I see. And is it worth your health?'

'In this case I would have to say yes.'

'Even if, in putting your own well-being at risk, you might also threaten the health of your children?'

Kate hadn't thought of it like that. She never thought of it like that.

'Is this what you're thinking about at night when you cannot sleep?'

'No. I mean, yes, sometimes. But mainly it's just that nameless fear. That something will happen to one of them.' Kate got up and stared out of a gap in the curtains into the dark night beyond. A mortal enemy about to storm the room. 'And, I suppose, yes, fear of abandonment, I guess you might say, so much worse since my husband left.'

'Understandably so.'

'Yes.' Kate watched the slow progress of a man with a selection of small dogs on leads. 'It's made worse every time I see my mother. In the last twenty-four hours alone, she has shifted from being kind, considered and thoughtful to spiteful and utterly poisonous, with a healthy dose of racism thrown in.'

'Your mother is, by the sound of it, a very damaged woman.'

'Yes, I see that.'

'She cannot care for you because she is too busy wrestling with her own demons. That is the cycle you must break. As I said to you the other day, you must learn to reassure yourself.'

'But if I know how toxic it is to see her – and, believe me, I do – then why do I always go? I can't resist it.'

'Your mother has always been a critical voice, when what you wanted – what any child needs – is reassurance and support. That is the paradigm. The more she denied you praise, love and assistance, the more you craved it. This is the essence of all emotional abuse. But this is the cycle we must break.'

'Why don't I just stop seeing her?'

'It would make sense to restrict your visits for a while, but as your mother is unlikely to change, it is your psychology we must focus on, so that you see your mother for the sad and damaged woman she actually is, not the instrument of your torture.'

'The thing is, I *know* that,' Kate said, 'but I haven't been able to change the way I think and feel about it.'

'That is the purpose of this process. I would like you to think about the serenity prayer – whether it's a faith you follow or not is beside the point. *O Lord, give me the serenity to accept what I cannot change, the courage to change what I can and the wisdom to know the difference.* You cannot change your mother, or her behaviour, so you have no choice but to accept it. However, you can change the way you think and feel about it – and in so doing you will liberate yourself from the mental prison that the abuse has created for you.'

Kate sat down again. 'I do understand,' she said. 'I've been trying to visualize the conversation you talked of and it does make sense. And about the time off work, I will think about it.'

'Do. Or it may be taken out of your hands.'

Kate didn't like the sound of that. 'Will I get better?'

'I'm afraid I can't answer that. All I can say to you is that many people do. But you must commit to the process – to recovery – with the same determination you have approached your working life. Then, I think, there is a high chance of success. But no one else can do that work for you.'

'Yes . . . Thank you.'

'I'll check with Sarah when your next appointment is and I'll see you then.'

Kate ended the call. She put her phone down, placed her face on her knees and closed her eyes.

17

GUS BLEW IN through the door with rare loquacity. 'I've been made captain of the As,' he said.

Kate sat up, feeling dazed. If she hadn't slept, she had nevertheless been lying on the sofa in a kind of trance. Perhaps that was where you ended up: perpetually caught between wakefulness and sleep. 'The what?'

'The As. Mr Jenkyns just told me. Next term.' He took in her confusion. 'Cricket, Mum!'

'Oh, of course. Yes, sorry. Congratulations.'

'Do you mind if I call Dad?'

'Ermmm . . .'

'I'd really love to tell him. He'll be so pleased.'

Kate couldn't see a reason to refuse. Gus dialled from his own phone and it was a revelation to her that he had Stuart's new number in Moscow. 'I've been made captain of the As,' Gus said, without introduction.

She watched her son listen for a moment, his face aglow with his own and his father's pleasure. 'Mr Jenkyns said it was between me and Horsington and that I had shown a much greater degree of maturity. I'm still going to open.'

Gus laughed at something his father said. 'It's cool,' he said. 'Thanks, Dad. I wish you could come and watch. Maybe we can do a tour to Venice!'

Kate felt like she was intruding, but she couldn't drag herself away. She watched her son revel in the news with his father in the full knowledge they would never share in the game. For the first time, she wondered if she had been right to insist so resolutely that she and Stuart could have no future together. Gus looked up at her and handed her his phone. 'Dad wants to talk to you.'

With that, Gus discreetly disappeared into the kitchen. 'Hello . . . Stuart?'

'Kate . . .'

'Yes, what is it?'

'Isn't it great about Gus? He'd never have admitted it to either of us, but he's been holding out for that. It'll mean the world to him.'

'The pleasure on his face was something to behold.'

'He needs a bit of a boost. They both do.' Kate didn't know what to say to that. 'All I have to do now is persuade the school to televise all under-fourteen A games and we'll be away.'

'Is there something I can do for you, Stuart?' There was a coldness to her tone that did not, she thought, reflect the way she felt.

'I just wanted to hear your voice.'

Kate closed her eyes. 'Please don't do this.'

'I'm not doing anything, love. I'm just lonelier than I've ever been in my life and hearing you or the kids on the phone is all I live for.'

'I'm sure there are many women in Moscow who would be only too pleased to console you.'

'That's a bit beneath you, if I may say so. I'm not here wallowing in self-pity, just telling you the truth. Do you have any idea when I might be able to see the kids again?'

'You mean after the last time went so well?'

'That was hardly my fault. And, from what I could gather, it might have been the making of your career.'

It was said with some edge to it. Stuart had always accused Kate of putting her work before their family. 'I have to go,' she said.

'How is Fiona?'

'She's fine. She's staying with Jed.'

'Blimey. I'm surprised you're allowing that.'

'You might be surprised at a lot of things. But it all changed the day you left.'

'All right, fair enough. I suppose I deserved that.'

'Goodbye, Stuart.'

'Goodbye, love. I miss you, though I know you don't want to hear that.'

'I don't. And if you keep saying it, I won't take your calls.'

Kate pressed the end button and walked through to the kitchen to give Gus back his phone.

'How was he?'

'He's missing you,' Kate said.

'You mean all of us?'

Kate looked at her son, who occasionally exhibited a maturity that surprised her. 'He's very lonely there. But . . .'

'He made his bed, so he has to lie in it?'

'I don't think I'd put it quite like that.'

Gus held up his phone. 'Anyway, thanks for letting me speak to him.' He headed for the door.

'Do you talk to him often?' Kate asked.

He turned back, looking shifty. He was certainly not a good liar. 'I guess so.'

'Every day?'

'Most.'

Kate forced herself to smile. 'That's good. I'm glad. It's exactly as it should be.'

Gus smiled back at her, his face flooded with relief and warmth. 'Thanks, Mum. You're the best.'

He disappeared up the stairs. Kate fed Nelson, who picked at his food with disdain, and started to think about supper. She put on some music and gradually felt the tension ease in her shoulders, losing herself sufficiently in the therapeutic process of cooking to miss Rose's key in the front door. 'Sorry I'm late,' her aunt said, as she placed her bag on the side and hung up her coat.

Kate swung around. 'You gave me a shock . . . You're not. Late, I mean.'

'Good day?'

'Er . . .' Kate thought about what she could say without giving away her true intentions. 'I had lunch with Sir Alan, who's just managed to get Alice home. He didn't seem in great shape, as you'd expect.'

'I know. Poor man. Did he take you to Grumbles?'

'Yes.'

'Must have been important to spare the time in a week like this.'

Kate recognized this as her aunt's subtle way of asking a question. 'Yes, but I suppose I'd better not go into it.' She thought of raising the matter of Maja's extraction from Belgrade, but decided to avoid that as well.

'Have you heard the news?'

Kate shook her head.

'The Germans have already dispatched an expeditionary force to Estonia. The French say they'll follow suit. The foreign secretary described it as sensible, the prime minister as rash. Cabinet discipline seems to have entirely broken down in this country.'

'It's all just signalling now the Russians have backed off,' Kate said. She turned to face her aunt. 'I'm sorry to have to ask another favour,' she said, 'but I have to go to Finland for a few days. Could you bear to hold the fort one more time?'

'Finland?' Rose exclaimed. 'I guess I shouldn't ask.' She smiled. 'At some point, I'd better reacquaint myself with my husband or Simon will divorce me. Are you sure you're up to it?'

'Yes. I'm fine. Really.'

'Have you been sleeping?'

'Yes,' Kate lied. She carried on cooking. Rose poured two very large glasses of white wine.

At supper, Gus was garrulousness itself, regaling Rose with his plans for the Compton House under-fourteen A cricket XI. They meant nothing to Kate and not, she suspected, much more to Rose, but neither said so.

Kate had texted Fiona repeatedly over the course of the evening and received no reply, so she set out after dinner for the brief walk to Jed's house. She was surprised to spot a car on her tail. Surely her watchers at the Security Service didn't think she was stupid enough to meet a Russian agent handler when she knew she was under surveillance. But that was their business.

Jed's parents were a charming couple in their late fifties, who lived in a spacious top-floor apartment overlooking Battersea Park on Prince of Wales Drive. They offered her a glass of wine and politely avoided displaying any sense of puzzlement at the way Kate's daughter had taken up residence in their home.

Fiona and Jed were both allegedly absorbed in homework and didn't appear for half an hour – and then only, Kate suspected, at Jed's insistence. His diffident, kind manner hid a touch of steel in the soul, which she was coming to be very fond of.

Fiona kissed her mother and sat in a corner while the rest of them made polite small-talk. They discussed the NHS, the fracturing of politics and the collapse in governmental discipline. Kate told Fiona her brother had been made captain of the Compton House As, in which she showed no interest whatsoever.

Eventually, Jed's parents politely withdrew, followed a few moments later by their son. Kate couldn't help but notice how thin her daughter looked. Clearly, living temporarily with two doctors had not convinced her of the health benefits of eating. 'What do you want?' Fiona asked.

'Nothing,' Kate said. 'I just have to go away in the morning for a few days, so I wanted to check you were okay.'

'I'm fine. Where are you going?'

'Finland.'

'What are you going to do? Invade Russia?'

198

Kate tried to smile. Sometimes she had to admit to finding her daughter's humour baffling. But perhaps she should be grateful Fiona knew enough geography to be aware the two countries were neighbours. 'No. Just a routine thing. I shouldn't be away long.'

'I'll be home at the weekend,' Fiona said, offering an olive branch.

'Great. I'll really look forward to it. Shall we do some cooking together?'

'Okay.'

'Anything you'd particularly choose?'

'I like that new Indian book Rose gave you.'

Kate smiled again. Her daughter was a born-again vegetarian. She couldn't help recalling the days when their conversation had routinely flowed with such ease. What had become of them? 'Do you speak to Dad much?' she asked.

'Why?'

'It's just Gus said tonight that he and Dad talked most days and I thought that was . . . well, very good. I hoped you did, too.'

Fiona sensed a trap. 'I do speak to him, yes.'

'Then that has to be a good thing, doesn't it?'

'Of course.'

Kate could see she wasn't going to get much further tonight. She stood, happy to bank such incremental gains. She wanted to tell her daughter how much she loved her, how she missed the easy familiarity they had once known. But the kitchen of her boyfriend's parents' home hardly seemed the place. She hugged Fiona and was pleased that she got at least a half-hearted hug back. 'Night, my love,' she said.

'Night.'

'I'll really look forward to the weekend.'

'Me too. Enjoy Finland.'

Kate walked back down to the street outside, some spitting rain and her ever-present watchers. She spent the journey home working out how she was going to lose her tail in the morning without her pursuers discovering her escape so that they put out an alert on all aliases she had on file, which would certainly prevent her passing through Heathrow. It was not going to be easy.

18

KATE WOKE EARLY and sat at the kitchen table, drinking tea and going over the provisional plan she had come up with the night before with the aid of an old London *A–Z* she'd located on Stuart's bookshelf. It still seemed the most viable option in the cold dawn light.

She assumed that, if MI5 was tailing not only her but the head of the Service, they would have secured the legal permission to deploy a range of measures from the home secretary, including electronic interception – which was why she'd needed the *A–Z*, rather than Google Maps. But this gave her the chance to lull them into a false sense of security, too, particularly if they felt she was heading somewhere expected and routine.

So, she began the day with an early call to Dr Wiseman's secretary, asking for an urgent appointment. She left a message, explaining she'd had another night without sleep and would be coming up to Ealing now, in the hope he could fit her in.

Then she left the house on foot, with a gym bag over her shoulder. The last impression she wanted to leave her watchers was of a woman off on a lengthy journey.

She walked north, skirting Battersea Park, crossing the river, then heading east with the flow of commuter traffic. She wove through Pimlico and finally disappeared underground and into the tube at Victoria. She'd estimated a team of at least four, but probably no more – resources were always tighter than anyone might imagine, even in the search for traitors – and she spotted the first man in the surveillance team as she swerved away from what seemed a full carriage at the last minute and ducked into the next one along. He was bald and wore blue jeans and a green Patagonia fleece, but he mistimed his lunge and only just made it through the doors. One or two commuters looked at him in surprise as he stared at the floor. Kate smiled. Amateur.

She picked out the second in the next carriage along once she had changed trains to the Central line at Oxford Circus. He was leaning against the side, reading a copy of *The Times*. He was wearing brown walking shoes, a grey outdoor shirt and a Gore-Tex jacket. But who goes to work in rush-hour dressed like that?

She'd noticed in the transfer between lines at Oxford Circus that the bald-headed man had disappeared from view. Clearly he'd sensed he'd been spotted. She moved closer to the man in the Gore-Tex jacket now, as if to let him know that she'd sussed him out, too. He paid no attention.

Part of the reason why using Dr Wiseman had appealed to her was that Ealing Broadway lay at the end of the line.

And, since she had also picked the very last carriage in the change at Oxford Circus, the numbers began to thin out beyond White City. The man in the Gore-Tex jacket got off at West Acton. She saw him muttering into his lapel mic as he walked away down the platform.

Kate sat down to survey the rest of the passengers. There was an art, of course, in doing so without being seen to do it, which made it a slow process.

As the train rattled towards its final destination, she had mentally given the remaining passengers the all-clear, but she changed her mind at the last moment about the couple at the far end of the carriage. They'd been chatting amicably, a passable imitation of lovers going to work, but what were the chances of two people in their twenties heading to work at the same tube station at the same time?

A workplace romance, perhaps. But somehow she doubted it. Their conversation had been too intense, too consistent. Couples who were that garrulous were also physically all over each other, in the first flush of love. She made a mental note to check that the pair did not appear anywhere on the journey beyond Dr Wiseman's office.

She left the train at Ealing Broadway and walked down the platform towards the barriers. She kept her gait easy and relaxed – it had long been a part of surveillance training to learn instinctively to spot changes in how a suspect held him- or herself – and, ten minutes later, hurried through Dr Wiseman's reception without so much as a sideways glance.

The doctor's secretary was on the phone, so, without greeting or explanation, Kate walked on to the bathroom at the back. She closed the door, opened the window, climbed through and dropped noiselessly into the suburban garden beyond. It was tougher to get over the fence on the other side without incident – she ended up having to commandeer a wheelbarrow – but she calculated she was into the street beyond in less than thirty seconds.

She allowed herself to look back, then carried on briskly along the route she'd memorized from the *A–Z*. Her phone, now switched off – as you would expect of a woman in an appointment with her psychiatrist – was no longer able to give away her progress.

The only part of the operation she had not been able to plan was how exactly she would get from there to Heathrow, but in the end her luck was in and she hailed a taxi shortly after she re-joined Madeley Road in search of a bus.

Kate waited for Julie as agreed at Pret A Manger on the other side of security at Heathrow. She had booked her own ticket for the next flight to Helsinki as soon as she'd arrived, having checked that there was another seat available for Julie. Her heart still thumped hard after the adrenalin rush of beating the surveillance team. The coffee did little to calm its rhythm. She'd resorted to a double dose of zopiclone the night before and the four hours' sleep it had afforded her barely touched the sides of her fatigue. She still felt like death, and for a few brief moments she considered calling off the trip to St Petersburg – then immediately thought better of it.

Julie arrived, flustered, with a copy of *The Times* tucked under her arm. 'Sorry, it took me ages to shake off the Security Service guys.'

'I think they've changed their teams.'

'Makes sense. Suzy must have advised them to. That girl is an absolute snake.'

'She's needy and insecure, which is not a great combination. You sure you lost them all?'

'Yes. You?'

Kate nodded. 'There was a couple I only spotted at the very end, but I've been watching carefully. They've not re-appeared. Did you book your ticket okay?'

'Yes, the flight's nearly empty by the looks of it. You want another coffee?'

Kate shook her head and Julie returned with a double espresso. She flipped over *The Times* so that it was headline up. It referred to the split in the NATO alliance between the boldness of the Germans and French and the caution of the British prime minister. 'I accept we both have our doubts about the wisdom of this trip, but you're right. We don't have a choice.' Julie gestured at the headline. 'I've been thinking about the sacrifices all our forefathers made in the last war. And for this, a world in which our leader is an immoral traitor in league with our enemy? We're growing uncomfortably accustomed to things being fucked up, but we shouldn't.'

Kate shrugged. What else was there to say?

'Are you sure you don't want me to come all the way with you?'

'I'll need some back-up here.'

Julie nodded and left it there. It was true enough and they both knew it.

Julie finished her coffee and they made their way towards Passport Control and security. They glanced at each other as they approached the border checks, but they passed through without incident and breathed a sigh of relief. By the time MI5 realized its mistake and caught up with them, they would, with any luck, be well on their way to the Russian border.

The flight landed at Helsinki in a hailstorm, the plane buffeted so violently on the approach that Julie's knuckles went white as she gripped the armrests. But the sun had broken through dark clouds by the time they had hired the car. Leaving the airport, they drove east beneath a spectacular rainbow. 'It's a sign,' Julie said, smiling.

But the risks inherent in what Kate was about to do weighed heavily on them and they passed most of the rest of the journey in silence.

They stopped at the coffee shop in Kotka where they had parted company when Kate had made her fateful journey to Sergei's dacha on the Gulf of Finland six months before. It was not a place with comfortable associations. They ordered sandwiches and coffee and looked out at the tall ship still berthed on the quay. The clouds had almost cleared now and the sun glinted off the water. 'I can't shake the feeling that this journey does not lead to happy outcomes,' Julie said.

'Me neither.'

'You think we should turn back?'

'I can't.'

'I'd still rather come with you.'

'I know you would and I love you for it.' Kate smiled at her friend. 'What are you going to do about Ian?'

'Does it matter?'

'I'm trying to take my mind off what lies in wait the other side of that border.'

'Well, I'll definitely report him to HR if he even thinks about firing me for this, or you.'

Kate smiled. She swirled the milky remains of her coffee in the bottom of the cup. 'How about a last fag?' They stepped outside, where a chill wind was blowing in off the water. Julie took a packet of Marlboro from her pocket and offered it to Kate. 'How's your sleep?'

'Chemically induced and not at all restful.'

'You're really not in a fit state to go. You know that? In fact, you look like you should be checking into a health farm for the rest of the year.'

'I tell myself I'm doing it for Rav and that makes me feel better.'

Julie drew deeply on her cigarette and turned away to blow the smoke up towards the clear blue sky. 'You ever think Suzy might have a point about Stuart not being Viper?' she asked.

'Stuart was Viper, I'm sure of that. She might have a point that he's not the only person who's been betraying us.'

'You, me, C, Danny or Ian: it's not the most encouraging collection of fucking suspects, is it?'

'It's also possible, as C says, that there is no one else and the questions are no more than conjecture, coincidence and paranoia.'

'Does it ever bother you that he and the prime minister were close friends at school?' Julie took another drag. 'I mean, I forget about that inconvenient fact for long periods and then I suddenly remember and think, Fucking hell, that is *weird*.'

'Why?'

'I don't know. It's just, if they were friends, I mean really *friends*, and James Ryan had been recruited by the Russians, wouldn't it be a natural next step to bring his old mucker in on the action?'

'You seem to forget that Sir Alan has been right behind us in everything we're trying to do. It's Ian who's taken a stance one might suggest is helpful to Moscow.'

'Ian's not a Russian spy, I can tell you that much.'

'What makes you so sure?'

'He's far too weak. He wouldn't dare and the consequences of being caught would terrify him so much he wouldn't be able to get out of bed in the morning.'

'What if he was blackmailed or bribed?'

'How? His wife is rich, so he doesn't need the money. I can tell you he's straightforwardly and vigorously heterosexual, and I don't think he has any particular kinks beyond the average – and I'm not sure even evidence of an affair, or several, would have been enough to push him to take the risk of working for Moscow. He's basically just a child.'

'Although that, in itself, might be a good cover.'

Julie thought about it. 'Maybe. But still . . .'

Kate threw away her cigarette. She smiled. 'Thanks for this last conversation. It's encouraged me no end.' She hugged Julie. 'Wait only two days,' she said, as she walked to the car. 'If I'm not back then, return to London and confess. What will you do?'

'Try to go off grid and see if I can avoid our pursuers from the Security Service once they catch up with us – for my own amusement, if nothing else.'

'Trailing us here would involve a lot of manpower and expense,' Kate mused. 'They might just sit tight and wait until our return.'

'You think Ian, or even C, will be so relaxed?'

'You should call them. Give Ian a holding statement. A lead came up. We had to preserve operational security so—'

'They're never going to buy that.'

'Agreed, but they'll know damned well what I've gone off to do and they won't want to do anything to jeopardize my safety.'

'Showing a lot of faith in them both,' Julie said, 'but suit yourself.'

Kate found herself glued to the rear-view mirror until Julie had dwindled into the sinking sunlight. A farewell to security, for the immediate future, at least.

The journey through the endless pine forests passed swiftly, as she turned over the last conversation in her mind. It was better, perhaps, not to chase one's tail in a state of doubt and confusion, always seeking yet more agents of the enemy: it had undone so much good work in intelligence agencies all over the world, from the days of the CIA's James Jesus Angleton onwards. But Julie had had a point when she'd raised the schoolboy friendship between Sir Alan and the prime minister. On some level, it bothered her too.

It was dark by the time she reached the Vaalimaa border crossing, the European and national flags cracking crisply above it in the breeze on the Finnish side as she waited behind a long line of lorries. The wind blew in from the Baltic in great gusts, buffeting the hire car and unsettling her. It was half an hour or more before she was presenting an Irish passport in the name of Kate McGillis to the stony-faced young man in the glass booth on the Russian side of the crossing. *'Dobrý den,'* she said.

He didn't look up. He swiped the passport through the computer and glanced over the accompanying paperwork.

All her passports – she had six at any given time – had in-date tourist visas for Russia.

The young man, his skin as flawless as his expression was impassive, stared at his screen for what felt like an age. 'Drive your car in to the right here and step out,' he instructed her in English. 'My colleague wishes to speak to you.'

Kate did as she was told, her heart thumping. By the time she had parked, a woman was waiting for her. She was young too, with blonde hair pulled back tightly and bright blue eyes. 'Please come this way.'

She ushered Kate into a room with a table and two chairs on either side of it. The woman sat, the passport and accompanying entry form in front of her. She might have been pretty, but for the angular set of her chin and skin marked by childhood acne. 'What is the purpose of your visit to Russia?'

'I have always wanted to visit St Petersburg. I'll only be here for a few days.'

'Where are you staying?'

'At a hotel on Admiralty Embankment.' Kate pointed at the form she had actually filled out in the office in London before she'd left. Then she took out the Expedia booking confirmation and pushed it across to her.

'Do you have friends in St Petersburg?'

'No.'

'You travel alone?'

'Yes.'

'When did you arrive in Finland?'

'This lunchtime.'

'Why did you not fly direct to St Petersburg?'

'I had a friend in Helsinki I wanted to see. We had lunch together.'

'Where?'

That caught Kate off guard, but she didn't blink. 'Well, she actually lives between the capital and Kotka, so we had lunch there, in a café on the quay. I can't remember the name of it.'

The woman stared at the passport and the piece of paper beside it, as if both were a mystery, the truth of which would soon be revealed. 'What is your occupation?'

Kate pointed at the piece of paper again. 'I work for Oxfam.'

'In Dublin?'

'In London.'

'You do not sound Irish.'

'My mother is English and I was brought up in London. But my father is still alive and lives in Dublin.'

'What is his name?'

'Dermot.'

Another silence. This time, it took on a more threatening air.

It's just routine, Kate told herself. How could they know anything? SIS's passports and back stories were legendarily efficient. They had to be. There was even a man called Dermot McGillis in Dublin who would agree he was her father if asked, and she had his number in her phone.

'Is something wrong?' Kate said. She allowed a trace of irritation in her voice. A real tourist would be annoyed at the delay by now.

'Wait here,' the woman said. She left the room, closing the door carefully behind her.

Kate looked up at the clock on the wall. It was seven and the night had long since closed in, the wind rattling the windows and rushing beneath the door. She was cold and longed for a cigarette.

She waited. The deadpan, slow, deliberate obfuscation of Russian officials was designed to unsettle the guilty and she could see no logical reason yet for concern.

Time dragged. Five minutes crawled past, then ten.

Until the woman stood before her again. 'You may go,' she said abruptly.

Kate resisted the temptation to ask what that had been about and got back into her car. 'Thank you,' she said, smiling at the woman. She headed off into the night.

The journey on to St Petersburg was long, featureless and sodden from the rain that had recently doused the perpetually potholed roads. But as she closed in on the old Russian capital, the temperature dropped and the episodic bursts of spitting rain became steadily drifting snow. At first, it melted on the damp tarmac, but by the time she had made her way through the industrial outskirts to the city's grand European centre, it had blanketed its streets in the magical winter coat Kate remembered so well.

She parked outside the front entrance of the hotel, which was right on Admiralty Embankment, and checked into the sleek modern reception area. She asked the valet to take care of parking the car and made her way to her room on the fifth floor.

The décor was a temple to modern Russia's celebratory absence of taste: a riot of purple, with an expensive television and a cream sofa from which to watch it. Kate pulled back the net curtain and gazed out at the River

Neva, almost lost in the blizzard. She glanced up and down the embankment.

She took a small bottle of whisky from the minibar and swallowed two zopiclone with its contents.

All she was aware of, as she turned out the light, was the rapid beating of her heart.

19

KATE DIDN'T BOTHER with breakfast. She put on her coat and the beanie she had stuffed into its pocket and walked out into the Arctic winter chill. She'd been up since dawn had broken and had remained at the window ever since, watching the sun creep steadily across the Neva and the grandiose buildings of Vasilyevsky Island opposite.

Kate walked across Palace Bridge, stopping to lean over the side at its centre. The spire of the Peter and Paul Cathedral glistened in the bright sun, the river flowing steadily beneath her, not yet frozen despite the biting cold. Palace Square was almost deserted, the tourists not yet having emerged from their expensive hotels. She lit a cigarette and sucked in the smoke with the fumes of the morning traffic. It made her feel resolutely wretched, but she worked her way through half of it before finally flicking the remains into the river below.

She started walking and immediately stopped. What was she doing here? The carefully constructed operational arguments folded in the face of the loneliness that gnawed away at her. She knew damned well why she was really here and it made her feel foolish, nervous and naïve by turns. She was back to being a fourteen-year-old girl preparing for her first date with Pete Carter, the trainee anarchist.

She glanced at her watch. She walked on past the Rostral Columns – once primitive lighthouses for river traffic on the Neva – the great massif of the former Stock Exchange, the honey-coloured buildings of the university and the severe grey beauty of the Academy of Sciences. At this end, close to the Strelka, the island still bore the hallmarks of the grand administrative centre the city's founder, Peter the Great, had once intended. But the further you walked from the Neva, the greater sense you got of the mercantile past that had been its true destiny. Sergei had liked to summon an image of its Tsarist heyday, when the summer air was filled with the whistling of winches, the cries of seagulls and the shouts of the ships' crews as an avalanche of varied cargoes was unloaded from all over the Russian Empire and well beyond. The days of a great Russia, he'd said, how different things might have been but for the Revolution.

It was why she'd always called him a dreamer.

The island had been laid out in lines, and from Kadetzs-kaya down to the fifth line, it maintained a fairly well-bred air. From there to the fourteenth had been the middle class and commercial district, and beyond, the tenement houses of the poor – and each part of the island still bore the mark of its history, in spite of, or perhaps because of, the brutal decades of Soviet rule. Kate skirted St Andrew's Cathedral and browsed through the rudimentary food on offer in a morning market, killing time.

She slipped into a café that had existed since Tsarist times and ordered coffee. On the walls, there were pictures of the last of the Romanovs at Livadia, their estate in Crimea. Alongside them, in pride of place close to the door, hung a framed portrait of the current Russian president, as if his connection to the former royal family was perfectly obvious.

When she could contain her patience no longer, Kate walked on to eigth line and the still grubby tenement building that housed the apartment that had once belonged to Sergei's grandfather, an important Communist Party official and officer in the city's maritime section, who'd somehow managed to keep his head and position throughout Stalin's reign of terror.

She climbed to the top floor and knocked. She could see her breath on the air. She pushed her hands deep into her pockets.

The door opened just a fraction.

Either Kate's memory wildly deceived her or Sergei's mother, Olga, had shrunk dramatically. If never exactly overweight, she had been a well-built, handsome woman far removed from the bent, shuffling figure that peered at Kate now through the mists of time. 'Yes?' she asked, with the strong Kiev accent that betrayed her familial origins. 'Can I help you?'

'Olga, it's Kate.' She spoke in Russian, and stepped backwards into the light from the landing window. 'Sergei's student friend from England.'

The old woman's face lit up. She opened the door wide. 'Kate?' The smile had all of its old welcoming warmth. 'Can it really be you? After all this time? Come in, come in.' Kate stepped into the gloom. Olga gripped her arms. 'Let me look at you.' There was light in those old eyes now. 'How well you are,' Olga said. 'What are you doing here?'

'Just passing through . . . on business.'

'But after so long!' Olga shook her head in confusion. 'Come in,' she said again, beckoning her further into the flat.

Kate followed her down the hallway to the living room. 'What can I get you?' Olga asked.

'Whatever you have.'

Olga took her coat, placed it on a chair in the corner and disappeared into the kitchen to put on the kettle. Kate took a seat by the old gas fire. This room was like a step back into Soviet time, the curtains and chairs grey and dark red with an old-fashioned wireless in a Bakelite case. Kate glanced at the walls around her, still filled with pictures of the St Petersburg ice-hockey team, whose stadium Olga's husband Pietr had managed, and photographs of Sergei, the couple's only child.

Olga returned with two cups of black tea and a plate of homemade *pryanik*, a kind of flat honey bread that Kate had developed rather too much of a taste for in her time as a student. She smiled as Olga offered her the plate. 'You remembered.'

'Of course.'

Olga spooned sugar into Kate's tea without question, then leant forward to take her hand again, eyes bright. 'Tell me everything! Sergei says you are married.'

'Was.'

'Ah, I'm sorry. But these things happen.' Olga and Pietr's devotion to each other had been legendary. 'Children?'

TOM BRADBY

'Two. Fiona is nearly sixteen and Gus – short for Angus
– thirteen.'

'You have pictures?' Kate fumbled for her phone and
flicked through it until she found a photograph of Gus and
Fiona. It had been taken on the terrace of the hotel in Venice.
Olga nodded approvingly. 'Such a pretty girl. Like you.'

'Ha, I'm not so sure.'

'Do you work in Russia?'

'No.' Kate realized she had lied too quickly. 'Very rarely.'

Olga's beady eyes gazed at her steadily. A former teacher,
she was a hard woman to fool. She could and did switch
from Russian to English and back again, but Kate continued
to speak to her in Russian. 'If only he had won your heart,'
Olga said heavily.

Kate stared at the floor. 'I'm not so sure he didn't.'

'I mean truly.'

'Perhaps if I had not been already committed to someone
else . . .'

'And now, it seems, you are free.'

'Yes, I suppose I am.'

'Is that why you have come?'

The directness of the question had Kate suddenly lost for
words. 'No . . . I don't think so. Not specifically, but in the
hope of seeing him perhaps. He was always a great friend to
me.' Kate looked at the photograph of Olga's husband on the
dark dresser beside her. It was from his days as a soldier in
the Soviet army. 'How is Pietr?'

'Only the dead can know.'

'Oh . . . I'm so sorry.' Kate could feel her face reddening.
'When did . . .'

'A few months ago.'

'I'm sorry, Olga. I know how close you always were.'

'Sergei is devastated. I think somehow it is even worse for him. He worshipped his father.'

Olga retreated into her thoughts. Kate turned to the window. It seemed indelicate to intrude further. 'Is Sergei here in St Petersburg?' she asked, as innocently as she could manage.

'He came to visit me yesterday. It is difficult now he has to spend so much time in Moscow.'

'Do you know where I can find him? It would be great to share a cup of tea at least, for old times' sake.'

Olga's expression was inscrutable. Kate had the disconcerting sense this kindly old woman was in some way laughing at her. 'Where are you staying?' she asked. 'I will let him know you are here.'

'At a hotel on Admiralty Embankment,' Kate said. 'But please do tell him. He has my number. It would be great to see him if he has time before going back to Moscow.' The words didn't sound like her own. She stood, too hastily, tipping her tea on to the floor. 'Olga, I'm so sorry.'

The old woman waved away her concern, and as Kate set off to get a cloth from the kitchen, Olga gripped her wrist with surprising strength. 'It is all right,' she said quietly, looking directly into Kate's eyes. 'It is all right.'

Kate stood, but Olga did not let go of her. 'Why are you really here, my dear?'

'Some business. I . . .'

'After all this time?'

'After all this time, yes.'

'You look . . . alone.'

'I am.'

'We have one life.'

'And I have made a mess of mine.'

'It is not too late. It is never too late.' Olga released her. 'I will tell him. What he makes of it I cannot say.'

Kate retrieved her coat. Olga accompanied her to the front door. 'Be careful, my dear, won't you?'

'Of course.' Kate had no wish to enquire in what way the caution had been intended.

The wind was still biting outside and Kate huddled in a tenement doorway to smoke a cigarette. She glanced at her watch. It was not even ten o'clock.

She started walking again, back to the bridge and the Admiralty Embankment. She headed for Nevsky Prospekt, on the grounds that at least there would be life there at this time in the morning. Shoppers seemed thin on the ground – the Russian economy was all hard grind unless you happened to have an oligarch's bank account – so she installed herself in the Literary Café, once the Wolf and Beranger, the restaurant from which Pushkin departed for his fatal duel in the 1830s. She ordered coffee and some smoked-salmon blinis, which came with sour cream, gherkins and onions. She pushed them around her plate without much enthusiasm, thinking she was turning into her daughter.

She switched on her phone for the first time since she'd left London. The only messages were from Suzy – a successive string of texts asking where she was and what she was doing, presumably sent at the behest of her friends in MI5. The silence from colleagues in Kate's own organization was ominous. Sir Alan and Ian must, she surmised, have guessed her intentions. There would be hell to pay when she got back.

She'd not had a single message from anyone else and she couldn't help drawing a contrast again with the days when Stuart had held the home front, her days and nights punctuated by the steady ping of messages, the sentiments of which ranged from amused to exasperated. No one prepared you for how lonely parenting became with divorce.

She killed as much time as she could in the café, then continued her promenade down St Petersburg's main shopping street. She was aware that fatigue was making her sloppy, so although she had seen and sensed nothing to rouse her suspicion since she'd crossed the border, she attempted some basic dry cleaning. The Russians were good at surveillance on home turf, and she had to acknowledge they might well have outfoxed her.

She passed the Stroganov Palace and moved at leisure through the Lutheran church. She crossed the road and wandered through the grandiose Corinthian columns of the Cathedral of Our Lady of Kazan, then walked on over the Griboyedov Canal and turned into the striking arcade of Gostiny Dvor, St Petersburg's main bazaar since the mid-eighteenth century. The shops and stalls here were more sophisticated than she remembered. She bought some retro Soviet-era T-shirts for Gus, Fiona and Jed, and then crossed Nevsky Prospekt again to the beautiful Style Moderne building that housed the delicatessen Yeliseev's.

She took her time there, then emerged again to cross the Fontanka river. She walked through the Moscow railway station before returning to Gostiny Dvor and installing herself in one of its corner cafés. She was just resisting the temptation to look at her phone when it finally pinged.

It was a WhatsApp message from Sergei. *Hey, hear you are in St Petersburg. Great news. A bit pressed today and have to catch the night train to Moscow tonight. You want to come with me?*

Kate stared at it until her vision started to blur. *Why not?* she replied, before she'd had time to consider the implications.

Great, he pinged back. *See you on the station's central concourse at 11 p.m.*

20

ST PETERSBURG'S MOSCOW station had changed markedly since Kate's last visit; the triangular Soviet-era ceiling that had once seemed so gloomy was leavened now by modern lighting. But the map of the rail network of the old Soviet Empire still had pride of place, and Kate was gazing up at it when she heard the familiar voice behind her: 'Look who it is . . .'

She spun around. He stood before her, every inch the student she remembered. He wore black jeans, a dark blue T-shirt and a black leather jacket, with expensive-looking suede loafers on his feet. He hadn't shaved, the stubble along his handsome jaw the same lustrous black as the thick, wavy hair on his head. He was wearing glasses for the first time, with a tortoiseshell frame. 'Nice shoes,' she said, looking down at his feet. His love of expensive footwear had been a private joke between them as students, since he'd once admitted to stealing more than a few pairs on his trips to the West.

'Tod's,' he said, smiling at her. 'And what is more, I paid for them myself.' He glanced at a bar in the corner. 'Come on, let's celebrate.' He moved to a steel table, dropped his bag on the floor and leant over the bar to order a bottle of vodka.

'What are we celebrating?' Kate asked.

'Our reunion. Here in Russia. After all this time.' He smiled again. 'You must be mad to come here.'

'Or desperate,' she said.

'For what?'

'Let's not go there.'

He poured two glasses. They toasted each other. *'Nostrovia,'* they said together, downing the shots in one.

'You look well,' he said.

'I look knackered, clapped out and old, but nice try.'

'You haven't changed.'

'Liar.'

'Same smile, same angular cheekbones, same delicate nose.'

'More lines, more bags and a hell of a lot more baggage.'

'That makes two of us.'

'Oh, yeah? Do you have an ex-husband?'

'No, you have something on me there.' He refilled her glass. They drank again.

'Are we going to carry on like this all night?' she asked.

'Why not? Moscow always looks better with a hangover.'

Kate glanced up at the board above her. 'Why are you taking the train?'

'Have you flown Aeroflot? Besides, I love the night sleeper. It reminds me of childhood holidays in Yalta. The romance of the long journey, the sense of freedom in time suspended . . .'

'Ah, yes,' she said. 'I remember you invited me.'

'Balmy nights, ethereal light, the magic of old Russia. I was convinced you would finally succumb.'

'Perhaps I would have done.'

'So close and yet so far.'

This time it was Kate who refilled the glasses. She suddenly had an overpowering urge to get wildly, blindly drunk. 'Do you ever think of what might have been?' she asked.

'Not as often as I used to. I mean, not more than once a month.'

'I'm sorry,' she said.

'For what?'

'Leading you on. You would have had every reason to hate me.'

'But I loved you. And I still do.' His megawatt grin – its evident sincerity, the way it seemed to transform his face – still had the ability to floor her. 'But it has been so long. I'm not saying I have been waiting for you. There have been other women. Just none who matched up.'

Kate stared into her glass. 'Damn,' she said.

'Is that what you came all this way to hear?'

'I don't know why I came.' She looked up at him. His gaze was locked on to her. She dived for safer territory. 'It was good to see your mother,' she said.

'She was overjoyed. She always thought I should have proposed to you and gone to live in the West.'

'I'm sorry about your father. He was an incredibly kind man.'

'He could be. Especially to strangers, who might think well of him.' Sergei's relationship with his father had always been complicated, a consequence, Sergei had once said, of the old man's thwarted ambition. But he had been only kind and charming to Kate.

She glanced at the clock on the wall. It had just gone a quarter past eleven. 'Come,' he said. 'We'd better board.' He took the bottle of vodka and the glasses with him.

Sergei led her out of the station concourse to the platform. The Red Arrow train bound for Moscow was a long, sleek machine in red and grey livery to match its name. Women in red coats with black felt and fur hats stood on the platform waiting to welcome their passengers to first class, and Sergei seemed to know where they were heading. He presented their tickets, climbed aboard and led her down the narrow corridor. 'Don't take this the wrong way,' he said, 'but I booked us into the same cabin. I figured after all this time we would spend most of the night talking anyway.'

Kate didn't risk an answer.

The first-class cabins were a resplendent rich red, from the bunks to the curtains to the velvet seat backs. Sergei stored his case and Kate her slender gym bag, careful not to bump into each other, and then they sat on opposite bunks. Sergei poured two more glasses of vodka. 'All right,' he said. 'Now we really begin. *Nostrovia.*'

'*Nostrovia*,' she replied, and they drank again. Her head was starting to spin.

The train shunted a few times, forwards and back. And then it began to move slowly away from the platform, the urban grime beyond it softened by a thin dusting of fresh snow. 'I was sorry to hear about Stuart,' he said.

'Were you?'

'Yes. I know how important your family is to you.'

'Have you seen him?'

'In Moscow?' He shook his head. 'By all accounts, he cuts a sad figure. The officers of the SVR don't have a great reputation for looking after their agents and defectors.'

In the long silence that followed, she held his gaze. 'Who do you work for, Sergei?'

'You know the answer.'

'But that's the thing. I'm not sure I do.'

'I work for the Russian government.'

'The GRU?'

He didn't reply, but in this case she took his silence to indicate consent.

'Why did you tip me off that Igor, Vasily and the others would be on that yacht in Istanbul?'

'Does it matter?'

'Yes.'

'To help you.'

'Why?'

'Because in all this time I have not been able to get you out of my head.'

'My colleagues think you told me what was to happen on that yacht in an attempt to discredit your rivals in the SVR.'

'And you? What do *you* think?'

'I . . . don't know.' And as she said it, she was aware that she really didn't. Not honestly. 'I don't believe you would cynically mislead me.'

'What else do we have to rely on in life but our instincts?'

Now Kate was wishing she'd gone a lot slower on the vodka. 'All the same, that leaves the possibility that you told me the truth, which also happened to be in your interests and those of your organization. There would be nothing dishonourable in that.' He was looking out of the window, at the snow falling across a ghostly landscape. 'I need to ask you something else,' she said. 'Is it true that Vasily Durov has been deposed as head of the SVR and is under house arrest?'

'He's not under house arrest. Not yet.'

'But the Kremlin has turned against him?'

'There is a battle. It is not clear who will come out on top.'

Kate searched those big dark eyes. She was not sure how much longer she could keep up the pretence of professional detachment. 'We have been offered evidence of our prime minister's treachery.'

'What kind of "evidence"?'

'The details of how and when payments were made and a copy of the sex video used to entrap him, filmed with under-age girls while he was an army officer serving in Kosovo.'

Sergei nodded, as if entirely unsurprised. 'Who has offered it? Durov?'

'Igor and his son. They also feel under threat as a result of their alliance with Durov and are convinced the net is closing in on them here. They are prepared to give it to us in return for asylum in the West. So is the video real or fake?'

'I don't know. But you need to be careful, Kate.'

'Of what?'

'You think, after all these years, that your husband was the Russian state's only asset at the heart of British intelligence?'

'Who else?'

'There are secrets even I do not know. But you took a huge risk coming here. It was brave, but also foolish. What if they have been following you?' Sergei took another sip of his vodka and came to sit beside her, half twisted on the couchette seat so that his knee was touching her thigh. Then, quietly, 'If you pursue this, it may cost you more than your career. You must know that. A reason to live for tonight, though, if ever I heard of one.' He took the glass from her hand and placed it on the table. He reached behind him and flicked the lock on the door.

He faced her. Kate's head swam, her heart thumping as it had when she had been a student in that dacha aching for this moment. He touched her hair, her cheek, the white, freckled skin at her neck.

And then he kissed her.

The smell of him, the taste and warmth of his lips . . .

She'd not thought of sex beyond an academic curiosity since she'd learnt of Stuart's betrayal, but now desire exploded inside her. They moved with the urgency of the condemned, his firm, sure touch on her leg, beneath her skirt, pushing up her thigh until her blue polka-dot dress was rucked up at her waist to reveal long slim legs above blue socks and scuffed sneakers.

He unclasped the back of her bra with practised skill and kissed her stomach, working steadily downwards. She arched her back, aching for him, and he gently freed her until all she saw was her white underwear wrapped around one leg, before losing herself completely in him.

It had never been like that before, was all Kate could think as she lay lazily in his arms afterwards. Never with Stuart – not in all honesty – loving and marvellous and fun as that had so often been. And certainly not the first time with Pete

Carter, which had been painful and mortifying by turns, or with the young boys who'd followed him episodically before she'd met Stuart.

It was as if, in some strange way, this secret had been revealed at the time of life when she needed it most.

She was so lost in her reverie that it was many minutes before her total failure to reach for any kind of contraception struck her. She rolled off the bunk in a hurry, retrieved her underwear and rearranged her dress and bra into crumpled respectability.

'What is it?' he asked.

'I just need the loo.'

'You're an incurable romantic.'

'Back in a second. Don't go away.' She reached the door, glanced back at him. 'It was worth the wait. That's all I'll say.'

He smiled at her. 'It was a pleasure to discover you like to make love with your pumps still on.'

'I always knew you were a pervert.'

Kate skipped down the corridor and didn't think about the possibility she might be pregnant again until she had been sitting on the toilet for quite some time. What was she trying to do – shake it out?

She cast her mind back. Her last period had been . . . Shit, how long ago? Maybe a month. No, two. Perhaps even three. She'd always been irregular at times of stress and it had taken a long time to get pregnant with both Fiona and then Gus.

She couldn't be pregnant. She probably wasn't even still ovulating.

But what if she was? She couldn't even begin to imagine explaining the circumstances to the children. What would she say? That she'd had a one-night stand with an old flame on a trip to Russia?

There was no way she could have an abortion. Ever. Not after the joy both children had brought her. And probably not even before that, either, if she was honest. My God, what had she been thinking? She stared at her underwear on the floor and at her offending blue sneakers. She'd have to get a morning-after pill. From a chemist in Moscow.

Yes, why not? It made sense. She'd ask Sergei to take her to one. And, anyway, the extra time together might even prove useful: it would give her the chance to tease out of him more information as to what was really going on in Moscow Centre.

She pulled herself together both physically and meta-phorically, washed her hands and walked back down the corridor with the pleasant certainty that, conception or not, this was unlikely to be the last time she had intercourse with Sergei that night.

'You ready for dessert, sir?' she asked, as she pulled back the door. But the sight that awaited her smashed every last sentiment from her except instinctive, animal panic.

Sergei lay naked on his back, his lean body covered with blood, his throat sliced from one side across to the other.

21

KATE SAT DOWN on the bunk opposite him. The walls were splattered with blood from Sergei's severed artery, which had been sprayed across a wide arc in his violent death throes. There was blood on the window, even on the vodka bottle, as he had evidently scrambled to get hold of some kind of weapon with which to fight back.

Who had killed him? Where were they?

She stood again, yanked the door shut and locked it. She sat down, trying to think straight against the tide of far too much vodka. Her heart thumped like a jackhammer in her chest.

Where was the killer?

Gone. He must have been waiting for Kate to leave before attacking. If he'd wanted to kill her, then . . .

He would have. He'd have murdered them both. Surely. No, definitely. But who was behind it. The GRU? Sergei's colleagues, infuriated he might spill their secrets? In which case, why not kill her, too?

The SVR? Its supposedly departing head, Vasily Durov? Igor Borodin and his son Mikhail?

The Russian Mafia?

But why *not* kill her, too? Why wait for her to leave and kill only him?

Somebody passed outside. Christ, what about the guards? What would they do when they discovered this? She'd be arrested, tried, sent to prison for more than a lifetime . . .

She had to get out of here. Now. Her DNA was everywhere – all over every inch of him and the carriage. No attempt at a clean-up was likely to do any more than deepen a state of suspicion as to her true intent. She took her bag from the rack, opened the door and looked up and down the corridor. It was dark, save for the night-lights and the moonlight reflected off the snowy landscape beyond.

She pulled the door firmly shut behind her and walked away down the carriage. She went through the connecting door to the next. It was quiet, but for the rattle and hum of the wheels on the tracks below. At the end of the corridor, she heard two attendants chatting quietly in their galley, but she flitted past them into another carriage. And then another, until she could progress no further. She put her bag down by the door and simply waited.

She pulled down the window a fraction and lit a cigarette. She smoked it as she looked out at the endless succession of snow-covered pines, fields and houses.

Kate waited for the consequences of the terrible scene she had witnessed to take their natural turn, but the strangest part of it all was that nothing whatsoever happened. The train did not stop suddenly at a small station in the middle of nowhere. No police stepped on board. No guards came running.

After an hour, or perhaps two, a guard came to his galley at the far end of the train. He caught sight of her and put his head around the side to ask if she was all right. She shrugged, pretending not to understand the language, and he left her in peace.

In the dead of night, nothing stirred. She smoked cigarette after cigarette, then closed the window and sat on the floor, resting her head uncomfortably on the wall of the carriage.

Dawn broke. The train clattered on through the grubby outskirts of the Russian capital and eventually glided to a halt inside Leningradsky station.

Kate was the first off. She did not look over her shoulder, because they knew where to find her if that was their intention, though she did have the clarity of mind to reflect on how little idea she really had of who 'they' were. Tired, distraught, shocked as she might be, nothing made any sense at all.

She almost ran through the bright concourse to the pedestrian section of Komsomolskaya Square beyond. She stopped by the line of yellow taxis and looked back over her shoulder at the clock tower above the station. It was eight thirty. She glanced about her. If they were watching, she certainly wasn't in a fit state to pick them out from the huge thronging crowd of early-morning commuters. She briefly considered getting into a taxi or heading straight back to catch a return train to St Petersburg.

She brought up Google Maps. She needed somewhere to sit, to think. She found Sokolniki Park was only a short distance away and walked there fast, oblivious to the people around her.

There was an Orthodox church adjacent to the park, so she installed herself in a pew at the back and closed her eyes. The moment she did so, she conjured an image of Sergei's face, his eyes bulging with the pain and shock of his sudden death. She hadn't seen any particular sign of a struggle: had it been someone he knew, expected even?

Who could have killed him? And why?

She wasn't on the passenger manifest but they must have watched them get on the train. If so, why had she been spared? Kate tried to pull herself together. She looked around the empty church.

She walked to the entrance and peered out. Two women in long trench coats leant against an iron fence by the road, as if waiting for her. She retreated again.

On an instinct that she later spent a great deal of time try-ing to analyse, Kate decided to call Stuart. He answered on the third ring, as if he had somehow been expecting her call. That was almost enough to prompt her to ring off straight away, but not quite: she was desperate. 'Hi, love,' he said, 'how nice to hear you.'

'Where are you?'

'Er, at home. Well, if you can call it that. In my apartment in Moscow.'

'I need your help.'

There was a momentary pause. 'Of course. How?'

'I'm in Sokolniki Park. There's an Orthodox church. I'm sitting at the back of it. Please come and get me.'

'In Moscow?'

'Yes.'

'Jesus, Kate, what are you doing here?' If he had truly expected this call, then his surprise was well faked.

'I just need your help urgently. I don't know if it will cause trouble for you and, well, I'll understand if you want to turn me down.'

'Of course I'll help you. I'll leave now. Just keep your phone on.'

Kate went back to the entrance and peered through the doorway. The two women had moved off. She stepped out and looked up and down the street, but there was no sign of either of them.

It took Stuart almost an hour to reach her and her first thought was again how incredibly well he looked. He was wearing a dark green T-shirt, but the same black jeans and leather jacket as when he had met her in Venice only a few weeks – or was it days? – ago. 'I'm sorry,' he said. 'The traffic is horrendous at this time of the morning.'

It was all Kate could do to prevent herself throwing her arms around him. He looked so . . . safe. Just like he always had: her Stuart. For a moment, they didn't know whether to kiss or hug. Kate eventually put him out of his misery by brushing his cheek. 'Can you take me to your apartment?' she said. 'I just need some time . . .'

'To what?'

'Please don't ask any questions.'

'Of course.'

He led her to his car, a battered old white Fiat. A man in a dark North Face raincoat, jeans and trainers stood just beyond it, smoking, as if waiting for something or someone. Her, she assumed.

They got into the car and pulled out into the morning traffic. Kate glanced in the side mirror. She watched a black

BMW 5 Series saloon turn out behind them. 'Everything all right?' Stuart asked.

'Fine,' she lied.

Their progress was slow. The capital's roads might be filled with many more shiny new cars since her first visit as a student in the early nineties, but they didn't move any faster. Kate kept a nervous, watchful eye on the side mirror. The BMW dropped back, but never out of sight. She bit her nails.

'Everything all right?' Stuart asked again.

'Yes,' she said. 'Fine.'

Stuart's apartment was out in Taganka, on the twenty-third floor of a concrete block that looked forbidding against a dark grey Moscow sky. The landing smelt of urine, and the wind had gathered rubbish into its corners. Kate glanced over the railing to see that the BMW had parked outside the block opposite. She averted her gaze before Stuart could remark upon it.

He let her into a small flat that had all the antiseptic appeal of a serviced apartment. It was clean and newly painted, but spartan and infinitely depressing. There was a small kitchen, with cheap Formica cupboards and a tiny table pressed up against the window, a single bedroom and a small sitting room at the end, with a cream leather sofa and two chairs in front of a large widescreen TV. 'It's not much,' he said, 'I know.'

Kate felt like bursting into tears, for him, for them, for the mess she was in. But the warmth of his smile stalled her. 'I can stretch to tea, though,' he said. 'English Breakfast or Earl Grey?'

'English Breakfast would be great,' she said. She was look-ing at the wooden dresser, which was full of photographs of the children, but also of the four of them as a family and of Kate. The one at the end was his favourite, taken on the day of their graduation, overlooking the river. She'd been drunk and happy, carefree in a way she could scarcely remember. 'I told you,' he said, following the direction of her gaze. 'Memories are all I have.'

He withdrew to make tea. Kate tried to divorce herself from her emotionally loaded surroundings in order to make sense of what had just happened.

Who had been watching Sergei? Why had they let her live?

What in the hell was she going to do now? She moved to the window and looked out. The BMW was still there.

Stuart returned with two mugs of steaming tea and a plate of biscuits. He'd made it strong for her, as she liked. 'How are the kids?' he asked, as he sat on the sofa opposite her.

'They're well. Gus was very thrilled about being made captain of cricket.'

'I know. It's going to break my heart, not being able to watch. You'll have to send me some video.' He smiled again, clearly keeping up a cheery façade at some cost. Kate was thinking about the men in the BMW downstairs. Were they waiting for back-up, for others to join them? Was the idea now to kill both her and Stuart here in this flat? Would that be a double problem solved? 'How about Fi?' Stuart asked.

Kate tried to concentrate on the conversation. There was no point in alarming Stuart. 'She's difficult to reach still. She spends a lot of time with Jed, but I'm not sure that's a bad thing. He's a very nice young man.'

'Despite the tattoos and piercings?' He was smiling again. She gave him a weak grin in return. 'I don't mean to pry, but I assume you're in some kind of trouble.'

'I need to sleep,' she said. 'Then I'll work out what to do.'

'Of course. Just finish your tea. I'm afraid I only have one bedroom, but if you don't mind, you can sleep next door . . .'

'I'm grateful for anywhere to put my head down right now.'

They sipped their tea during another long and surreal silence. 'Just so I know . . . I mean, I don't mind, but forewarned is forearmed and all that. Am I going to be in trouble?' he asked.

'I doubt it. Something just happened. I don't know how, still less why. I need time and space to think before I work out what to do next.'

'Of course. I understand. What are you doing here in the first place?'

'I was meeting someone.'

Stuart couldn't hide his hurt at that. 'I think I can guess who. What happened?'

'I'm really sorry, I just need to rest.' She put down her tea.

He leapt to his feet. 'Of course,' he said. 'Of course. I understand.'

He showed her through to his bedroom next door, which had a small en-suite bathroom with a loo and shower. There were more photographs of the family on a bookshelf, and by the bed there was one of Kate alone, taken only a few years ago in the Italian Dolomites. Kate didn't know what to say. This was not how she had imagined him living here. 'Do you mind if I take a shower?' she asked.

'Of course. I'll leave you to it . . . Anything else you want, just shout.'

'If you need to go to work or—'

'I don't have a job to go to. I'll be reading a book next door. I'll leave you to sleep for as long as you want.'

He retreated. Kate undressed, stepped into the shower and tried to shake off the sense of guilt she felt as she washed away the legacy of another man with her husband's favourite mint shower gel and Australian shampoo.

She dried herself and cleaned her teeth with his brush. She took the top off the Acqua di Parma aftershave and sniffed it. She'd given him his first bottle in a Christmas stocking almost a decade before and he'd stuck to it religiously ever since. That was Stuart, loyal to a fault. Except, as it turned out, in the one way that really mattered. Kate dried herself, put on a clean pair of knickers and a T-shirt, and sat on his bed. She took half a dose of zopiclone this time, since she wasn't sure how long she should sleep.

She pulled back the curtain and checked the street outside once more. The BMW was parked there, still, but the men inside did not appear to have been joined by anyone else. Who in hell were they?

She lay down and tried to ignore the light streaming in through the thin yellow curtains and the sight of her own cheery face gazing down at her from the table beside the bed. Was it conceivable Stuart had put these pictures out after her phone call or did he really have this beside his bed all the time?

Her thoughts led inexorably back to Sergei. She could think of no reason why they would kill him and let her live. What had he planned to tell her? What would she have found out? She thought of his final few words: *If you pursue this, it may cost you more than your career. You must know that.*

There could be only two candidates for his murder, surely: either it was the GRU shutting down a renegade officer who'd had no motive but to assist the woman he'd always loved. (What was it he had told her? *You think, after all these years, that your husband was the Russian's state's only asset at the heart of British Intelligence?*) Or it was Mikhail, Igor and those close to them trying to protect their exit strategy.

She turned it over and over in her mind. Was it Sergei they had been watching, or had they been tipped off that she was on her way and followed her from the moment she'd crossed the border?

Kate flopped over, so that she was face down; the way she traditionally slept. She could smell her husband in the sheets and the sensation was comforting.

They'd known she was coming. That was what she kept returning to. And they'd killed Sergei before he could give her a full account of Moscow's men – or women – in London.

But he might already have done so, in which case why not kill her, too?

Because to murder her would cause them problems. There would be an international outcry: a British civil servant killed on a Russian train. Too much trouble, perhaps. Better to send her back confused and disoriented.

They were protecting someone. They'd been tipped off she was coming and they'd closed down her source.

That much seemed clear to her. Concentrate, she told herself, on the pieces you can see and understand, not the many parts of the jigsaw you can't know and may never know.

Kate shut her eyes. She tried to think of something else. She breathed in hard again and attempted to transport herself back to the carefree days of her life with Stuart. She turned from one image of him to the next: walking along Constantine Bay in Cornwall the summer before last; Stuart laughing his head off, roaring drunk, on the night the picture beside her had been taken in the Dolomites.

After a while, she noticed the sheet beneath her was damp with tears.

She pressed her face down harder, trying to clear her mind, as she waited and waited for sleep to come.

In the end, the chemicals did the trick, but, as ever these days, not for long. When she awoke, the clock on the table beside her told her it was just after midday. Kate got up and pulled back the curtain to reveal shards of sunlight glinting off the rows of concrete tower blocks. It was bright. The BMW had disappeared. There was a white van further along, parked with its engine running. Perhaps they planned to kidnap her.

She sat on the bed. She felt grim, but was gripped now with at least one clear thought: she had to get out of here, right away, by any means possible.

She pulled on a pair of jeans and packed her dress into her bag. She brushed her teeth again and emerged to find Stuart reading his book next door. 'Did you sleep?' he asked.

'A bit. Thank you.'

'You looked like you needed it.'

'I did.'

'Cup of tea?'

'Why not? I might actually drink it this time.'

He went to the kitchen and returned with a sandwich as well as tea. 'I figured you'd probably need to eat.'

She was ravenous, so she didn't argue with him. He watched her eat in silence. She finished, and sipped her tea. She was aware his eyes had yet to leave her face. There was a hunger in them she'd not seen since the first days of their courtship. She tried to suppress the wave of pleasure it brought. And in that moment, she knew he would do absolutely anything she asked. 'I understand if you don't want to do this and I wouldn't blame you. But could you drive me to the border?'

'Where?'

'Finland. In fact, St Petersburg, because I need to pick up my hire car.'

'Wouldn't it be quicker or easier to fly or catch the train? I can come with you to help allay suspicion if that's the issue, but it's a very long—'

'I'd rather go by road and I'm in no fit state to make the drive alone, as you can probably tell.'

He looked at her for what felt like an age, his mind evidently turning over this strange twist of fate. 'I'd do anything for you,' he said. 'Anything at all.'

Kate went to the window and looked out once more. The van had moved off. She scanned the street outside carefully, sweeping one way, then the other. If they were still watching her – and they must be – she could not see how. 'All right, then,' she said. 'Let's go.'

'Now?'

'Yes.'

22

BEFORE THEY LEFT Moscow, Kate said she needed to go to a chemist. Stuart was resistant: if she really was in trouble, shouldn't they leave straight away? But Kate was adamant and would not give a reason. In the end, he took it in mute silence and she half suspected he guessed why it was a matter of such urgency. She bought a bottle of water and swallowed the morning-after pill before she got back to the car. The only thing that worried her was that the last time she'd relied on this last resort against an unwanted pregnancy – ironically on that skiing holiday to the Dolomites when they'd supposedly been using condoms until they'd both got too drunk on the last night – she had bled profusely and for a long time. She'd also bought two large packets of sanitary towels.

If Stuart had guessed at the truth, or something like it, it might have explained the long period of silence. It was as if he was nursing a hurt and trying to find a way to broach the subject. 'It must have been quite some reason to take the risk of coming here,' he said eventually.

'I can't really talk about it,' she said. She glanced into the side mirror once more. The Volkswagen Golf she'd thought was tailing them had turned away at the last traffic lights and her suspicion had landed instead on a dark Volvo that appeared to be hanging back at a steady distance. 'Tell me about your life in Moscow,' she said.

'That's going to be a very short conversation.' They'd reached the outskirts of the capital now and were driving north towards a portentous, brooding sky. 'What do you want to know?'

'Are you still hunting for a job?'

'Yeah.' He shrugged. 'I met my "handler" – if that's what you'd call him – last week and I complained to him about my lot. He seemed quite sympathetic and promised to see what he could do. They've said they're going to ask me to lecture new recruits on how Western bureaucracies work. I think it would be different if I was you. Then, I guess, they'd be looking to put me to use, but an awful lot of what a civil servant does is well known to them. My guy did seem quite interested in my read on the PM and Imogen and the current state of British politics, so maybe something will come of that.'

'Do you have friends here?'

'You mean a girlfriend?'

'No. I was just—'

'Well, the answer is no and no. I've mostly been feeling sorry for myself, I'll admit. It's been very depressing. I spend a lot of time in the local gym and that's about the only thing that's keeping me sane.'

'You look fit,' she said. It was true. She'd found it hard not to admire his bulging arm muscles when he'd been sitting in his T-shirt in the flat. 'So what do you do all day?'

'I get up. I have breakfast. I read the British newspapers online and congratulate myself on escaping the crazy crock of shit that is our politics before feeling unbearably home-sick. I go to the gym for a couple of hours. I'm tight for money, so I come home for lunch . . . I watch TV in the evening, but I try to spend the afternoons reading a book. Otherwise . . .'

'Haven't they helped you at all? I mean socially or . . .'

'Not really.' He forced a smile. 'It's like I've fallen off the end of the earth. I'm not complaining. I've made my bed, so I have to lie in it. Those couple of nights I spent with Imogen are turning out to be just about the most expensive in his-tory.' He shook his head ruefully. 'I know there's no way back. Somehow I have to make it work here. I need to find a life, friends, whatever. I've asked if there's an SVR football team I can join. If not, there are a few other expat organiza-tions I can maybe fall in with. It's just . . . there's a lot to let go of and I'm not there yet.'

It started to rain, first with a few drops and then in great thumping balls of water. The Panda's windscreen wipers struggled to keep up. Kate's gaze was drawn relentlessly back to the side mirror, but the Volvo had disappeared from view and she could no longer be sure they actually had a tail. If anything, it confused her still further.

'Was it worth waiting for,' Stuart said, his gaze resolutely dead ahead, 'your night with Sergei?'

'Were your trysts with Imogen?'

'No,' he said emphatically. 'Not that it will make any dif-ference, but she wanted more. It was me who cut it off. I felt unbearably guilty, of course, but it was also just . . . second rate, mechanical, by comparison.'

'Just for the record, it doesn't make any difference.'

He peered closer to the windscreen. It was misting up now so he put the fan on full. 'You didn't answer my question,' he said.

'I don't need to, do I?'

'And yet you're here in my car. I guess I'm taking quite a risk driving you wherever it is you're really headed. So it would be polite at least to try to indulge me with an honest—'

'Sergei is dead.'

She watched the colour drain from Stuart's face. He tugged at the stubble on his chin, a sure sign he was nervous. 'Christ,' he said. 'Jesus Christ, Kate.'

'I didn't come here to have sex with him. I came to ask him a question that only he would conceivably be able to give me an answer to. This morning, I found him with his throat cut.'

'After you'd . . .'

What was it with men? Kate thought. Why were they so obsessed with the act of sexual intercourse? 'You mean after we'd had sex?' He didn't answer. 'Yes, if you want to torture yourself with the truth, after we'd had sex. I didn't intend it to happen. I didn't especially want it to. But I'm lonely, too, and strung out, and bereft and confused. In the maelstrom of all that, I finished what I shouldn't perhaps have started all those years ago. And, yes, also, the earth did move for me, not better or worse than making love to you, just different.'

She saw the hurt in his eyes and wished instantly she'd held her tongue. 'Is that what you wanted to hear?' she asked.

'Of course not.'

'Then don't ask a question if you don't really want to know the answer.'

There was another long silence. 'I did want to know,' he said. 'Thank you for telling me the truth.'

'So that you can torture yourself with it?'

'Perhaps it will release me.' He turned to her. 'That picture of you by my bed wasn't for show, Kate. I've never stopped loving you, not for a single second.'

Regret flooded her now: for his betrayal, for their estrangement, for the life they'd had and the future that might have been, for the brutal honesty of her tongue. 'I'm sorry,' she said again. 'I should have kept all that to myself.'

'I think I had it coming.'

'That doesn't make it any better.' She thought of the flat they'd just left and the window it had offered into his life here as it was and as it might be. The barren, hopeless bleakness of it chilled her.

'Won't they come after you once they've found the body?' he asked. 'Why haven't they come already?'

'It depends who you mean by "they".'

'Well . . . I don't know – the police, the Mafia, the SVR, whoever was involved.'

'The police certainly, I'd guess.'

'Does that make me an accessory to murder?'

She didn't answer that. Sitting there now, Stuart's crimes, which appeared to amount to a couple of nights of careless sex with Imogen Conrad, didn't seem to match the punishment Kate was putting him through. Regardless of whether she made it out of the country or not, there was a reasonable chance he might be made to pay a very heavy price.

Bleak as his current life in Moscow might be, it barely held a candle to the prospect of a long stretch in a Russian prison. "I'm sorry,' she said again. 'I shouldn't have dragged you into this.'

'Stop saying you're sorry. I knew exactly the risk I was taking getting into this car with you. And I'd do it again, a hundred times over.' He forced another smile. 'Besides, I trust you. Aren't you James Bond?'

Kate tried to grin back at him, but doubted she managed more than an awkward grimace. They lapsed into silence after that, but they were only about three hours north of Moscow before the onset of heavy bleeding forced her to ask him to stop at a truck-stop diner.

She disappeared into the filthy toilet, and by the time she emerged, he was sitting at a metal table by the window with two mugs of coffee and a sandwich each. 'It's going be a long night,' he said. 'I thought we could use this.'

Kate slipped on to the tattered red plastic bench opposite him. The chrome and steel décor was supposed to conjure the image of an American roadside diner, but, like many imitations in modern Russia, it was way off. Kate sipped her coffee and stared out at the traffic thundering past. It was still raining heavily, the light gloomy and visibility limited.

'You had to take the morning-after pill,' he said, gesturing at the packet of sanitary towels on the seat beside her. 'I remember you travelling home from the Dolomites with a bagful of them after that last night in the hotel.'

'You have a good memory.'

'For all the best moments. And there were a hell of a lot of them.' He swirled the coffee in his mug. Kate was suddenly desperate for a cigarette, but they'd given up together at least a decade ago, and she was too proud to admit she'd fallen off the wagon.

'Tell me honestly,' he said, still staring into his drink. 'Is there even the slightest chance you might one day forgive me, that we might . . . I don't know, be friends, or . . .' He trailed off, though she knew well enough what he was asking.

'If you want to know if we can ever be a couple again, as we were, then the answer is no. You betrayed me and you know who I am, how I am. You understand why it matters so much to me, however black and white you might find it. But you'll always mean something to me. Just in a different way now.' It wasn't the answer he'd hoped for, she knew, and he gazed disconsolately at the table, brushing his fingertips to and fro. 'I can't give you what you want. I can't take back time, or change the passage of events. But I can see how bleak your life here is and I'd like to do something to ease it.'

'Oh, yeah? And how are you going to manage that?'

'I don't know yet. The Service is quite happy to have you in Moscow. The last thing they would have wanted was to put you on trial. In time, when the way ahead is clearer, I think we can use that to our advantage.'

'How?'

'I can make it an argument about the children's welfare. They'll never let you come back to the UK, but it is just about possible I could persuade them to turn a blind eye to you living somewhere else in Europe – in France, perhaps, or Spain, somewhere you can build a proper new life for yourself and the children can visit regularly.'

There were tears in Stuart's eyes now. He wiped them away brusquely. 'I don't deserve you, that's for sure,' he said.

She reached out and put a hand over his. He slowly turned over the palm until their fingers were interlocked. 'I can't help, though, if you keep wanting to take it beyond friend-ship,' she said, but she was aware as she did so that the finality of her words were at odds with the emotion cours-ing through her. She removed her hand.

He wiped the tears from his cheeks. 'Thank you,' he said. 'Thank you. I'm never going to forgive myself for what I did to you. Sometimes I think it would be easier to stay here and punish myself. I just don't know what I was thinking. I must have been out of my mind.'

They finished their coffee and sandwiches and hit the road again. Kate half expected Stuart to ask her to drive, but he seemed to expect to soldier on. The rain stopped and, once in a while, a few rays of evening sunshine glinted off the pooled water on the tarmac.

And when they were finally swallowed by the night, Kate felt fatigue creep up on her until her head was lolling uncomfortably between the side of the seat and the cool glass of the window. At one point, Stuart reached over and put his sweater beneath her cheek. 'Where are we?' she asked.

'Just beyond Tver,' he replied, and then she drifted off again, a bleak, dreamless sleep, so that every time she was shaken awake, she felt more tired than she had been before.

Kate was dimly aware of a petrol stop somewhere, but it was two in the morning when Stuart shook her properly awake again. 'I'm sorry,' he said. 'I can't keep my eyes open and it's getting a bit dangerous. I'm just going to grab a coffee and something more to eat. You want to stay here, or come in?'

His arm rested easily on her shoulders. 'I'll come in,' she said.

The long, dark building was a no-frills café without the pretences of the previous diner. It had metal chairs and tables and a battered linoleum floor. A pretty, dark-haired girl leant against the counter and indicated they should take a seat. A much older man – perhaps her father – was asleep against the wall behind the bar.

'What can I get you?' she asked in English. Kate asked for coffee and something to eat in Russian. The girl gestured lazily at a counter along the far wall and Kate understood well enough: at this time in the morning, they weren't going to get anyone to cook for them. Perhaps not at any time in the morning.

Kate went to take a look. The breakfast spread ran to a selection of cold meats, cheeses and gherkins that looked as if they had been sitting there for ever. 'Rather you than me,' she reported back. But Stuart was made of sterner stuff. He returned with a plateful. She watched as he worked his way through it.

'What have you been thinking about?' he asked.

'Nothing.' She certainly didn't feel like admitting she'd been unable to get out of her mind the feel of his fingers locked in her own.

'You've got something you want to get off your chest.' He piled meat and cheese on to a slice of bread and took an enormous bite. He had never been an elegant eater. 'That's the advantage of having been married to someone for half a lifetime.'

Kate weighed what she had been proposing to say. She wouldn't have imagined it even an hour ago.

'We're almost there, so . . .' he smiled at her '. . . speak now or forever hold your peace.'

Intuitive as he was, he was not about to guess this. 'What if I said there was a chance – a very, very slim one, but the glimmer of something at least – that I might be able to find my way back to how I felt before?'

The colour drained from his face. The shock was palpable. 'I'd do anything,' he said, 'absolutely anything you asked of me.'

'It would require you to be honest about something. Completely honest. And I'd have to be certain you were telling the truth.'

'Of course.'

'Even then, I'm not offering any guarantees. The road would be long and hard and we might not get there, but . . . it might open the door.' He waited, spellbound by this unexpected turn of events. He scratched nervously at the stubble on his chin. His yearning for a second start was not in doubt. 'I need to know what you told your handlers in Moscow.'

'About what?'

'Everything.'

For a moment, she watched something – a flash of resentment, a warning, a moment of doubt – slip through his conscious mind before he faced her again with unalloyed eagerness, but whatever it was, it triggered a counterbalancing reaction in her own mind: was her offer real? Did she mean it? Was it even possible? Or was she just using him? Even she didn't know the answer to that one.

Kate took the plunge nevertheless. She nodded. He downed a last swig of his coffee and answered her. 'I know it may not seem much, but I mostly talked to them about Imogen and British politics. They were interested in her ambitions, particularly in my take on whether she was ever going to realize them and, if so, how, when and why that might happen.'

'Did you get the impression they wanted her to be promoted?'

'They were careful never to ask leading questions. They just seemed genuinely interested in my views on the polit-ical scene.'

'Did they ask for papers?'

'Sometimes, yes. If I was on the circulation list for any-thing that was unusual or interesting, I'd hand it over. I was trying to keep them happy, you know . . .'

'What did you tell them about the Service?'

'Nothing.' He was clearly aghast. 'For God's sake, Kate, I'd never have betrayed you like that.' Kate was almost tempted to say that fucking their friend was a rather bigger betrayal, but this time she held her tongue.

'They must have asked.'

'They did, but I just said you never, ever talked about your work at home – which was true, most of the time.'

'Did they ask you to access my phone or computer?'

'Yes, but they're all password-protected and I told them that. To be completely honest, they didn't seem *that* incred-ibly interested.'

'What do you mean?'

'Well, they asked about you, definitely, but I didn't feel that I *had* to deliver any of the detail they requested or they'd expose me. When I said I didn't know or couldn't find out, they didn't press me.'

Kate thought about this. It was certainly not what she'd expected to hear. 'Did you tell them about the operation in Istanbul?'

'What operation?' If his confusion wasn't genuine, Stuart had turned into an amazingly competent actor.

'"How did it go in Italy?" you asked me. "Istanbul," I answered.'

'I don't know what you're talking about, Kate. I can't remember that at all.'

'What about when I went to Greece a few days later?'

'What about it?'

'Did you tell them about that?'

'No! Why would I have done?'

'Did they ask about it?'

'No.'

'Did you tell them the former PM had prostate cancer?'

'I didn't even know he had it until he made that announcement in Downing Street.'

He was obviously confused now. But not half as disoriented as Kate was. Even as he spoke, her mind was spinning. If Stuart hadn't told Moscow about Operation Sigma, who the hell had?

'To be completely honest with you,' he went on, 'I sometimes wondered why they wanted to recruit me at all.'

She looked up at him again. 'Why do you say that?'

'When they cornered me – blackmailed me – it all seemed incredibly urgent and elemental. They were brutal. They said they'd show you the video of Imogen and me and destroy our love and marriage. I absolutely believed them. They seemed ruthless, determined. But almost as soon as they'd got what they wanted, it was as if their interest waned. I mean, we'd meet up – about once a month, on average, I suppose – but even then they'd quite regularly postpone one or other rendezvous. Every time I was so relieved and started to convince myself they'd lost interest.

'And even when we did meet, they didn't seem that interested in what I had to say. It was like going to lunch with a benevolent but distant relation, who was trying to feign interest in everything you do.'

Kate shook her head. 'I don't understand.'

'It was almost as if the purpose of recruiting me was to tick a box, or meet a target. As I said, we talked about politics and Imogen, who was up and who was down. I discussed policy in some of the areas I was working on, but they weren't at all interested in that. They asked about you or the Service only rarely and when I said I didn't know anything, they didn't pressure me to try to find out more. I didn't tell them anything they couldn't otherwise have picked up from watching the news.'

Kate was looking out of the window. A lorry had pulled up and an enormously fat driver stepped down and waddled towards the diner. She was pretty sure now that they were not being tailed, but she couldn't make sense of why not. Did they intend to pick her up closer to the border? Perhaps they had a tracking device on Stuart's car.

'Did I say the wrong thing?' he asked.

'In what way?'

'For a shot at redemption.'

'It isn't about that,' she said, though in a way it was: a test of whether she thought he was capable of telling her the truth. 'What you say is . . . surprising.'

'Why?'

'Their disinterest.'

'I know. Sometimes I think it would have been easier if I had been passing vital state secrets. At least that would have felt important. They ruined my – our – life for nothing.'

Every time Stuart veered into self-pity or self-justification, she felt her hackles start to rise. She could have pointed out, and very nearly did, that it was his decision to screw Imogen Conrad rather than their exploitation of it that had ruined their lives, but what was the point? It made her sound and feel shrewish and embittered, and it was a train of thought and emotion she was trying to choke off.

Instead, she tried to make sense of what he had said. It occurred to her that Stuart might indeed have been a box-ticking exercise or, more worryingly, a red herring to disguise a much more important agent somewhere in Whitehall or perhaps even MI6. So perhaps Stuart had really not been Viper, after all.

Which meant, of course, that Viper was still active.

How easy it was for Moscow to throw Stuart to the wolves when suspicions started to sink in that there was a mole somewhere in the system.

But even this train of thought rested on a basic premise: that Stuart was telling the truth.

'Did you mean what you said,' he asked, 'or was it just a trick to get more information out of me? I wouldn't blame you if that was the case. I deserve it. But it would help to know.'

There was a long silence. Kate had to suppress another deep craving for a cigarette as she watched the young girl behind the counter light one and suck the smoke deep into her lungs before blowing it towards the blackened ceiling. The lorry driver had disappeared, apparently to the toilet. 'I did mean it. In a curious way, despite the awful circumstances, these few hours we've spent together have been the greatest peace I've known since the day you left.'

'For me, too.'

'But I can't change the fact that you wounded me deeply. The trust we had, the unique bond, is broken. For ever. We can't repair that. So, in truth, I don't know what I want. I miss you. I miss what we had.'

'My sparkling wit.' He was smiling at her.

'Everything but that. So I . . . don't know. I'm opening the door. Partly for the kids' sake. I'm not certain that I'll ever be able to walk through it. I can't give you any promises. Perhaps we can find a way back to friendship. I'd hope that was possible. I don't want to hate you. I don't want the children to have that bitterness and rancour in their lives. But as to whether something more than that ever develops, I really can't—'

'That's enough for now. I don't want to push it.' He put his palm over hers. 'I know it's going to take a long time.'

Kate withdrew her hand. If his touch had thrilled her earlier, she now couldn't bear it. 'I'm sorry,' he said. 'What did I say?'

'It's not what you said, but what you did. I . . .'

He nodded. 'I understand. I'm sorry.' He stared at his hands. She couldn't help noticing how fine they were, always one of the most attractive things about him. 'I'm here for you,' he said. 'Always. If ever and whenever you need me. That's all you should know. I have nothing else in my life, and if I never have anything else but your occasional friend-ship, that's enough for me.' He smiled at her, and the genuine love and warmth in his gaze brought tears to her eyes. She brushed them impatiently away.

'How would it work?' he asked. 'This friendship, this new life, just to give me some hope to live for.'

'I don't know. I'd have to do some thinking about it. I'd need to persuade the Service to turn a blind eye to you mov-ing permanently to take up residence in France or Spain or Italy, perhaps.'

'France. It's closer.'

'Okay. You'd have to work out where you wanted to go. Then we could try to make a plan so the kids could come over once or twice a month. Maybe sometimes I could come along.'

'Sounds great.' His smile was broad. She found herself smiling back, the warmth spreading through her. 'Come on,' she said. 'We'd better get going.'

Back in the car, most things were the same: the intermit-tent rain, snow and hail, the poor visibility, the condensation on the windscreen and the gloom of the drab Russian night.

But something was different. Hope had transformed their demeanour. Kate could hear it in Stuart – he was mentally far away, but humming old songs from the eighties – and feel it in herself. She found her mind roaming through the possibilities she had just outlined. Where would he go? What would he do? She found herself excited already at the prospect of getting on a plane with the kids to spend a weekend with their father in the South of France. Not for love, much less for sex. But the prospect that a true and decent friendship held, well, that was something to hold out for.

She thought about sex. She'd changed her sanitary towel in the disgusting toilet in the last diner and, while there was certainly some bleeding, it was nothing like as profound as the last time she'd taken the morning-after pill. She allowed her mind to roam worriedly over the possibility that it might not have worked. Christ, what if she really was pregnant?

All of which led her back to the thought of Sergei's slaughtered body in that carriage. The momentary sense of well-being that had enveloped her evaporated in an instant.

They barely spoke for the last leg of the journey, as Kate wrestled with what she would tell her superiors back home.

What did all this change?

They reached Kate's hotel on Admiralty Embankment. The weather had closed in to the point where Vasilyevsky Island was barely visible through the driving snow. They got out of the car and, for a moment, neither of them spoke. 'I'll follow you up to the border,' Stuart said.

'Why?'

'Just in case there are any issues. I have a Russian passport, after all. I'm officially a citizen. Maybe that might help.'

'It's fine.'

'I'd like to, just to see that you're okay.'

She nodded. 'Thank you for your help.'

'It's been the best twenty-four hours I've had since I left. I'll be high on it for days. I'll go home and start researching places to live in France. That's exciting. I mean, really thrilling. It gives me something to live for and I'm grateful.'

'Let's not get too ahead of ourselves. As I said—'

'I know what you said, love. But this is going to save my life. What happens after that is in the lap of the gods. I understand that.'

'You may have some trouble when you go back.'

'I may, but I don't care.'

'Will you tell me if they come looking for you?'

'Probably not. They've already robbed me of everything I care for, so I don't mind what else they do to me and they know that.'

A gust of wind whipped the snow into Kate's face and she brushed it from her cheeks before she leant in to kiss him. 'Bye, then,' she said. Stuart gripped her, wrapping his great arms around her and pressing her to his chest. It brought tears to her cheeks again and, as soon as she was free of him, she brushed them away.

'I'll be thinking about this journey for weeks,' he said. 'A pretty strange turn of events.'

Kate tried to smile at him. Without another word, she walked to her own car, got in and drove away. She did not look back. And, within minutes, she was crying so hard she had to pull over to the side of the road and press her aching forehead to the steering wheel. She cursed softly, took out a face-cleaning cloth from her bag and wiped her eyes. She glanced at herself in the wing mirror and attempted to apply some lipstick and mascara. But no amount of touching up was going to magic away the impression of complete exhaustion.

She pulled herself together and drove off before Stuart could come along and ask her what was wrong. She was grateful for the comforting sight of his headlamps behind her. She could still see no sign of any other tail.

There was only a short queue at the border crossing, but as she edged towards the barrier, Kate had only one thought: if they had put out an alert for her after discovering Sergei's body, then her image would already be plastered up on the wall in every exit point all over Russia. Tail or no tail, was there really any chance they would let her leave?

23

THE BORDER GUARD either had a keen wit or no sense of irony at all. 'Why do you want to leave Russia?' he asked.

'I'm sure I'll be back,' Kate said, though she doubted it.

'They say it rains in Ireland all the time.' He was a lugubrious man, in his forties or fifties, with large spectacles and cheeks like a bloodhound's. He stared at her passport and scanned it into his computer. Kate watched the snow twist and turn in tight eddies just the other side of the barrier.

She wondered what would happen if she had to hit the accelerator and drive for her freedom. She turned around to see if Stuart was still behind her, but he had disappeared. 'Irish?' the guard asked, as if genuinely challenging the evidence in front of him.

'Yes.'

'I went to Dublin once, and Belfast.' His English was remarkably good. 'I don't remember much about it.'

'That's often the way.'

He stared at the screen beside him. 'What have you been doing in Russia?'

'I was just in St Petersburg, seeing the sights.'

'Did you go on to Moscow?'

Kate hesitated a moment too long. 'No.'

There was a long silence. He was evidently waiting for some instruction from his computer. Kate leant closer to the windscreen and peered ahead into the gloom. They'd open fire on her if she drove for it, that's for sure, but it was only a hundred yards at most. She looked at the guard by the barrier, his assault rifle idling at his hip.

'You are free to go.' The guard smiled at her. 'Come back soon.'

'I will,' Kate said. The barrier went up and she drove on with a heavy sigh of relief and still more questions. It had felt as though the guard was waiting for a specific instruction but, if so, why would it have been to let her go?

Julie was waiting for her in a beaten-up old Volvo saloon just beyond the barrier. Kate didn't get a chance to ask how long she'd been there before Julie threw her arms around her. 'Fucking hell, Kate.' She released her, held up her phone. 'I had literally just decided to give you ten more minutes before I pressed the nuclear button.'

'I'm sorry. It took a lot longer than I thought.'

'There's been hell to pay from London. Ian guessed the truth immediately, as did Sir Alan.'

'It's all right. I've got enough to make it worth it.'

'What the hell happened?'

'I'll tell you in the warm.'

Kate glanced at Julie's car. 'I hired it for cash from a guy I met in a bar in Kotka. It's quite the place, as it turns out. I have to drop it back so I'll see you in the café by the quay.'

Kate followed her and, by the time a few rays of sun finally burst through the morning clouds, they were both slipping into a corner table for breakfast. 'You want caffeine or nicotine first?' Julie asked.

'Nicotine.'

They stepped back on to the quay and watched a long line of students walking up the gangplank to the tall ship. The sun shimmered through its rigging. Julie lit up and gave the cigarette to Kate before producing another for herself. Kate sucked the smoke deep into her lungs and exhaled into the sky above. 'Shit, that feels good.'

Julie watched her. 'You going to explain, or am I going to have to wheedle it out of you?'

'What happened in London?'

'Ian claims to have kept the dogs in MI5 at bay by quoting operational security. But he says he's going to enjoy firing you when you get back. Now, spill the beans. Did you meet Sergei?'

'Yes.'

'Where?'

'He was travelling to Moscow, so I went with him on the night train. It was the only way I was going to be able to see him.'

'And?'

'We talked. I told him the truth about what we'd been offered and why, and asked him whether he thought what Mikhail had said to us about his father was true.'

'How did he respond?'

'That it was.' Kate took a last drag of her cigarette and stubbed it out beneath her shoe. She'd thought of little else but what she would say to Julie since they'd left St Petersburg, and at no point on the journey had she come to a firm conclusion to tell this exaggerated version of what Sergei had really said, but what purpose would the truth serve?

Either the video and the accompanying financial evidence that Mikhail and Igor offered was real or it was an incredibly convincing fake. They would never know until they got it to London and ran all the appropriate tests.

Sergei had, in truth, offered her nothing *conclusive* on the political ups and downs of Moscow's intelligence elite, only that some kind of internal civil war was under way. So why burden Julie, Sir Alan or still less the foreign secretary with further doubts? What they wanted was certainty. So she had resolved, on instinct, in this moment, to give it to them.

'Christ,' Julie said. 'So it's all on the level. For sure?'

'Nothing is for sure. I told him what Mikhail had said, and he agreed that it was in line with the rumours he'd heard. That is as good as we're going to get.'

'What will you tell London?'

'Exactly what we agreed. I came here to Kotka to meet Sergei. It took him a few days to get across the border and I stayed out of communication because I didn't wish to compromise his security. But he made it over, I met him here for an hour – and he told us what we needed to know. We don't have to admit that I went into Russia.'

'You think it will be enough?'

'As I understand it, from Sir Alan, the issue now is mainly about removing the foreign secretary's excuses. We need to line it all up for her so she has no choice. This is the last piece of the jigsaw.'

Julie threw away her cigarette and they went inside to warm cold hands with hot coffee. 'What are you not telling me?' Julie asked.

'About what?'

'I don't know. You're holding something back. To do with Sergei, I would guess. Did what I think happened finally take place?'

Kate didn't answer. She hadn't liked lying to Julie in the first place and had no wish to compound it with further evasions, half-truths or outright falsehoods.

'You've waited long enough,' Julie went on. 'So I guess you slept with him.'

'I was followed after I got off the train,' Kate said, changing the subject. 'I managed to lose the tail in the subway, but it spooked me. Moscow is a long way from home. I weighed my options and decided my best bet was to call Stuart and ask him to drive me straight to the border.'

'And he agreed.'

'Guilt goes a long way.'

Julie shrugged. 'I'm not sure I entirely believe you, but it's your business so I'll let it go.' She looked directly into Kate's eyes. 'Just so long as you're absolutely on the level about what Sergei told you.'

'Of course I am.'

'Then why are you not meeting my gaze?'

Kate looked up into her friend's eyes. She could feel her cheeks colouring. 'There are things you don't know and don't need to. In fact, for your own sake, it's much better that you don't. It was my decision to go in there and mine alone. I knew the risks. So if there is any fallout, I'll face it alone. All you do need to be sure of is that we have little choice but to accept this defection and face the consequences. I cannot go the rest of my life knowing we allowed a cowardly set of politicians to wriggle out of the implications. If we're going to do that, we might as well all pack it in and work in the City.'

'If that speech was meant to reassure me, I should probably tell you it was a total failure.'

'I got what I needed. That's all you have to know.'

'Well, maybe,' Julie said. 'Whatever happened in there, you're an absolute fool to keep it to yourself.'

'We go back to London with one clear message, as I have outlined. Agreed?'

Julie gazed right back at her, those big green eyes full of doubt, fear, possibly even suspicion. But, eventually, she nodded. 'Agreed, boss. For better or for worse.'

They spoke little for the rest of the journey to Helsinki airport. After turning in the hire car, Kate suggested Julie contact Sir Alan and Ian to give them the basic agreed outline of what had happened and to arrange the necessary meeting with the foreign secretary so she could sneak home on their return to London.

She found Fi and Gus eating dinner with Rose at the kitchen table. They all seemed very pleased to see her.

They chatted idly for a few moments before Rose said she needed to get back to Simon and quietly slipped out. 'We missed you,' Fiona said, as soon as she'd gone. 'I mean, Rose is lovely, but we've been really looking forward to you coming home.'

It was enough to have Kate reflecting once again on the strange shifting currents of teenage emotions, but the warmth of her own response perhaps explained her spontaneous decision to share more than she'd intended. 'I saw Dad,' she said.

'My God, where?' Fiona asked.

Kate had her son's rapt attention now, too, and their evident devotion to their father touched another chord within her. 'In Moscow.'

'What were you doing there?' Gus asked.

'I had to go into Russia for work. Things didn't go quite the way I'd planned, so I had some time on my hands. I called Dad and we agreed to meet up.'

'Where?' Fi asked.

'I went to his flat in Moscow, which is, in all honesty, a very depressing place. It's tiny, cramped, soulless and on the umpteenth floor of a grim Soviet apartment block.'

Gus was staring at the table, as if he was about to burst into tears. But Fiona could sense her mother had more to impart.

'I don't want you to get your hopes up unduly, but it was clear to me that this was not a reasonable way to go on for any of us.'

'What do you mean?' Gus asked.

'You miss him. If I'm completely honest, I miss him, too. And he's miserable.'

There was a stunned silence as the pair absorbed the implications of this. 'So what are you saying?' Fiona asked eventually.

'That, in the first instance, I want to get him out of that terrible place to somewhere he can be much happier and you – *we* – can visit him.'

'Like where?'

'He suggested France.'

There was another silence as they registered what she'd said. Kate got up and went to get a glass of wine. There was half of an open bottle of rosé in the fridge, so she helped herself and returned to the table.

'Where in France?' Fiona asked.

'That's up to him. Somewhere he can get a job and make a life for himself – and that's easy to reach from London.'

'So we could visit him, like, every weekend?' Gus said.

'I think every weekend would be stretching our resources a bit thin now. He doesn't have a job and may struggle to find one. He doesn't speak much French, so far as I know. But every other weekend, perhaps.'

'You said "we",' Fiona chipped in.

'Like I said, I miss him, too.'

Fiona and Gus looked at each other, bewildered, their hopes and fears fighting for traction. 'Are you going to get back together?' Gus asked.

Kate worried that she had gone too far – much too far. But seeing the hope in his eyes – and perhaps it was, after all, only a reflection of her own – she didn't quite have the courage, or will, to row back. 'I'd rather not say that, because the truth is I don't know. I think it's unlikely. His betrayal hurt terribly and I'm not sure I can ever feel the way I did before.' She gulped some wine. 'But I miss him. I'd like to see him – not as a wife, or partner in the first instance, but certainly

as your mother. I think we can find our way back to friendship. I don't know yet whether more than that is possible.'

'But the door is open?' Fiona asked.

Kate hesitated. Was it? Was that really true? 'Yes,' she said.
'It might be.'

As soon as she uttered the words, Fiona burst into tears
and left the room. 'Yes,' Gus said, standing and punching
the air. 'Yes! I fucking knew it.'

'Language,' Kate said, though she was struggling to wipe
the smile from her face.

She followed Fiona upstairs and knocked softly on her
bedroom door. 'Not now,' her daughter replied, but Kate
thought that, for once, she could probably get away with
ignoring her. She slipped in quietly and sat beside Fiona on
the bed. 'It's all right, Mum.'

Kate put a hand on her shoulder. 'I'm sorry, my love,' Kate
said.

'For what? There's nothing to be sorry for.' Fiona straightened, wiped her eyes with the sleeve of her baggy sweater.
'You have no idea how much Gus and I have prayed to hear
those words.' She looked at her mother. 'I hope you meant it.
Neither of us could take being let down again.'

'I told you how I felt. That's not the same as promising
any kind of outcome. I can't say that we'll be together again
as a couple, much less that we can recreate what we had
before. But I think we can, with enough goodwill, be friends,
and that would greatly improve all our lives, wouldn't it?'

Clearly, it wasn't what Fiona wanted to hear. Like her
brother, she yearned for what they'd once possessed. 'It's
enough,' she said. 'For now. But how will it work? I thought

Dad wasn't able to stay in Europe except for very brief visits.'

Kate stood and moved towards the door. 'Dad is guilty of treason. If he ever sets foot in this country again, they'll put him on trial and he'll go to prison for a very long time. But that would also come with an avalanche of bad publicity for the Service that it would be keen to avoid. I negotiated them turning a blind eye for that trip to Venice. It's possible I could do the same for a longer period – perhaps indefinitely – so long as he agreed never to return to the UK.'

'So he can't ever come home?'

'Never.'

Fiona's gloom seemed to return at being reminded of this fundamental truth and she took to staring at her hands.

'I have to go to the office briefly,' Kate said. 'Would you mind holding the fort here with Gus?'

Fiona looked up and gave her a broad smile. 'Of course not.' And, as she walked down the stairs, Kate tried to recall the last time she had seen her daughter smile like that. A long while ago, that was for sure.

24

IT WAS JUST past eight by the time Kate reached SIS head-quarters in Vauxhall, and the third floor was deserted. She walked through to her office in the corner, switched on the desk lamp but not the overhead light and fired up her computer. She logged on, pulled up the electronic version of the Operation Sigma file and punched in the passcode.

She read through it slowly, methodically, trying to view it through fresh eyes. If Stuart was telling the truth about the relative paucity of the material he'd passed on to his handlers, that left two possibilities: either the Russians had stumbled upon Lena's presence on the yacht through luck rather than judgement, or Sergei was right and they had a much more important source than Stuart in or close to London Centre.

Kate checked through the timeline carefully once more. It was possible that someone in Athens had spotted her coming through the airport and alerted the Russians. But why would they have immediately scrambled a wet team from Moscow?

She went backwards again to the original operation to get Lena and the electronic bug on to the yacht in Istanbul. She stared at the screen. It had long troubled her that the *Empress* had departed her buoy close to the Kempinski Hotel in the middle of the night. Why would the captain have done that, unless they had been alerted to something amiss?

She pulled up the phone logs, which Suzy had attached, and tracked her own movements. After returning from Istanbul, she had entered the SIS building that day at 15.58. She had gone straight to the meeting with Ian and Sir Alan. There had been plenty of time in the course of the evening for someone to have alerted Moscow.

Kate stared out of the window into the darkness. Did she *actually* believe Stuart, or did she just *want* to believe him?

She went back to the file and continued scrolling through it. She read the coroner's report on Rav's death. Verdict: suicide.

There was no sign of foul play and no indication anyone had entered his apartment on the night he'd died.

It was a conclusion that had appeared to suit everyone, including his partner, Zac, who seemed determined to blame himself. And although Kate did not believe the verdict for a single second, she had the uncomfortable sense it might have suited her, too, as she wrestled with the collapse of her marriage.

She opened the account of Rav's movements, such as they could be determined, in Geneva in the twenty-four hours before his death. Suzy had also attached the CCTV log from a newsagent opposite the entrance to the offices of the lawyer Rav had said he was going to see. It confirmed that, whomever he had met, he had not been there.

She read Suzy's report of the events in Berlin. It ended with a simple conclusion: *On the balance of probabilities, it seems likely the Russian state security apparatus had been tipped off to expect us.*

Kate thought about the last chapter in this file, which she had no intention of writing: that somehow they'd known she was crossing into Russia to meet Sergei.

'You could say they've been expecting us at every turn,' Suzy said.

Kate spun violently around. 'Jesus, you gave me a shock.'

Suzy stood by the door, arms crossed, eyes fixed upon the file open on the computer. Her petite, slender face was much less pretty when she was angry. 'Julie said you were in Finland meeting a contact.' Kate didn't confirm or deny it. 'I don't appreciate being kept in the dark, Kate.'

'Incredibly, not everything is about you.' Kate turned back to her computer. The questions the files seemed consistently to ask were preferable to those from her subordinate.

'It would have been courteous at least to let me know you'd be gone for a few days. I've looked a total idiot.'

Kate didn't bother to answer that. She had many problems. Suzy's bruised ego wasn't one of them.

'At any rate,' Suzy said, 'it doesn't change the question those files keep on asking.'

There was a long silence. 'I just need a bit of time to think,' Kate said.

But it was going to take more than that to force Suzy to withdraw: she leant back against the filing cabinet, as if settling in for the long haul. 'Either someone is tipping them off as to your every move,' she said, 'or they're actually tracking you.'

'Perhaps they found a way to inject a microchip into me.'

'Stranger things have happened.'

Kate glanced at her. 'This is real life, Suzy, not the movies.'

'You ever consider the possibility that this has been a set-up from the very first moment?'

'Of course.'

'No, I mean, really, that they've planned every stage of it methodically: the original tip-off about the meeting on that yacht, the news that the former PM had cancer, conveniently true, the idea that the leading candidate to replace him was working for them and now, suddenly, the "proof" that it must be true in the form of a sex video.'

'You've spent too much time listening to Ian.'

'I mean, I know you have this great source and—'

'How do you know that?'

'Ian told me.'

Ah, so that was it. It shouldn't have surprised Kate that Suzy had chosen to throw in her lot with Ian. That much had surely been inevitable.

'Don't you think it feels like a classic Moscow long play?' Suzy asked. Now she was using some of Ian's favourite language as well.

'I'm tired, Suzy. Do you mind if we discuss this another time?'

'I'm just trying to help.'

No, you are not, Kate thought. 'I know,' she said. 'Thank you.'

'What did the source you went to see tell you? I'm assuming he or she was the person who tipped you off in the first place.'

'Our agent told me Mikhail's account of what has happened to his father is accurate. I'll be briefing the foreign secretary to that effect in the morning.'

Suzy gave her a thin smile. 'I guess it's your call.'

She slipped away into the darkness. And it was all Kate could do to stop herself punching her computer. But she couldn't quite persuade herself to log off and go home. She stared at those pictures of the *Empress* leaving the quay in Istanbul in the middle of the night. Who had known enough to warn them? Sir Alan, Ian, Julie, Danny. That was it.

But only Julie could conceivably have tipped off the Russians about her trip to see Sergei.

Unless Sir Alan had guessed what she was intending to do.

Kate got up and went down to Operations, where Danny was on the night watch. He had his feet on the desk, a cup of tea resting on his chest. 'Here comes trouble,' he said easily.

'You here on your own?'

'No, I have someone from GCHQ on attachment. I sent him to get us a takeaway. From north London.'

Danny was idly flicking a pound coin with his thumb and forefinger. Kate sat and watched him. 'Did you and Rav always cheat at Spoof?' she asked.

Danny flipped the coin once more. 'Of course.' It was something of a field tradition that operational staff always played Spoof – a game in which you have to guess the number of coins people have in their hands – for the dinner bill.

The first time she, Danny and Rav had worked together, on a trip to Turkey, northern Syria and then Mosul, Kate had lost almost every time. 'Why do you ask?'

'I was just thinking about it the other day. How did you do it?'

'Secrets of the subordinates, Kate. I'm not telling you that.'

'Whose idea was the laundry trolley?'

He smiled at the memory. 'Rav's.'

On the last night of what had been a long, arduous and dangerous trip, Kate had accused them of cheating at Spoof and left them to pay the bill in an Istanbul restaurant. They'd blocked the exit of the restaurant until the owner got angry and then they'd bombarded her with calls when she got back to her room. When she finally switched off her mobile and unplugged the hotel phone from the wall, they'd persuaded the porter to open her door, then bundled her into a laundry basket and wheeled her around the hotel. 'God, I miss him,' she said.

'Me too.'

'You were a nightmare together.'

Danny flicked the coin one last time, caught it in his palm and bunched his fist. He sighed heavily. He'd frequently called Rav a blood-brother and claimed him as the family he'd never had.

'Could I ask you a favour?' Kate said.

'Depends what it is.'

'I need some internal phone logs.' Kate gave him the date and then a piece of paper with the names she wanted checked. He almost spat out his tea. 'You're joking?'

'Not exactly, no.'

The laughter lines around his eyes had disappeared. 'I can't start rooting around in the chief's phone records.'

'I just need to rule him out of something.'

'You know we're all officially suspects, right? A team from Five came to my apartment last night.'

'Yes, I do know.'

Danny stared at the sheet before him for a long time, as if it would make the problem miraculously disappear. With a frustrated grunt, he logged on to the computer beside him and went hunting for what she had requested. She watched as the electronic dots darted around the screen before him. 'In the office until eight p.m. Then at home in Pimlico.' He closed in on the screen. 'No activity at all there until the phone goes off at eleven p.m.'

'How about Julie?'

'Are you really going to do this, Kate?'

'I have to.'

He checked Julie next. The screen remained blank all night. 'Phone off.' Kate nodded. 'Who next?'

'Ian.' He pulled up the log. 'Busy between five and six,' he said, 'something going on.' The dot on the screen clearly located Ian in his office.

'Then . . .' The dot moved across London now and Danny closed in on its final destination. 'Chelsea . . . That's home, right?'

'Frith Street, yes.'

'Okay, yeah, so home. One more burst of communication at nine p.m., then phone off.' Danny turned to her. 'You haven't asked for my phone log.' There was a strange glint in his eye. He was smiling knowingly at someone over Kate's shoulder.

She whipped around to see Julie's departing wisps of auburn hair. She turned back. 'Another complication.'

'What kind?'

'Anything going on between you and Julie? I know that look.'

'No!'

'Are you sure?'

'I think I'm entitled to say it's none of your business.'

'She's only just broken off with Ian.'

'Nothing's going on.'

'I'm not going to ask if you know what you're doing.' She smiled at him and stood. 'Thanks for your help.'

'Remember me when I've been sacked,' he said.

She'd got almost to the door before she had a final thought. She turned back. 'Could you just do one other thing? How about the logs of Rav's phone for the weekend before his death?'

Danny pulled them up. Rav's phone was consistently located at his home on Sunday, but it was switched off all day on Saturday. 'That's . . . odd,' Kate said.

Danny nodded. 'I guess so.'

'Why would he have his phone switched off all day?' she asked.

He shrugged. 'Maybe he just wanted some peace. Maybe he had another phone.'

Kate thanked him again and went to get her bag from the office. She ran out into the rain and caught a taxi to the Fulham townhouse that Rav's former partner, Zac, shared with his wife. They and their children were gathered around the kitchen table, a picture of familial warmth in a pool of light on this dreary night. She almost lost her nerve, but she rang the bell before she could change her mind. Zac came to answer and the expression on his handsome, youthful, slender face moved from neutral curiosity to visceral hate. 'You,' he said.

'I'm so sorry to trouble you, Zac.'

'I have nothing to say to you.'

'I don't blame you. But there's just something I really need to ask.'

She had expected him to slam the door in her face, but he held his temper. 'What?' he asked.

'Would you mind if I came in?'

He stepped back to allow her inside. He ducked his head into the kitchen to explain to his family that he would be a few moments and led her through to his study at the back of the house.

It was a wood and glass addition, which stretched out into the garden. It might have been bleak and dark on that gloomy, rainy night, but it had been decorated with the same refined but austere flair as the rest of the house. Kate took in the photographs of their ideal family, which appeared to cover every tiny scrap of available space. There were no photographs of his dead boyfriend.

Zac closed the door and sat opposite. A picture of his wife in a swimsuit in what looked like the South of France loomed over his shoulder. He did not seem to be conscious of the incongruity. 'What do you want?' He had long, feminine eyelashes and brooding dark brown eyes. But petulance didn't suit him.

'I'm really sorry,' she said again.

'You can't ever be sorry enough.'

There were so many things Kate could have replied to this, not least that no one had forced Zac to return to his wife and shatter her old friend. But what was the point? 'I'll make this quick,' she said.

'Good.'

'We're still looking into various issues relating to Rav's death.'

'Like what?'

Kate was trying not to be put off her stride by his hostility. 'He was murdered, as you know.'

'The coroner found no evidence of that.'

'The fact that there was no evidence doesn't change the reality that it is the most likely explanation for his death.' Zac breathed in deeply. 'He may have been upset with you,' she went on, 'and me, for that matter, since I should never have told him you'd been staying back here with your wife. But that wasn't why he died. He did not kill himself. Rav would never have done that.'

Zac shook his head. 'I've been through this with the police, with MI5, with your people. And I'm sick of it. He's dead. He's still dead. And the hows and the whys just don't matter to me any more. I'm trying to move on.'

'I understand that. I have only one question. What was he doing on the Saturday before he died? His phone was off all day.'

'I told the police that.'

'Would you mind explaining it to me, too, and then I can leave you in peace?'

Zac stared at the floor. Kate glanced around the room again. Rav's absence here was quietly devastating, as if he had been airbrushed from existence. Zac looked up and seemed to divine the direction of her thoughts. 'I can't,' he said. 'I just can't. She'd kill me.'

'I understand.'

'I used to have a picture of him on my desk, but it upset my eldest son and . . .' He stared at his hands. 'I'm sorry . . . My God . . .'

He started, very quietly, to sob. Kate didn't know what to do. She stood and moved to comfort him but he raised a hand to prevent her. She watched as he brusquely wiped the tears from his cheeks. 'I'm sorry,' she whispered.

'There's nothing to be sorry about. Look, there isn't much to say. I did see him. He was very angry with me when I got back to the apartment on that Friday night, as he had every right to be. We argued. I came here. The next morning he was waiting when I went out to get a newspaper. He was regretful, tearful. He begged me to have a coffee with him. We went to a café just up there on Fulham Broadway.'

'What did you discuss?'

'He said he understood that I was conflicted, uncertain. I told him I didn't know what to think. I was confused. I loved him. I told him I always would, but I didn't want to abandon and let down my family, not just Emily but the kids . . . I was all over the place. He was actually incredibly thoughtful and kind, as you would expect. He kept saying he understood and would support me – be my friend – whatever I decided . . .'

Zac was still wrestling to hold back the tears. Kate waited until he had regained control of himself. 'Do you know what he did for the rest of the day?'

He seemed confused. 'No. We hugged in the door of the café. I said I needed some time, space. He said he'd always love me and then he was gone. That was the last I saw or heard of him.'

'He didn't say what he was planning to do?'

'He said he was driving to the West Country. He'd been trying to track down a former school master there.'

'At Sherborne?'

'I don't know. It was the place the prime minister went to school.'

'He was still investigating him?'

'Not him. The other one, your boss, Sir Alan whatever his name is.' Kate gasped. 'Are you all right?' he asked.

'I don't understand.'

'What?'

'It's just . . . How can you be so sure that it was Sir Alan he was investigating?'

'He was a bit obsessed with him. I told him it wasn't a very good career-development strategy.'

'What do you mean he was obsessed with him?'

'He was always asking me about public-school friendship.'

'In what way?'

'He had this conviction that there was no way you could become best friends in an experience as prolonged and intense as boarding school – based on my descriptions of it, though Eton is a bit different in various ways – and suddenly not be friends years later. He kept on referring to it as an unbreakable bond. He had tracked down the house-master and said he was going to talk to him about Sir Alan and his friendship with the prime minister . . . Are you all right? You really don't look well.'

Kate insisted she was absolutely fine. She thanked him and left. She caught an Uber and asked it to stop about half a mile from home. She needed to clear her head.

It had started to drizzle. She stood for a moment in the darkness and let the cool water land on her cheeks, then run in tiny rivulets down her neck.

The same thoughts circled in her head until she felt dizzy.

Was Stuart telling the truth?

What had prompted Rav to become fixated on investigating Sir Alan's past?

She walked for a while, then stopped beneath the shelter of a beech as the rain thickened. She watched it thump on to the pavement beside her. It reminded her of all those childhood days when she had sat in the kitchen with her father, waiting for the rain to cease so she could go out and climb the beech at the end of the garden.

How she yearned now for the comforting and warm certainty of his love, for his ability to magnify her hopes and banish her fears. She closed her eyes and could almost feel his arms around her, the roughness of his bristles on her cheek and the comforting smell of his aftershave.

God, she felt alone. Why had she told the children she could be friends with Stuart again, that it might work, implied that she would even consider welcoming him into the marital bed as her lover? She must have taken leave of her senses. 'Get a grip, girl,' she muttered, under her breath.

She straightened, heading home to what was left of the bottle of rosé – or perhaps open a second – and another hefty dose of sleeping pills.

She would have downed both at the double, but Fiona was waiting for her at the kitchen table, her bright face shining with newly found contentment. 'I spoke to Dad!'

'Great!' Kate said, without thinking, as she headed for the fridge. She found she'd all but finished the half-drunk bottle earlier and fetched another from the cupboard. She filled a glass with ice and sat opposite Fiona.

'Are you all right, Mum?'

'I'm fine.'

'You're drinking a lot and you don't look well.'

'Work is complicated,' she said. But not nearly as difficult as life, she felt like adding.

'We got out a map and everything. He's keen on the Dordogne in France. Far enough south to be a bit warmer – which would be great – but near enough to make it possible to drive, if we wanted to. We looked up flights and Gus and I reckon we can easily get to Bergerac, or maybe Bordeaux.'

'That's good news.'

'He's not sure what he's going to do for work. He said he reckons he'll have to think outside the box about that.'

'Would it not be easier to go to Paris? Dad is very bright and I am fairly certain he'd find work there.'

'He likes the idea of somewhere warmer. So do we. He said there's a lot of English people in the Dordogne and they even play cricket there, so Gus was super-excited about that.'

Kate washed down two sleeping pills with a slug of wine. 'Roll on the future,' she said, with as much sincerity as she could muster.

'Do you take those every night?' Fiona asked.

'Erm . . . not every night, no.'

'Honestly?'

'All right, too often, yes.'

'I know you're worried about me, but it's yourself you need to be paying attention to.'

Sometimes Fiona was capable of wisdom well beyond her years, Kate thought. 'You're right,' she said. 'But I can't think about it right now.'

She finished her wine, kissed her daughter and left her nursing a cup of tea at the kitchen table as she went up to bed. For once, she was asleep almost the moment her head hit the pillow.

25

AS ALMOST EVERYONE who has ever had even mild insomnia will attest, four hours' pill-induced sleep is not enough. Watching the dawn light creep through the shutters and across the kitchen table several hours after she had risen, Kate had quietly promised herself that, as soon as Mikhail and his father were safely brought into the UK, she would request time off work and make a concerted attempt to sort herself out. She had grasped that her job was breaking her. And that, in turn, might have influenced her decision to keep the morning's rendezvous with the foreign secretary simple.

With Sir Alan's wife now hovering between life and death, the meeting took place in the kitchen of his Pimlico home, one floor beneath the bedroom in which Alice was being nursed night and day. That lent the proceedings a surreal and distinctly uncomfortable air, which, it was clear, none of them was immune to. The foreign secretary, Meg Simpson, arrived last and didn't bother to take off her long, fawn rain-coat, as if she were going to run at the first hint of news she didn't want to hear. She took a seat opposite her permanent secretary, a strikingly young-looking man with wavy blond hair and a bright tie. He must have been forty, but looked twenty-five at most.

Opposite him sat Ian and Kate. Sir Alan was at the end of the table, beneath an enormous watercolour of a Cairo street market. Kate recognized, but could not quite recall, the artist. As in so much of the rest of his life, Sir Alan had exquisite taste in art.

'I'm very sorry to force you to meet like this,' Meg Simpson said. 'Kate, you take the floor.' Like the rest of them, Sir Alan had no wish to extend the meeting a second longer than was necessary.

'You asked for more evidence,' Kate said, facing the foreign secretary, 'so I activated a source whom I believe to be completely reliable. At considerable personal risk, he agreed to travel out of Russia to meet me near Helsinki in Finland. We talked for about an hour and he confirmed, in essence, what Mikhail, Igor's son, told me in both Venice and Berlin.'

'What do you mean, "in essence"?' Simpson asked.

'He was honest about what he didn't know. He couldn't be certain of exactly what had happened in terms of the internal dynamics of the very top tier of individuals close to the Kremlin. But he confirmed that Vasily Durov and Igor Borodin were under house arrest and that the widely held view was that the Kremlin had concluded both they and the SVR in general were becoming too arrogant and over-mighty.' Kate stared at the spotless oak table before her.

'So he confirmed the GRU had been engaged in some kind of coup against its rivals in the SVR?' Simpson asked.

'Yes.' This lie was coming harder than she'd imagined. Kate studied her hands. There was a long silence. She finally looked up and watched the faces around her. A grim group they assuredly were. Surprisingly – or maybe not, given the relentless nature of his ambition – Ian was the first to break ranks. 'This really leaves us with no choice, Foreign Secretary. I've had my reservations. You know that. But this is crystal clear: a reliable agent, talking to one of our most experienced and able officers. We have no choice but to pursue this to its logical conclusion now.'

Simpson gave him a withering stare, but he didn't back down. If this was to go ahead and ruin a prime minister, he wanted to own it. 'My advice is that we must proceed with all due speed.' *My* advice. He made it sound like the most weighty and significant thing in the world. Meanwhile, Sir Alan gazed out of the window.

'It doesn't assuage any of my doubts,' Simpson said. She was visibly squirming now. She'd taken her glasses from around her neck and was tapping them nervously against her knee.

They waited her out. 'If the video is fake, the ramifications are horrific. Your source can't verify it, can he?'

Ian had rolled up his sleeves. He leant forward, elbows on the table, intent on taking control of the meeting now. 'The truth is we have done all we can, Foreign Secretary.' He gestured towards Kate. 'Kate has done a frankly amazing job, which we should all acknowledge. If there is an inquiry . . .' He let that hang. It was his standard way of cornering politicians. '. . . then we will be required to show that we acted at every turn in good faith. This looks like due diligence to me.'

'I am fully cognizant of the possibility of an inquiry into all aspects of my work at any point, now or in the future,' Simpson said acidly.

'I understand that, Foreign Secretary, but this is surely about the balance of risk. Because of Kate's good work . . .' My God, she thought, he's laying this on thick. He was making sure the blame game was well advanced if subsequently it all went wrong. '. . . we can characterize with confidence the worst that can happen.'

'Which is?'

'You are completely right about the video. As we have discussed before, there is the real possibility that it is a "deep" fake and that the financial information they say they are going to provide will prove to be a long and misleading trail to nowhere. But if we conclude they are misleading us, we have a choice: simply to let them be and ignore them or throw them out.'

'Except they will have hired the most expensive lawyers in the country to make that impossible,' the permanent secretary said. He had a very deep, steely voice.

'All right. The worst that can happen is they get an unwarranted passage to freedom and security in the West. Not ideal, but they're hardly public figures. Who is ever going to know?'

'Are you familiar with British politics and our press?' the permanent secretary shot back.

That seemed to silence the room. Simpson had taken to staring out of the window too. 'This is so fraught with risk and complication,' she said, 'that every political instinct I have rebels against giving the go-ahead.'

'Perhaps you should pay attention to them,' her permanent secretary muttered to her.

'But you leave me no choice.' She looked at Ian. 'As you have so helpfully pointed out, any subsequent inquiry will make inaction look like cover-up, or worse.'

'Are you sure?' the permanent secretary asked.

'Sadly, yes.' She stood, looking squarely at Kate. 'I hope to God you know what you're doing.'

Simpson and her permanent secretary walked out, leaving Kate with Ian and the chief. Sir Alan hadn't said a word. 'You want coffee?' he asked eventually.

'I'm fine,' Kate said.

Ian declined. 'How much longer?' he asked Sir Alan softly.

'A day. Two. Three. Soon, in any event.'

'I am so sorry.' It was said with quiet sincerity.

'I'm going to have to leave it to you both,' Sir Alan said. 'I know it's a lot to ask, and in normal circumstances I'd be with you in the trench, but I can no longer pretend that we're in anything but the very final chapter.'

'We can handle it,' Ian said confidently. 'There's no reason to think it will be anything but straightforward.'

'Nothing like this is ever straightforward.'

'I understand that. But we'll do our best.'

They left him to the gloom of his thoughts and circumstances. Kate found herself dwelling on how she would feel if she were told Stuart had terminal cancer and only weeks to live. It was hard to keep conversation with Ian going as he started to try to discuss every aspect of the operation. He had a spring in his step and she found it difficult to work out exactly why. Was it his chance to prove himself to Meg Simpson, or had he some other outcome in mind?

Suzy and Julie were waiting in the office and Kate briefed them on the decision that had been taken. Suzy appeared thrilled until Kate told her that she would have to remain in London. She argued about it until Kate put her foot down, at which she retreated into a barely disguised sulk.

Julie slipped out with her. Kate closed her door and sat with her back to it, eyes shut as she tried to still her thumping heart. The pain in her stomach and central back had grown in intensity again. She felt about a hundred years old.

Ian had made clear he was going to run the operation and had already insisted on deploying himself to Tbilisi with her, but Mikhail was her contact, so there was plenty for her to work through. She took out her phone and sent him a message, using Signal this time, as all staff were advised to do from time to time: *Green light. We will arrive in Tbilisi tomorrow.*

She got a reply in seconds. *Good.*

Kate logged on to her computer. She started researching Kazbegi, deep in the Caucasian mountains, where Mikhail had indicated his father would cross the border. She had lost herself in the task when Julie burst in. 'Have you seen?'

'What now?'

'Go to the ITV website. Someone's leaked it.'

'Leaked what?' Kate asked, in exasperation, but Julie didn't dare answer and, as soon as she pulled up the site, Kate could see why. She stared at the headline, as if it belonged to a different world entirely: *Russian Defector Offers MI6 Sex Video Evidence PM Is Moscow Spy.*

Kate stood, physically backing away from the screen. 'I'm counting down to your phone erupting,' Julie said.

Kate was hardly able to grasp what had happened. How long ago had she left the meeting? Half an hour? Forty minutes, at most. Who could possibly have picked up the phone to the media? The foreign secretary? No, surely not: this seemed destined to end her career within minutes. Her permanent secretary? But what could conceivably be his motive? 'Who in the hell . . .' Her voice trailed off.

'Ian.'

'What?'

'Of course. Every which way he wins. He tips off the PM. He tips off the press. Then he tells the PM's people the leak came from the foreign secretary's office. She is screwed, Sir Alan is embarrassed, the PM is grateful.'

Kate shook her head. 'Even he isn't that brazen.'

'Of course he bloody is! Can you think of anyone else with the sheer brass neck to do something like this within an hour of your meeting?'

Kate didn't have time to give this a lot of thought. Her phone rang. It turned out to be the Downing Street switchboard. 'Mrs Henderson, I have the prime minister for you.' Kate waited, her heart thumping.

'Good afternoon, Mrs Henderson,' he said. 'May I politely ask what the fucking hell is going on down there in Vauxhall?'

'Prime Minister—'

'I'm not going to trouble your chief. I'm aware his wife is dying and I've known him long enough to be sure this isn't his doing. With my next call, I intend to unceremoniously fire the foreign secretary for gross incompetence, not to say disgraceful disloyalty. So I'm going to need someone to offer me an explanation. And I have a hunch that person is you.'

'Prime Minister—'

'Get your pretty little backside in here right now. I'm in my office at the Commons. I'll expect you within ten minutes.' He ended the phone call. If you could slam down a mobile phone, it had sounded as though he had certainly done so. 'Who was that?' Julie asked.

'The PM.'

'Holy shit.'

Kate sat down. She closed her eyes, tried to gather herself. 'I have to go,' she said. Julie didn't dispute it. 'I have to go,' she repeated.

'I know!'

Kate got up, pulled on her coat, slung her bag over her shoulder and walked through the outer office. Suzy was nowhere to be seen, but Maddy stood in front of the TV screen, transfixed. It was tuned to Sky News and the strap at the bottom read: 'Foreign Secretary Fired Over Fake Sex Video'. News moved so fast these days.

26

KATE WAS GRATEFUL for the fresh air and decided to walk up to the House of Commons. Streaks of morning sunlight cut through the bank of dark cloud and gave the Mother of Parliaments a golden hue. She crossed Lambeth Bridge, slipped across Victoria Gardens and went through security like any other visitor before making her way to Central Lobby.

A taciturn but pretty young woman with straight black hair came to meet her and escorted her to the prime minister's office behind the Speaker's chair. 'I don't know what the hell you people are playing at down there,' she muttered. Kate wondered again at the supreme – and annoying – self-confidence young special advisers attached to Downing Street were wont to exude, as if they had just inherited the earth.

The prime minister rose from behind his desk as she entered and guided her to a seat in the deep green chair by the door. He didn't bother to offer her tea or coffee. 'Well?' He sank on to the wide sofa opposite.

He ran a hand through his dishevelled hair as his special adviser curled up on the sofa opposite, long legs and short enough skirt just revealing the tops of lace stockings. She hadn't offered her name. 'You asked to see me, Prime Minister,' Kate said, glancing at all the weighty tomes lining the bookshelves in the old-fashioned wood-panelled room. Kate thought of the much greater men and women who had occupied the office before him. How had it come to this?

'Of course I asked to bloody see you.'

Kate wasn't going to make this easy for him. If her career was to expire, as seemed likely, if not frankly inevitable, it was only reasonable to derive some enjoyment from its dying embers. She waited. So did he, but not for long. He could barely contain his rage and it was the first time she had ever really witnessed it. His temper was legendary. 'Well, are you going to offer me an explanation or not?'

'Of what, Prime Minister?'

'Are you totally deranged?' the PM said, as his special adviser glared at Kate, shifting in her seat, so that her skirt rode up another notch. He surely couldn't be having an affair with her as well, she wondered idly.

Kate thought of that terrible video. Real or fake, true or false? So much seemed to ride on her judgement, her instincts. Had she believed in its credibility because she thought the character of the man she'd seen in it matched exactly that of the one before her? 'We've been trying to do our duty,' she said quietly.

'Don't be absurd,' the special adviser spat at her.

The PM leant forward, elbows on knees, so his eyes seemed hooded and brooding as he awaited an answer. Kate thought he was ageing rapidly. 'The former leader of the Russian SVR, Moscow's equivalent to SIS—'

'Yes, yes, I know what the bloody SVR is by now, for God's sake. That's something you have achieved in your determination to give yourself a starring role in my life story.'

'He offered to defect.'

The PM just stared at her. *'And?'*

'There appears to have been some kind of coup at the heart of the Kremlin. It is incredibly unusual – not to say unheard-of – for such a senior official to offer himself to us. He'd bring with him a treasure trove of material on all aspects of their operations in the UK and everywhere else in the world. It was our judgement, and that of the foreign secretary, that it was an offer we had to explore.'

'What does this fellow want?'

'Asylum.'

'So, do you want to explain to me how ITV has this story today and what it is about?'

'The man in question, Igor Borodin, has been one of the most influential intelligence figures in Russia for the last decade or more. I have been dealing with his son. It was he who first approached me to explain what had happened in Moscow and to offer his father's services in return for asylum for his immediate family.'

'And?' The PM still looked as if he was about to explode, puffing out his cheeks nervously.

'Among other things, they said that you had been recruited into their service many years ago while you were serving as an army officer in Kosovo. The son, Mikhail, played me a video that purported to show you having sex with three underage girls.'

The PM looked as if he was ready to leap up from his seat and throttle her. 'And you believed this disgusting codswallop?' The special adviser had uncurled herself and sat upright on the sofa, the colour drained from her face.

'The video was incredibly convincing. Now, it's possible that it's what we would call a "deep fake". Because motion-capture technology and AI are so advanced, it's possible, for example, to have a public figure say and do things that never actually happened. But there is no way of assessing that until we can get the video back into our labs to test it in the most thorough possible way.'

'You're talking, Mrs Henderson, as if I'm not here. Unless I'm mistaken, this grotesque fake is of *me*.'

She looked at him steadily. 'I understand why you're so upset and angry, Prime Minister—'

'Angry? I'm bloody livid!'

'I understand that. And, in your shoes, I would feel the same. I am merely trying to explain the reality of the situation we found ourselves in as dispassionately as I can.'

'And you and your colleagues, in your wisdom, decided to take this seriously?'

'There are many factors here. We could possibly have chosen to ignore the video—'

'God's blood, it's not of me!'

'—purporting to be of you, and all the other evidence, which they suggest they would bring with them, including detail of the many financial payments made over the years.' He was shaking his head now. 'But, ultimately, none of these things was material. The crucial fact is that an offer to defect of this kind is a priceless intelligence jewel. We had to pursue it.'

'Without my knowledge?'

'The foreign secretary was fully informed.'

His eyes bored into her. 'In all honesty, that is not the kind of mealy-mouthed crap I expected of you.'

'I'm sorry to disappoint you, Prime Minister.'

'And neither is that! For God's sake, Kate. I thought you were a good egg. Is this your friend Imogen Conrad's doing?'

'She's not my friend.'

'You could have fooled me.'

'You may recall she had an affair with my husband.'

He shrugged. 'Fair enough.' He got up and paced behind his desk. He picked up a squidgy stress ball and pumped it hard in his fingers.

His special adviser had curled herself up again. 'No one will believe it,' she purred soothingly. 'You've wanted to get rid of Meg for an age.'

'She's never coming back. Never! Bloody bitch.'

Kate's experience of government at the highest level had been of such exaggerated formality that the Prime Minister's relentless foul mouth was a shock, if not necessarily a surprise. It made her reflect on just how well he hid his true nature behind that easy-going affable exterior. 'You know what the worst of it is?' He was looking at Kate, waiting for an answer.

'There are quite a few aspects of this that would qualify as "the worst of it", Prime Minister.'

'All right, drop the "Prime Minister" crap. It's not very authentic.' He leant back against his desk, tossing the stress ball into the air and catching it. 'The worst of it is that I sense you believed it. You thought it was true.' He picked up two more balls from his desk and started to juggle. He was rather good at it.

'Believing what you see is a basic human instinct. But I'd like to think I'm smarter than that. It wasn't my job to form a view either way on the video.' Kate reflected as she spoke that she had, which had perhaps been a mistake. 'In the end, for us, it was simple: we couldn't turn down this kind of offer. Everything else is incidental.'

'Not for me it isn't.'

'Look, I'm extremely sorry about this leak. I don't know what happened. It occurred within an hour of our meeting with the foreign secretary this morning and the fact that it happened is absolutely inexplicable to me.'

'I doubt that. And, if so, you don't spend enough time around politicians.'

'I don't see how Meg Simpson benefits—'

'A safe pair of hands if I fall.' He put down the stress balls. 'Surely even you can see that.'

'I don't think Meg Simpson leaked this.'

'Really? She's not as cosy as she looks.'

He came to sit opposite her again, landing with a thump. 'All right, Mrs Henderson, let me tell you this. We're going ahead with your operation. We'll accept Igor Whatever-His-Bloody-Name-Is into this country with open arms. And we'll expose exactly what our friends in the Kremlin have been up to.'

Kate stared at him. If he had a reputation for being unpredictable, she sure as hell had not expected that.

'You look shocked,' he said.

'It wasn't entirely the outcome I expected.'

'Exactly. Because your world view is unfortunately limited enough to conflate those men who enjoy the company of women too much with those who seek to abuse them.'

Kate could feel her cheeks reddening. In his case, that was indeed exactly what she had done.

'I hereby authorize you to do whatever you see fit to expedite this defection. But do it quickly. I intend to brief the press in full as soon as this man is in the country and we have established to your satisfaction that what he has to offer is as fake as the Hitler diaries.' He returned to his desk and took a seat beyond it. 'You are dismissed!'

Kate got up and walked out. The special adviser led her down the long corridor beside the Commons chamber. 'You didn't expect that, did you?' she said. 'You people aren't nearly as smart as you think. I love the way he outmanoeuvres you.'

It was all Kate could do to refrain from punching her. 'I can find my way from here,' she said icily.

'I need to see you out.'

'I can manage, thank you.'

The woman turned away in irritation and Kate marched on towards Central Lobby. But there was one more surprise in store for her on a day that had already held too many. Imogen Conrad stood waiting. 'They said you were here,' she said, without any other form of greeting.

Kate didn't break her stride and Imogen fell into step with her as she swung right towards the entrance.

'I've just had a text from the PM, asking me in. What the hell is going on?'

'I really can't talk about it.'

'Come on, Kate, for God's sake . . .'

'If he's texted you, perhaps it would be an idea to go and see him.'

Imogen took Kate's arm and brought her up abruptly. They were close together. And, not for the first time, Imogen's olive skin, full lips and wide eyes annoyed her: she was too damned pretty for her own – or anyone else's – good. 'Is he going to offer me the job?'

'How on earth would I know?'

'Did he talk about it?'

'No.'

'But you were in seeing him, right?'

'I can't talk about it.'

'Well, if I'm about to become your boss, I can instruct you to do so.'

'Once you do become my boss, you can call the chief, or one of his deputies, and request a formal briefing on any subject you like. But in the meantime the answer is no comment.' Kate started to walk away.

'You are absolutely infuriating,' Imogen threw after her, but without much conviction, and it occurred to Kate that one of her friend's – if you could call her that – more redeeming features was her utter imperviousness to all criticism or insult.

She burst out of the House of Commons, wove through the tourists outside and marched away down Millbank with grim purpose. She had no idea what to think. The operation had been green-lit and Imogen was about to be made her direct boss. You simply couldn't make it up. She took out her phone and glanced at a news alert. Below the item about the 'so-called sex video' and of the foreign secretary's departure there was a report that the US president had cancelled a state visit to Denmark because it wouldn't sell him Greenland.

The world was laughing at her.

Imogen Conrad had been formally appointed foreign secretary by the time Kate returned to the office and she had already given up being shocked: one politician mired in scandal over a sex video appointing another formerly mired in scandal over a sex video. Perhaps they would make one together.

Kate gathered together Julie and Suzy. She called Ian, who practically ran down the corridor. '*What* is going on?' he said, as he burst in, which more or less confirmed her – or, at least, Julie's – suspicion that he must have been the cause of the leak.

'I've just been summoned to see the prime minister.'

Ian looked put out. 'Kate, it really isn't your place to—'

'He wasn't handing out gold stars, Ian.' Kate was enjoying the sense of being at the end of her tether and felt better than she had for a long time. At some point on the walk back, she realized, she had taken the decision to resign from the Service in search of a quieter life once this was over. The relief made her feel light-headed. 'He has authorized the operation.'

There was a stunned silence. 'He did *what*?' Julie asked.

'He said the sex video is a fake and he now has to prove it.'

Ian was ahead of the others. He had a superhuman ability to sniff out the political ramifications in all things. 'He'll say it's fake anyway.'

'What do you mean?' Suzy asked.

'If we bring Igor in, the PM will insist the video is examined by experts he appoints and they will conclude it's a fake. He'll come out looking like the victim of a wicked plot, not the wretched traitor he may very well be.'

This was injudicious, for Ian, and Kate saw the surprise in Julie's eyes in particular.

'It's a trap,' Suzy said.

'Of course it is,' Ian said. 'But we still have all the cards. We'll have Igor. We'll have the video and evidence of the payments he's been receiving. If Downing Street wants to play games with this, they've chosen the wrong people. Game on.' He nodded at them with schoolboy enthusiasm and strode away down the corridor. Suzy went after him. Julie and Kate watched them go.

'What's got into him?' Julie asked.

'I don't know,' Kate said. And it was true. Ian's conversion to their cause was perhaps the most worrying turn of all.

27

THE AIR FRANCE flight banked smoothly and straightened as it followed the course of the Mtkvari River on its way into Tbilisi, the ancient Georgian capital that had served for so many centuries as the crossroads between East and West and gateway to the Caucasus and Central Asia.

By the time they disembarked, the sky was a rich dark red beyond an old Russian Tupolev plane silhouetted on the far side of the runway. There was a newer Boeing 747, too, painted white, with 'Cargo' emblazoned in bright orange on its side. It looked like some kind of rendition flight. Perhaps, Kate thought, that was appropriate under the circumstances, though the Service certainly didn't run to hiring a Boeing to fly out a defector.

The old Soviet terminal was banished behind a barbed-wire fence across the apron, so they were bussed to the shiny new gateway to Georgia, which looked like a couple of stacked pancakes. There was nothing but gambling ads for casinos in the baggage waiting area, but immigration was painless – a country that actually welcomes visitors, Kate reflected – and their bags arrived swiftly enough to have them in the car Suzy had organized from the hotel within minutes.

Their driver was a big, burly man, probably younger than he looked. Ian immediately engaged him in fluent Georgian, which he insisted on answering in English, to Ian's visible irritation. He launched into an unstoppable tirade on the greatness of his nation, its friendly people, its varied landscape – 'Visitors say Georgia has everything, why would you ever leave?' – and its courage: 'We are very, very old country,' he said. 'We protect our lands against Turkish people, Iranian people. Many times. Many times.'

They were packed into a new minivan, but he insisted on trying to drive it like a Ferrari, so Kate attempted to distract him by asking where he was from. 'Kakheti,' he said. 'Georgia best wine-growing region.' It turned out he had been brought up and schooled in the dying days of the old Soviet Union and, like many men and women of his generation, he had mixed feelings about their former Russian overlords. On one level, he was irritated by their continued interference in Georgian affairs, but on another he recognized the value of Russian tourists and was fighting a losing battle to persuade his children to learn the language. 'French, German, Spanish, English, of course. They would rather learn anything but Russian.'

After that, he couldn't be stopped. He talked about his love of rugby, but mostly seemed to want to curse his government – all governments, in fact – as well as Turks and Iranians. As they roared towards the centre of town, he had to swerve to avoid a couple crossing the road. The woman was wearing the *niqab*, which elicited another muttered insult. 'I'm sorry,' he said. 'I just don't like them.'

They were speeding past Tbilisi old town and Kate looked out at the brightly painted houses with their striking exterior balconies, many of which appeared to hang in mid-air. This gave Ian a chance to play the role he'd adopted as Suzy's caring and thoughtful tour guide, holding her hand through 'her first major foreign assignment', as he put it, though it wasn't and she didn't need her hand held. Berlin had proved that. 'They really are quite something,' he said, pointing out a particularly spectacular example of the local architecture. 'I had a house just up here with the most incredible courtyard.'

As a transparent and not especially subtle attempt to make Julie jealous, this flirtation was surely doomed to failure – 'He's a moron,' she'd whispered to Kate on the flight from Paris. 'I can't imagine what I saw in him' – but Suzy appeared to be lapping it up.

'Tbilisi was destroyed by the Persians in 1795,' Ian told her, 'so it turned to Imperial Russia for protection. They reneged on everything they'd agreed, but made it a place to be reckoned with, a true crossroads between East and West. Most of the old houses you see are essentially a mixture of cultures and styles.' He was warming to this theme. 'You get these amazing exterior staircases that literally cascade down the hill, following the natural contours of the slope.'

'Tbilisi very old, very beautiful,' the driver chimed in, not to be displaced as tour guide. They were racing away from Freedom Square down Rustaveli Avenue. 'Here is Parliament building. Heroes butchered in 1989.'

'So was Georgia always part of the Russian Empire?' Suzy asked Ian. Perhaps it was her imagination, but Kate had the sense she already knew the answer to this perfectly well. If she was playing him, he took the bait.

'No, it declared independence at the end of the First World War, after the Tsar had stood down. But it only lasted about a year before Lenin ordered the troops in to take it back. It was why it was one of the first Soviet republics to declare independence when *glasnost* got going.'

'I thought the Georgians had a pretty good run of the Soviet Empire?'

'They did, if you can ignore the deportations, mass shootings and trips to the gulag. Stalin was their man, too, of course, so they have rather mixed feelings about him now. They maintained a pretty strong sense of national identity throughout, so maybe it was no surprise they were among the first to want out.'

They arrived at the hotel. Suzy had booked it through the Travel Department and Kate thought she must spend much of her life on the Mr & Mrs Smith website, since Rooms Hotel Tbilisi bore a striking resemblance to Das Stue in Berlin, and was another study in low-key luxury. The central lobby had floor-to-ceiling bookcases on both sides, though all of the books appeared to be in English – a sign of the direction the hotel, and perhaps the country, was facing. They walked over polished red and cream tiles, past a curved green velvet and wood sofa and renaissance chandeliers until a bellboy in red hat and jacket, with a gold tassel on the shoulder, leapt at Kate's small shoulder bag and insisted on escorting her to her room.

She rummaged in her pocket and produced a twenty-lari tip.

It was a big room with a free-standing iron-clawed bath, sumptuous green velvet curtains and bold black and tangerine wallpaper. The lighting was low, the atmosphere moody. It was comfortable, luxurious even, and so clearly designed for couples in the first flush of lust as to be the last place on earth Kate felt like being. She thought painfully of the night on the train with Sergei and found it hard to push the image of his distorted face from her mind.

She washed her face and went downstairs to wait for Julie in the bar. She ordered some kind of lavender cocktail – made with gin and coconut – and sat beneath a giant painting of a woman seated backwards on a zebra. It was that kind of hotel.

Kate's cocktail arrived, shortly followed by Julie. 'What is *that*?' she asked.

Kate sipped it. 'Too sweet for you.'

Julie waved at the waiter. 'Gin and tonic, please. Hendrick's, if there's a choice.' As he disappeared again, Julie took in their surroundings. 'A stoner's paradise,' she said. 'Have you spoken to Mikhail?'

Kate took out her phone, checked the Wi-Fi hadn't hooked up to the hotel's system, then sent him a Signal message. *We're here.*

She got a reply straight away. *Good. Will let you know where to meet tomorrow 10 a.m. Be ready.*

Kate answered: *Would rather we set venue.*

But Mikhail was obdurate: *No, this is our backyard. Do as we ask.*

'I bet you a hundred quid he shags her on this trip,' Julie said.

'He's just trying to make you jealous.'

310

'That may have been his original intention, but he's loving the attention. He won't be able to resist. You know what it's like, the excitement of your first big foreign gig. She'll be all over him like a rash.'

'He's not that stupid.'

'He absolutely is and you of all people know it.'

Kate thought about having a word with Suzy and warning her off. But she actually felt a little sorry for both of them. Their loneliness was so transparent. 'Would you be upset?' she asked Julie.

'Not in the slightest.'

'Are you sure about that?'

'One hundred per cent certain. Every time I look at him, I feel a bit sick at what happened between us. I can't imagine what I was thinking.' She could see the scepticism in her friend's face. 'Genuinely, honestly.'

Kate was struck by her colleague's ability to cleave off a set of unwanted emotions. No wonder Ian was so shaken by it.

Ian and Suzy arrived together. Perhaps he'd continued his tour of Georgian history all the way to her room. Suzy had booked a restaurant a short walk from the hotel, and since it was still a balmy evening, they took a table just beyond the rose-covered pergola on the terrace. Ian demanded a menu in Georgian, rather than English, and ordered for all of them. The food – tender green beans with soft walnut paste, beetroot quenelle and lightly fried corn bread, a Georgian speciality – was better than the conversation. Ian marched on with his history lesson, gesturing wildly at the twinkling lights of the city beneath them. He'd arrived in 1990, the Service's first man in – 'an incredible opportunity for an ambitious young officer' – and he gave Suzy a blow-by-blow account of that era, from Gamsakhurdia's departure for Armenia and Chechnya to the long rule of Eduard Shevardnadze, Gorbachev's foreign minister, of whom Ian was an unreconstructed fan.

But just when Kate's thoughts had wandered inexorably back to Sergei's stricken face, Ian turned to her. 'Have you been in touch with our man?' He glanced around them to check they were not overheard.

'Yes. He's here.'

'What about his father?'

'I assume so, but I didn't ask.'

'Where are we going to meet?'

'He said he would set the venue, but to be ready to move at ten a.m.'

'No. I'm not having that. We'll set the meet point.'

'I tried to insist, but he said it was his backyard and they would pick the venue.'

'Then tell him different. We have the whip hand.'

Kate could tell Ian was trying to show off to Suzy, but she wasn't in a mood to indulge him. 'We have to be careful. We don't know what their agenda is, we don't know what they're dealing with from their side, and we don't know who else they have been talking to—'

'What do you mean?'

'If you were them, wouldn't you have cast the net wider than just us? If we delay, or prevaricate, or muck them about in any way, there's a chance they'll bolt and pull the lever somewhere else.'

'Doesn't that sound a lot like the operation that went so badly wrong in Berlin?'

'Yes, but we don't have a choice.'

'We're not the ones trying to escape a lifetime in a Russian prison, or worse. I'd feel a lot more comfortable if we were setting the parameters.' Ian shook his head to underline his disapproval. 'Have you discussed this with Danny?'

'Not yet. I was going to talk to him when we get back to the hotel.' Danny and his team were staying at the Marriott, just a short walk down Rustaveli Avenue. They'd come in via Istanbul earlier in the day.

'All right. Julie will go with you.' He was pointing at Kate. 'I want both surveillance teams deployed. I'll play quarterback.' Ian rolled up his sleeves. 'What about the plane?' It was directed at Suzy.

'It arrives the day after tomorrow. We've told the Tbilisi authorities we're picking up a film location crew. We've filed a flight plan direct to London for eight p.m., but we can change that. We can push back by about twenty-four hours, but after that we start to have issues with the pilot.'

'What have you told Sarah?'

This was directed at Julie, who had been instructed to liaise with Sarah Creaven, SIS's Tbilisi station chief. She left her reply just long enough to make her insolence felt. 'That we need to extract someone and it's conceivable there may be issues, but we didn't want to inform the Georgians and hoped it would pass off smoothly.'

'Did she guess?'

'I don't know. I didn't ask her.' Kate nudged Julie under the table.

'Does Mikhail know there's a time constraint on the plane?' Ian asked Kate.

'Not yet.'

'You should tell him.'

Kate wasn't enjoying being given direct instructions on what had been her show from start to finish. 'They're in a hurry to get to London. I don't think they need to be told that we're keen to get it over and done with too.'

Ian nodded. 'We're in good shape,' he said, then ordered more wine and embarked on a long soliloquy about how Georgians made theirs differently.

Kate took another double dose of zopiclone when she got back to her room in the hotel and undressed quickly. She asked herself when she would next dare to attempt to sleep without chemical assistance, but knew that this was neither the time nor the place.

Her head had been down barely five minutes when an argument broke out down the corridor. She heard Julie's voice and hauled herself out of bed to intervene.

Julie was in the doorway of her room, leaning against the frame in a black, see-through nightgown. Ian stood before her still fully clothed, part supplicant, part bull in a china shop. 'Ian!' Julie shouted.

He had his foot in the door. 'I just want to talk,' he pleaded.

'Hey,' Kate said. 'Come on . . .' It was like her friend to answer the door without bothering to put on a dressing-gown just to provoke him. She felt a flash of resentment at having to be the grown-up in this equation.

'I've told him a hundred times,' Julie said. 'He just won't listen.'

'We owe it to each other to talk,' Ian said, ignoring Kate entirely.

But Julie kept her eyes on her friend. 'You tell him!'

'Keep your voices down, both of you,' Kate said. 'This is not the time or the place—'

'Why does she answer the door like that, if not to make a point?'

'Ian,' Kate said. 'No woman is required to dress in one way or another when you bang on her door in the middle of the night.'

'It's only just past ten.'

'Go to your room.'

'After everything that has passed between us, it's just bizarre she won't agree to sit down and talk things through for a few—'

'What do you mean, "everything that has passed between us"?' Julie asked. 'You mean sex, normally in the missionary position, which is about as far as your imagination ever seems to stretch.'

'For God's sake . . .'

'Stop it, Julie.' There was steel in Kate's voice now. 'I mean it.'

'I'm going straight to HR when I get back from this trip. I've told him a hundred times I do not wish to talk to him about this ever again. I don't know what part of his tiny brain can't grasp—'

'You think I give a damn if you report me? You can stick a copy of your complaint in the post to King Charles Street and Downing Street as well for all I care! All I am asking for is a bit of respect. Like it or not, we have been in a relationship for more than a year and—'

'It was just fucking sex, Ian, and lousy sex at that.'

Ian looked as if he was about to explode. Or cry. Or both. But they were saved by Suzy's appearance. She'd taken off

315

her make-up erratically and her cheeks were stained with mascara. 'Is everything all right?' she asked.

There was a brief silence, before Ian pulled himself together with lightning speed. Perhaps it was the potential loss of professional respect from the newcomer, or that he'd already identified her as his next conquest, but he managed a very quick turnaround. 'All fine. Still debating who sets the meet point tomorrow. I was uncomfortable with the way we left things, as you know, but . . . I can see we have no choice. Goodnight.'

He walked away, down the corridor. Suzy retreated in the opposite direction. 'He's a cunt and she's welcome to him,' Julie hissed, so that both of them could hear, before she closed the door without ceremony.

28

KATE AND JULIE sat on the plush velvet sofa in the Rooms Hotel reception area. 'You nervous?' Julie asked her.

'A bit.' And she was, too. But then, when had the stakes ever been higher?

Mikhail's text came in bang on time. Kate showed it to Julie and they left the hotel. 'The Peace Bridge,' she said quietly, into her lapel microphone. 'We'll walk.'

'Get a cab,' Ian barked. But she ignored him. She got a greater feel for things on foot. She offered Julie some chewing gum and they strolled down Rustaveli Avenue easily, past the buskers and the beggars, the restaurants open on to the street and the market stalls selling quite sophisticated tourist memorabilia. They took the underpass beneath Freedom Square, where Julie pointed out, with a smile, a shop selling handguns, and came up at the corner of the old town.

Julie had been in charge of mastering the topography, so Kate let her lead the way down towards the river. It was hard not to be impressed by the crumbling splendour of the centuries-old city that Ian had been so enthusiastically lecturing Suzy on. This section was like a microcosm of the country, with pockets of sophistication, style and wealth cheek by jowl with evidence of the neglect and decay of the Soviet years. Painted balconies on old houses, with delicate Moorish latticework, or Ottoman yoke arches, stood side by side with crumbling bricks and ugly Russian iron staircases.

It had started to rain, and as they reached the incongruous glass and metal Peace Bridge, they took shelter under a tumbling vine in a street full of boutique hotels, stores and restaurants aimed at Tbilisi's ever-expanding tourist trade. Julie lit a cigarette and shared it with Kate. They didn't need to tell their watchers where they were, or that the waiting was dragging out. Kate's phone buzzed. She glanced at it. *Walk away down Erekle II Street. Keep going.* She showed the message to Julie, who nodded. 'You need to look it up?' Kate asked. Julie shook her head.

They started moving again, walking across a car park, then beneath a line of cypress trees as they passed a section of the old city wall. This was the heart of the tourist old town, the houses newly painted and the restaurant tables sheltered beneath plants overhanging from shady terraces. They passed a church and found themselves in a square with Tbilisi's famous clock tower. Kate's phone throbbed again: *Go down to the river, get a taxi to the Dry Bridge.*

Kate called him via Signal. He answered immediately. 'I'm not doing this again,' she said.

'The Georgians have been watching me here in Tbilisi. I have to make sure they are not following you.'

Kate ended the call. 'Moving to the Dry Bridge,' she said quietly. Julie was still checking this on her phone as Kate was relaying the instruction to a taxi driver on the quay. He seemed to understand.

It was only a short journey and the taxi disgorged them into what looked like a flea market that stretched along the riverbank. Kate and Julie browsed the stalls in the morning sunshine. It was as if every citizen of the capital had assembled every piece of junk that had ever been in their possession to sell to tourists. There was a stall offering plugs, adaptors and every kind of electrical accessory, another selling old tools. An old man had a huge selection of knives laid out on a long table, a woman next to him a ten- or fifteen-feet-wide section selling old crockery. Behind them both was an old Lada so full of debris there was no possibility of even a cat squeezing inside it.

Kate and Julie kept walking. They found an old man selling Soviet film posters, another offering medals and Soviet badges. Julie lingered on the posters. 'I love these,' she said.

A new black four-wheel-drive Toyota Land Cruiser roared up. Mikhail was in the passenger seat. 'Get in,' he said. 'Both of you.' They did as they were told. He leant behind him. 'Turn off your packs,' he said. 'They're going off grid, whoever is listening. We know where you are and we'll contact you when we are ready to leave.'

'We can't go off grid,' Kate said.

'It wasn't a suggestion. My father's order. I think you will concede he knows this part of the world better than any of you are ever going to.'

'Do *not* agree to go off grid,' Ian instructed in their earpieces.

'Now,' Mikhail said.

Kate glanced at Julie. She nodded and they both switched off their packs. 'And your phones.' They took them out and powered them off. Mikhail nodded with satisfaction and Kate couldn't quite suppress a moment's pleasure at the thought of Ian's reaction. 'Where are we going?' she asked Mikhail.

'Out of town. My father will cross the border tonight. We have a house nearby. You will meet him. In the morning, we will make the run for the airport.'

'How far out of town?'

'Not far.'

Mikhail nodded at the driver and he roared off again. They lapsed into silence as they spun past the hard evidence that this ancient city had not escaped the depredations of the Brezhnev-era central planners, with concrete housing, block after block, leavened only by the occasional splash of colour.

If the Soviet Union had succeeded only in making every one of its citizens poor, independence had clearly made a tiny number of Georgians rich. They passed a Porsche garage and one for Jaguar Land Rover, as well as a smart-looking shopping mall, with the French supermarket Carrefour advertising its wares with a giant sign on the roof, but the overall impression was of poverty and neglect.

Eventually the housing blocks petered out, to be replaced by shabby single-storey dwellings, and then they were out of the city altogether, following the foaming waters of the River Terek. 'How far are we going?' Kate asked.

'A few hours. Three, perhaps. It depends.'

'Where are we going?'

'Relax.' He turned and smiled at her. 'Have you ever been to the Caucasus?'

'We're not here to take in the sights.'

'I told you, these are our lands. We are safer here.'

But safer seemed a distant prospect. They were following the Georgian Military Highway, the long single-track road that had allowed the Russians to dominate this southern republic for two centuries. It was full of potholes and packed with lorries, all of which made glacial progress, so the driver felt compelled to dice with death at every turn in the long and winding road.

By the time they reached the Jvari Pass, the weather had closed in, reducing visibility to only forty or fifty yards in the sleeting rain. That didn't deter the driver from over-taking at will, so they were frequently forced to duck back in to avoid a lorry or truck coming the other way with only inches to spare. 'Does he always drive like this?' Kate muttered, but Mikhail did not answer and neither did Julie, who was gazing out of the window.

They passed the Gudauri ski resort, which looked like a drab construction site lost in the mist, and then the Russian-Georgian friendship mural at the highest point in the path, which had been made in 1983 to celebrate the long relation-ship between the two countries, and ignored by every Georgian since.

They started to descend again and it wasn't long before they broke through the dense cloud into a wide, lush valley. This was the landscape that had so inspired Russian writers from Lermontov and Tolstoy to Pushkin and Gorky: rich green valleys linking rugged mountains that reached for a dramatic cobalt sky.

The sun danced off a reservoir nearby, bringing an even greater majesty and grandeur to the landscape. Kate and Julie stared out in silence all the way down to the village of Kazbegi, or Stepantsminda, as it had been renamed, which had the air of a modern-day Klondike, mining the new gold rush that was international tourism.

They swung off the main road, past guesthouses, cafés and tin-roofed shacks with market gardens, and roared on up the hill to a long wooden building that appeared to have been newly restored. 'Check in here,' Mikhail said, as they came to a halt at its entrance. 'I will pick you up later. Do not switch your phones on. I will find you.'

Kate and Julie got out and walked into one of the strangest places Kate had ever seen. It turned out to be the sister establishment to the Tbilisi hotel they'd stayed in, a former Intourist site that had been the subject of a dramatic make-over to turn it into a kind of Soho House in the Caucasus. Only the Intourist poster by the lift – *Welcome to the Soviet Union* – had survived its past, as the interior was an open, stylish expanse of wood and leather all the way up to the bar at the far end of the room. Large brass binoculars on stands by the floor-to-ceiling windows gave guests the chance to gaze up at the wonders of Mount Kazbegi, which towered high above its surroundings on the far side of the valley.

Kate and Julie agreed to share a room, but went straight out to order coffee on the wide wooden deck in front of the hotel. They sat in silence for a while, watching the clientele, who seemed to represent a rainbow coalition of different nationalities, from the blond Norwegian family sitting next to them to a large group of Chinese tourists and two Iranian women in the *niqab*. If Georgia had always been a melting pot, it seemed determined to turn that heritage into the widest possible flow of visitors and tourist dollars.

'Is it too early for cocktails?' Julie asked.

'Yes.'

They ordered Diet Coke and sat soaking up the sun. A crisp wind whipped away the last remnants of cloud to reveal the summit of Mount Kazbegi, the legendary heart of the Caucasus, to whose flanks Prometheus had allegedly been chained.

Gergeti Trinity Church, which sat atop the hill directly opposite, was bathed in sunlight, the landscape a riot of brilliant green meadow. 'This may very well be the most beautiful place I have ever been,' Julie said.

'It is awe-inspiring,' Kate agreed. They ordered food, which appeared promptly. 'You shouldn't provoke Ian,' she said.

'You're not my mother.' Julie was eating an enormous slice of traditional Georgian cheese bread, as if it was set to be her last meal on earth.

'No, but I am your boss.'

'I didn't ask him to come to my room in the middle of the night.'

'And you definitely shouldn't be answering your door in a see-through nightie.'

'If he's going to shag Suzy, I might as well remind him of what he's missing.'

'I thought you didn't care.'

'I don't.'

'Well, you sound as though you do.'

'No, I'm just being mean. Given what a twat he is, I'm en-titled to punish him.'

'It's beneath you.'

'It so bloody isn't and you know it. Besides, wouldn't you relish the chance to rub Stuart's nose in it?'

Kate thought about this. The complexity of Julie's emotional landscape was a challenge much too far for Ian's schoolboy simplicity, though perhaps that had been why he'd fallen for her so hard. She could be quite cruel when she wanted to be, and Kate wondered if Danny knew what he was getting into.

She watched Julie finish off the last of the cheese bread. 'I need some pudding,' she said.

She ordered Soviet cake and Kate sat back, stared at the mountain and thought about what her friend had just said of Stuart. With the benefit of some distance – geographic and with the passage of time – she had started to regret her recent commitment to Stuart and the children. She was by no means convinced she wanted to give her marriage another try or would be able to. She thought of Ian's childish petulance last night, the plaintive cocktail of wounded ego and bruised pride. How was it so many men seemed not to have progressed beyond the emotional maturity of small boys? Were they just spoilt, mollycoddled, smothered?

She wondered if that was what she was doing to her own son. It was hard to imagine, since he rarely let her close enough to love, let alone smother him.

The Soviet cake came. It was a grey sponge made from condensed milk, so sweet Kate almost gagged. 'How can you possibly eat that?'

'It's delicious.' Julie wolfed it down.

After that Kate lay back in her chair, her face turned up to the sun. She was told to take her feet off the table by a waiter, who ignored the rowdy Georgian kids nearby, playing their music loudly on a portable speaker. 'Dick,' Julie said, as he departed.

Julie stared at the kids next to them with growing irritation. They looked like they were stoned or high, dancing around the table self-consciously. Kate made a mental guess as to how long her friend would last and had it right at about three minutes.

Julie marched over to them. 'You want to turn that off?'

They were startled to have been challenged so abruptly and they instantly complied, as meek as lambs. Julie was a formidable presence.

Kate sunbathed for about an hour. Julie grew bored and wandered off down to the town. Kate borrowed a swimming costume from the hotel and did some lengths in the basement pool. It had floor-to-ceiling windows, as if the hotel's designer had been determined that at no point should you be deprived of the magic of that view.

They met for drinks before dinner and Kate insisted they stick to Diet Coke. After dinner, they went back outside and wrapped themselves in rugs left out for the purpose. They gazed up at the stellar night sky, the snowy peak of Mount Kazbegi majestic, even luminous, in the crystal-clear air.

They had both dozed off when Mikhail shook them gently awake. 'Sorry, sleeping beauties,' he whispered softly. 'Time to go.'

29

AS FAR AS Kate could tell, there was no one behind them. But the driver gunned through the village of Stepantsminda, as if the entire Russian intelligence community was in hot pursuit.

They roared up the hill past Gergeti Trinity Church and on into the valley behind.

There was only one house here, a set of twinkling lights high up above Gergeti, in the lee of Mount Kazbegi. They pulled through a set of security gates that seemed spectacularly incongruous in the middle of nowhere and then Mikhail led them up the stairs to the terrace above.

The house was done up in a similar style to the hotel opposite – a temple of oak, fur and glass – with a roaring fire on a giant raised hearth. A woman in a black skirt and white shirt hurried forward to offer them a drink in fluent English. They both declined. Mikhail warmed his backside against the fire. 'How was your day?' he asked Kate.

'Pleasant. It's quite a spot.'

'We used to come here a lot when I was a child.'

'When did you build the house?'

'Six years ago.'

They lapsed into silence. Mikhail appeared uncharacter-istically nervous. Kate went out to the wooden deck and looked back towards the rear of Gergeti Trinity Church. Julie appeared beside her and offered her a cigarette. Kate couldn't resist. 'I'm definitely giving up when we get back.'

'Me too.'

'Mrs Henderson.' Kate spun around to see a bull of a man striding across the lounge towards her. He wore blue jeans, cowboy boots and a scuffed leather jacket. He looked like a tougher, fatter George W. Bush, his hair greying at the tem-ples. He exuded purpose, confidence, as men in his position often did. 'Thank you for coming all this way.'

Igor Borodin had been such a remote and legendary fig-ure in the shadowy world of espionage for so long that Kate was momentarily lost for words. Bright blue eyes scrutin-ized her with barely concealed curiosity. 'You'll need a drink,' he said.

'No, thank you.'

'It wasn't a suggestion.' He went to the table, poured four glasses of vodka and brought them on a tray towards them. They all dutifully toasted and drank. 'Welcome to the land of my forefathers,' he said. He returned to the fire. 'Sit,' he said. That wasn't a suggestion either. 'What happened in London?' he asked. It was directed at Kate. When she didn't answer immediately, he put a booted foot on the sofa next to him and leant on his knee. 'We are capable of reading the news.'

'The foreign secretary authorized this operation. Then someone leaked it.'

'Who?'

'We don't know yet.'

'And then?'

'The prime minister personally authorized that it should go ahead.'

Igor seemed surprised by that. He dropped down into the sofa, put his boot on to the long oak coffee-table and gazed into the fire. 'Why?'

'He'll find a way to take control of the authentication of the video and make sure it's pronounced a fake.'

'And what does that mean for my son and me?'

'Nothing. Your defection is an enormous coup for SIS in any event, so you will be safe. None of us can really be sure how the politics will play out in the end, but it won't make any difference to you.'

'If it is pronounced a fake, the pressure to send us back where we came from will be irresistible.'

Kate shook her head. Sometimes, even the most sophisticated of opponents were wont to underestimate the strictures of the Western democratic system, in which no amount of politics was permitted to overwhelm the law. 'You'll have the most expensive lawyers money can buy, which is saying something, and our courts will never send you back to Moscow.' She glanced at Mikhail. 'You know that.'

'The leak compromises the operation.'

'Strangely, it forces the prime minister into a position where he has to accept your defection.'

Igor turned to her. 'You were very foolish to seek out your friend Sergei Malinsky. The GRU has its own spies in London. They knew you were coming.'

'Who are their spies?'

'If I knew the GRU's secrets, I would not be sitting here.'

'How do you know I came to meet Sergei?'

'Everyone in Moscow is aware of it.'

'Why did they not kill me as well?'

'Because we protected you, for long enough to get you out of the country.' He gave her an icy smile. 'You are our passport to the West. We just did not expect you to do something so foolish.'

Kate avoided Julie's gaze. She stood, placed her glass carefully on the table. 'The plane will be ready to go at five p.m. tomorrow. I think we should leave here in the morning, so that we are ready just in case it comes in early. We have a secure room at the airport.'

Igor nodded. Now she came to think about it, he had all the warmth of a reptile. 'Mikhail will show you to your rooms,' he said.

Mikhail did so and bade them goodnight. Kate hadn't had time to sit on her bed before Julie burst through the door. 'When were you going to tell me about Sergei?'

Kate put her fingers to her lips, to indicate there was every chance the room was bugged, but Julie just shook her head in incredulity. 'You think it matters?'

'I didn't tell you because it would have served no purpose.'

Julie was genuinely furious. 'What happened?'

'I told you. I took the train with him to Moscow.'

'Yes, but you left a mildly important bit of the story out.'

'About halfway through the night, I went to the loo. When I came back, he was dead. They'd cut his throat. There wasn't much sign of a struggle, so I think it was someone he knew.'

'You think . . .' Julie pointed to indicate Igor.

'I don't know.' Kate sat on the bed, fatigue overwhelming her. 'That was why I called Stuart. I had to get out of there. But I have no idea who killed Sergei, or why they spared me and let me escape.'

'Maybe it was like he said. They were protecting you.'

'Who knows? Perhaps they saw me coming, just as they apparently did in Andros and Berlin. I've been over it a thousand times. I've looked through the files. Suzy is not wrong: the unanswered questions are legion. But that is in the nature of our business. What we don't understand will always be greater than what we do. There are many things we can't see and may never get to find out about. So, I've decided to concentrate only on the fundamentals before us.'

She stood up. 'This offer of defection is unrivalled. Why would Igor want to come to the West unless the story he tells is real and his offer of cooperation genuine? I've seen the video. They have promised evidence of the many payments. We have no choice but to proceed.'

'What do you mean – they saw you coming?'

Kate shook her head. 'I don't know if Stuart was Viper or not, or if he was, whether someone bigger and more important was left behind. He swore to me on our drive to St Petersburg that he never passed on any important operational details about my work.'

'And you believed him?'

Kate went to the window, pulled back the curtains and gazed up at the snowy peak of Mount Kazbegi. 'I don't know. I wanted to.'

'But he's lied to you and cheated on you before.'

'True, but he's desperate for reconciliation.'

'He says he is.'

'He's not a good actor.' Kate turned to face her friend again. 'Perhaps they've just found a way to track my movements that I have yet to work out. I don't know. We may never know. If you're asking me, I suspect Igor or some of his people were alerted to my presence in Russia, perhaps by someone at the border, and resolved to eliminate Sergei lest he undermine their story or spoil their plan to defect in any way. Nothing else makes sense to me.

'So, I return always to the same point. I think this offer to come over to us is real. The video looked credible. The politics of what happens after this may prove very complicated and, the way I feel, I might not want to be around to witness it. But that's a battle for another day.'

'What do you mean, you might not be around to witness it?'

'I have to sleep.'

'If you're resigning, so am I.'

Kate was already reaching for the zopiclone in her bag. Julie took the hint and withdrew.

Perhaps it was the purity of the mountain air, but Kate slept until about eight the following morning. There was no sign of Igor and Mikhail, so she helped herself to coffee and a croissant from the lavish breakfast laid out on the dining table and ate it on the terrace. After that, she left by a side gate and walked down to the Gergeti Trinity Church, which was thronged with tourists even at that time of the morning, the monks fussing around the under-dressed women, demanding they cover their legs and heads.

By the time she returned, Igor and Mikhail stood by the SUV, with Mikhail's wife and young son. Another was just pulling up behind it. 'We need to go,' Mikhail said.

'What's the rush?'

But he waved away the need for an answer. Julie came out, still eating her croissant, and they got into the back of the second SUV. 'What's going on?' Julie asked Kate, as the doors were closed on them. Kate shrugged.

They reversed out on to the gravel track beyond the gate, then followed Igor and Mikhail's lead towards the valley floor. The weather was better, but the return journey was no less terrifying. Soon enough, though, they were back on the course of the River Terek as it found its way down towards the capital, the dramatic mountain scenery replaced by dilapidated houses hidden behind the ash, poplar and syca-more trees that lined much of the road. It was just after midday as they passed through the city centre and, not long after that, pulled into the old Soviet-era terminal building that served as the waiting area for private flights. Ian and Suzy were already there and the former's smile at his cap-ture of this huge intelligence fish, and the credit he would no doubt claim for it, could on its own have powered the plane.

After the introductions had been made, Igor retreated with his family to the far side of the room, pointedly indicat-ing he had no desire to engage in small-talk.

Ian strode over to Kate. 'I told you not to go off grid.' She didn't bother to answer and she didn't need to, his excitement overriding any temptation for further recrimination. 'This is coming off like a dream,' he said. 'Any sign of problems?'

'Not yet.'

'Anyone on your tail?'

'He wanted to move earlier than we expected this morning, but I wouldn't read too much into that.'

'Excellent.' He looked at his prized catch. 'What a bloody coup,' he said softly to himself, barely hiding a note of self-congratulation. 'The plane is coming in early,' he said. 'Should be here any moment now.'

And so it was, landing in the distance and pulling up within fifty yards of the terminal entrance. There was no security, of course, their only brush with officialdom a tame Customs official, whom Sarah Creaven had brought to check their passports, including the fakes that had been supplied to Igor and his family.

Kate gossiped with Sarah, whom she'd worked with in Lahore for a while, and then they were all walking towards the plane. They climbed aboard, Ian dropping into the battered leather seat beside her. He glanced at their surroundings. 'Only the finest on Her Majesty's Secret Service,' he muttered, then peered out of the window to check that no one was steaming in to intercept them. 'Like bloody clockwork,' he said again.

Kate's phone buzzed. It was a WhatsApp message from Fiona. She opened it with a smile to find a video of her daughter. She put in her headphones, attached them to her phone and pressed play. Fiona was tied to a chair, with her brother, in some kind of warehouse, both stripped to their underwear. They looked terrified.

'Mum,' Fiona said, crying. 'They kidnapped us, blind-folded us, took us somewhere miles away . . .' Fiona glanced nervously off camera. 'They say they know what you're doing and if that plane takes off with the defeater . . .' another terrified glance '. . . the defectors aboard, then they'll behead us both. Please, Mum . . .' She and Gus started to weep. 'They'll let us go if you leave the defectors there in Georgia . . .'

The screen went black.

30

A MINUTE LATER, Kate stood opposite Ian on the tarmac, an afternoon breeze tugging at her hair. The engines were already running, so they'd had to walk away from the steps to be able to converse. And Ian was shaking his head. 'We can't,' he said.

The panic in Kate's chest was so intense she felt as if she were about to have a heart attack. Ian forestalled a tirade with a raised hand. 'We'll find them,' he said. 'We'll throw everything at it, but this operation is a matter of national security.'

'They have my children!' she shouted.

'And we'll stop at nothing to track them down.'

She gestured at the plane. 'We have to leave them here.'

'Kate—'

'For God's sake, Ian. The operation is compromised. Someone has told Moscow when, where and how we were intending to extract them. They are threatening to kill—'

'And we'll stop them before they have a chance even to think about doing that, but we have absolutely no indication your children will be any safer if we abandon this operation. In fact, the reverse may be true. We will immediately have lost any leverage.'

'We have to leave them!'

'Kate, just think about this for a moment. If we depart without them, whoever has your children will have no incentive whatsoever to keep them alive.'

'I'm calling Sir Alan.'

'No! Do *not* do that. I am in operational charge here and I expressly forbid—'

She walked away from him.

'Kate! I'm warning you!'

She pulled up Sir Alan's number and dialled. Ian tried to take her phone away and she rammed her shoulder into his chest. 'For God's sake!' he yelled.

Sir Alan answered. 'I'm making the assumption this is a matter of life and death.'

'They have Fiona and Gus. They've just sent me a video of them both stripped to their underwear and tied to chairs in what looks like a warehouse. Fiona says they'll be beheaded if we take off with Igor and Mikhail onboard.'

Sir Alan was silent for a moment. 'Is there any possibility the video they sent you was faked? Have you tried to get hold of either of them?'

Kate had not even considered this possibility. Her heart skipped a beat. 'No, I—'

'Have you told Ian?'

'Yes, he's here. He's trying to insist the operation goes ahead.'

'Establish your children are missing. If they are, you'll have to call the operation off. Tell Igor and Mikhail we'll come back for them. I'll call the ops room and press the emergency button.'

He rang off. Another call came in, this time from Fiona and Gus's school. 'Hello, Mrs Henderson. I do hope every-thing is all right. We're just checking why Fiona and Gus were both absent from school today.'

Kate didn't wait to hear what else she had to say. She called Rose. Her phone went straight to its message service. She tried the Finance Department.

'Celine Jones,' a woman said.

'Celine, it's Kate Henderson from the Russia desk here. Is Rose there?'

'No, Mrs Henderson, she is not. I was about to call you, actually, because I know she's been staying at your house this week. She hasn't come to work today and her mobile phone goes straight to answering machine. I was wonder-ing if everything was all right.'

Kate ended the call. She turned to find Igor Borodin strid-ing towards her. Ian tried to interrupt his progress, but Igor swatted him away as if he were an irritating distraction. 'What is going on, Mrs Henderson?'

'They have taken my children. They're threatening to behead them if we take off with you onboard.'

'My former colleagues will have subcontracted the work to Serbian or Albanian gangsters. As soon as they know in Moscow they have thwarted this defection, the gangsters will cover their tracks. The only chance your children have is to take us on that plane with you.'

'We'll come straight back for you.'

He glared at her. For the first time she thought that what she saw in those eyes was fear. 'If that plane takes off without us,' he said, 'we are dead. And so are your children.'

'I've told her the same thing,' Ian said, but Igor Borodin continued to ignore him, his gaze locked on Kate.

'I've spoken to the chief,' she said, as much to Ian as to Igor. 'I have the authority to make a decision. I can't take off with you onboard. If you can wait here in Tbilisi or close to the border, I give you my word we will return for you as soon as I know my children are safe.'

Igor took her arm, led her roughly away. Ian followed. 'Stay there!' Igor bellowed at him. He dragged Kate to the corner of the terminal building, so that they were out of earshot. 'Your children are safer with us onboard,' he said. 'Believe me.'

'I can't take that risk.'

'You have no choice.'

'I'm sorry. It's my call. You would do the same.'

Igor's gaze never left her face. 'Your prime minister works for us,' he said. 'I recruited him myself in Kosovo. If I don't get on that plane, you will never prove it and the truth will die with me here in the Caucasus.'

'I understand that.'

'You have a duty to your country to take us with you.'

Kate shook her head. 'Let me talk to Ian for—'

'No!' Igor gripped her arm furiously again. 'That joker. You want to know how we have been aware of your every move? The operation in Andros? Your deputy Rav on a plane to Geneva?' He gestured contemptuously at Ian, who was dancing from one foot to the other in a bid to contain himself. 'Because that useful idiot is so desperate to be C, he tells your prime minister everything and always has, even when he was foreign secretary. And what Ian told him, James Ryan passed on to us.' He shook his head. 'There was no other source, as you have been wondering, but just your superior's relentless ambition and loose tongue.'

Kate felt dazed. 'But I never told Ian I was coming to St Petersburg and—'

'Come on, Kate. Wake up! The GRU has known for a long time your Russian lover Sergei was leaking material. It was all we could do to get you off that train in one piece. I saved your life. Now you must do the same for me and my family.'

Kate looked back at Ian. Of course. It explained so much. How could she not have imagined he would do anything – anything at all – to make it into Sir Alan's chair? 'I can't.'

Igor leant closer. His cheeks were bright red now. 'This is your last chance, or the truth dies with me.'

'I'm sorry. I can't.'

'You're a fool!' Igor spun away from her.

'Mr Borodin,' Ian pleaded, as he stormed off. 'I will call the prime minister . . .'

But Igor paid him no more attention. He stalked towards the plane and, moments later, he, Mikhail and the rest of their group hurried back towards the terminal. 'For God's sake, Kate,' Ian said. 'I need to speak to the PM. This is a catastrophe.'

Kate called Danny. 'I need you,' she said. 'We're in the private terminal.'

Kate climbed back onboard. She ignored Ian, who was in a state of advanced panic, swinging wildly between fury at her, feigned concern for her children and fear as to the impact of this debacle on his career.

Danny arrived and, from then on, Kate entered a narrow tunnel, the intense terror that gripped her giving everything she said and did vivid focus. They started by pulling up the CCTV all around her house in Battersea as the plane took off.

Danny broke into the closed-circuit system of the newsagent on the corner and they all watched as Rose, Fiona and Gus were bundled into a grey van. Julie and Ian – who had given up flapping around and was now sitting on the floor beside them, his own laptop open – started tracking its progress through the road and traffic cameras all over the country. Suzy spoke to the Metropolitan Police to enlist their support and kept an open line between their ops room and SIS headquarters in Vauxhall.

They called out its progress. 'Wood Green,' Julie said.

'Enfield,' Ian added. 'Now Harlow.'

'Stevenage,' Julie called back. 'Where the hell are they going?'

'Luton,' Ian answered. 'They're in Luton.'

Kate had her eyes fixed on Danny's laptop. He'd closed in on the men marching her children to the van in the dawn light. One had a snake tattooed on the back of his right hand.

So Danny was now working through all the databases at his disposal, from those at SIS to those kept by the Met, MI5 and the National Crime Agency. Only in the last did he get a match, and the file it connected them to made Kate want to throw up.

Arlind Sadiku, the man with the snake tattoo, was an Albanian gangster renowned for his control of the London cocaine trade and a penchant for extreme violence.

The last road camera the van had passed was on the way into Luton. The process of tracking it beyond that grew more complicated as Danny was forced to hop from one private CCTV system to another. Julie, Ian and Suzy joined him in the work and they eventually located the van in a car park outside a nondescript warehouse.

By now, the entire machinery and power of the British state were hurtling towards this small group of Albanian thugs. Sir Alan had been as good as his word and they were told that a team from Hereford was on standby.

Ian, who had picked up the role of point man inside the plane, wanted to know that he had Kate's authorization for the SAS to go in. She nodded. What choice did they have?

They waited. Ian and Danny tracked the progress of the rescue through the SIS ops room, which was taking a video feed from SAS headquarters in Hereford. 'Helicopters airborne,' Ian said.

'Three minutes,' Danny said.

And then they counted down. Two. One. Thirty seconds. Twenty. Ten.

'Roping down,' Ian said.

'Blowing doors,' Danny added, a few seconds later.

'Dogs in.'

There was silence. How long did it last? Ten seconds, twenty, a minute?

It felt as if it would never end.

And then, from Ian: 'No one there. Damn. They've flown. They've gone. Jesus. How did they get away?'

There was no time for recriminations or doubt. They returned to leapfrogging the CCTV systems. Somewhere, somehow, they'd missed something.

The plane eventually landed at Northolt. Danny and Kate were still gazing at his laptop as they boarded a helicopter on the tarmac, bound for a Cobra meeting in London.

It was MI5 who eventually found the missing link: CCTV footage from a dry cleaner revealed that, just by a round-about, the gangsters had pulled over a for a few seconds to perform a very slick changeover, switching their cargo – now prostrate in body bags – into the back of a lorry. 'They're dead,' Kate shouted, against the noise of the helicopter.

'Unconscious,' Danny said. 'They wouldn't move them any other way.'

They began the process of tracking them again, this time to an industrial park on the outskirts of Luton. It was Danny who got there first, just before they ran from the helicopter to a waiting car at Battersea heliport.

Danny got into the back beside Kate. Julie was in the front, Ian in a car behind with Suzy. 'We can't risk a rescue,' Danny whispered to Kate, as the car roared away.

She looked at him, confused.

'The moment they hear the rotors, they'll kill them.'

Kate's phone buzzed. She opened a video from Fiona's WhatsApp account. It showed her daughter's terrified gaze for only a moment, before her face was pushed down. Someone held up a huge blade and began the process of beheading her.

Kate screamed, dropped the phone.

Danny picked it up. 'It's fake,' he yelled, above the sound of the rotors. He gripped Kate's shoulders, looked her in the eye. 'They're screwing with us. It's fake!'

'No . . . No . . .'

'Look at it. Look at the quality of the pictures. I told you! There's a weird sheen to those images.'

Kate could not bring herself to examine the footage. Julie turned. 'What about the sewers?' She put her computer on Danny's lap. On it was a planning application that detailed the sewage arrangements for a huge industrial park.

Danny nodded. 'They'll expect another airborne rescue. They probably left someone behind to see what happened at the place the other van went to.'

'I'll text Ian.'

Kate was too paralysed to think straight. 'I don't know . . .'

'It's the best way, Kate.' Julie turned to her again, vivid green eyes staring into Kate's own: firm, friendly, certain. She radiated steel and confidence. 'We have your back.'

They reached Whitehall and were whisked down the stairs towards the Cobra room in the Cabinet Office. But as they reached the last security barrier, Ian turned to her. 'You can't come in, Kate.'

'What do you mean?'

'They are your children. We can't allow you to be in the meeting.' His manner was kindly, reassuring. 'We'll do everything we can. Julie's idea is a good one. The director of Special Forces is looking into it right now.'

'No, I have to be in there—'

'You can't be. You know that.'

'But—'

'Please trust us.' Kate had never seen Ian like this before. There was a calm sincerity to his demeanour that was entirely surprising.

But still she rebelled against it. 'I can't just sit here.'

'We'll get the car to take you back to the office. Julie can go with you.'

'No, no—'

'Or we can drive you up to nearer the scene.'

'I'll stay here.' She nodded. 'Tell me as soon as you hear anything – anything at all.'

Ian squeezed her arm once more and handed his phone to the security guard, who checked his name against the list and allowed him through.

Kate leant against the wall and sank to the floor. She placed her head in her hands.

A few minutes later, she looked up to see the prime minister standing over her. 'Are you all right, Kate?'

She started to get up. 'Stay where you are,' he insisted, but she stood anyway. 'I'm so sorry,' he said. 'This is a bloody awful business. I just wanted to say we're doing everything we possibly can.'

'Thank you.'

'I know how terrifying it must be.'

'Yes.'

'Sir Alan, the Special Forces chaps, everyone is very confident, so I don't think there's anything to worry about. You know how good they all are.'

'Of course.'

There was an awkward silence. 'Look,' he said eventually. 'Why don't you come in? I know it's against all protocol, but, as prime minister, I can probably overrule that.'

The PM nodded at the guard, who let them both through the barrier.

Everyone was in the anteroom, grouped around a screen that carried the video feed from Hereford.

The lead soldier was charging the rear of a building. A man alongside him blew out the lock with a Hatton round, and then they were inside a cavernous warehouse, full of pallets stacked with cement and other building materials. Agitated warnings in Albanian bounced off the tin roof and echoed around the building. A man rounded the corner with an Uzi and was instantly silenced with two rounds from a Sig 556 high-velocity rifle.

They were into a corridor. Kate held her breath as the lead soldier – with the camera on his head – passed one open door, then another.

They reached the last room. The soldier moved forward as he and the man next to him 'sliced the pie', covering the room in an arc with their weapons as they moved through the doorway.

Gus and Rose lay on the floor, bound and gagged but conscious, their faces frozen in a grimace of pure terror. But between Kate and her children stood a nervous young Albanian gangster, tattoos all over his arms, who was using Fiona as a human shield. The lead Special Forces soldier did not hesitate, delivering an instant double tap – two shots – through the lower jaw to the part of the brain that controls the spinal cord. The gangster dropped immediately.

And there, in the middle of the screen, was the face of her bound, gagged daughter, whose mouth was wide open in a silent scream.

Epilogue

IN OTHER CIRCUMSTANCES, Kate might have cracked a smile at the sheer irony of it.

How many weeks had it been since she had sat in that same corner office interviewing Suzy Spencer for the role as her deputy? Four? Five? And yet here she was being questioned in return, their roles – even their seats – neatly reversed.

Alongside Suzy loomed the tall, angular, lugubrious Shirley Grove, the cabinet secretary, a woman so devoid of charisma she might have merged with the wallpaper. Kate was learning too late that these were the most dangerous mandarins of all.

'So, if we could recap,' Grove said. 'In the beginning, you thought Sergei tipped you off about the original meeting on Igor's super-yacht out of . . . friendship?'

'Yes.'

'Though you considered it possible he was also acting on behalf of his bosses in the GRU?'

'That's correct.'

'As a result of a power-tussle at the heart of the Kremlin, as they tried to gain the upper hand on their rivals in the Foreign Service, the SVR?'

'Yes.'

'In other words, a win-win for Sergei. He pleased his bosses and the woman he loved?'

'Something like that.'

'You therefore thought the conversation you recorded on Igor's super-yacht genuine?'

'Yes, of course.'

'And that James Ryan was the Russian spy or agent of influence?'

'Yes.'

'So when you were later told that the GRU were coming out on top in this power struggle and that Igor wanted to defect, in return for bringing you hard evidence of the prime minister's treachery, that seemed perfectly credible?'

'Yes.' Kate wondered how long this history lesson was going to last.

'You were further convinced that Stuart was Viper, the agent mentioned in that original overheard conversation?'

'I don't think there's much doubt that Stuart was working for the Russians.'

Grove nodded. She turned the page, moving on. The issue of whether there was another Russian mole at the heart of Whitehall was a much more open question, of course, but Kate wasn't going to raise that now. Her priority was to get out of there fast, with the minimum chance of any recall.

'The foreign secretary was reluctant to accept Igor Borodin's defection at face value,' Grove went on. 'She wanted more evidence. That was why you went to St Petersburg and then Moscow in search of Sergei?'

'Yes.'

'He confirmed your supposition at the time, that Igor was losing the power struggle and needed to get out of Russia?'

'Yes.'

'And you believed Igor Borodin killed Sergei to prevent any potential interference with his planned defection?'

'Not immediately, but I came to that conclusion shortly after it went wrong.'

'Why?'

'It was the only explanation that made sense to me.'

'*At the time.*'

'At the time, yes.' Kate would dearly have loved to find a way to make Igor pay for Sergei's murder. But it was too late for that.

Grove turned another page. 'When Mr Borodin told you on the tarmac at Tbilisi airport that the prime minister was definitely working for Moscow and that Ian had unwittingly passed on information to our enemies by keeping him informed at every turn, you believed that too *at the time*?'

'I did, yes.'

'So, in short, when you took off from Tbilisi, you were firmly of the view that the PM was a traitor and that Ian Granger was, at best, an indiscreet and ambitious fool who had unwittingly assisted him.'

Kate glanced out of the window at Ian, who was pacing the corridor. 'Yes.'

'You have not heard anything from Igor Borodin *since* that conversation on the tarmac?'

'No one has. Not us, not GCHQ. He and his family have vanished off the face of the earth.'

'Where *did* you think they had gone?'

'I assumed that, if the GRU had won the power struggle and he was caught in the act of defecting, he and his family were probably in a Siberian gulag or dead already.'

'I see,' Shirley Grove said, without emotion. She turned over another page and cleared her throat as she approached the climax of this charade. 'And yet you *now* say that everything you once believed in relation to this case was *wrong*?'

'That's correct.' Kate met her deputy's flinty glaze. How slow she had been to realize that Suzy's true purpose – as instructed by Grove and her master, the prime minister, no doubt, and, of course, aided and abetted by Ian – had not in fact been to open up the Operation Sigma file but to find the means and the method to ensure it remained closed. *For ever.*

'So to be clear,' Grove went on, 'you are now saying it was a set-up, right from the start. A great big Fabergé egg of a fake. Far from being rivals, the GRU worked *with* the SVR to sell us – to sell *you* – the mother and father of all intelligence dummies. The prime minister was never working for the Russians, the sex video was a fake, Stuart was the only agent working in Whitehall – and he was easily expendable in the cause of creating terrible chaos, confusion and mistrust at the heart of our democratic system?'

It was a moment before Kate realized Grove was expecting an answer. She certainly was exacting her pound of flesh. 'Yes,' Kate said. 'Absolutely.'

If the price of escaping all this was to flip everything she really believed on its head, she might as well do it with conviction.

'Sergei was killed just in case he blurted out the real truth to you on the train – that you had been deceived and manipulated *right from the start*?'

'Yes,' Kate said again, with excessive conviction. 'That *is* correct.'

Grove tapped her pen on the file. 'A cynic might note, Mrs Henderson, that you have announced you wish to leave the service with immediate effect. This way, the case is conveniently closed. There will be no committee of inquiry, no torturous, complicated, draining search for the truth. Just closure. The prime minister recovers his reputation, the Service can move on and you . . . well, you walk away, with your reputation and references intact. Free as a bird, one might say.'

'I'm not a cynic,' Kate said. And when she realized that Grove had truly no sense of humour, she went on: 'Ian was right all along. It's not easy to admit that, but it's true.'

If nothing else, she thought, she was becoming a much better bloody liar.

'We shouldn't blame Kate in any way,' Suzy chipped in. 'It was all so plausible. Who wouldn't have jumped at such a sensational story? If true, it would have been the most amazing intelligence coup of the modern era, enough to make anyone's career.'

Kate didn't dignify this with an answer.

Grove leant forward, her reading glasses brushing against her clipboard. There were a lot of ticks on her checklist now. 'After all this,' she said, 'you suddenly wake up one day and decide that Ian Granger was right all along and that you *were* duped?'

'Yes.'

'You didn't meet anyone, see anyone, receive any new information before experiencing this Damascene conversion?'

'No, but when I had time to reflect, it was the only explanation that made sense.' She forced another smile. Given they all knew that Grove's sole aim here was to bury this file in the darkest recess of the Service's vaults, her show of probity was beginning to grate. 'You know as well as I do, Mrs Grove, that in our world we never get hard and fast answers. There is no black and white. When you have ruled out all other potential explanations, what remains is the truth, however unlikely. Upon reflection, I decided Ian had been right. I feel no shame in admitting it.'

'So you accept this matter is closed?'

'Absolutely.'

'Good. Good.' Grove nodded sagely. 'We appreciate your cooperation, Mrs Henderson. I know this has been a tough time for you.'

'And the prime minister.' Grove looked confused. 'I mean, to have been falsely accused in this way,' Kate said. She was laying it on really thick now, but why not? She might as well enjoy it.

She glanced up at the light above her, in which she suspected a microphone was hidden. Whoever was listening – MI5, certainly, perhaps even the prime minister himself – she hoped they appreciated the effort she was putting into her show of contrition.

'Yes, yes. Monstrous. Very difficult.' Grove stood. 'Thank you, Mrs Henderson.' She offered her hand. 'A relief to all of us, I'm sure, to have this matter finally resolved.'

Kate took the proffered hand. She even kissed Suzy, though she didn't grace Ian with an answer when he asked her in the corridor outside how it had gone. Let his ambition sweat a moment longer.

'Kate,' he said, as she turned her back on him. 'Thank you for your contribution.'

She faced him. 'To what?'

'This inquiry. And the Service, of course.'

'Is that some kind of joke?'

'No, no. I wanted to thank you for all you have done.'

Kate retrieved her bag and walked away, without bothering to offer him a reply.

She found Julie waiting for her by the lift. 'Don't,' Kate said, raising a hand to forestall any show of emotion, for which she no longer had the stomach.

'I'm not going to cry,' Julie replied. 'Not now, anyway.'

'One day soon we're going to meet up and get very, very pissed. And we're never going to talk about any of it again.'

'You did the right thing, Kate.'

'You don't think that. And I'm not convinced I do, either. So I need to get out of here before I change my mind.'

'I do think it, actually.'

Julie launched herself into Kate's arms. They held each other until Kate released herself and belted for the stairs before the emotion welling inside her could find expression. She was damned if she was going to be seen leaving the building for the last time in tears.

Sir Alan was at the last security barrier, readying himself to leave to get back to the hospital. Rose was beside him, her arm still in a sling from the kidnap. The doctors had made clear to all of them that the mental scars would take much longer to heal.

Rose touched Kate's shoulder in support. Sir Alan did not appear to know what he should do. 'I thought I'd better pipe you out,' he said.

'Off, I think.' He looked confused. 'Don't you pipe someone off? It's a naval term.'

'Yes, yes, perhaps so.' He stared at the floor. 'I'm sorry it had to end like this, Kate.'

'I'm not. I should have made this decision a long time ago.'

'Are you certain you're doing the right thing? I'm sure my successor—'

'Your *successor*?'

He glanced at Rose, as if it was a decision they had reached jointly. Not for the first time, Kate wondered just how far the friendship between her aunt and their superior extended. But she choked off the train of thought. Not her business. 'I've taken the decision to stand down,' Sir Alan said. 'The search for my replacement has already begun.'

For a moment, Kate was less sure of her own decision. Perhaps it was the old competitive spirit or, as she would have preferred to see it, her conscience. 'So Ian got what he wanted.'

Sir Alan glanced at Rose again. 'We can make sure there's a future for you here, Kate.'

She wavered for only a moment more. 'No,' she said firmly. 'To answer a question Stuart once asked of me, I don't think in the end it *is* possible to be a warrior for truth and the mother I'd like to be. And if I must choose, then I know what it has to be.'

Kate could have told Sir Alan – and, indeed, Rose – that an agreement to allow Stuart to come and go unhindered in continental Europe had been the explicit quid pro quo with

Shirley Grove for lying through her teeth a few minutes ago or, as Grove herself had put it, 'telling the complete truth of the entire affair'. But they would, no doubt, have guessed as much.

Kate kissed Sir Alan. 'Bloody good luck, my friend,' he said.

She hugged her aunt, who whispered only, 'See you at home.'

She nodded at the security guard, who let her out of the building for the last time.

She swung right and headed westwards towards Battersea in the drizzle.

It was a gloomy night, but warmer than it looked, a close humidity wrapping the capital in its suffocating embrace. Kate shrugged off her coat, slipped it over her arm and glanced back at the organization to which she had devoted most of her adult life.

She walked on, faster and with greater purpose. Tonight, she had her own version of truth or, rather, of her role in this universe.

She was going home.

Where she belonged.

She picked up the pace and burst through the front door of the house to find Fiona and Gus waiting in the kitchen.

Kate took them in her arms, their warm hands wrapped tight around her. 'It's over,' she whispered. 'It's all over now.'

Acknowledgements

My primary thanks, as always, to my incredible wife, Claudia, my partner in life and work. I'd also like to thank my brilliant agent, Mark Lucas, and wonderful editor, Bill Scott-Kerr – and indeed Eloisa Clegg and all the fantastic team at Transworld. Thanks also to Rayhan Demytrie for her help in Tbilisi. And thanks to those in the Security Services who assisted but would prefer to remain 'in the background'.